PARLEY POLE

All about a village

Neil Jagger

Published by New Generation Publishing in 2015

Copyright © Neil Jagger 2015

Illustrations by Nina Turner and Anne Mason ©

First Edition

www.newgeneration-publishing.com

ISBN 978-1-78507-213-0

 New Generation Publishing

For the grandchildren

CONTENTS

TALC

Denton Cheney was recorded by the Normans. The village is unusual in having two manors, one of which also owns land in Dunton, an adjacent, smaller hamlet. This anomaly has turned the villages into half brothers, promoting a permanent rivalry. Despite being situated within a few miles of the county town, which spreads ever closer, the settlement is in an officially designated 'rural area'. Twenty miles from an original Roman road, the village remained isolated until the early sixties when a nearby north-south motorway junction placed it prominently on the road map of Britain, bringing its reluctant residents under the influence of modernisation.

As a cluster of nearly three hundred dwellings with about seven hundred inhabitants the village remains compact having grown around a tiny, but reliable, stream. Public houses, of very different character, cater for the social side of life, while the residents support such a variety of societies, clubs and sports associations that I lose count. Like most independent villages Denton Cheney has a popular, parochial infants school, a well kept church dating from Saxon times - though much refurbished by the Victorians, a seventies village hall, and a combined post office/shop adjacent to the central main green with its sad, weathered memorial to the accumulated sacrifices of two world wars. Demographically, the population is older than the national average and a majority of its inhabitants work locally.

Underlying a wide variety of houses is a stratum of soft sand laid down by a considerable pre-glacial river. Prompted by a nearby, early nineteenth century canal, some of these deposits have been worked commercially. One manor and one large farm still retain, and cultivate, most of the remaining grade two agricultural land which surrounds the village and supports a mix of both animals and crops; through it are many ancient, sign posted footpaths and bridleways which are used by locals and dog walkers – more especially in summer.

The settlement has managed to retain a strong sense of identity. Its residents stated overwhelmingly - in a 'parish plan' put together by the parish council - that they 'wished to remain a village separate from the town and other villages.' Located where they are, with a sense of history, convenient but cut off, its inhabitants, with their aspirations, interests and problems, may be taken to represent what is still thought of as a desirable, typically English community.

There follows a two year account of life in Denton Cheney. Better informed, you may soon be in a position to decide if living in a village is an attractive option, worth the housing cost premium and loss of privacy one has to endure, or whether it is only an idyllic image, successfully promoted by Agatha Christie's detectives, Jane Austen's novels, country calendars, chocolate box lids and the English Tourist Office.

YEAR ONE

GYPSUM - SUMMER

If an alien were to approach the village from space, or use an internet mapping site, he would see Denton Cheney as a compact group of buildings surrounded by a band of open countryside - two kilometres wide at its narrowest.

The tiny window stood wide open; it was set in fifteenth century, lime pointed masonry. Upstairs, the roof was supported on nineteen seventies matching sandstone. Sadly, when the second storey was added the work preceded new regulations, allowing thatch to give way to Welsh slate. High on the chimney breast, a small pewter sun can be seen. When Rectory Cottage was a single story priest's home owned by the Church of England, it was insured and this plaque, unnoticed by most, bears witness. The Sun has watched over the old building for three hundred years and no fire has dared to harm its fabric.

Mrs Faulkner, known to friends as 'Auntie' Dot, wasn't born in Rectory Cottage but in a similar, nearby house which she regretted seeing demolished. Having spent her whole life in the village, Dot knew it well.

In early May, her home already felt hot and she reflected that it was never like this when she was growing up. Dot and her late husband Nathanial had added oil fired central heating out of the lump sum he received on retirement from British Railways; now the climate was warmer, she wondered whether it had really been necessary. She pushed open the front stable door, wedging it with an old fire iron to let in a moist breeze. On the linoleum lay a folded paper; stooping to pick it up Dot noticed it was two sheets stapled together and sat down to read it in her father's favourite, polished oak armchair. Mrs Faulkner had no need for glasses now that her natural, country woman's long sightedness had regressed under the dual influences of time and television.

The missive was from an action group; a list of members was given, some of whom she knew and respected. It stated that a large secondary school was proposed just outside the village, gave a list of reasons why this was undesirable, and asked for her support to resist it. The attachment was a typed proforma letter of protest, already addressed to the district council; she only needed to add the date, her name, address and signature before posting it in. The old lady failed to see any need for such an establishment. Village children had always attended the parochial primary school by the old green and, following that, were bussed to a large, well thought of comprehensive in another much larger village. The idea made no sense – Denton Cheney was smaller now than when she was a girl. Dot hunted out an envelope, did what was needed in a rounded hand, collected her walking stick and set off to get some stamps, all the while wondering how much they would be this time.

The post office was housed in an extension to a detached red brick, between wars house - so out of character in Denton Cheney she thought. The news was bad; not only had second class stamps gone up two new pence but the owners had received advance warning that government was intending to consult nationally with a view to closing all unprofitable, inadequately supported offices. Admittedly, the timetable set was two years hence, but Dot was shrewd enough to realise that the branch in nearby Dunton was within walking distance for the fit, and that, at long last, there was a reliable, half hour bus service between the two villages. Recalling wartime rationing and fifties economies, she immediately concluded that one of the two would be sure to go.

As Dot walked slowly back - taking the longer route to enjoy the fine weather and the fact that it was cooler out than in - the new proposal set her thinking about all the changes that she and Nathanial had seen during their long married life. Cars were common now, even eighteen year olds needed them. Shank's pony, or sometimes a real pony and trap, was all her dad used - but then small farmers were always a bit behind the times. Returning from a day in the fields after the sun had set, a radio was their only diversion - when reception was good and they could tune it in properly; a great big heavy thing it was, with all those glass valves that collected dust and needed replacing at regular intervals! Now, people had television, sometimes a set in each room - even the children's bedrooms; she didn't approve of that and frequently said so. Telephones were rare and a shared line was, for years, all they could obtain. She had watched men erect fir poles to carry two thin wires up from the main road. Now, there were mobile phones, more in the country than people who used them - or so the papers said. Apart from phones there was this internet thing her grandson had shown her; it was astonishing that farmers could order their groceries, fertiliser or seed potatoes in the evening without leaving home. Yes, life had become easier in the countryside but, as her sons advised, there was no longer any money in farming. That's life, she thought, some things improve but others get worse.

The loss of the village post office would be most inconvenient; with her bad leg and inflamed varicose veins, getting to Dunton was near impossible. Well, maybe it wouldn't happen - the other lot might get elected and change it all, or perhaps, by then, she would have gone to join Nat. She laughed at her depressing thoughts. 'I'm not a gloomy person,' she muttered. 'Come on Dot, it's a beautiful day and you still enjoy life. Must be positive like that Mr Churchill said.'

The name of the nation's saviour in World War Two reminded her of something and she glanced across towards the distant churchyard on its small rise. The acorn from Blenheim Palace which she had seen planted to commemorate Churchill's long life was now a massive, spreading oak. 'Such trees grow slowly,' she mused, 'it will long outlive me, I just hadn't realised how big it had become.' Close to it, villagers had placed a brass tablet attached to a rock, she wondered if it was still there and determined to go and look. Those were awful times but, thanks to that great man, the country had survived. Winnie was always right.

*   *   *   *   *

'This right of way is ancient. It was used by the Saxons and appears in the Domesday Book.'

Looking back over his shoulder the inspector smiled slightly but continued walking. The narrow, uneven track had been cut through a field overgrown with yellow flowering rape.

'There's Spring Farm,' said Jeff, pointing. 'It was derelict, but has been redeveloped tastefully into several businesses and two houses. They've also planted a tree screen on the motorway side.'

Topping a slight rise the three men paused. Beyond the farm a church steeple rose above a colony of noisy rooks in a copse of towering ash.

'This was once the only link between the two villages,' advised Jeff.

'It runs directly from one steeple to the other. Literally as the crow flies!' added Mike.

The inspector retained a professional distance. It was his task to give an independent opinion. He mustn't be too pally with these villagers, well intentioned though they were.

'I've seen enough,' he concluded. 'No need to go any further.'

The two friends turned. Respectfully following the tall, angular figure, they retraced their steps into the wind and back through the animal feed.

'It's strange how this stuff appears to be rolling towards us - like an ocean,' observed Mike.

'A parting of the yellow sea is letting us return to our village,' laughed his fellow protester and, raising his voice for the inspector's benefit, added. 'We consider Denton Cheney as a sort of 'promised land' – that's why we want to keep it that way. This proposed ten year long sand extraction would ruin it.'

The inspector deigned to comment but the point had hit home. Yes, he reminded himself, he must remain objective when drafting his report for the Minerals Inquiry in Public, making a mental note to keep his diary up to date when he returned to the pub at which he had booked in for three night's bed and breakfast.

* * * * * *

Aaron was bored; it seemed he always was. In the present good weather he could, at least, kick a football with friends on the playing field and, when it grew dark, move to the wooden bus shelter near the green which made a good goal – only problem there was that people sometimes came out to complain. Right now the school holiday was nearly over and his days of freedom were dwindling – as the song said – to a precious few. The imminence of being organised once again compounded his feelings of frustration. Looking back, the summer hadn't been too bad, really. He and his brother Joe had gone camping with dad and mum and their dogs Barry and Robin – named after the Bee Gees. The site was on a lake where there had been rowboats, canoes, and a swimming area with a slide, and rope attached to a tree from which one could swing out and jump in. A bit cold but good fun. Even the dogs went in, paddling along with their noses just above the surface. Their heavy, old canvas tent had stayed up this time, so Mum was happy, and the boys had found plenty of teenagers to join in games of football, or teach touch rugby to - for they lived in an area where rugby had always been the more popular game.

After all that fun Dad had gone away, driving his truck in Europe somewhere for days at a time, and Mum was back helping at the Phoenix old people's home till all hours. This had left him and Joe to moon about around the village. They couldn't afford the bus into town, and there was nothing there anyway that didn't involve spending money. Locally, they saw Sam and Dave from time to time. Sam, having just completed his schooling, had begun day shift work in one of the cavern like warehouses - distribution centres they were called – that had proliferated around the motorway junction; but they were about six miles away and effectively out of reach.

Fortunately, the brothers got on well together and managed to while away their unproductive hours fairly well, always provided they could burn up energy outside where Aaron, the elder and more imaginative usually took the lead while Joe enjoyed being his obedient follower. When it rained hard, which according to Mum was now more often, they were stuck inside the small council house with only 'the box' as company. Neither read much; they'd tried, but nothing their teacher recommended had caught their fancy, and without Sky so they could follow the cricket and golf, the summer television programmes did not appeal. To fill in time they made paper darts and threw them at each other or played endlessly on hand-held Japanese-made electronic games.

On one such long day there was a knock at the door. Hidden behind net curtains in the bay window Aaron checked the Norfolk porch to see who was there - just the way his mother always did. He discovered a wet looking Sam and Dave standing coatless in the slanting drizzle and opened up to let them in.

'Are you coming out,' asked Sam, adding hopefully, 'it's nearly stopped?'

Glad of an excuse to do something the brothers pulled on matching, unfashionable sweaters that had been knitted by Grandma, and battered, high-sided trainers, stuck hands deep into pockets and shut the door carefully behind them.

'You not working?' asked Aaron.

'Given up,' replied Sam, who, realising an explanation was expected, continued, 'all fucking pricks over there. No respect.'

'What will your dad say?' wondered Joe. Sam looked anguished.

'He'll be mad, I know, say I must stick it out - to be expected when starting at the bottom. Anyway, it's my problem, not yours.' He brightened, 'What say we go find Eddy? Here!' He ripped two cans off a plastic wrapped six pack and threw one to each of the brothers. Sam and Dave were already sipping from opened tins; they smelt of lager.

Eddy was a skinny, shadowy figure. Wearing a baseball cap pulled well down over his eyes, he turned up regularly in a dirty white van which he parked in the village hall's shingle covered yard, hidden from passers-by behind the wooden bus shelter and parish council notice board. Eddy appeared to have no income, yet ran this set of wheels and never seemed to work.

'He said down Glebe Lane about 5.00,' Sam recalled. The appointment had already been fixed.

'OK,' agreed Dave who followed Sam everywhere, acting like his lieutenant.

The four youths set out for the stately oak under which there was a passing place, well used as a tryst and always littered with dirty, plastic supermarket bags, condoms and half empty beer cans. As they approached the van it was facing away from them but there was no sign of life. Drawing level, they made out Eddy slumped in the driver's seat; he noticed them but made no attempt to get out. Finally, he opened the side window a few inches. Fumes of stale alcohol rushed out. In his left hand, near the floor, he held a half drunk bottle of white coloured liquid. For a big person Sam was surprisingly deferential.

'Eddy, do you remember your promise? You said we could try some of those pills. Did you bring them this time?'

'As your go-between I expect a please,' snapped what could be seen of the thin, white face.

'Please,' mumbled Sam.

'You'll have to say it nicely,' insisted the slurred voice from inside. 'This is your last chance; if not you'll end up in the water like that other fellow.'

'In the water? What do you mean?' responded Sam defensively.

'Oh, nothing to do with you,' muttered Eddy, adding hastily, 'something on the telly.'

'Alright, alright,' repeated Sam, 'for you I'll say please.'

'I don't have none today. You'll have to pay me in advance. It's a tenner for twenty.'

'But, Eddy, be fair,' bleated Sam. 'You said we could try them first, and I've just quit my job.'

'Well, more fool you,' scolded Eddy, quickly winding up the window and starting the engine. The mud spattered vehicle did a wheel spinning, three point turn and headed back towards the main road, leaving Sam a much less impressive figure than only minutes earlier.

'What was that all about?' asked Joe, who had only overheard a part of the conversation. 'Does he push drugs?'

'Shush,' warned Sam, 'It's illegal. Don't tell nobody.'

The brothers were a bit bemused, suddenly realising that they hadn't really wanted to get involved. It was only boredom and bravado that had made Sam's proposal sound interesting. They looked at each other cautiously and began to turn away.

'Where you going?' mouthed Sam, desperately trying to cover up his temporary humiliation.

'Our dad's coming home soon,' said Aaron. It was all he could think of.

All four stood silently still for a minute looking at the ground before Aaron, reassured that there would be no violence, moved slowly off. Joe followed, neither looked back.

The brothers reached the tarmac road and, after checking there was no sign of pursuit, Joe asked, 'What was that?'

'Drugs,' Aaron informed. 'I thought it might be interesting – liven up our days a bit.'

'But, Sam said it was illegal. Is he right? We'll get the cops after us.'

'It's not very likely. Everybody in our class at school seems to think he's a dealer, but he's never been caught. Have to say it's not good. I don't like it now. Best stay the way we are. That sort of stuff leads nowhere.'

Joe listened attentively. He didn't disagree. They walked on morosely, side by side. Suddenly, Joe stopped.

'Why don't we join the scouts? Give us something to do. I have a mate who goes, says it's a laugh. It's every Wednesday, in the hall and free!' Aaron looked unhappy.

'It's a lot of posh people. We'd feel out of place, I reckon. Anyway, you need a uniform and Mum couldn't afford one.'

'You don't,' Joe disagreed. 'Nigel – that's my friend – goes in his school clothes. At least we'd know someone.'

'Alright, you win. Let's give it a go, but, if I feel uncomfortable, I'll just walk out.'

'You can't do that! Promise me you'll stay to the end and not act daft - or I won't go.' Aaron remained doubtful. He suspected the scouts were naff, but, seeing his brother was keen, relented.

'I promise,' he said, and meant it.

*   *   *   *   *

Mrs Oldham parked her small, tired station wagon outside the church
- after the village had been bypassed there was little traffic during the
day. She lifted a steel latch and opened one side of the heavy, oak lych-
gate. Just recently the leaves had begun to stick, making it a hard push
for an octogenarian. Inside, was a short shingle path set with recent
commemorative stone tablets; it led between grassy banks to the south
porch and main entrance. Mrs Oldham noticed that fresh flowers had
been laid on some and couldn't help but read the chiselled names; she had
known them all. Reaching into her canvas satchel she took out the large
key on its cumbersome wooden tag – as one of three church wardens
she kept it handy at all times in case of emergency – and turned it in the
well- oiled lock.

A fusty, damp smell rushed out to greet her, it emanated from the fading
flower arrangements for last week's wedding which she had come to take
away. She collected the vases, took them outside and tipped the water
out into the grassy churchyard, thinking that after so much rain, it would
benefit from a cut and tidy up. In her bag was a list of flowers required for
the next wedding which the bride's mother had passed to her a few days
earlier. For religious festivals or church events she either brought blooms
from her own garden or received regular donations from other villagers
– like her friend Dot Faulkner – placing them in the various containers
as tastefully as she could in a manner taught by her mother. These days,
couples getting married had money and tended to appoint a florist in the
town who not only provided bouquets and buttonholes, but also brought
in all the arrangements for the registry, church and pew ends. Apart from
letting the florists in and showing them where to go, this recent trend
had made her almost redundant - not that she minded less work. Her
compensation was seeing and learning the names of new varieties of the
often un-seasonal plants from overseas which the professionals ordered
and used to such good effect.

As she stood looking about her she was struck by the lack of facilities
in the old building. Mrs Oldham had learnt from the vicar that, under
recent health and safety rules and regulations, it was no longer possible to

organise large or lengthy fund raising events inside Saint James - it simply was not up to the required standard. It was apparent to Mrs Oldham, who even on this warm day was beginning to notice the internal chill of the stone flagged church, that having somewhere smaller - perhaps with toilet facilities - which could be heated separately from the cavernous nave would be sensible. If the parochial church council wanted to pass on a viable, properly funded building to future generations of villagers, they could not stand still. What they needed was an inspiring concept.

*   *   *   *   *

Alan had been in the village for six years but still felt a stranger there, even though everybody he met asked him if he was 'all right'. After a spell in Australia he had finally retired and felt ready to occupy himself by doing something useful. On his way around the streets to get some exercise he spotted a new sheet pinned on the parish council's notice board. Two co-opted members were being sought to make up its numbers to the full complement of nine. He wondered why they were short. Was the work so demanding that nobody wanted to do it, had somebody died, or was there just a general level of disinterest in this busy modern age? Such an opportunity seemed the right sort of thing but, after continuing his amble, he had second thoughts. He didn't know anybody on the council, and, aware that local government in the United Kingdom was famously bureaucratic and unrewarding, he held back - finally deciding to make a start by attending a meeting to discover what it was all about. As a responsible citizen it was the least he could do.

The council met on the second Monday of each month and he duly turned up at the village hall. The barn like building, clad in locally quarried iron stone, dated from nineteen seventy three – or so said a plaque by the entrance. It was rectangular in shape and the plain open, main hall had a raised wooden stage at one end. There was a small side annex - which doubled as a store for sets of folding, metal-framed tables and chairs, a meeting room and a rather dated kitchen. As Alan approached, only five minutes before the start time, the hall was dark and looked deserted. He was beginning to think he'd got the date wrong,

14

when a burly, bearded man arrived carrying a key. The ruddy cheeked newcomer, who resembled an ex-naval boatswain, spoke to him curtly.

'What are you here for?' he asked. Alan was taken aback.

'I thought the public could attend your meetings,' he answered, but received no reply.

Four other silent men and women appeared out of the evening glow from across the shingle forecourt; Alan followed them inside. One councillor set out a few chairs and all five sat down around a folding table. Finally, a younger, long-haired woman came in carrying a battered lever-arch file and took the last unoccupied seat. Alan stood awkwardly by the door, watching what had clearly been expected to be a private get together. The 'bo's'n', who sat in the middle and appeared to be acting as chairman, looked him over.

'People don't usually come here,' he announced in an intimidating voice.

This was too much for Alan and he decided to stay - unless someone physically threw him out. Never having attended such a meeting before, he didn't know what to expect. The councillors were all well over sixty and chatted together in low voices with strong local accents, which he found hard to follow. He noticed that the young lady was readying a ball point pen and preparing to take notes on a ruled pad. She appeared to have an agenda sheet – which nobody else did; he concluded that she must be the secretary or clerk. After a hidden signal the councillors deliberately rearranged their chairs so they had their backs to Alan, and anyone else who might wish to attend; finally, ten minutes late, the meeting began.

Jack, the chair, did most of the talking; as he spoke Alan noticed the smell of alcohol. No one else said much and nothing was discussed; after an hour it was all over. Curious to know what, if anything had transpired he asked if there would be any minutes, only to be rudely told, 'No'.

During the following weeks he regularly consulted the parish council's notice board, but no record of that, or any other meeting, was posted, and the delaminating plywood behind its cracked, dirty glass remained totally bare. Alan was glad that he'd made the effort to attend, and pleased not to have volunteered to join what, to him, had seemed both disorganised and pointless. But he couldn't let it rest – something was wrong – and he resolved to return in order to get more of a feel for what was happening, what decisions were being made – if any, and to discover whether proper accounts were being kept. Then he thought, 'Perhaps all parish councils are like that!' It was, after all, a rural area. Nonetheless, Denton Cheney deserved better. After a lifetime in private business and a daily need to judge other people's competence, he knew there was a problem; the next step was to identify it and arrive at a solution.

Pondering his conclusion, Alan arrived back home to find a single sheet of folded A4 paper lying on the front door mat; it was an action group's request for support to resist the siting of a school on a field immediately adjacent to the village. He didn't recognise the signature, but there was an evident, deep felt concern about the future of Denton Cheney. Here, perhaps, were like minded people whom he could assist.

* * * * *

Dogs and the English go together like horses and carriages; as may be expected, the village was well populated with them. Few residents walked Denton Cheney's streets and lanes without one or two, either in tow or – if the animals were large, being towed. But 'Lady' was small and timid, she kept Arthur going. His wife of forty happy years had died a few months earlier and, to provide him with company and another living thing to care about, his daughter had bought him the puppy. She was a small King Charles spaniel with big brown eyes, and he had no hesitation in naming her 'Lady' - after Disney's heroine, the bosom friend of 'Tramp'.

As Lady grew he took her for walks along Glebe Lane, but often had to carry her back as it was simply too far. After he twisted his ankle the two of them were on a par and could be seen, mornings and evenings, moving slowly between the hedgerows. The little dog appeared so delicate and weak that even a rabbit would frighten it; her caring owner worried after the slightest wheeze. On the garden gate of his ground floor council flat Arthur had fixed a lovely, coloured, ceramic likeness with a single word announcing her name. The postman was always careful to close the gate behind him before bending down to reach the low level letter box; he was spared this effort in summer when Arthur left his front door ajar to let in the cool breeze which allowed Lady to wander out and enjoy the shade of an old apple tree on the neat front lawn.

Today, Arthur had received the appeal from the self-styled action group. After watching how the deliverer, when he left, had taken care to check that the latch was properly engaged, he felt an instant empathy. Lady didn't bark and wasn't snappy - the postman would testify to that - but Arthur, out of politeness, nevertheless called her in if he heard someone coming; the effort of communicating made him feel less alone. Of course, he was against the school - it would be built on and destroy the leafy lane he and his dog used so much. Arthur dragged a ladder-back, straw seated chair up to his dining room table, dug in a drawer for his wife's still scented pad and used a fountain pen to write a personal protest. This rural village must not be spoilt by a noisy comprehensive with lots of yobbo teenagers causing trouble and dropping litter everywhere, nor plagued by the cars of their parents. Where would he and Lady have left to go? His poor health meant they couldn't walk very far, and taking a pet by bus for a stroll in the country seemed silly when one was already living there.

*　*　*　*　*

'Sunny' sat, perched gloomily on a high stool behind the narrow counter, surveying the empty space and depleted shelves. The nickname was inappropriate; it had been coined - if that is the word - by his brother, somehow, despite the odds, it had stuck.

Fewer people came into his shop after the government's decision to pay pensions directly into bank accounts, or used the tiny post office in the opposite corner where Shiva, his ever patient wife, sat silently behind bars, caged, yes, but only for security – those were the rules. After making the bold decision to leave interfering parents behind in Islamabad and try his luck in Britain, a shaky arranged marriage had become a successful partnership. Since running a post office and general store was a full time commitment, they only returned to Pakistan for family deaths and marriages. Nobody visited from back home – it was far too expensive.

Sunny knew he had been misnamed - it simply wasn't his natural demeanour to be cheerfully positive. Too many years of immersion in the English culture of chat and complaint had, perhaps, worn off from his customers, many of whom came in primarily to find a captive audience and moan about some aspect of their daily lives. He was stuck there, but by choice and happily so. Both he and Shiva liked the peace and politeness of this green village, preferring it to urban noise and rudeness. Yes, in town their turnover had been more than double, but there had been intimidation and hassle. They concluded it was better to be bored and just scraping by, rather than rich and stressed out. This country had been kind to them and they appreciated it. The move had allowed them to bring up three well educated, well behaved children - two sons and a daughter – all of whom had now left home, but were energetic and supportive, well able to fend for themselves in today's demanding world.

The couple decided to reduce stock to items which moved quickly, retaining only a minimum of perishables - like milk and butter. Previous owners had provided a full grocery and newsagent service, but, in those days, the post office had been elsewhere. Now that most people had a refrigerator, could afford to run a car, and bus times to town had improved, demand was minimal – mainly from locals calling in for items they had forgotten to get during their weekly supermarket visit. As a result the shelves only displayed cigarettes for the adults, treats for the youngsters, and some sliced white bread, augmented by staples like baked beans, tinned peas and half bottles of spirits.

Household and women's magazines sold well, as did racks of cards for every occasion. Daily and Sunday newspaper delivery to Denton Cheney and Dunton supplemented their income which was consolidated by the post office, without which they could not have survived. This fine Monday afternoon it was almost time for the village primary school to close and a flurry of mums, with a few dads, would be coming in for sweets and chocolate. Ice cream, Sunny didn't stock – it was too seasonal and there was anyway a travelling van whose meagre trade he had no wish to usurp.

Sunny had not been well recently. He became upset when head office sent him a confidential internal memo announcing that, because letter delivery was being subsidised annually by many millions of pounds, a review had been put in hand with the possibility that some branches would be closed. The criteria were to be usage and distance to the nearest alternative office, which, in a rural area, had been set at three miles. This he accepted was a walkable distance for the healthy, but many from the village reached his shop along the footpath on motorised invalid carts or tricycles and, although the closest village – Dunton - had a thriving post office and store, it wasn't easy to get there – simple on a map but rather different in practice. Shiva was quick to point out that the government wasted vastly more on foreign wars, fraudulent tax credits and failed computer software. She thought that a post office – especially in villages – should be seen as a public service rather than a business, it was after all, a natural meeting place and at the very heart of rural life.

A copy of the action group's circular had been handed to Sunny during the morning with a request to please respond and then display it in the shop window. Although the proposed new school would generate more profit just before their retirement, on balance neither of them wanted such a change. Money wasn't everything. After they had finished working Sunny wanted to remain in this relaxed, isolated village with the people he knew, where he was accepted as English and not seen as foreign at all. Yes, they would willingly support the protest. While Shiva stuck up the circular prominently in their big window, Sunny signed the proforma letter, dated it, wrote their address at the top, took an envelope, added a second class stamp and put it in his mail bag ready for the daily 5.00 pm collection.

As he closed the bag another thought struck him. Perhaps he could enlist the action group's support to publicise the post office's new policy and discover whether people agreed. Letters to local government had to be recorded and taken account of, why not the same for policies originating in Whitehall? If this branch remained open he could retire at a time of his own choosing and not be pushed out before he was really ready. He decided that, when someone came in whose name was on the action group membership list, he would acquaint them with the threat and see what they advised. Never mind the memo's needless, bureaucratic insistence on secrecy, it was his duty to keep the customers informed - they were, after all, friends and neighbours; it was only appropriate that they should be the ones to determine his future.

* * * * *

A large, printed banner had appeared on the end gable of the big black barn; it was easily visible as the building was located in one of two central fields which formed part of the village conservation area.

Denton Cheney was fortunate: the loss of population brought about by the steady mechanisation of agriculture had left it with an open figure of eight configuration rather than the more typical single high street, which often became a busy main road, effectively dividing the community in half. Long, straight principal thoroughfares had developed where settlements lay astride main coaching routes. Inns had not only to accommodate travellers but organise changes of horses. If a brewer wanted to be sure of trade he needed to build convenient premises right on the highway. Located in low lying, fertile land, the village had never been close to arterial routes which always favoured the drier hills. As a result of this isolation the village had, until quite recently, remained a random collection of family homes, all of which were involved in country activities of one sort or another.

Yellow capitals stood out against dark paint and announced: 'Fun Day June 18'. A further reminder of the event appeared in the parochial news sheet which covered the three villages for which a peripatetic vicar was responsible, and was delivered to all households by a series of volunteers. Apart from the date no further details were given. The organisers evidently expected that only locals - who knew exactly what to expect - would be interested; as a newcomer, Alan certainly didn't. When the designated day arrived he was none the wiser, so he and Carol decided to go along after lunch. As residents, they felt an obligation to support village events and wondered what it was all in aid of.

The sun shone down from an empty, limpid blue vault, but a strong breeze mitigated its effect. In the quietness, mellow, brown stone houses slumbered behind abundant, flowering gardens which were just approaching their best. Alan felt that his choice of a place to retire into was fully vindicated; he resolved to return later - if the weather held - to begin a record of the village by photographing all the listed buildings.

On the way they passed a grand country mansion on whose original paddock their own house had been built. Its boundary was a high, rust red, brick wall which had cracked and bowed out towards the single narrow footpath; alarmingly fresh chips of lime mortar lay on the tarmac, forcing them off the kerb for safety. At regular intervals the wall contained the round, cast iron plates of tie backs which, he was told, had been installed when the road had been lowered so that the house's owner could no longer see the carts and horses of passers-by - it was a sort of 'ha ha', but for humans rather than cattle.

Further on, they took a short cut along an unmade, overgrown footpath - known locally as a 'jetty' - between the tall, ancient, stone walls of what must once have been a narrow concession for villagers granted by adjacent landholders. From there the close packed houses opened up revealing St James on a small mound, its tower and temperamental clock framed by ancient yew trees - which predated it - and the stately oak that Dot admired so much. Immediately in front of the west entrance lay the fun day field, it was a hive of activity.

The junior school had set out various busy competitions where teachers recorded times so mums could contribute cash towards small prizes and discover whether their offspring were the fastest or the most skilful. A mini-league football match was also in progress. Stalls sold donated items - such as children's books and toys which they had outgrown, or general bric-a-brac retrieved from the attic or barn. An enthusiastic lady with protruding teeth and a large nose rushed about offering multicoloured raffle tickets for a draw to be held later in the day; Carol hoped that the undisclosed prizes would be rather better than the items on the stalls.

Country pursuits were represented by a garden tent containing dozens of delightful, just hatched chicks - 'partridge,' the man said in answer to Alan's question - all kept warm by a propane heater; small children giggled and asked if they could pick them up. Just outside one could bet on the outcome of a ferret race. At a signal, four of the sharp toothed, furry animals were released into intermittent, parallel lines of small

21

diameter drainpipe; the first to reappear was the winner. Occasionally, a ferret would decide not to race, and much fun was had by adults and youths alike in trying to corner and catch it.

An open area had been laid out with white plastic chairs and tables where beer, soft drinks and tea could be bought cheaply from an adjacent canvas tent. This attracted the elderly or less mobile who sat about in the sunshine cheerfully discussing previous village happenings. The ridge roofed, corrugated-steel clad barn had one open side from which the farmer's tractors and harrows had been removed, which allowed the cheeses game to be borrowed from the Fox and installed under cover. One pound bought five attempts to knock down all ten skittles using three Edam shaped wooden 'cheeses'. Lots of cheering had drawn a happy crowd of watchers and the takings soared. Beside it was a queue attracted by the mouth watering smell of frying sausages. Locals waited patiently while Joan, the competent farmer's wife, produced hot dogs in fresh, soft rolls with slightly burnt onion rings and ample helpings of English mustard or tomato sauce, according to taste.

Carol tried to open a conversation with Joan but fumes from the cooking oil and the press of onlookers made it almost impossible.

'Best thing today,' praised Alan as he handed over the money.

'There's an ox roast this evening, and barn dancing,' advised Joan with her usual economical use of words.

They didn't know and couldn't go, but volunteering such information to people still deemed strangers was appreciated. It was the first time an 'old' villager had spoken to them apart from a predictable, 'Are you alright then?' as people passed one another in the village streets – one was never sure whether they had recognised you or just said it automatically.

As they moved away, munching contentedly, Alan noticed that the great barn had been erected on the lowest part of the field; it bestrode a covered stream which he realised must once have performed the very same function that Hercules achieved with the one he diverted through the Aegean Stables. Nobody had enlightened them about the purpose of the 'fun day' and he guessed it was a village tradition, a rare break from the daily grind of rural labour where the idea had been simply to enjoy oneself. Later, he discovered that no accounts were ever published

22

– honesty was assumed - and that previous practice had been only to break even. In effect, on this one special day, richer locals subsidised their poorer neighbours, allowing everybody to relax. 'And, why not,' he thought.

* * * * *

The basic idea had come up at the pub – as all the best ones invariably do. A week later, nobody could recall whose it was.

During the annual, game bird shooting season Henry worked as a beater for several different landowners; the job included helping to ensure that clients had a successful outing. He noticed that it was becoming an increasingly expensive day. His family had lived in this rural area for generations, further back than he had been able to trace in existing records; many relatives were buried in the churchyard, their algae encrusted headstones flaking away and the chiselled lettering almost lost. As a true countryman Henry could turn his capable hands to almost anything and had all the many skills modern farming demanded; with the next generation migrating to the towns there was no shortage of work. Cheerful, strong and reliable he was always busy and, when away from the farms and estates, was sought after for his house building skills, especially where local stone was specified.

After a few pints at the 'Fox' somebody had suggested that they get together, pool their resources, breed their own pheasants and enjoy the shooting – as a hobby that is, rather than a business. Henry pointed out that the biggest village farmer owned most of the land thereabouts and would probably let them shoot across it without charge; prudently, they decided to ask his teenage son to join them. Tim, the proprietor of a free range egg farm at the outskirts of the village said he would like some winter sport and a change from shooting foxes, and volunteered the free use of a surplus field on which breeding pens could be erected. Mick, a recently married, occasional pub visitor who rented an upstairs flat in the old council estate with wife Susan and baby Damien, expressed an interest; he couldn't contribute a lot, but was a pleasant, open young man and the others felt a bit sorry for him. By consensus, Henry, who had all the required 'know how', and energy to spare, became their organiser in chief.

'That's a start,' said Henry, summing up. 'Nearly closing time anyways and we all have to be up early. I'll sound out Chad, and his dad. Let's think it over a bit more and talk again the next time we're all here.'

He drained the glass, collected his bike from the wall outside and cycled home in the fading light. There was no need to make hasty decisions - ones they might regret later.

CALCITE - AUTUMN

Fish nibbled at the bloated face; for them it was just an easy meal, not the result of an event destined to disturb the equanimity of the local population..

* * * * *

Three members of the village hall working group sat around a scrubbed, pine table in the kitchen of a large, internally gutted and modernised, thatched stone cottage. It was their chairman's home; he had arrived there after moving from a nearby village in which his second wife - a Croatian - had found it difficult to settle. Despite her strange accent Sanja regarded herself as English and had adopted all the behaviour and causes of the comfortable middle class.

The old house was next door to the hall which dated from 1975 and had been incorporated as a trust whose founder members included all the major clubs and societies of Denton Cheney – but, strangely no representative from the established church or parish councils. When the previous chairman had resigned - owing to ill health - it had been only natural for him and the trustees to invite Vincent, a former Home Office civil servant of many years' London experience, to chair their committee.

Apart from their chair, those present were: June - the caretaker, who was strong and capable and doubled up as cleaner; Ernest - the secretary, and a stooped, balding, tweed- jacketed former school teacher; of the other members somebody called Ian had tendered an apology. Generally, there was very little business and, as a consequence, the meetings were infrequent and poorly attended. Under Vincent it had become accepted practice that no minutes or decisions were made public or advised to the trustees, the workings of the group were a mystery and had become a talking point all around the village. For quite some time the trust had bumbled along, tolerating these secretive ways. Nobody really cared to get involved, although most agreed that the situation was unacceptable; whilst the elected parish council - who owned the land on which the hall stood - had become inward looking and disinterested in putting matters right.

The stage was last used in the eighties to present plays by schools and amateur dramatic societies. In winter months the poorly attended badminton and short mat, carpet bowls clubs utilised it on three weekly nights, the more active scouts and youth club took one night each. In summer, when the evenings were lighter and the television sports programmes better, the main hall was under-booked. This high ceiling room, with adjoining kitchen, was reached from the entrance through an annex used to stack sets of folding tables and chairs – it was where Alan had attended the disastrous parish council meeting. Except for rather basic toilets at the rear, there were no other rooms.

This potentially useful facility stood on ground donated by the owner in 1967 after an enclosed yard of decrepit cottages had been demolished. After a long fund raising effort, led by the parish council and the late husband of Mrs Cecil, the trust was set up. The building was completed ten years later.

Vincent's wife Sanja had brought a fresh pair of eyes to the problem; she was quick to point out that the hall was dowdy, run down, and not up to twenty-first century standards, apart from which it was barely paying for itself. She was correct: the electricity supply was through a meter into which florins - the old two shilling coins - had to be fed and then taken out by the caretaker for reuse; the only heating - from infrared lamps high on wooden roof trusses - was ineffective and wrongly sited; the rusting steel framed windows fitted badly and let in draughts; the stage was unused, and without a pleasant, private room no organisation could reasonably be expected to meet there. Vincent brought the gathering to order.

'Welcome,' he began, 'I think we need to discuss and agree a long term plan for upgrading our hall.' The words fell into a stony silence, but finally the schoolteacher spoke.

'Is that really necessary? The premises are often booked. With the monthly village draw, and income from clubs, we can just break even. Anyway, we have no money for capital works.'

Ernest spoke up. 'It's all Ian and I can do to patch the place up- we sometimes resort to persuading small local subcontractors to work for nothing. I agree that its time to do something, but where is the funding to come from?'

'People are so much better off today than when the hall was built,' replied their chairman, 'and there are grants available for such work - often on a pound for pound matching basis, or better. We can hold events to raise money – my wife has lots of ideas she tried out in London. If we don't make a start the hall will become a liability. Don't forget that the trust's purpose is to provide up to date facilities for the benefit of all villagers. I fear we are in danger of failing in our duty!'

Ernest cautioned, 'We need to put this to the other members – four of us aren't a quorum. If we want to go ahead, such a policy would require approval from a majority of the trustees - at least in principle. Who's going to produce a plan? We need somebody with expertise in modern building work, one who understands the current regulations.'

'We do,' agreed Vincent, 'but that's a long way off. What we need first is a programme of imaginative fund raising. Let me sum up for the minutes. As I see it we have agreed to put the need for refurbishment to the rest of our members and trustees – I'll do that by phone. If there is general acceptance I will call a further meeting to seek ideas for a series of fund raising events, and volunteers to implement them. Gentlemen, I think that's as far as we can go tonight. This meeting is closed. Let's say, using Mr Churchill's famous wartime words, that it's 'the end of the beginning'.

'An ambitious project,' commented the teacher, 'but, you're right Vincent, something must be done. I've been convinced, let's hope the others are.'

The chairman smiled, he liked to get his own way and he knew that Sanja would be pleased. He beamed at the two men and began to uncork a bottle he had brought with him.

'Won't you join me in a celebratory glass of wine before you venture out into the rain?'

* * * * *

'BODY FOUND BY CANAL'

announced a strident, full page headline in the weekly Advertiser. Overleaf, the article continued: 'An early morning dog walker made a grizzly discovery near the Grand Union Canal at Denton Cheney. A body was floating face down in a stream. Mr Turner, a shocked local resident, said, 'I was out early with Rex – my long haired setter – when he ran off and wouldn't come back. I climbed down from the tow path to see what was wrong and saw a body lying in the weeds. Although only a flat hat and denim jacket were visible I felt there was something familiar about him. I didn't touch anything, and phoned 999 on my mobile. The police came quickly. We walk the canal regularly but don't usually go so far from the village.'

Detective Inspector McAlister appealed for anyone who was in the area during last Friday night or Saturday morning to come forward. He said the case was being treated as a missing person, asking locals to advise him if anyone they knew had failed to return home.

At the scene early today a white tent had been erected over the stream and the area taped off while investigations continue; two policemen were in attendance. Later, our reporter saw police cars and an ambulance parked along the nearest road about four hundred yards away. It is thought that the body has already been removed.'

The paper was widely read in the rural area and delivered to most houses during Saturday afternoon. Talk at the shop and the Fox and Hounds inevitably centred on this item, though it was no surprise; most villagers having already heard some version of it by word of mouth. All sorts of theories were advanced but, on examination, none seemed very plausible. Nobody appeared to have noted any neighbour or friend as unaccounted for. At least, none had been reported to police community support officer Sheena, who, with Sergeant Smith, was making systematic calls at every house. They were concentrating on those of known dog owners, fishermen, regular walkers or cyclists, and taking statements. Later, their search was expanded to the surrounding villages. The body was rumoured to have been several weeks old and only found when Turner's dog picked up the smell of decomposition.

The unpleasant discovery appeared on both the BBC's main and regional television news, and most of the commercial channels, as cameras and reporters descended on the usually sleepy village. After a week, with nothing new, they all departed.

Village opinion soon decided that the victim was a loner, perhaps a tramp or drug addict who had collapsed and drowned - probably somebody that nobody would miss and unworthy of further interest.

* * * * *

The baby was always crying, putting Susan into a permanent state of tension while she anticipated possible complaints from downstairs. Not that there had been any - it was just knowing that Jim below worked shifts and took his sleep at odd hours. The small flat was part of the council estate, built, in two phases, by the Atlee led government in order to provide better living conditions for poorly paid, farm labour. There were only a few such 'up and downs', the rest were semi-detached houses most of which, after Mrs Thatcher's generous offer, were proudly owner occupied by the original tenants. Entrance was from open, exterior

29

concrete steps. Once inside they had a living room, kitchen, bedroom and separate bathroom. It was cramped but adequate, all they could afford on Mick's wages at the farm - though he had recently brought home a nice summer bonus which had helped provide the essential baby things.

Baby was putting on weight - doing well, said the health visitor – so Susan had no special problems beyond making ends meet. Fortunately, the tenancy included the use of half the garden, which was huge. On fine days she could put Damien outside and go down to feed him, which made a welcome break from being stuck inside. Before her pregnancy Susan had been a clerk at the district council offices, about four miles away and needing a bus ride. While there she had made enquiries about affordable housing, discovering that it was council policy to provide it for families with strong connections to the area and household incomes which prevented them from getting onto the 'housing ladder'. After attending interviews and filling in all the forms, Susan was encouraged to hear that suitable houses and flats were being built by independent housing associations as small developments in nearby rural villages. It seemed that one purchased only as much equity as one could obtain a mortgage for and paid rent on the outstanding value. If it became necessary to leave then the accommodation was sold and you received the full market value of your initial share which could be taken away as cash. Susan and Mick quickly realised that, if house prices rose, they would at least get a part of any windfall, rather than just endlessly paying rent with no long term capital gain.

Armed with this valuable knowledge, and assisted by council officials, the young couple struggled through the application process, managing to become selected - provided their circumstances remained unchanged - as candidates for the next 'appropriate development', as the formal letter advised. Unfortunately, when Susan enquired about a likely date she was advised that there was nothing in the pipeline near enough to be of use to them, and nothing specific in hand at Denton Cheney or adjacent villages. The housing officer told her that, even after obtaining planning approval, it would take at least two years to complete for occupation. She was disappointed - a home of their own was still years away, but she had Damien, who was whole, healthy and lovely, and they had their names on the list. She reconciled herself to patience. Things could only get better - her parents had waited ten years for a council house, and that was only to rent.

*   *   *   *   *

The bare stone pantry was always the coolest room in her elegant manor, which explained why the old lady had chosen to sit there. She stooped over a genuine campaign desk, one that had once been used on the northwest frontier by an earlier Cecil, a Colonel of Foot, and now served as a practical place at which to deal with the household accounts. Today, a copy of the 'Advertiser' was spread out across it; the paper had been passed on to her by a neighbour who had drawn attention to its shocking headline.

'Well I never,' she exclaimed to herself. 'I often walk down there. Such a find makes me nervous about going out. I wish Auberon were here.' Feeling it necessary to talk to somebody she picked up the phone and dialled her son's number, but, before he could answer, put the receiver down. 'What am I doing?' she scolded herself out aloud. 'He won't be interested and will only think I'm getting silly and can't look after myself. People die all the time, but I find it strange that they don't know who it was.'

The house was large with three stories but no basement; in more prosperous times it had been decorated on the north side by the addition of a symmetrical Georgian front from which her late husband had removed the cement stucco to expose buff coloured stonework. She much preferred it this way, but had a twinge of conscience that they had never sought planning approval, even though it was Grade 2 listed. The building was surrounded by several acres of garden, all laid out in the 'separate room style' of the twentieth century arts and crafts movement; after living there for close on sixty years, walking around it remained an adventure. Immediately opposite and just across the lane was Home Farm which was rented to her estate manager and his family. The farm-house stood amongst a cluster of irregularly placed, more or less derelict barns, pigsties and outhouses which now served only to garage agricultural machinery.

Farm and manor were at the edge of the village, having been cut off from her remaining two hundred acres when a bypass was constructed in the fifties. For Mrs Cecil the road was a terrible daily inconvenience but Denton Cheney had benefited from it. The planners had little alternative but to issue a compulsory purchase order, since to pass by on the further side of the village would have involved twice the length and twice the cost.

A rap on the front door demanded her attention. In the porch were two uniformed police officers, one was the cheerful, female PCSO, whom she had often noticed around the village.

'Mrs Cecil?'

'Yes', she confirmed.

'You will have heard about the body in the stream,' continued the officer, very politely.

'Yes,' she repeated, adding, 'only just.'

'We're calling all around the village. Have you been in that area recently, or know of anybody who is missing?'

'Come into the parlour a minute,' Mrs Cecil suggested, 'it's hot out there.' The big oak door opened straight into the reception, there was no hall. 'I took a stroll by there two weeks ago. It was a Wednesday – after my keep fit, the twentieth - such a lovely day. I didn't notice anything, but then I wasn't looking.'

'Did you go down by the stream – near where it joins the canal overflow?' asked the sergeant.

'No. That was where I turned back. The water was very clear, rushing by.'

'Thank you. If anything occurs to you that you think might be useful, then please call us on this number,' said the sergeant handing her a leaflet. As she let them out Mrs Cecil had a question.

'Was it a man or a woman? I'm searching my mind for anybody I haven't heard from recently.'

'It was a woman,' responded the policeman guardedly, 'but any information would be of interest to us. Thank you for your help.'

After they'd gone she remembered, 'That's strange,' she thought, 'old Turner said it was a man.'

32

* * * * *

'It's time we had more trees in this village,' suggested the voice to nobody in particular. Jeff stopped to listen. The man continued cheerfully, 'We planted some in the Lake District a few years back.'

As an active newcomer, really a city dweller, Jeff felt he should be sympathetic towards country practices. While taking a stroll he had attempted to behave more like a local by wishing this villager a brisk, 'Good morning'. The man's car was parked on a drive and, while he was passing, its door had suddenly opened, allowing a pair of long, corduroy clad legs to swing out. The comment had followed. Having revealed his ignorance Jeff mentally kicked himself. He'd forgotten the standard words, which made the friendly response even more surprising. A nod in acknowledgement had been the most he had expected; now he had a proposal to consider.

'I must say, all I hear is of people chopping them down for fear they might affect their houses or walls, or insurance. Nobody plants any!'

The man looked up knowingly, 'I'm Chris. I don't think we've met?'

'No,' agreed Jeff, proffering his hand in formal business style. Receiving only an awkward grasp in response, he realised he'd done the wrong thing again, but his new acquaintance remained positive and, for want of doubt, repeating himself, 'Chris.'

'Jeff,' he acknowledged with an awkward grin.

Chris appeared to have sensed some sort of compatibility, perhaps a similar accent or style of dress.

'I was in the Cotswolds this summer, Stow-on-the-Wold. Do you know it?' Jeff nodded. 'They had the most lovely flower planters. We could do something similar.'

'Why not,' agreed Jeff. 'But - there's always a but – we need some money.'

'This is a rich village,' Chris continued enthusiastically. 'If others can do it, so can we.'

'Perhaps we could get some of the village businesses to sponsor a box each – the shop, the old peoples' home, the pub?' suggested Jeff.

'We could put out a leaflet asking for donations,' continued Chris.

Jeff paused, 'It could be done, but first we need some brochures with costs so we can select the best.' His new friend was evidently pleased to have found such instant support and warmed to the idea

'I've got a file of stuff I've collected - just never got going. Want to see it?'

'Why not,' Jeff began to realise that Chris had already done the planning but, without a partner, had faltered. His awakening interest had served to move things forward.

'If you hold on I'll get it,' suggested Chris.

Minutes later Jeff walked away with a red folder and a feeling that, having got involved, he had to make it work.

After some phone calls information began to arrive. Both favoured moulded plastic for its durability, clean look and, hopefully, proof against vandals, rather than steel which rusts and needs regular painting, or wood which rots and requires varnish. One of the collected catalogues offered tough, black planter boxes with a built in water reservoir, a permanent wick feed up into the soil and the option of elegant lettering for the village name - all at a reasonable price.

Pleased to find something suitable, Jeff decided that it would be wise to begin at all four of the main village entrances. This concept was easy to grasp and would probably avoid disputes about why a particular street or house had been favoured. Chris was in agreement, which set a monetary target to be achieved before the following summer's flowering season. After trying to gauge the level of interest by leafleting the whole village they were delighted to receive a number of positive phone calls and, as a result, decided to forge ahead.

Small contributions from individual residents formed the bulk of the donated money with the less well off often the most generous. These were supplemented by unexpectedly large amounts from active village societies and clubs. Jeff was surprised to find so many separate organisations in a settlement of only three hundred households, but they were most welcome.

Aware that the parish council had become inactive, they consulted the district council by sending them a plan of the proposed locations. The response indicated that they must refer to the county council and obtain permission from any house that would overlook the planters. Chris was cautious and recommended that written approval should be obtained before any money was committed; as a civil servant he had bad memories of English people who had been unreasonably difficult over anything connected with their house, car or garden. Jeff was surprised – he'd been out of the country on and off over many years – but accepted that the concern was valid. As a consequence they spent some time sending out letters with tear off acceptance slips at the bottom; nothing came back. The vast lethargy of the silent majority had become all too apparent. It was only by following up each letter with a personal visit that they managed to collect all the required approvals, passing copies onto the county council for their records. An apparently obligation free retirement had turned into hard work.

* * * * *

The knocks on the door were persistent, demanding; then a female voice, 'Is anybody home? It's Sheena with Sergeant Smith. We're checking to see if residents have any information on that recent canal death.'

'It's the fuzz,' whispered Sam.

'Let's get out the back,' suggested Dave. 'It's us they really want. They know your dad and mum are at work.'

'No,' said Sam, restraining his friend. 'Open the door and let them in.'

The PCSO'S large boot crossed the threshold, followed by the taciturn, skinny sergeant.

'This isn't about what you may or may not have done,' Sheena began reassuringly. 'We need information on that body. You two know all the youngsters and get around the countryside in your spare time. Has anybody mentioned anything unusual to you, strangers in the locality, cars lurking about – that sort of thing?'

'No,' replied Sam, serious all of a sudden – he enjoyed being taken as someone responsible. 'It's been quiet about here all summer – too hot – but I'll ask.'

Dave still hadn't uttered a word but lingered there, listening and looking around like a startled pheasant, aware that public relations weren't his strength.

'Is there any sort of reward?' he asked, 'one to loosen tongues.'

'No son,' said the sergeant, at last finding something he could deal with, 'and there won't be.' He blundered on, undoing the good start his colleague had made. 'Good citizens help their local police, they don't need incentives. Just remember, we know who did that job at the petrol station kiosk, even if we can't prove it… yet. Something useful from you two might help keep you out of court.'

The veiled threat having been delivered, Sheena continued the 'good cop bad cop routine'.

'Some help would be appreciated,' she concluded pleasantly as the two officers let themselves out, pulling the door to behind them.

'What do you think?' asked Sheena.

'They're telling the truth this time,' admitted Smith. 'I think they might even do some detective work of their own – bit of fun type of thing. We can always hope.'

$$* \quad * \quad * \quad * \quad *$$

The letter had been addressed to VASE and sent to his home. 'Villagers against sand extraction' was the pressure group he and Mike had founded to resist the development of a minerals site close to Denton Cheney. Jeff slit it open with a thin, ebony paper knife which he vaguely remembered his father bringing back from Egypt when demobbed in 1945. Inside, were several sheets which had been clipped together; they covered each scheduled session of the imminent, ten day Inquiry in Public, giving times, allocated rooms, details of who was to present the case for and against each of the proposed mineral sites and who, apart from the inspector and his clerical assistant, would represent the county council – originators of the controversial 'Local Minerals Plan'. Yes, they had been accepted as a consultative group and were asked to present their case verbally on the sixth day during a two hour afternoon session.

'Whoopee,' he yelled out aloud, and immediately headed down the hall to reach the phone. 'Mike, it's me. We did it. Good news.' His fellow member was more cautious.

'I expected it. At least we've met the inspector. Now we have to prepare our points and agree who says what. Do you realise that the enemy will have a tame barrister to speak on their behalf - paid for out of our council tax! It's hardly fair and even.'

'Well no, but I've some confidence in that Brian Findlay guy. He's a middle-aged civil engineer, nobody's fool. In my judgement, someone mature and even handed.'

'Let's hope so,' said his friend doubtfully. 'Can we meet at your house on Thursday to sketch out our first draft?'

'Right, Coffee at eleven, see you.'

The whole thing – this involvement in the democratic planning process – had begun by chance. Jeff had noticed that, according to the town's weekly paper, a large sand pit had been proposed at a site within their parish. It was less than a kilometre from his house and in the direction of the prevailing south west wind. The article had come as a surprise. He'd never heard mention of it before; his solicitors hadn't advised him of it in their search when, having moved away from a part of England scarred with slagheaps and run down collieries, he and his wife had purchased in the village. Jeff thought he'd moved into the countryside but opencast mining was coming back to haunt him.

On exploratory walks around the village he had noticed several areas, heavily overgrown with thickets and nettles, which appeared to be at a slightly lower level. Prior to the Minerals Plan he hadn't given them a second thought, but realised now that they were the abandoned workings of old sand or gravel pits. On making enquiries he discovered that the football club ground was one such abandoned excavation which had been backfilled with surplus spoil from the nearby motorway, and understood why the public playing field, with its ancient swings and slides, was about three metres below the adjacent road. Now, the topography all made sense.

Seeking further background he approached their district councillor, an attractive middle-aged lady, to whom he had been introduced at the Conservative Association's pig roast. Brenda was pleased to note his eagerness to see if further desecration could be prevented. The proposed new pit was huge; it would take about ten years to work out and probably be left as a dangerous area of swampy ponds. Jeff realised that the extra traffic generated must pass through either Denton Cheney or Dunton, both were equally old, unspoilt and rural.

Confidential advice from Brenda was that organising a protest was properly the duty of the parish council but, as the present one was poorly constituted and led, it was better if someone set up an action group – like the one that was fighting the school. Such an approach could have advantages over even a good council because a separate entity would not have any of the constraints incumbent on an elected, representative body. Jeff took the point and, after teaming up with his golfing partner Mike and recruiting two part timers, had formed VASE. Although the acronym didn't immediately define their cause it was catchy and easy to remember.

Never previously involved in, or even interested in, local government they experienced a steep learning curve. Everything was new but, with a belief that commonsense should prevail and his own professional expertise as a geologist, added to Mike's local contacts and management know-how, they had succeeded in stirring villagers up into writing letters of protest. This support had led to the recognition of VASE as a legitimate consultative group within the community.

Jeff briefly attended earlier Inquiry sessions in order to understand the procedures and gauge the atmosphere. This experience made him glad they had accepted the advice to form an independent unit since the parish council had been noticeably under-represented; he couldn't help but wonder if any of its members had an interest in the fields designated as the potential minerals site. The grapevine told him that, in villages, everything was done or decided by a small clique of long term resident families and farmers; he hoped that, if they did exist, they would leave him alone. Fears of 'accidentally broken' windows or damage to his car or the garden wall had crossed his mind, but he daren't tell his wife Jean who, having a very 'black or white' approach, would either panic and tell him to desist or tick him of for overreacting. Right now it was better to just press on quietly, but with determination.

He phoned Brenda who was, as far as he could discover, unlikely to reap any benefit - whatever the outcome. She said the site had been one allocated as a potential source of soft sand in a previous 'local plan' but that planning approval had never been sought. Although the extent of the reserves had been proven by borehole sampling and shown to be of good quality, they lay mostly below the water table. Another problem was access. Contractor's trucks would need to exit through one of the twin villages whose lanes were far too narrow. As the town's railway link passed close to the site, one proposed solution had been to load the sand onto rail cars. As far as Jeff could ascertain no binding restrictions had yet been placed on means of access, lowering of the water table or refilling and restoration of the pit, which led him to conclude that the best defence was to ensure that any extraction would be as expensive as possible and continue to remain commercially unviable.

Armed with this information Jeff prepared a speech which listed, should the site be used, all the adverse environmental impacts he could imagine, asking for them to be mitigated by development control criteria which specified exact methods of working, levels of acceptable dust and air pollution and protection of adjacent properties. He also raised the need for independent weekly monitoring to ensure full compliance.

The venue for their inquiry session was a conference room at the town's rugby club. In the professional era the latter had, under the guidance of a local entrepreneur, been transformed by massive investment in both male and female, user friendly building development and new stands, all supported by the reliable cash flow generated from a team in the first division. With a town centre site, and its own large, adjacent car park, the facilities had proven useful for meetings of all sorts and were readily transformed into large, member only bars for home fixtures.

Jeff drove them there in his aging, but reliable, Honda; it had eighty thousand miles on the clock but he was loath to replace it. They were early. Outside, the press had gathered, awaiting the conclusion of an earlier session which had attracted a colourful 'rent a crowd' mix of idealistic unemployed students and pensioners; both had time to spare. The main doors swung open and microphones were thrust under the noses of leaving participants whose faces immediately registered expressions in which suspicion of the media was overcome by the pleasure of becoming, for the first time in their lives, the centre of attention. Jeff and Mike watched in surprise as home made placards on garden stakes bobbed in a circle around a brown, duffle-coated journalist who held his black microphone towards a serious looking, partly bald man in a grey suit. The surrounding, handwritten messages read: 'No gravel from Grendon' and 'Grendon has done enough'.

Before they could approach close enough to catch the interview, it was over and the previously animated throng began dispersing towards the street in a seemingly disorganised way.

'What was all that?' an intrigued Mike asked a nearby spectator.

'It was Charlie - from the radio car – we had to fit into his morning programme slot but were a bit late. At least he turned up. Once before we waited for an hour but he got stuck in traffic – or so he claimed.'

'Oh,' said Jeff, discovering during further explanation, that Charlie's outside broadcasts were a popular feature of the regional BBC station. They looked at each other, and Mike grinned ruefully.

'Seems they're doing a lot more than us.'

'Yes,' agreed Jeff, suddenly feeling guilty, 'come on – we've only five minutes to go.'

They clattered up the bare concrete stairs, following Xerox copied A4 sheets sellotaped to the whitewashed, brick wall and arrowed with 'Public Inquiry'. On the second floor an official asked them to sign in on a clipboard paper, headed unambiguously, 'Day 6 - Afternoon'.

'Name and organisation, please,' he insisted as they hurriedly recorded their details.

Formalities completed, they entered the room which had been arranged confrontationally in parliamentary style. Rows of chairs faced each other; between them, at one end, was a head table with two vacant, more comfortable, upholstered seats, and two name signs – 'Inspector' and 'Secretary'. They hastily took up positions on the right. Those opposite being already occupied by four, smartly dressed officers from the county council and, as they were soon to learn after the introductions, a rather pompous barrister.

'We're heavily outnumbered,' whispered Mike.

'It's quality that matters,' retorted Jeff.

The enemy suddenly stood up as the two adjudicators walked in to take their seats. Unlike the council, who had already been through several days of this, Mike and Jeff were unaware of the decorum but quickly followed suit.

'Do you have any objections if I tape record the proceedings?' queried the secretary.

They didn't.

'Will the representatives from villagers against sand extraction, VASE, please put their case?' invited the tall, bespectacled Inspector in a sympathetic tone.

Mike kicked off by reading from their prepared notes, handing over to Jeff for the more technical arguments. It didn't take long.

'And may we have the council's reply?' intoned the Inspector after clarifying some of the points raised, mentioning his own visit to the site, and pointing out that it was crossed by an ancient footpath which connected the two, sister villages.

The barrister had the best delivery, as befitted his profession, but to Mike, the poorer case. He reminded himself that this advocate was being paid for out of the villager's council tax. Why couldn't the planning officials speak for themselves? It wasn't fair - VASE couldn't afford such a service.

'Does anyone wish to raise any further points?' asked the secretary. Nobody did. 'In which case I declare this session closed. You will all be able to read the result in Mr Findlay's report - he expects to conclude it within three months.' Jeff put up a hand.

'Yes?' called the secretary.

'Will that document be available to us for comment?'

'Available – yes, for comment – no. The report, and its recommendations, will be considered by the county council and each part either accepted in whole or rejected. You and all the others will be able to make representations on their decisions - which they may then consider. For us the Inquiry will be complete.'

Jeff nodded his understanding and stood up with Mike to leave. All that work and yet it still had months to run! Worse still, the county council, as originators of the plan, were not even bound to accept the results. After all the Inspector's effort and judgement his learned comments in a sixty

41

page document could be totally ignored. Jeff thought it a laborious and unhelpful process, well intended – yes, but, in the end almost futile since the results were not binding on anyone. He couldn't believe that so called democracy had been allowed to fall this far.

*　*　*　*　*

The thin, but spry old man placed a large wicker basket of freshly cut runner beans onto the kitchen table.

'That's about it Dot. Take what you need to freeze, the rest can go to the old people round at Phoenix House. Apart from some late flowers for the church, I don't think we can help much more this year.'

'Have you any further news about that poor woman in the stream? The Advertiser said a man - at least they corrected it in the next issue. Any gossip?' Dot knew that Roy picked up all sorts of talk as he did his gardening tasks around the villages.

'Nothing at all, which is unusual, I must say,' answered Roy as he disappeared back into the well kept vegetable garden to begin the annual clear up.

'Yes, it's been a productive season,' thought Dot. After early warmth, rainy days had alternated with hot sunny spells, causing most of their standard planting to grow vigorously. 'Perhaps it was a result of this global warming everybody is concerned about,' she pondered. 'Certainly, the winters are much less cold than in the nineteen twenties and thirties; of that there is no doubt.'

The tasks were shared out between them. Since becoming a widow, Dot, with help from her brother-in-law Roy, had managed to carry on with the vegetable patch. In early spring they had dug over the whole plot, rejuvenating the earth with bags of chicken manure collected from Tim at the egg farm. Although it smelt awful, none of the neighbours had ever complained; provided it was dug in deep, the odour soon disappeared. Good stuff it was, but the garden soil, although originally the paddock of the grandest house in the village – apart from the two manors that is – was thin and sandy, needing nourishment to provide a decent annual crop.

Prior to the First World War, Denton Cheney reached a peak population of over a thousand – not counting all the horses. Villagers had contributed twelve young lives to that awful, misnamed 'war to end all wars'. Afterwards, with the introduction of efficient, petrol-engined tractors, mechanised farm machinery, trains and country bus routes, young people had drifted away to the towns, seeking less arduous, better paid work. Their wartime experiences changed participants for ever, taking them away from their narrow rural roots and opening their eyes to the world beyond - its good and its bad aspects. They had survived, now they wanted - thought they deserved - a better future.

After World War II ten more names were added to the memorial on the green. As nobody in 1919 had expected this further, wider conflagration, no space had been left and a separate plaque had to be fixed higher up the sandstone column, spoiling the monument's overall symmetry and forever looking like a less important afterthought. The new list included a number of families whose sons - they were all male – had also appeared on the original; one was an officer from the main manor house. To Dot these further lives had always seemed like an unreasonable double sacrifice. In the first war all the villagers had joined the same unit, willing to preserve the rural scene - the England we still love - with their own lives. 'Of course,' she thought, 'we were ignorant then. Why did we show such patriotism in 1914 for that avoidable and unnecessary cause, whereas in 1939 it was just a job, a case of survival?'

Following that war the Labour government rose to power and decided that the housing stock needed upgrading - too many families were living in unhygienic, unsanitary, overcrowded conditions. Her parents' house, which she had always liked and regarded as a home with character, fell into this category. This ancient building had seen many uses during its long life, beginning as a crude dwelling for the grooms and stable boys who tended the many horses that served the deCourt family, and becoming a general shop - one of five in the village - as that noble family fell on hard times during the industrial revolution. When the shop failed, her grandfather – a mason by trade – bought it and converted it into a respectable home with an upper floor, well water, a pump, and septic tank.

At Denton Cheney this socialist insight had resulted in mass demolition of ancient cottages; at least thirty percent of the housing stock was raised to the ground. German bombs could not have done a better job of permanently changing the character of the village. Although Dot herself always hankered after a traditional, stone built, village home, the decision to re-house the occupants of the many run down properties in a brand new estate of council houses had proven popular. These semi-detached properties had three bedrooms, generous gardens, Formica kitchens, inside toilets, electric power, mains water, a sewer connection and controlled rents - ideal for a low income population, the majority of whom still worked either on the land or in country pursuits.

Octogenarian Dot, then in her early twenties, belonged to one of the first needy families to be uprooted. After the move she shared a bedroom with her elder sister, Alice, while Mum and Dad had, for the first time, a room of their own, and the twins another. Not long after this, Alice, the clever one, had left to board full time with an aunt while attending a teacher training college in London. Soon afterwards, at a dance in the village hall, she had met Nat, a farm labourer from Dunton. Within a year they were married at St James All Souls - only a short walk away - and returned to occupy her old room and share the rent at her parent's modern house. This arrangement had served them well, but another bathroom would have been useful.

After Mum and Dad had passed on, and been interred side by side in the churchyard at St James, they had taken advantage of Mrs Thatcher's amazing offer, becoming only the second sitting tenants to purchase an estate house from the Tory government. Dot had said at the time, 'I'm so glad Dad isn't here. He would never have agreed with anything the Conservatives did.' It turned out to have been a sound investment. Ten years later they received inside knowledge - from the village grapevine - that the owner of another shop – one similar to her original family home - wanted to cease trading and return to town. After discussion they sold up and bought their present house. Externally, it had real character, reminding Dot of her demolished childhood home; internally it had been totally modernised. The circle was complete and a rural couple were, once more, living in one of the few remaining listed buildings.

She often looked back at the wanton destruction of those poky, linked buildings which, given today's affluence and awareness, would have been combined together, upgraded and retained. 'What a shame it was', thought Dot, 'what a short term policy! Nonetheless,' she had to admit, 'at that time of poverty and post war depression, with people living four and more to a tiny room, it had been the right decision.'

As a householder and respected old villager, 'auntie' Dot worried about the threat of mass housing. Nothing much had been built in Denton Cheney for thirty years. The action group argued that development would follow the construction of a proposed new secondary school, swamping the surrounding green parish. This must be resisted. What did twenty two brave young men die for if not to keep their homes as part of a lovely village set in the countryside?

* * * * *

It was an odd feeling - this being retired. Away from the hour by hour, week long, stresses and strains of the business world, but both fitter and healthier than he had been for several years, Alan's uninvolved mind kept dwelling on sex. Carol had gone off to see a friend and he went into the kitchen to make a 'pot of tea', or less anachronistically, he thought, a 'stainless steel container of tea'. Their old, shiny electric kettle - a wedding present he recalled - hadn't survived its journey back to England, or was it the hard limestone water? As a replacement his wife had acquired a much less attractive, tall plastic 'jug' which sat on a short, stiff post. Every time he filled it beneath the cold tap and dropped it into place, it conjured up a vivid and, admittedly, enjoyable vision of a beautiful, naked woman sitting down on …. If only!

Clearing his thoughts, Alan checked the list of action group members, found the chairman's name and began to look for it in the local Thomson directory, but it wasn't there. Next, he tried the area's BT phone book with more success, and a busy housewife found time to give him the mobile number he needed. He realised that, in his absence abroad, it had become fashionable for self-important people, and those serving the public, to become ex-directory. Contact was made and his offer to join accepted - subject to checking with the others, which was not expected to be a problem. The next meeting was - 'Due in three days time at David's place.' He said he could make it.

The detached house was neo-Georgian in style and in one of two, small, sixties cul-de-sac developments within the village confines. He learnt that, since them, nothing further had been proposed until a planning application for the school appeared out of the blue.

'Our present parish council is inept,' explained John, the chairman, 'we have to do all the work by ourselves. It does, however, have the big advantage of being able to avoid playing by the rules!' He continued, 'As from today I'm standing down as chair,' explaining vaguely, 'I have some health problems. David is taking over.' Noticing Alan's doubtful look, he added, 'Don't worry - you'll find him more than competent.'

Alan mentioned his experience at the disastrous parish council meeting and agreed that it was better to proceed independently and avoid sharing their intentions. Sitting in the pleasant room were - a self-employed accountant, an ex-policeman - now a security adviser, and a solicitor turned businessman who had spent his whole life in the village. Not available was the Hon. Mrs Cecil - described as a robust, elderly lady and stalwart supporter of their cause, she was from one of the manor houses; their retiring chairman owned the Grange, another grand residence.

This is a strong team thought Alan, but all of similar age and class. How he hated the designation 'class'; it was an awful word, not much understood in other countries, but, here in England, still widely recognised and binding. He reminded himself never to acknowledge such a socially destructive concept.

Glasses of chilled, Rhine wine were offered by David's German wife and gratefully accepted - despite some having driven the short distance there. The chair advised that a check of case files at the district council office had revealed a good response to their circular - seventy eight letters had been received so far. He would now contact and remind people he knew who had not yet replied, could the others do the same? The solicitor raised the issue of the action group's right to speak on behalf of the villagers, he pointed out that some sort of mandate was essential and proposed organising a public meeting in the village hall. His idea was that the decision to protest could be put to a show of hands and the expected majority result carefully recorded. It would also be appropriate for questions to be taken and help sought, thus providing an opportunity for members of the group to be seen and identified by everybody at an open forum. Somebody asked about notifying the local papers. A general agreement was reached that they should be invited and a suitable press release prepared. There being a consensus, David phoned the village hall chairman, there and then, to book a Thursday evening, two months ahead, a date which allowed sufficient time for publicity and preparation. After he switched off his mobile he advised them that, as it was a village event, Vincent had agreed to waive the hire fee.

Alan went home impressed. These people were competent. If they fought hard there was an outside chance of success, despite advice from their elected, and supportive district counsellor that the county council's education department had already narrowed their choice down to one of two sites – both of which were in or near their village – and were not expecting any opposition.

* * * * *

The classic Mercedes saloon pulled off the motorway, delving, almost immediately, into twisting B roads, its occupants exchanged pace and monotony for dawdle and interest. Anesh passed the quaint village sign and the limestone church before negotiating some narrow streets to reach Phoenix House, a residential home for the elderly. He and Amita had purchased it three years ago.

In India, before partition, his grandfather had been a pioneer of private, secular, residential care; Anesh remained proud of his achievements. Becoming weary of the seemingly endless religious extremism and unrest in their own country they had migrated to England soon after getting married. The decision was hastened by inside knowledge from Anesh's father that the state government was thinking of closing down all privately run homes and insisting that they be provided only by religious foundations. The couple knew they had the experience to provide a

47

useful service and had learnt that, in England, government policy was to shut down state run homes and expect private ones to replace them. A large mortgage needed feeding, but cash flow was good and Anesh foresaw a day when the home would be all theirs.

Every weekday they drove up early from the capital and back again in the evening. Willing, but inexperienced, part-time staff from the village had been in place when they took over. After supplementing them with two full-time professionals and a rota of trained carers from the town, it was quite practical to be there only during normal office hours. In north London they had started with a small hotel acquired by means of a family legacy, but this was now efficiently managed by their son and his wife who had joined them five years ago. The success of this arrangement had left Anesh's energetic, do-gooder wife, by her own admission, with 'too much time on her hands,' and had led to the purchase of Phoenix House. It provided a new challenge and, what was important to them both, a contribution to the wonderful nation in which they had settled and were so happy.

Dealing with the ever burgeoning bureaucracy and paperwork was Anesh's main task. There were regular visits from the district council, the Health and Safety executive and officious inspections by staff from its kitchen hygiene department. If notified in advance such visits called for a bit more effort on the preceding afternoon, or if by surprise, led to a day of tension and note taking. Of course, there was always something that needed attention - such as replacing old equipment or retraining staff; dealing with it disrupted their daily routine. Meantime, his wife did all the cooking, which she enjoyed, and provided an interface with the residents, while he was stuck at a desk set up in what had once been a small store room on the ground floor.

Among the papers in Anesh's tray today was a note which puzzled him; it was from a village 'action group' who were concerned about a proposed new school. Even though they only visited by day, both liked the secluded rural atmosphere where horse's hooves could sometimes be heard clip-clopping along the street outside and flocks of baaing sheep brushed past the wall. Although mostly tied to the business they had come to enjoy being a part of Denton Cheney, having acquired a sense of belonging it was an easy decision to write in and support this protest. Impatient to discover what progress had been made, and needing to answer the concerns of his paying guests, the majority of whom had been brought up in Denton Cheney, Anesh called the number given on the action group's sheet. A man answered in very King's English with a crisp delivery. It was a voice similar to those with which his father had become very familiar during the British Raj, and one he himself had inherited. Yes, it was the right number, and yes, a lot of protest letters had been sent in already - as of yesterday precisely two hundred and fifty one.

'A good result,' he ventured. The man hesitated.

'I've arranged for the leader of the county council to come and see us at my home next week. We need to tell him, face to face, what a nonsense this is. For your information, a site was originally allocated in Upton Park – that new development of a thousand houses south of here. It's still available and better placed to serve the children, most of whom would have to travel to Denton Cheney by bus, all paid for unnecessarily out of your, and my, council tax.'

'I see,' exclaimed Anesh, who well understood the political negotiations that democracy involved. He remembered that, in the India of his parents, bribery was the accepted means of achieving one's objective, and asked, 'Who's behind all this?'

'Don't know. All we can do is get the residents to send in letters - under consultation rules the council must acknowledge and take account of them. Then, lobby our elected representatives to support our view point, and chat up the Advertiser - our town's weekly paper – who love to expose bad decision making and waste. We've achieved one thing, an inter-party committee has been appointed to review the decision – which was made in camera by the majority Labour party 'cabinet', or executive, without seeking a confirmatory majority at a full council meeting. The committee's report will go to such a full meeting – it is open to the public – for a final vote in about eight weeks time.'

'You've done a lot,' Anesh interjected into the confident flow of words. He was genuinely impressed; it was the sort of procedure one would expect in this fair minded country, a place he had admired from afar, long before becoming a citizen himself. 'Is there more we can do?'

49

he asked, as Amita tried to attract his attention - someone was sick.

'Get everyone you know to write in,' was the reply. 'Bye.'

Gladys, at ninety three their oldest resident, was lying on the floor in the lounge. Blood trickled out of her mouth and one ear, making a dark red stain on the grey, fitted carpet. Six other people remained slumped in their chairs, many were too weak to stand without aid, the rest so assailed by Parkinson's or other diseases of senility that they could barely communicate. The large, bright television screen acted like a drug in keeping them all sedated, helping to solve the ever present problem of maintaining twenty four hour staffing.

Anesh reached the spot quickly. 'What happened?' he asked, but received in reply only silence and the confused stares of those who are neither in this world nor the next.

Then came a melodic voice from the deepest armchair. 'It's Gladys. She fell out of her chair.' It was Ellen, at eighty five still the most active and helpful of the residents.

'Thank you Ellen,' said Anesh. Crouched on the floor he turned towards his wife, 'Best call the doctor's surgery. Say - urgent. We've already had one death in the area, we don't want another!'

A coded system of alerts had been pre-agreed with the local, six doctor practice in Denton, barely a mile away. This message would bring a prompt response.

'Don't move her,' cautioned Amita unnecessarily as she dialled the number.

'No, I'll cover her with some blankets and wipe up the blood – it seems to have stopped. She's unconscious but breathing steadily.'

A rather short, overweight lady appeared in the doorway; she was dressed in a blue tunic. 'Not Gladys again, she's fallen down about every other day.'

'Dorothy, did you report that – put it in the book?' queried Anesh. 'We must keep a record and show it to the doctor.'

'I did,' replied the woman.

It reminded Anesh that today only one fully-trained carer, who hailed from the village's council estate, was there. Dorothy wasn't so bright but more than made up for it with a good attitude. Fortunately, she knew all the health difficulties and personal idiosyncrasies of the incumbents.

During the doctor's visit no long term problem was diagnosed and Gladys recovered well after going to her room with Dorothy in attendance. Anesh beckoned Amita into the office and shut the door.

'We must write straight away and inform her son that she had a fall – it's required by Health and Safety. The trouble is she's had others which we haven't notified. Our staffing is inadequate. We make do with too few. One day we'll be in real trouble and closed down. How upset my father would be then!'

'Anesh, you're right. It's time we took a long term view. The economy in this area is strong – unemployment is only two percent. The NHS competes with us by recruiting possible local carers as hospital assistants. Soon, we'll have nobody. I already feel bad about our standards.'

'There's been a lot on the television about immigrants. Why don't we apply for qualified people from the European Union - Poland for example? If we get one or two to begin with they can probably bring their friends - help keep them happy. If we rent a house they could all live together nearby.'

Amita was in favour. Secretly, she was relieved, 'What about the cost?'

'I'll do a budget and talk to the Home Office. Also look at the various web sites.'

'Good. In which case I'll take the car into town right now and speak to some estate agents.'

Amita could, at last, see a permanent solution. Just as she stood up to leave, the floor jarred beneath their feet as a dull thud, followed by a scraping sound, rent the usual village silence.

'What on earth…' began Anesh, just as Dorothy rushed in.

'It's outside,' she announced.

The owners looked at each other and headed for the front door. It led out into the street via an enclosed garden where two elderly men with dull expressions were sitting on a bench.

'Must be drunk,' one declared as Anesh ran past. At the gate the cause became all too apparent. A green, heavy goods vehicle, carrying a forty foot container marked COSCO, and pulling a trailer with a smaller container, had jammed itself up against the outside of their high, stone wall. It was the narrowest part of the village and there was no footpath. The podgy, boiler suited driver approached them, frantically waving his hands about and talking in a language neither could follow. Dorothy joined them

'He's Italian – there's a letter 'I' on the back.'

'Quite a few stones dislodged,' said Anesh. 'We need to check if it's safe. Call the police,' he instructed Dorothy. 'He'll need some help to get out. What's he doing trying to come through here? There's a sign by the church saying: 'Narrow road, unsuitable for lorries', or something similar. I'll go and call our insurers,' he announced.

Left behind on the street Amita was caught gently by the elbow and led towards the cab. The driver indicated she should climb up. His expression showed he was eager to declare his innocence, so she complied. The Italian sat next to her in the front seat and pointed to the glowing face of an instrument where a coloured map could be seen.

'Look,' he seemed to be saying, 'I followed that stupid thing.'

'A sat-nav!' she declared aloud. The man nodded and sighed. 'But, you idiot,' she continued, 'you need to use some commonsense. This isn't the first time it's happened, or the last I expect - unless we can get the council to do something.'

The Italian shrugged, realising that he was unpopular, and they both got out. Thorough as always she smoothed out her sari, produced a pencil and paper and wrote down the owner's address in Milan, the truck's registration and the time of day. 'Name?' she asked. 'Nom?'

The driver understood French. 'Stephano,' he replied, looking worried, and spelt it out. Headlights blazing, and a flashing blue roof beacon, signalled the arrival of a yellow and blue BMW station wagon containing two fluorescent, yellow coated, peak capped policemen.

'Bit jammed up there,' commented the sergeant with a smile towards the driver, before engaging him in a flurry of words which he, clearly, but nobody else, understood. Notes were taken and the policeman approached a puzzled Anesh who had reappeared at the accident surrounded by a group of curious locals.

'Me and the wife go to Sorrento every year. Love it. Didn't think I'd meet a Napolitan in, what do you call it, Cheney?'

'Denton Cheney,' Anesh corrected.

'Leave it to us,' reassured the sergeant. 'We'll get a breakdown truck to assist him back to the motorway. Sat-nav problem - as your wife saw. No real damage to your property, I think, but I'll ask the Highways engineers to check it out and let you know.' He focussed his attention on the onlookers. 'Alright you lot, move along. The fun's all over for today.'

Amita indicated to the Italian, using sign language, that if he came in he'd get a cup of coffee. Happier now, the driver followed the care home owners back through their gate, leaving the competent, multilingual motorway patrol team in charge outside.

* * * * *

Spring Farm was at the heart of Denton Cheney; one of its walls had been built directly against a cottage, better known now as the 'Fox and Hounds'. Both buildings were still thatched and shared a common history. The pub was once the home of a yeoman farmer who, as a result of the eighteenth century enclosures, had fallen on hard times, selling out to the farming family next door and entering their service. Between world wars an attractive offer was received from a Cambridge brewery and the neighbouring houses had, once again, become separately owned. In recent years the family had found there was less and less money in farming and gave up working their acres: 'Not worth the effort,' was their complaint, 'Too many EU edicts and British regulations. We just work like dogs doing the wishes of remote bureaucrats. It's daft.' But, in case their fields were required by builders, they held onto ownership and, to obtain a steady income, rented them out to others - shrewdly, on a month by month basis.

New Labour decided that a national housing shortage was to be addressed by home building on a massive scale in two principal areas - north Kent and around the nearby town; each would be orchestrated by a new quango or 'development authority'. Following this announcement everybody with a local square chain, acre or hectare saw golden figures coming up in the slot machine of life. Committed, long time farmers suddenly developed backache and a desperate need to retire. Ten year options were soon being sold to the highest bidders, who proved, like moths to a flame, not hard to find. Spring Farmhouse – all of its outbuildings had been pulled down - carried several handwritten 'House for Sale' posters, followed by a few printed 'For Rent' signs and, by the autumn, a pair of wooden 'For Sale' boards from different estate agents. According to the regular drinkers and darts players next door who knew the exact price, they were asking far too much. The publican was wiser; he reckoned that by year's end the booming market would have rendered the huge figure attractive. Right on cue both signs were duly taken away, but nobody knew which of the competing agents had been successful.

Speculation immediately began about the identity of its new owner. Stories abounded: he, or she, was related to old Ben in Phoenix House; he was a retiree from London; he was a rich business man; she was a widow from the north come to be near her sister; they had won the lottery. On one thing all were agreed, the purchaser was either mad or naïve in wanting to live next door to a popular public house.

Towards the middle of December a gnome-like, silver-haired man with matching goatee beard, was observed from the narrow lane, or jetty, that ran behind the 'Fox'. He was sitting in an open, grey sports car parked right outside the farmhouse. It wasn't Santa Claus but, as villagers were soon to discover, it was a Christmas present. The man they saw was aptly called Rector - Christian name Keith, and his arrival led to all sorts of confusion.

Denton Cheney, having been without a dedicated vicar for three years, was required to share the one at Dunton; now they had both a vicar and a rector! To make matters worse Mr Rector explained that he was indeed what his surname announced - a retired, ordained priest or, more correctly an ex-vicar. He had been educated at one of the Oxford colleges, he did quote a name - which, although not recognised, nobody dared to query. Following this he trained in holy orders and worked for a long time in a Birmingham parish, finally becoming dean of his old college where his main preoccupation had been the raising of funds.

Of course, everybody expected that Keith would be an embarrassment to their real rector - a sort of competitor for the souls of villagers, but he made it clear that he had already introduced himself to the Reverend Johnson, confirming that the two holy men, being from a common background and of similar ages, got on well.

* * * * *

You parents have always worried about daughters. Come on, admit it! It's nothing to be ashamed of - even in this age of women's liberation. After all, apart from paedophilic homosexuals, not too many crimes are committed against boys or youths. Yet mass murderers regularly kill women all over the front pages of our newspapers. We men are more concerned than our wives. Having found slim, young female forms attractive all our lives we can relate to the need for some males to do more than just look. A short skirt or a flash of cleavage is often enough to catch our attention, spark our basic instincts and make us want to touch and feel. Most of us never grow out of it.

Sunny Ibrahim was no exception to this male way of thinking. Despite having lived in the Midlands for more than twenty five years he knew, somehow, that daughter Ayesha was unable to choose a good partner all by herself. That she must have a husband and protector was not in doubt – look at all the reports of attacks on women. Even worse, there had now been an unsolved murder close by, out here in the quiet country where nothing ever happened. Ayesha needed a nice young man. When she was home he had become afraid to let her go out alone, even in daylight. How could she, at only eighteen, have his and Shiva's wisdom? They would have to do it for her. After all, it had worked for them. His marriage to a girl chosen by his parents in Pakistan and sent to him 'sight unseen', had provided him with a loving, faithful wife.

Their daughter was half way through the first year of a fashion design course at Bristol College of Art. She had refused to apply for a similar course in the local town, one to which she could have travelled each day from home and which would have allowed some parental surveillance over the friends she made.

'Dad,' she had said, 'it's the British way. Students leave home. Everybody says it's good for you - helps on your c.v. I was born here. I must follow the ways of this country, not yours.'

Her argument had been persuasive. But now, at half-term, she had phoned to say she was staying at her hall of residence with a friend and completely refused to clarify whether the friend was male or female; 'What a silly question. I'm not going to answer it.'

Their two older sons had been little trouble, each having gone on to university - away from home, yes, but there were none within commuting distance – and had always behaved well. Each had discussed his choice of subjects with the parents before applying and had registered at the mosque in their adopted city. One never heard anything bad about the boys and they insisted on coming back to see Mum whenever they could. The wider family was justifiably proud of them. Compared with either of them Ayesha was wild, a rebel.

One evening, after they had closed up the shop and post office, Sunny took Shiva's arm and gently directed her away from the usual task of checking and recording the day's takings.

'Come into the lounge and sit down for a moment,' he insisted. Shiva smiled. He was a good husband and they worked well together but, right now, he looked worried.

'What's wrong?' she asked kindly.

'It's Ayesha. Maybe I'm over concerned, but she's so stubborn, so independent. I worry that she'll take up with the wrong sort of fellow. It's acceptable, I suppose, if it's just a phase, but such a pretty young lady will attract offers of marriage.'

Shiva laughed derisively. 'You men! You should admire her. She's got more 'get up and go' than our sons, clever though they are. Girls are free to do what they wish here. We mustn't return to our ancient customs – it's a different society. Most modern Muslims accept it. You don't want to be labelled 'old fashioned', do you?'

By now Ibrahim was beginning to look and feel a little awkward, 'I hear you, and I want to believe you, but it's hard to shake off my worries.'

'She admires you Sunny. Never doubt it. She sees you as a role model, someone to emulate. Don't force her to disobey and split the family.'

Usually, Ibrahim had the greatest respect for his wife's pragmatism and logic, but that very morning something occurred which had caused him to pause. When he had retreated into the living area for the lunch break he noticed a new paperback on the table - it was Bill Bryson's 'Made in America'.

'That's entertaining,' he had exclaimed, 'I think we've read it before – library maybe?'

'Oh,' she had replied, 'I was looking for 'The Thunderbird Kid' which is about his early life, but I saw that one and thought that was it.'

The complete mindlessness of what Shiva had readily admitted to having done made him wonder if she was seeing things clearly these days. Perhaps he should no longer take her comments so seriously.

'Alright, I won't say anything to Ayesha, but I'll secretly contact my brother – he's still at the bank in Mumbai – and ask him to interview some possible husbands – professionals like himself, from good families - and make out a short list.' Shiva's face registered her disapproval. 'Nothing final,' he added quickly, feeling uncomfortable, 'just exploratory, just in case.'

His wife remained dubious but restrained her comments, thinking, 'Maybe Ismail will refuse, or be too busy, or find nobody 'suitable', which means it's all over and no harm done.' Aloud, she said, 'As you wish. I won't tell her. Just make sure no evidence is left lying around or we'll have a major bust up. She could even leave home.'

Ibrahim walked back into the shop with a look of indecision and sat down behind the counter. Agitated and uncertain, he got to his feet again and reached for a pad of airmail writing paper and a black biro. Holding one in each hand, he began to walk slowly around the small shop in the weak, yellow street light which filtered in around the edges of roller blinded windows.

* * * * *

The village was surrounded by rolling, mixed farmland, much of it tenanted out. Evident every spring was the hard graft of lambing as the farmers took away in trailers those ewes that were about to give birth and installed them temporarily in their barns. This process was soon followed by yet more new life as cows gave birth to their calves unassisted and

57

alone – usually singly, occasionally to twins. Villagers often alerted the responsible farmer who arrived quickly, but watched from a distance, well aware that, if he approached the animal, it would try to stand up, which only made things more difficult. Sometimes, the vet was called out, but, as most of the mothers were already experienced, problems were rare.

To add confusion to the rural scene it was becoming common to transfer cows and their tiny, ear-tagged calves from farm to farm, paying for the period until the youngsters were weaned, separated from their mothers and sorted out into female – kept for long term production, or male – heading for immediate slaughter.

Nobody reared pigs on a small scale any more. The sties in the centre of Denton Cheney were abandoned in the seventies. Much to the relief of residents, that acrid, ever pervasive smell had finally gone. The solid brick buildings had been whitewashed and were now used as garages. The rambling, adjacent farmhouse, around which the village had grown, had become disconnected from land that, for centuries, had financed it; now the outbuildings were a series of pretty, thatched, weekend hideaways. The family had no further interest in working their fields and, encouraged by government's designation of the area as a focus for long term growth, made it no secret that they were courting offers from major housing developers. Economics and the EU's common agricultural policy, or 'CAP', now ruled everything in the countryside.

It came as a surprise to Alan when, on one of his regular walks along Glebe Lane, he saw four horses grazing peacefully in one of the meadows, enjoying the lush, late summer grass. This was a change from the regular annual pattern of usage and he became concerned that it might be a temporary measure while the field awaited approval of a planning application submitted by some unknown new owner, resolving to check whether the village action group were aware. Crude, felt tip written notices had been posted on the gate and fence: 'Private land, keep out' and 'Horses. Please drive quietly'. His eye was caught by blue tarpaulins thrown over the leaking roofs of a set of run down, brick sheds, which were evidently being used as stables, and by an almost hidden grey caravan with bright red gingham curtains – probably, he thought, for shelter and tea on a rainy day.

A week later, he passed by again. Three women, all wearing matching jodhpurs and riding hats, were emerging awkwardly from a battered mini. Avoiding conversation was impossible.

'I'm pleased to see the horses. They're a welcome addition to our village. Will they stay?'

'Oh yes.' The reply came from one who appeared older, and rounder. 'We're going to buy a pony from the travellers - maybe two.'

They seemed to assume that he knew all about them. Then he remembered, everybody in the country knew everybody else's business - it was taken for granted, the fewer the population the better they were informed.

'Great,' he smiled as they busily unloaded brushes and buckets, 'I can see you're busy!' and walked on.

* * * * *

It was nearing closing time. Chad and Mick had been out since dawn at what was still known as the deCourt estate – though the family had long disappeared - preparing for the beginning of the pheasant shooting season. Tired and footsore they were enjoying a few slow pints of refreshing abbot ale at the 'Fox'.

The 'Fox and Hounds' claimed to be the real village hostelry and had some facts on its side. Built as an oak frame it was originally in filled with wattle and daub - since replaced by brick and render - and could be reliably dated to the civil war when, to its later detriment, the countryside around supported the royalist cause. The village historical society had unearthed documents donated to the county records office by the Hope family, they mentioned sums of money set aside to relocate two houses which blocked the view of a lake from their manor; further research indicated that one of them had become a public house.

The 'Fox' had competition from the 'Maltings', a larger, much adapted and modernised inn which had once formed part of a brewery. This rival hostelry lay on a bypass road which allowed the ever increasing through traffic to avoid Denton Cheney. It served a decent menu of food: 'All day, eight days a week.' As a consequence, their clientele consisted mainly of people from town who drove out to enjoy a meal - especially on summer weekends when they could eat outside on extensive shady lawns next to an attractive, carp and goldfish stocked pond. By contrast those drinking and playing cheeses or darts at the 'Fox' were regulars who walked or cycled there. At the 'Fox' locals went along knowing who was likely to be there and where they would be sitting, whereas at the 'Maltings', visitors booked a table in advance and brought their friends with them.

Tim approached them, 'Sorry guys, I intended to be here before this but I had to get out the shot gun – foxes again!'

'Get him?' queried Chad, who was an expert shot.

'Yeah, lucky I guess. A young one - had to bury it right away. Time for another pint?'

Mick nodded and Chad didn't disagree - he liked Tim's company. Big, bluff and reliable, 'the egg man' bothered nobody, finding his new way of life vastly preferable to the car factory production line to which he had been tied for fifteen long years. Tim made only a meagre living, but accepted it. Husband and wife were proud to be independent, both appreciated the privilege of living in the countryside.

Tim transferred three tall glasses from a beer wet, tin tray to the already sodden mats on their table. 'Here you are,' he announced as he sat down to join them. 'Get a lot of birds?'

'Went well,' said Mick. 'Good day's shoot. I'd love to have a crack myself. I've helped to rear them for years now. Them Hopes make a good living from it all.'

'So can we,' said Tim. 'You know what was agreed.'

'Yes,' said Mick, 'but it will cost!'

'I've given it some thought. We could club together and buy the eggs – that's what the estates do now-a-days - and rear the chicks in my field, let them go at nine weeks – I think that's right – and have our own shoots at weekends.'

'We could,' said Mick enthusiastically, 'but we need an incinerator, sorry an incubator, to hatch out the eggs.' He looked at Chad, 'Also permission from your dad to trample across his fields.'

'No problem,' said the farmer's son. 'I've talked to him. At this time of year there's nothing to damage.'

'I heard most of that,' noted a cheerful rustic voice. 'It's what I like to hear – no problems.'

'Henry! You've come at just the right time,' said Tim. 'I'll research the price of an incubator on the internet - that's our major outlay - and maybe you three experts can work out the cost of eggs and feed, and where to get materials for a pen - I won't charge for the space to erect it.' Tim drained his glass, he could see that the others were on board, their weather-beaten faces shone with enthusiasm.

'Must go, meet you here next Tuesday – nine say – to finalise it?' said Tim, but stopped reflectively. 'We may need others to contribute - depending on the budget. You've all lived here longer than a townie like me; can you think about that? Henry, you're usually finished and have cycled home by about four thirty. Could you do the daily feed and make sure the chicks are kept warm?'

'I can,' confirmed Henry. 'Gets me out in the fresh air - I need to take the dogs for a walk anyway. Why not? I just need someone to help me out from time to time.'

'I'll share it with you,' volunteered Mick. 'I'm short of cash - the baby takes a lot - but I can do the work.'

'Good,' concluded Tim, standing up, 'see you Tuesday. Next year we'll be in business.'

Henry was well known and well liked in the village, his family had lived there for at least five generations. He and his wife owned - well mostly – their house; it was a corner plot which provided a huge garden in which he kept chickens and grew enough vegetables to feed themselves and their two teenage daughters. The grapevine said that his partner was the smart one. Kelly had installed a computer in one bedroom, and was connected to and familiar with the internet. She worked from home on out-sales, data collection and marketing for a London based cosmetic company, and filled up two days a week as an administrative officer at the tax office in town – known as a secretary before government job titles were upgraded as a means of holding down wage demands. Her employment provided a steady income. Henry's country based occupations varied from season to season, whenever he was offered a contract to build a house or an extension he took it.

The following week's get together was productive, all four of them were committed. Although Kelly was doubtful, Henry felt sure he could scrape together enough cash for the incubator - provided they all agreed to share any loss of value when it was sold. He had solved the pen problem by agreeing with Lord Hope's gamekeeper that they could borrow some spare frames of wire netting for the side walls and a large rope net for use as a top cover, but they needed to organise transport and return the frames in good condition at the end of the breeding season. So, the main requirements were settled.

A decision was made to have at least two shoots to which they would invite paying guests, and do the beating themselves. That way most, if not all, of their external costs - like the outlay on feed for the birds and bottled gas for night time heating - could be recovered. A clinking of glasses sealed the deal and they all looked forward to the following spring and a whole new adventure.

Of course, none of this was written down - in the old fashioned, rural world of trust it hardly seemed necessary.

* * * * *

It was an unusually warm day as retired rural policeman Robert strolled towards the 'Fox'. Windows stood jammed open, doors were ajar and the excited voices of children echoed around the village streets. He intended to indulge in a light lunch, a glass of bitter and some topical conversation about the mysterious corpse with whoever was present. This looked like a case that would drag on until positive identification was made. From his own experience, unclaimed bodies turned up more often than the general public realised; usually matched with known missing persons who had invariably died from natural causes, there was nothing controversial for the press to latch onto. Today he was more concerned about the many opportunities that presented themselves for casual thieving.

Years ago when he had been a trainee, farming villages were places where crime was unknown. Householders knew their neighbours; outsiders who ventured into the lanes were soon noticed, resulting in doors being shut and a watchful eye kept. Robert missed most of that, in some ways, idyllic period when he had worked from home covering the three adjacent hamlets on his heavy Raleigh bicycle. In the fifties and sixties his imposing, ubiquitous, six foot two frame was enough to quell aggressive drunkards without a fight and his 'quiet words' with unruly teenagers, or their parents, damped down potential trouble before it began. In recent times he couldn't remember when he had last seen a policeman or woman; if they did visit it was only to drive through in a Panda patrol car. No officer now knew the local bad characters or had any respect from youngsters, they had become the remote, unfriendly representatives of authority.

Robert considered it his duty to be informed; he had the local paper delivered each afternoon but had no truck with the main, London based dailies which he considered to have become impersonal, simply reiterating and amplifying news flashes from the big international agencies. With time to spare he had made an effort to chase up his usual informers in an attempt to get a lead on the body in the stream, but nothing tangible had emerged; it really did seem to belong to an outsider – even the Advertiser had ceased to push that story.

As part of his quest to remain abreast of village happenings Robert attended parish council meetings whenever he could and, although concerned that these had become unfocussed, had found some of the invited, external speakers to be quite interesting.

The police superintendent for the county's southern area was one who had caught his attention. Despite an attempt to make them sound better – 'spin' they called it these days – the figures for burglary and house breaking were significantly up over the five year period since New Labour had taken control. These were the crimes that most affected people, often hurting them deeply when they lost, perhaps not valuable, but personal or family items to petty thieving; it was something the average person didn't expect and wasn't attuned to avoid. Robert was unimpressed, 'We could do better,' he'd concluded and had said so. The superintendent was sympathetic, he knew that Robert had been 'one of them' and was open in explaining that the constant reorganisations mandated by Whitehall, and burdensome additional paperwork, made it difficult for him to deploy his officers in the most effective way to both prevent and solve crime. He readily agreed that to provide more community policing would be the best policy, but...

The last meeting served to remind Bob that the parish council had become moribund; it no longer represented the silent majority. The good news was that, next spring, their four year term was up. Three years ago he had considered standing himself - surely he could do no worse. Now, he was much encouraged by the action group and VASE - both organisations were active, used modern methods, and were working in the overall, long term interest of Denton Cheney; he fervently hoped that some of their competent members would contest the April elections.

As a bachelor Robert lived a fairly solitary life. When on active duty as a constable, and later a sergeant, there was no way he could have admitted to being gay – a queer copper would not have carried any authority. Colleagues had joshed him for living alone, clearly suspecting the truth of his sexual orientation. He had always endeavoured to deflect their comments, often by saying that his elderly mother needed a lot of looking after. He lived for the job, it was his whole life. Robert knew he was popular but feared that if he was branded, or admitted to being, a poof, then the work he enjoyed so much would be at risk. Retiring into different, more enlightened times he was glad he could now be open, and even more pleased that the force no longer discriminated against his type - at least not officially – though he fully appreciated that it still represented an added complication for any serving officer.

The enhanced role and promotion of women had helped considerably to ease the way for homosexuals; they didn't care what one's orientation was - only how well you did your job. Perhaps this was why he especially admired Sheena's busy, pragmatic approach. Although a good listener, she also possessed a physical stature that could overawe at least the younger teenagers. The PCSO managed to track down the youngster who, to the horror of the whole community, had thrown stones through one of the church's original, medieval, stained glass windows. At first there had been a cover up and town policemen visiting village homes had not been well received. Those who knew weren't prepared to share their secrets with uniformed, outsider figures who knocked on doors in

64

an aggressive manner. The guilty mother was the leading member of a certain village clique, one which thought itself above any law, and whose members were feared by their neighbours. Sheena's ground roots investigation - patiently joking with and talking to children and youngsters, had gradually provided the clues - none of them wanted to get into trouble for something they didn't do.

The church authorities were reluctant to prosecute, but Sheena was able to make a powerful impression on both the lad - who was anyway too young to be taken to court - and his parents. In Bob's experience this was the best approach and the right solution. She had probably saved the culprit, and his family, from becoming entangled in a web of cover-up and deceit, which may well have alienated the parents and pushed their son into more serious crime. He felt it was his duty to write to his friend the chief constable and recommend a citation.

*　*　*　*　*

The friendly, panting, little dog came scampering up, only to be brought to a sudden halt when the long lead reached the limit stop inside its leather case. Jeff was delighted to see Lady and her owner Arthur, they had been noticeably absent for several weeks. The dog looked well but Arthur seemed to have shrunk back into his worn tweed jacket and the stoop had become more pronounced, still, he was out and about and had reached the canal towpath, that couldn't be bad.

'You always keep him on a lead?' observed Jeff.

'Her,' corrected Arthur. 'Yes, she's a bit younger than me. If she wandered off I mightn't catch her. I'm frightened of losing the only companion I have left.'

Nearer the village Jeff encountered a string of dog walkers who, on returning from their workplaces, had hurried out to exercise their pets before the light faded and the autumn chill intensified. There was the thin woman – rumour had it that she was recovering from bulimia - with her equally skinny greyhound, also on a lead, and the pale faced bespectacled man with a big labrador who, while putting the dog's unpleasant faeces into a plastic bag, advised Jeff that the village had no dog pooh bins, even though it was a designated 'scoop a poop' area. 'Your council needs to do something about it,' he insisted. Yes, he had raised it - long ago - but to no avail. 'That lot are useless. Any other council would have installed them years back.'

Another regular around the streets was a high stepping, curly haired terrier which looked to Jeff like something from the sort of children's nursery that Peter Pan visited - except it should have been on wheels. It was always led by a bored teenage boy or girl whom, he suspected, had this chore imposed on them by busy parents after arriving home from school. The lack-a-daisical way in which the task was performed made him doubt whether the resulting dog dirt was ever picked up - he had never witnessed it.

Farmer Jones' dogs were no household pets. Jeff had acquired considerable respect for them, based on their abilities and usefulness. They were a family of border collies - a mother and her two sons; lean and fit all three. When not busy they found places in the shade around the farmyard but were never allowed inside – not even in the huge farm kitchen which formed the daily epicentre of farming activity. Time and effort had been expended on their training and, as a result, they formed a natural team when it came to moving sheep or cattle from field to field around the village. Given very few prompting whistles from Jones, his dogs worked the big animals almost independently, aware exactly how close they needed to approach and where to position themselves for the task in hand. Jeff had often seen one or more of them getting its exercise while running along behind the farmer's old Daihatsu pickup as it trundled down Glebe Lane. More often they had a lift, balancing skilfully in the tray and looking out alertly as the four wheel drive bumped across the pock-marked rabbit fields. When only one dog was needed, Chad used his motorbike and one of the collies somehow found a precarious footing in front of him on the fuel tank. The three collies were wonderful working dogs with gentle temperaments, one couldn't help but like them.

FLUORITE - WINTER

McAlister had organised his men to check out every canal boat hired during the last six months along the Thames and Grand Union Canal. From this data boats that could have passed close to the village at the approximate date of death were listed, their hirers contacted and interviewed. Meetings were held with marina managers, canal officials and lock keepers; his team also called at cafes and pubs close to overnight mooring areas, always asking the same questions: Did you hear about any strange happenings or see anything suspicious when in the vicinity of Denton Cheney? Do you know of anybody who has gone missing?

There was a considerable amount of holiday traffic during the summer months so the work had already taken several weeks. Although the village was attractive, it offered no 'bed and breakfasts', no accommodation of any sort, no designated areas for caravans and no camping sites. Denton Cheney wasn't singled out in guide books or included on any recommended tourist route - even the two pubs failed to get a mention. As a result very few outsiders, apart from those passing through on the canal boats, ever had any reason to pay a visit.

* * * * *

The vicar, called his parochial church council to order. 'Sorry I'm a little late but there's a wedding coming up on Saturday and I had to meet the young couple. It took longer than expected to explain things as they don't live here and will need a special licence.'

The councillors sat down on the vestry's hard, cushionless chairs. When he arrived - admittedly it was a quarter past the scheduled hour - they had all been standing up.

'You weren't leaving?' he asked timidly.

'No', said the working farmer's wife in her blunt way. 'It's them seats. This ain't a good place for meetings. It's colder than my big kitchen of a morning, and less comfy.'

The other attendees were: Brian - a young man who managed a supermarket on the edge of town, Laura - one half of an apparently successful marriage of medical professionals, and Keith Rector - a retired clergyman who was new to the village - all those present were itching to ask if the name had led to his calling.

'Joan has already touched on our discussion subject. Tonight it's all about meetings,' opined Keith. 'What can we do to make our ancient church more attractive to the parishioners? Surely, the answer is - have it more widely used. At present it's occupied on every third Sunday for the routine services, on Saturdays for weddings – usually only in the summer months, and intermittently for funerals or commemorations. In other words, only for strictly Christian church business. I, for one, would like to see such a pleasant venue put to good use by the whole community during weekdays and in the evenings. The upkeep is high and we need more income. We are, I suppose, in competition with the pubs and the village hall which all have comfortable seating, better heating and, most critically, washrooms and toilets. What are your views?'

'Can we find room for a toilet within the existing Church building?' It was the doctor's wife speaking. 'Under today's regulations I expect it would have to be large enough to accommodate the disabled?'

'We'd best sound out the church authorities first - in an unofficial way that is,' suggested the young man, 'and check with the various ancient

68

monument regulatory organisations – like English Heritage - before we go any further. Such an addition may not be permitted.'

'Good point er...,' said the vicar who could never recall the enthusiastic young man's name. 'Can I put you down for that initial search?'

'He must investigate all that before we waste any time,' agreed Joan. 'These days nothing can be done to the original fabric without their say so, and that's before applying for planning permission - which will cost us money.'

'I'm sure it won't be straightforward,' said Laura, 'During your predecessor's time, when we wanted to repair the central heating – only a simple leak – the plumber wouldn't do any work without a formal agreement. It was a lengthy business.'

The vicar, on a short term assignment and close to his retirement date, was understandably reluctant to start up a long term project; his wife had made him promise a move to the south coast and he wouldn't be able to follow it through to a conclusion.

'Yes, it will need patience,' said Keith who, after opening the discussion, had been uncharacteristically quiet, feeling that he shouldn't come forward too positively. 'I had this problem at my last parish. Basically, no change was allowed - it's English Heritage, they're very strict. However, I have the advantage of having done something similar at my old college.' He paused for effect. 'Might I make a suggestion - perhaps a bold one? I believe we in the Church have to look forward, have to be creative. We live in a wealthy country – aren't they always telling us ours is the fourth biggest economy in the world. Perhaps we can raise funds for something more ambitious, rather than just a washroom! If we're brave enough God will help. The last major work on this building was in the Victorian era.'

'What had you in mind?' said their chairman in a quiet, wondering voice. He'd never met anybody quite as positive as Keith before.

'I've given it some thought. The idea hit me when visiting Winchester cathedral with my brother. I can't claim it's original.' By now he had their undivided attention.

'Why not add a chapter house. We could access it from the small, unused north door. Make it round and in local stone. In the connecting link we could incorporate a conventional toilet plus one for the disabled. A chapter house was originally an important and elaborate meeting room, ours can be simple. That side of the church is away from the road and is barely visible from any of the houses, so there will be no objections. If you think it possible, I could persuade an architect I know to give us a free initial sketch and budget.' His words trailed off into a stunned silence.

'What a brilliant concept,' acknowledged the vicar breathlessly, and paused. 'It might just work.'

Everybody was supportive. What a bold idea to add something to a building that had not seen structural change since the nineteenth century, and that was only an upgrading and new roof. Fancy contemplating new work at a place some said was in grave danger of closure through lack of worshippers and funding. It could reinvigorate the lovely old church by making it useful to the surrounding community, and inject an optimistic, forward look into the congregation and village. 'One has to dream big,' said somebody.

'Thank you,' said Keith very quietly. He was a little overcome by his own idea, already wondering if he had allowed his enthusiasm to overrule commonsense − surely the cost would be prohibitive - but he liked a challenge, and this would certainly qualify. 'Don't feel committed, think it over. Let's hurry slowly and look at a realistic cost before we mention it outside these four walls.'

There was instant assent all round. The councillors left the meeting engaged in animated discussion; they couldn't but help feel excited.

*   *   *   *   *

The horse was wearing a green canvas coat while nibbling at the threadbare remains of summer grass. The field had been cut to yield winter hay, after which a dry, cool period produced little new growth. Alan looked towards the horizon where its two similarly clad equine companions seemed thinner than usual. He had stopped against rusting iron palings, beneath a huge beech whose remaining crinkly, brown leaves reminded him that summer would eventually return. The stately tree had been preserved in the hedgerow of the narrow lane where two fields joined. All around was the sweet smell of manure. In the tree's shade was a brand new, galvanised steel hay dispenser and, lying beside it, two rectangular bales of compressed grass. With her white breath warming the chilly air a slip of a teenage girl in jodhpurs and a tight, ribbed, light blue sweater had just begun splitting one of the bales, ready to pitch-fork its contents into the crib. Alan could do no other than say, 'Hello,' adding conversationally, 'time for the hay? Animals become expensive at this time of year.'

The horse girl smiled warmly. He noticed an attractive, porcelain skinned, high cheek-boned face, in sharp contrast with the shiny black peak of her riding hat.

'Didn't I see you a few months back – three of you?'

'Yes,' she agreed, moving closer and ceasing work for a moment. 'We'd only just started then.'

Alan was curious, 'Are you part of a company; from a riding school?'

'Oh, no,' she responded, this time with a slight grin. 'Fiona's husband rents the field for us. She's always liked horses – it's a hobby. Sally and I just assist - when we can.'

'You're not from this village?'

'No, all from Barnswell,' came the reply.

In his discrete English way, Alan felt he had intruded for long enough. As he began to turn away, three teenagers approached, dressed in worn trainers, dirty jeans and hooded tops, they slouched rather than walked. He identified them as Aaron and friends. Together they appeared slightly threatening, but were, in fact, a diffident lot - a group of lost boys waiting for their Pan.

'Here are some people more your age,' said Alan. 'Do you know Aaron? Say hello Aaron,' he instructed wickedly. As he had expected, it left the young men embarrassed and rooted to the spot, not sure whether to ignore him and walk on, or try and say something. Before rounding a bend in the lane he glanced back to see if anything had resulted from the enforced introduction. Aaron had moved close to the fence while the others hung back, but there was no obvious communication. A momentary flash of envy passed across his mind. Yes, she was pretty! He wondered if these youngsters were capable of noticing. After recalling his own youth he decided that they probably already had. Whether they were, like he had been, too shy to do anything about it remained to be seen.

* * * * *

Patrick woke in a cold sweat, the events of the previous evening still fresh in his mind; noticing that Sara had got up he pulled on a dressing gown and rushed down the stairs. She was standing calmly at the kitchen table giving the children their breakfast.

'Your hand - how is it?'

'Seems alright, only one finger swollen.'

'Should we see the doctor?' Patrick was anxious. 'Don't forget it's Saturday and the nearest is at Ranwick - mornings only.'

Patrick grimaced as he recalled the accident. It was all that new hatchback's fault. After their usual Friday evening visit to the out of town supermarket with the two youngest in tow, they had stopped in the gloom of their drive. Outside it had become cold and, in a frenzy of unloading, he had slammed down the rear hatch when Sara, who was helping three year old Kirsty out of her car seat, had left one hand there to steady herself. The scream still echoed in his skull and he had visions of an urgent drive to Accident and Emergency at the town hospital.

When he looked up Sara had her fingers stuck under the closed steel door. Trying to remain calm he quickly reached inside the driver's side door to disengage it, put his arm around her and helped her into the house. There was no blood, so he sat his wife down on a chair and fetched a jug of cold tap water, telling her to keep her hand in it. By now she had calmed down. Aware of the effects of shock he put a warm coat around her shoulders, raced to the drink's cabinet and poured out a large glass of neat whisky.

'This will help,' he had insisted. When he looked up the youngsters were standing next to him, silent witnesses to their father's evident concern.

Back in the present Sara teased, 'The best thing was those two glasses of Red Label. Normally, you never offer me one.'

Patrick didn't know how to respond - they no longer drank at home except for an occasional glass of wine with the evening meal.

'I think you were fortunate. You have such small bony fingers, and that thick rubber strip around the edge cushioned the blow. But it was an awful sight.'

'Is mummy going to be alright?' queried Padraig, their nine year old, receiving in response a comforting hug and warm reply from the invalid.

'Yes, it was just an accident. I was lucky.'

Later, they left the family in the capable hands of his mother-in-law who, to release her own tension, needed to scold him.

'You could have broken her hand. Then who would look after the children? I can't come round every day – at my age, it's too much.'

Miffed, but telling himself it was only the expected reaction of a caring grandparent, Patrick restrained himself, merely nodding in acknowledgement. 'I know,' he agreed.

Patrick drove and they headed towards one of Leicester's newer suburbs. Both husband and wife were active members of the Liberal Democrats. Patrick had half heartedly inherited the allegiance from his father – with whom nobody dared to disagree – whereas Sara had been converted by a former boyfriend during her school days. Their allocated task was to meet local party activists and assist them with a day's leafleting in advance of forthcoming elections. This district formed part of the constituency where local elections were in hand, and for which Sara had been nominated as parliamentary candidate at the next general election - due in two years time. As the seat was held only marginally by New Labour, and would probably be targeted by party leaders, it was essential both to know it and be known in it.

They met in a vacant, glass fronted shop which had been provided, free of charge, by a believer for use as campaign headquarters. Exhorting posters in strident yellow adorned the huge windows, while inside, volunteers sat on borrowed chairs at borrowed tables placing individually addressed letters into handwritten envelopes, then sorting them out, street by street, for delivery by well organised teams. In parallel, nominated local district council candidates, who carried leaflets and were accompanied by party workers adorned with yellow rosettes, toured the likeliest wards on foot - well briefed to answer any questions raised by the electorate in regard to policy. There was going to be a lot of walking on hard pavements, but their joint efforts could serve to tip the balance on election-day.

Patrick, who had a degree in microbiology, had recently become disenchanted with his employer, owing to their, in his view, bullying and exploitative promotion of genetically modified food. As a consequence he had joined the town's red brick university - which had recently upgraded from a technical college - in a newly created post with responsibility for organising the alumni. This involved much less travel, allowing him to reach home earlier and lend a hand with the children. The change was welcomed by Sara who could now spend more time on her political commitments and ongoing ambition to become a Member of Parliament.

In his new appointment Patrick had unearthed within himself a gift for communication, the skills needed for the production and distribution of news sheets and the ability to organise year group get-togethers. He grasped the potential of the new electronic media, developing fluency with computers, desk top publishing and the use of the e-mail and internet - perhaps his famously voluble, Irish ancestry was reasserting itself. Sara commented that the church newsletter filled only one sheet and was extremely narrow in its coverage. Seeing how much her husband enjoyed his new work she suggested that he produce a more comprehensive one for the parish council. Patrick's response was that he wasn't inclined to support the present incumbents who needed removing at the first opportunity; fortunately, such an occasion was only a few months away.

* * * * *

Alan lay in bed, dosing. Everywhere was quiet, no, silent; it was what he most liked about the countryside. Yet, there was a downside - a noticeable unease had gradually permeated the village. The residents were less relaxed and open than when he had first arrived. Was it simply that, as he got to know them, their normal everyday cares and concerns became more apparent? No, it was more than that - the locals had become more

74

distant. He sensed a growing, unspoken anxiety about the strange body, and the realisation that the police had no answers. People had begun to look at each other more carefully, questioning neighbours they had known for years. As a relative newcomer he would be high on their list of suspects. Villagers wondered if they were sheltering a killer and checked that their doors were locked at night.

Despite this new development Alan was enjoying retirement, and still appreciated the luxury of not having to get up early - not having to get up at all if he so decided. His wife was ever more active, but today away visiting her elderly mother in Cornwell, consequently, he was not disturbed until the clatter of the metal letterbox flap prompted him to take an interest in the day. Still dressed in pyjamas, but with a heavy golf fleece pulled down hastily on top, he made his way downstairs barefoot. Realising that the house was chilly he diverted into the lounge to push up the thermostat on the gas fired central heating, pausing a moment for reassurance from its familiar start up 'clunk'.

There was no mail, only two, folded, typed sheets, which constituted a second missive from the action group - one similar to the letter that Dot Faulkner had pondered over. This time, the five strong organisation identified its members by name, an openness of which he approved. All were villagers, though to Alan their names meant little. The circular called for him to sign, date and send in an attached template letter which objected strongly to the proposed locating of a large secondary school at the edge of Denton Cheney. It advised that the planning application was intended primarily to service a newly completed development of nearly a thousand homes located about five miles away, and pointed out that the school should be located with the houses – as had already been promised to the residents when they moved in – which would allow most children to walk or cycle safely to and from classes, rather than spending half a million pounds annually on unnecessary bus transport. The group had even identified an appropriate site which they claimed had been reserved for such a school but dropped after pressure from developers.

Alan saw no sense in building this facility in a rural village of only three hundred houses with barely seven hundred, mostly elderly residents, it was illogical and expensive. He sat down promptly at the kitchen table and completed the proforma, before jogging back to collect an envelope and stamp from his makeshift, upstairs office, resolving to post it before the GPO announced yet another unofficial shutdown.

While eating his Weetabix and muesli he realised that he felt strongly about this silliness. As a person with time on his hands, a good education and some relevant business experience, Alan felt it was his duty to put some effort back. Yes, it was! Taking the local telephone directory he scanned it for the action group's names; beginning with the least common he soon identified an address only a street away and resolved to call round on his way to the letterbox before the 5pm collection time.

Alan had a recurring sense of guilt. On dark winter days – like today – when his wife was away and the house empty, his thoughts often returned to the demise of his parents. Although he knew death was, as his father stated when his wife died, 'an accident of life', such philosophy – brave and admirable as it was – had failed to assuage his sense of guilt at having been away too much. From time to time, small intimate things reminded him of his father: in a world atlas they used quite often was written a date and, 'To Alan for birthday and Christmas'; on a garden shed shelf were faded, brown tie-on labels for peat and fertiliser in the same unmistakeable hand; in his wardrobe hung heavy, wooden coat hangers that Dad had marked with his name for college, and the kitchen drawer contained neatly cut lengths of white string with a small bowline at one end - because they could be pulled tight, yet easily undone - his father had used them for securing almost everything. More personal was a sheet of writing paper retrieved from the hospital where Dad had spent his final days. It began quite tidily by being addressed to Alan, and had almost completed an explanation of what had happened when the writing trailed off down the sheet, never to be resumed again.

He began to get a grip on himself. As a poem said, echoing what he knew would have been his father's wishes: 'Think of me a little, not a lot.' It was easier said than done. To win this battle for the village would be some sort of compensation for his past, rather conveniently, self-centred life. Now he had the time, it was the least he could do. He sat back in his armchair realising that the fight wasn't the fundamental issue. If the parish council had contained someone with experience of construction, and had been well led and well informed, it would surely have anticipated this problem, mobilised the villagers, put up a strong protest, and nipped the ridiculous idea in the bud before a particular site was chosen and a formal planning application submitted. Yes, the parish council was the real, long term problem; it needed reforming. The village deserved to be represented by a group of decent, well intended residents who had the interests of the majority in mind and not, as he suspected, be in thrall to some developer who had taken out options on the surrounding farmland. The action group needed to look further ahead, to see past the school issue and stand at the next parish council election; his eyes lit up, of course, he remembered now - one was due in the spring.

Now he had a mission he began to feel more content. He could do some good for the silent majority who were about to be trampled on by a rampant bureaucracy. England, unlike the country he had lived in for so long, was a parliamentary democracy where people had rights and there was an underlying belief that things should be 'fair'. What had happened in this cradle of modern civilisation? Voters must surely have a means of influencing such arbitrary decisions. His priority was to understand how things really worked, how local government decisions were made and what were the opportunities for influencing them; as a relative foreigner in his land of birth it was all a mystery to him.

His morning of angst was cut short by a further clatter of the letterbox. This time, it was a single sheet of paper from VASE advising progress on a proposed sand extraction site. 'Oh no,' he thought, 'not another problem!' This second wake up call caught Alan in a mood for action. An idea came to him.

*   *   *   *   *

The meeting was set to change the future of Denton Cheney - VASE and the action group were finally to get together... but I'm getting ahead of myself. It came about like this.

After their efforts at the Inquiry, Jeff and Mike suffered a mutual sense of anticlimax. They were in for a long wait before any result would be known, and hadn't achieved much that was tangible; now, they sought an outlet for their enthusiasm.

'We should support this action group,' Mike had suggested as they drove home from the rugby club. 'A secondary school in our village is patently nonsense.'

'They haven't exactly done much for us,' snorted Jeff. 'We've had to work alone.'

'There's only so much time and energy,' replied Mike, who was always diplomatic, 'no doubt they've had plenty on their hands.'

'Alright then,' suggested Jeff, changing tack, 'why don't we join the parish council? That would cover both causes and be the proper way forward.'

'Yes, but everybody says they're useless. That's why these separate groups have formed,' stated Mike

'We could go along next time – it's allowed – and judge for ourselves? That's the fairest way.'

'You win,' conceded Mike. 'It's next Monday at seven - in the village hall. In fact they've just put a notice on their board and are looking to second two new members. It could be an opportunity for a pair of likely lads like us!'

'Right,' sighed Jeff, albeit reluctantly, 'I'll be there.'

The council met in a small, cold, badly lit annex which opened onto the main, wood- floored sports hall. Unfortunately, the badminton club had a parallel weekly booking and their heavy lunges, with accompanying shouts of woe, could be heard very clearly through the thin screen. The two friends arrived in good time and sat on hard wooden chairs against one wall, watching in astonishment as the councillors followed their usual practice of turning their backs towards the public; nothing had changed since Alan's visit.

The acoustics were poor and, with constant thumps from next door, it was difficult to hear all that was said. Exactly on time the gloomy silence was broken by a statement that the meeting had begun - the voice belonged to Jack. Although it was impossible to follow what was going on they noticed someone taking occasional notes in a small, black schoolbook. After three quarters of an hour a tall, slim lady appeared in the doorway wearing a plastic waterproof and immediately interrupted the session with a question.

'What about them roads, Jack? Some of those puddles could drown you.'

The chair explained that they never got anywhere with the county council, so he wouldn't do anything.

Jeff had done his homework and discovered that the meetings were obliged to incorporate a designated 'public session' at which anybody could ask questions – perhaps this was it. Emboldened, he queried, 'Is the council for or against the minerals site?'

Instead of a response he elicited only an annoyed silence. It seemed that no reply was merited, so he asked again.

This time the chairman spoke reluctantly but without turning round, 'Everybody knows there's nothing we can do.'

They waited for some explanation, but realised that the agenda had moved on when Jack told the clerk, 'With that body problem still hanging over us there's no point in entering the best kept village competition this year.'

After less than an hour the villagers got up and drifted away morosely, barely acknowledging one another. No one said 'goodbye' or 'goodnight.'

The two visitors were left alone, somewhat bemused. This was not what they had expected from the 'first tier of democratic government'- as the Home Office insisted on calling it; rather, it had been a pointless, unfocussed gathering of long term insiders who had no intention of doing anything, least of all welcoming strangers – 'new villagers' as they were called - into their midst.

'This place deserves better,' declared Jeff as they walked away along the High Street with hands deep in coat pockets to guard against a sharp easterly wind which had sprung up while they were inside.

'Hardly welcoming was it,' agreed Mike. 'It was all so negative. This country developed modern democracy. Parish councils must have a voice; if they don't fight for the village then nobody will take us seriously. The planners and builders will just walk all over us.'

'Did you realise there will be elections in the spring?'

'No. What? Parliamentary?'

'Local government,' Jeff explained, 'which includes parish councils – it's every four years, I think.'

'What happens if nobody stands? They're short now,' said Mike.

'Simple, those in office just carry on. In some parishes people hang on for a lifetime – they only have to attend a few meetings each year to retain their places.'

'Something needs doing. Correction, we must do something.' Mike emphasised the 'we'. 'Get sufficient decent, active, business savvy villagers to stand against that lot. Surely, we can make inroads and gradually bring in proper management.' He had the bit between his teeth.

'Yes,' agreed his friend, very pleased at this Damascene conversion.

By now they had reached the corner where their paths parted, and stopped beneath a convenient, but flickering, street light.

'Yes,' said Jeff, with a chuckle, noticing Mike's doubtful upward glance at the lantern. 'Lighting is also the responsibility of our council.'

Mike was not to be distracted. 'You saw what happened. When a councillor raised something that Jack bloke didn't like, he just called a vote and always had sufficient cronies to win. Changing things will be a struggle - but I'm with you. Practically speaking we need to enlist support from the action group and see whether, between us, we can't put up a full set of candidates. At least that will prevent automatic re-election because there are insufficient applicants.'

'Done,' said Jeff firmly, 'call me at the weekend.'

'We have common ground,' announced Alan as VASE founders Jeff and Mike were introduced to those of the action group who were available. 'I've only just joined – a new boy really – but we all agree that, if Denton Cheney is to survive as an independent village beyond the threat of the school, the sand pit, and, as I have realised, government's imposition of mass housing, then the parish council must be replaced.'

They were at Hamish's home; it was one of the village's two manors. For the sake of central control Duke William of Normandy had shrewdly split a powerful Saxon fiefdom - one dangerously close to his capital – leaving neither the original, nominally subservient, owner nor the new French baron entirely dominant. These Norman invaders were the only immigrants in English history to start at the top; as a consequence their main fear was that of losing power. A Tudor, stone floored room with tapestries, albeit modern, decorating the walls seemed an appropriate venue in which to plan a revolution. It reminded Alan it wasn't far from here that Gatsby had assembled and briefed the conspirators when organising the Gunpowder Plot.

Hamish was hardly Norman, though he was a baron – not of Denton Cheney but a town north of the border; it was an honorific title which had been purchased rather than inherited.

'I'm away a lot,' he began, 'but support the cause.' He waved a hand airily towards a positive looking man of medium height who was dressed in a pink, v-neck sweater, 'Alan, this is David – almost your neighbour I think. He's our chair and real organiser but, as I was in the village for a few days, it was convenient to meet here.' Hamish's manner indicated that he didn't favour a less grand venue. The only other person was an elderly lady who pressed forward and introduced herself breezily as Mrs Cecil. 'David will take it from here.'

'Now we are six,' began David, unintentionally plagiarising A.A. Milne. 'Thank you all for coming along. Being a rebel group we can't have any formal membership - no signing in blood and no notes! As residents who were concerned enough about the future of Denton Cheney to organise our own teams to fight the minerals and the school, it makes sense for us to cooperate in resisting unnecessary housing. Unlike the other two issues, this will clearly be a long term, ongoing battle for the village, one which a parish council is best placed to fight. We're all agreed that our parish council – which is the village's official body - needs strengthening so that it can lead this legitimate concern. In order to have credibility and clout with local government we need to demonstrate village support through the council. What I propose is that most of us stand in the next local election, if a few get in we can begin to influence decisions and steer it in the right direction. In the meantime, please try to commit. Let me know if you're willing and I'll get you the registration papers as soon as they become available.'

* * * * *

Keith Rector's friend was a semi-retired architect who worked in partnership with his son, Peregrine, unusually, they specialised in church renovation and repair. Their scope was often small, but it required taste and skill to integrate new construction into the existing fabric of the nation's often ancient, and already much altered, places of worship.

Peregrine began enthusiastically, 'Father sends his regards. Yes, your idea can be made to work - but you will need to appoint us officially. My dad always insists on a written agreement. Here's a standard format.' He fished around in a heavy, battered leather briefcase to extract and hand over a single sheet of type-written paper and a thin, brown booklet with RIBA prominent on its cover in embossed gold lettering. 'As you will see, it's simple. We know that representatives of the Church of England won't let us down and, given God's help, will always find a way to pay us.'

'I'll need to obtain the Reverend Johnson's approval,' said Keith. 'What are your fees?'

'For preparing initial details up until the project is approved in principle by all the relevant authorities, we charge on the hourly basis shown – it rarely comes to more than a thousand pounds. After that we ask for five per cent of the final building costs.'

'I see,' said Keith, who was familiar with such business arrangements. 'How long does it take to get through to final approval?'

Peregrine grimaced, 'You've touched on the critical issue. Could be a year - your diocesan people are difficult. Then there's Ancient Monuments and English Heritage to satisfy – the list goes on - before we can submit an application for outline planning approval to the district council, which one do you come under?'

'Shottle.'

'I've dealt with them previously - which will help. Finally, there's raising the necessary capital, but that rests with your side. You really do need a persevering, proven fundraiser; frankly, without one I would advise you not to start.'

Keith put on a serious expression and nodded, 'Point taken, we'll work on that. I'll try to get this signed and back by the month's end. Thanks for your guidance.'

The two men were sitting in the 'Fox', close to a well made log fire that crackled and banged cheerfully in an open iron grate.

'Peregrine, best you drink up the last of that cafetiere of coffee,' said Keith, and laughed. 'You wanted to see inside St James? I have a key, but I warn you, it's freezing at this time of year!'

'Hopefully, we can fix that problem,' replied the young architect seriously. 'I'll go ahead and draw up outline plans for your committee to review. My fees will be forthcoming – God will provide.'

Keith, as an ex-cleric, didn't know whether it was a joke or not.

* * * * *

'Middle, always in the middle,' thought Martin. He was in one of those reminiscing moments that come with age: 'Middle child,' - he had two brothers; 'middle row of the scrum,' – he was six feet four; 'Midlands,' – the village was near the nation's centre of gravity. He grinned, wondering how many more 'middles' he would find that were apposite. Yes, that one adjective could very well describe his way of life.

His duties as an opthalmic and vitreoretinal consultant at Radcliffe Hospital had, over recent years become ever more onerous. It was not so much the work, which he enjoyed, but the endless trivial reorganisations and futile directives that arrived weekly as government sought to improve the National Health Service without seeking advice from the experienced staff they employed. All this nonsense had impacted on his surgical work for which he had taken ten long years to qualify; frustrated, he had retired eighteen months ago. Laura was pleased. Martin had been growing thinner, more ashen faced, losing his once delightful sense of humour and ability to laugh off the irritations of a centralised bureaucracy.

Their neglected medieval, Grade I listed house and garden had kept him busy, built of rubble and earth, even the old brick extension was thatched with the requisite reeds from Norfolk. A barn to the rear provided a garage, but that had a slate roof which was of less concern - especially on bonfire night when celebrants let off all those rockets and star shells. Did nobody understand the risk?

A sociologist would find Martin, and wife Laura, a good example of the professional middle class - a diluted form of the Edwardian version when the population, apart from the landowners or 'upper class' - who ruled the country - were either tradesmen or labourers.

Laura was a proper churchgoer - something which involved more than a mandatory visit to the midnight Christmas mass – and, it goes without saying, Church of England. She hailed from a northern family of male engineers and female nurses – what else respectable was there for girls? Since their marriage Martin's wife had never changed; she just carried on with her well meant, sociable way of life and steady support for St James - perhaps unwittingly, certainly without any strong faith, it was simply the way she had been brought up. As a regular member of the congregation, and mainstay of fund raising through her garden party and raffles, it had been quite natural for the previous vicar to include Laura in the parochial church council.

Every summer she organised a formal well attended garden party. It was set out at wooden tables on a flagged terrace overlooking a freshly mown, weed free lawn which meandered away amongst mature, herbaceous borders. Her scones - made from a secret recipe handed down by her maternal grandma - had a drawing power of their own. Only the better off were invited - teenagers, babies and dogs were unwelcome.

A good appearance was maintained. Laura never left home without looking smart, even fashionable, but only in the country manner. Her hair was always tidy, well cut, and appropriately styled or tinted, and her outfits picked up the latest trends - like sleeveless sheepskin waistcoats or ankle length trousers – only to be abandoned when they faded from the press and television. That is not to say she was snobbish, merely in touch with current fashion and aware that, given her slim figure, she looked good.

Laura managed a long running book group of like minded women who met at her lovely home - in itself a reason to attend - on the first Thursday of each month at ten a.m. sharp. Despite the fact that most members lived within a few minutes walk, they all arrived in cars - generally expensive ones, making it difficult for the local, single-decker buses to get through. Of Pakistani ethnicity, Shiva had been singled out for a personal invitation as it was felt she needed bringing into the social fold of her adopted country. This good intention ignored the fact that Shiva had lived in Denton Cheney longer than most - with one son a scholar at Oxford University she was as middle class as anybody - and disguised the real reason, which was because she was the only member who needed to work.

In all countries, except England, good manners are employed to help people from different walks of life become more at ease with one another. Here, by contrast, they have been used to highlight variations in speech, education or wealth in a manner intended to make the less fortunate feel uncomfortable and know their place. Poor Shiva was treated, quite deliberately, in a way designed to prolong the divisions in society that most well intentioned people want to see disappear for ever.

In a similar way, Mrs Cecil at the manor house used the title 'the Hon.'; nobody knew why but it provided reason enough to treat her with unthinking respect - a bit like the Queen. In Britain the feudal system has been perpetuated in the handing out of 'titles' by political parties as a cheap way of rewarding supporters for favours given or donations made. All this process achieves is to perpetuate a hierarchy of status and aspiration in what is supposed to be a left leaning liberal democracy. Sadly, the village was no different from anywhere else and the 'middle class' fell over themselves to invite anyone with a rank or title to address their get-togethers at the historical society or women's institute, on the assumption that, somehow, such people were more capable or more interesting simply because they were 'sirs', 'generals', 'lords' or 'ladies'.

The Coopers were a typically kind, English couple. Secure behind high walls, and enjoying interaction with four children and numerous grandchildren, they drifted comfortably along, but would be among the first to complain if mass housing spoiled their environment or the police allowed their enquiry about the body to drag on.

* * * * *

Susan was in the garden pegging out the washing on her revolving clothes line – but no blackbird came down - while intermittently rocking Damien to sleep in his big, well sprung, enamelled pram. The 'perambulator' had been a gift from Mum and, although impractical for someone living in an upstairs flat, she couldn't refuse it, especially knowing it had been kept for all those years down in the cellar – 'Just in case'. It usually stood beneath the external concrete stairs covered with a tarpaulin but gradually losing its shine.

The day had begun cold and frosty but the sun now shone in an azure sky. Susan felt that, after several days of rain, Damien, who was well wrapped up in a blue, woolly jump suit, would benefit from some fresh air. She looked up to see movement on her steps as the long shadow of a tall figure passed across the outside wall. The man was wearing a short, brown leather coat over black corduroy trousers; in one hand he held a supermarket branded, plastic bag from which he took out a sheet of paper, folding it carefully before pushing it through her letter box.

As the man retraced his steps he suddenly noticed Susan, paused and offered a pleasant, 'Good day,' following it with an explanation, 'It's only an update from the action group. Some progress has been made. The residents of Upton Park have, at last, formed their own organisation - they want the school over there. The right place at last!'

She glanced up, noticing that a canary-yellow, knitted hat lent his pale, pinched features a chromatic glow. 'Are you from the council?' she asked. For Susan, all officials came from one of the many types of council.

'The action group,' was the reply.

'Oh,' she exclaimed, disappointed, 'I was going to ask if you knew of any progress on affordable housing – we're on the list. I'm pregnant again but this place is too small, and not private enough for a young family.'

'Ah,' said her visitor sympathetically – her comment seemed to have triggered something, 'some of us will be standing for the parish council in April. If we succeed I'm sure we can press for action. This village needs homes for young couples - if they want to stay then we don't want to loose them. It's a pleasant place to live, when people like you leave it will end up full of retirees - like me!'

Susan smiled - any encouragement was better than none. 'Mick works on Jones' farm, so we can't afford much. He can cycle or walk to work from here, which helps.'

Alan felt he wasn't wasting his time - there were things in Denton Cheney that needed doing. Now, he had a reason to get onto the parish council. He waved goodbye and posted a sheet to the downstairs flat next door where a yappy dog leapt up at his fingers. Bearing no malice, he left via a wooden picket gate, closing it carefully behind him.

*　*　*　*　*

'Still no positive identification?' probed the chief constable.

'No Ma'am. I've had them go through the UK's missing persons' lists, and we're now contacting Europe The face was badly disfigured – fish had been..., I won't continue – so we couldn't obtain a useful photo. I've alerted the local community policing team who have put up notices, talked with residents and asked about unaccounted for relatives or friends - but nothing to date. The parish council clerks of Denton Cheney and all surrounding villages within ten miles are aware and have been asked to publicise our search - again, no leads thus far.' McAlister summed up, 'We may have to conclude that this woman was an outsider.'

'I see,' murmured the chief constable, 'a body without an owner. What about finger prints and DNA. Surely forensic can assist?'

'That's all in hand. No matches for either from the data base, but I've widened the search to other police areas. There was nothing useful on the body – no keys or name tags, only a few British coins.'

'I presume it was a drowning?'

'We await the full autopsy report. Violence does appear to have been involved.'

'That's worrying,' said the superior officer. 'I suggest you chase them up. Who's on the case?'

'Apart from myself - Detective Sergeant Smith, two detectives, three constables, the local community support officer, and the usual specialists. It's our top priority right now – we need to clear it up.'　.

The chief constable had been standing in front of the inspector's desk, relaxed with hands clasped behind her back. Now, she grimaced, seemingly frustrated, 'Four weeks it's been, and we're no further forward.

Let me have a daily report. I need to brief the chair of the police authority - he won't be happy.'

*　*　*　*　*

Jane leant back from the desk in her padded, wooden armed, chair. She liked the study best of all. When she stood up and looked into the bottom half of the pier mirror it reminded her that the house was previously her father's; he had been so tall, an officer in the army whom the family had dutifully accompanied through many overseas tours. As a result she had been brought up in a separate, disciplined environment where the indigenous people were always ill-educated, incompetent or dishonest – sometimes all three. From all this early age travel she had developed moral certainty and a need for fairness, combined with total confidence in her own ability to achieve, despite the odds.

Apart from the cottage and wall mirror she had also inherited the desk, which, although too art-deco for her taste, would always be her main workplace. In the cold months, when it was dark and better to be inside, the two of them remained in the house but separated into their favourite locations. Her husband was usually in his workshop making useful things out of metal, or models of World War II fighters. Come spring, he switched to spending his days at the nearby, grass based aerodrome where he was a member of the flying club and kept up his pilot's licence by putting in more than the minimum number of hours using his own, small monoplane.

On a wing commander's pension, flying was an expensive hobby. Jane didn't want him to give it up, which had prompted her interest in re-entering remunerated work as an elected district councillor – Conservative of course. Although the role had been interesting, the need for party discipline and use of three line whips had clashed with her need to do the right thing. As a result, she had given this up in preference to becoming the clerk to a number of parish councils; it was an employment which not only provided a useful income but also brought her administrative skills, computer literacy and knowledge of local government regulations up to speed.

The paper work in front of her was confirmation of a successful protest she had been asked to lead. The main east coast railway line, which had become very busy, passed close to her village; the only way to the other side was by means of an ungated, traffic light controlled, level crossing. The parish council decided that this would be far too dangerous now that this minor road was to be upgraded into a major bypass. After a two year campaign which had involved demonstrations, lobbying of councillors and members of parliament, working closely with the local press and mobilising the community, Network Rail had succumbed by agreeing to provide a permanent road bridge.

She reflected that it was rare for one to feel satisfied when trying to right wrongs or remedy a patent injustice, but this time, the correct outcome had been obtained. 'Thank you' letters lay opened in a pile on the carpet, they had reinforced her belief in the power of democracy and the commonsense of the population. Then it occurred to her, she would need something to fill in the now available time and burn up her undoubted energy. Coffee was due and Bernard came in.

'Well done old girl, only you could have done that. Most thought it a lost cause, but not you.' Jane enjoyed the compliment.

'Maybe, but I'll need something to do when you're off with your flying chums. I had the idea of trying to unearth a lead on that drowning over at Denton Cheney. As a clerk I know the local villages well. I could raise the issue with councillors and ask them to use their network of contacts and report back on anything or anybody that seems out of place. It can't be on the agendas but I could raise it afterwards. It's something I could contribute. That crime, or perhaps it's just an identity mystery, needs clearing up so we can all get back to normal again; its affecting the whole district, everybody is talking about it.'

He put an arm around her shoulder, 'Surely not, you deserve a break. Treat yourself! A rest will do you good, enable you to think clearer.'

She looked up at her husband doubtfully, but realising he had a point, spun the chair around to face him, 'Yes, you're right, I already do too much. Come spring, I'll look around.'

* * * * *

'That's it!' announced 'Sunny' Ibrahim as he shut the shop door and pulled down the window blinds. 'Thank goodness for half day closing. I'm whacked and this heavy cold doesn't help. Meeting so many customers, I'm bound to pick up something,' he concluded gloomily. 'This year I had that flu injection,' he added, looking towards his wife for sympathy, 'but it was no use.'

Shiva was perched on a tall, round stool behind the narrow, barred post office counter, quietly balancing the day's business. She clicked the machine and tut-tutted to herself before finally locking the drawers and descending onto the floor, still neat in her amber sari and grey woollen trousers.

'Let's get in by the gas fire,' she instructed Ibrahim who followed her into their living quarters at the back.

'You realise,' began Ibrahim, comfortable now in his favourite armchair with sock encased feet extended towards the flickering heat, 'that this government is hell bent on closing down more post offices. You suggested talking to that action group; I did, and they were helpful. They came in to see me and are composing a circular to all villagers asking them to write in and protest, but, from what I've seen, it's only money that counts. This, so called, Labour government is worse than the Tories, they refuse to call us a necessary social service and only consider the subsidy they are paying. We can't win. Give it a year or two and we'll be gone.' Shiva looked surprised but he continued. 'Let's face it, there's one at Shottle, only a mile and a half away and right on the bus route. Unlike us, they also have a profitable general store where people stop on their way home from work. Admittedly, we do the papers - which they don't. Nevertheless, if push comes to shove, they will survive, not us.'

'Then we can relax a bit and enjoy an early retirement,' concluded Shiva. 'You've always said how much you like this village. I remember you turned down more prosperous livings in town because they were in rough areas.'

'I did, and I was right. With three children to bring up we needed a decent neighbourhood with nice people – like here. There is one problem though…' he paused to ensure his wife was giving him her full attention – she was, '…our income will fall, yet our only daughter is still unattached.

90

We must marry her off to a well off Muslim professional who can afford to look after her and take the burden away from us retirees.'

Shiva's face closed in anguish, she thought: 'Here we go again.' As she was about to object Sunny waved her away. 'We talked about this before but I did nothing. Now, I see no reason not to contact my brother in Mumbai, ask him to seek out some candidates and provide us with a short list. We can go out to India and interview them ourselves - it will make a nice trip.'

'Surely, you won't. It's all wrong,' scolded Shiva, but he was already looking for a writing pad.

'I've time this afternoon,' continued Ibrahim, suddenly motivated, 'I must do it now or we'll be too late. Tell me what I should specify – doctor, engineer, accountant...age twenty five to thirty...not previously married... not too religious...good family?'

Shiva threw up her hands in disbelief, got up and walked out in tears. Ibrahim was hurt, he loved his wife and they had got on well over so many years. But, he had decided, it was the husband's job to do the right thing, even if others disagreed. After a sigh and a minute's contemplation of the empty doorway, he began to write slowly and carefully, choosing words to suit the local context and customs, rather than those of his adopted country.

* * * * *

After serving several overseas postings in hot climates, where the sun set predictably between six and seven each evening, Chris found it difficult adjusting to the short, dark days. A widower, he had retired with a sound, index linked government pension and a large sum of money from prudent investment. Without elderly relatives to care for, he could have chosen to live anywhere in the world. However, when discussing the possibilities with his new partner, Sandra, she pointed out that her mother was still soldiering on and that all their family were based in England. 'What was wrong with staying here?' she said - they could afford to get away to somewhere less severe in the cold months. In Britain inflation was low and the pound strong, it made sense to remain where they were.

Chris saw merit in her arguments, but had preferred to work from the whole world down by a process of logical elimination, first making a short list of continents and then assigning points to each location to see which came out on top. It went something like this: Far East - mostly unstable and too hot ; Africa, except for South Africa, which had suffered from apartheid and would be tense for many years - was uncivilised; North America – by contrast was civilised, but he knew it well and had covered it systematically during a series of long vacations. It offered little different from the UK, except there was more of it and the population was less aware of the world outside; Europe - year round warmth came only in Spain's Andalusia - but what sort of a life would it be to join an exclusive club of British expatriates; South America, was a mystery and dangerous with too many failed states - somehow it had never appealed; Australia and New Zealand were similar, prosperous societies with the rule of law and mild winters, but neither country presented any sense of excitement - added to which they were a long way away.

So, England it was, and back to the village and house he had bought with his late wife who had died, far too soon, in a tragic airliner crash. Chris had kept the cottage in Denton Cheney as a base, reoccupying it between foreign postings and using it to display a collection of antiques and curiosities from around the world. After retiring, and before meeting Sandra, he had considered living in Bath, a visually pleasant city with good access to the west-country and a fast train service to London, but the thought of a move to an unknown area so late in life had deterred him. Following his chance meeting with Sandra – who was a local - he had abandoned that idea, deciding to make the best of the village.

The winter days dragged; with nothing to do outside, Chris felt himself sliding into a mood of depression. His thoughts drifted towards recent reading - Sterne's use of digression in 'Tristram Shandy' really did reflect the way one's mind worked. Like Shandy he was unable to prevent dramatic past events being freshly experienced.

Wiser now, and more experienced in life's problems, Chris realised, with hindsight, that he had never given himself time to properly understand his brother. The circumstances of Ken's death had been heartrending.

While at work in the Singapore consulate he took an unexpected phone call from his cousin Anne - no relatives had ever phoned before as it was expensive and difficult to get a trunk line. Soon after Ken had arrived on a visit to see her, he stated that he could see two images of his car through the window. A stroke was diagnosed by the paramedic and he was rushed to hospital. At first, Chris had felt no sense of urgency, but alarm tingled his finger ends when Anne's husband's unmistakeable, Somerset burr advised him to 'come soon', but omitted to give any sort of prognosis.

Chris was already booked to visit London that week in order to present a report at the Foreign Office; he was looking forward to this and had kept it a secret from his family so that it would be a surprise. He suggested calling in to see his brother at the beginning of the trip. Anne gave him the hospital's telephone number and a doctor to contact for a more detailed assessment; they talked, but there appeared to be no urgency. Coping with ill or injured people lay outside his experience. In the office he was accustomed to dealing with colleagues who were nearly all young, and, as a widower with no children, he had become insulated from day to day family problems.

Early on a March day Chris walked shivering along the aircraft tunnel and into the terminal, collected his case, put on a thermal vest and pullover in the toilet and booked a bus direct to Cardiff. Visiting time was that afternoon. His cousin told him how hard she had found it. When Chris noticed Anne preparing herself for what was clearly an ordeal, he realised, for the first time that this was more than a woman's over reaction; the situation was, evidently, one of real concern.

His brother was in a separate, grimly blackened, old stone building, in which there were only three beds, all set wide apart. The reality of this 'dying ward' only dawned on him later. It was gloomy inside and senior staff faded into the background as they approached a steel bed in which Ken's arms and handsome, suntanned face lay exposed. His cousin immediately took the lead, chatting away frenetically very close to the pillow, taking all his brother's attention. It left Chris to occupy an upright wooden chair on the opposite side, jetlagged, tired and uninformed, he was adrift in a nightmare world.

Suddenly, he felt a warm hand pressing against his arm. Not having grasped the seriousness of his brother's condition, he responded with a big smile, saying, 'My brother looks better than either of us.' To which Ken appeared to respond positively, though he couldn't talk. The patient then rolled his upper body convulsively towards Anne who held his shoulders and talked in platitudes, never once mentioning that Chris had come to see him. Very soon, the accompanying nurse said it was time to leave – they had been there long enough – and the two of them moved despairingly away like a receding tide. Once outside Chris, who was by now mentally exhausted, held his silence. This wasn't what he had expected. He hadn't asked the right questions, and everybody was reluctant to tell him the facts.

Days later he became dismayed that, during what turned out to be a final meeting with Ken, he had been so distant. He also felt guilty that his cousin had been through such a traumatic experience, one which should rightly have fallen to him. When thinking about the cause of the stroke he realised that, for a person who had been a heavy smoker with probable cardio vascular deficiencies, Anne's customary effusive, over the top welcome, had probably been the trigger of sudden excitement and high blood pressure. It was unsettling to realise that the unrestrained expression of love and affection shown by Ken's favourite cousin had led directly to his demise.

Chris needed a ledge on which to rest his battered thoughts. He searched the Sky sports programme and discovered Tiger Woods mastering yet another golf course with his ever determined skills. Tiger had just endured the death of his own father and mentor. It reminded Chris that nobody is immune to such a tragic experience, one which lies totally beyond their control.

This agonising wasn't helpful - he couldn't change the past but he could influence the future. He cleared his head and began to study some technical papers Jeff had lent him; they covered previous extraction of soft sand. Much to his surprise, he discovered that no less than seven pits had already been worked commercially within the parish boundary. Curious, he dug out his raincoat and golf umbrella and set off to see if he could still trace them. Physical action in the fresh air was the most effective panacea he knew.

The county police headquarters were housed in town at an old, decaying mansion; a cheap, sixties wing had been added to the rear and it was here where McAlister and Smith met the forensic pathologist.

'What news?' asked the Detective Inspector. 'We're struggling with this case.'

'I'll complete my report tonight, it isn't good news. There are clear signs of violence: damage to the right eye socket; a fractured right cheek bone and considerable bruising to the face and neck. Some of the latter could have happened when she fell into the stream, but not the facial injuries - they were made by a heavy blow of some sort. She drowned but was probably unconscious at the time. Age, about seventy - frail but otherwise healthy. One strange thing; there is an old injury to the left foot - obtained in childhood I expect. She may have walked with a slight limp.'

'Murder then?' speculated McAlister, his interest aroused.

'Not for me to say - that's your job. Certainly no accident,' she elaborated.

'They're all women now,' thought McAlister, '– at least, they are on television.'

'What are you doing about identification?'

'I've no choice now but to seek approval for DNA testing of all the village men. I feel sure there must be a local connection but we haven't found one so far. Having no birth marks or tattoos, and no face to speak of, has given us a problem,' admitted the inspector, adding with a sigh, 'I was hoping you would solve it for me. The limp might help, it's something. Come on Smith, let's get back to work!'

* * * * *

Each Wednesday in late autumn as the nights drew in, the clocks went back and outside activity became unattractive, the fourteenth county scout troop began to meet in the village hall. Ray, the scoutmaster, had been a Queen's Scout himself. Long term residents, but originally from the south, he and Emma had moved into the village from Kent after a transfer by the Ford Motor company - they had offered Ray the position of national spare parts manager at their huge, purpose built distribution depot adjacent to the M1 motorway, very close to its intersection with the A14 which led to the Felixstowe container port.

Ray had founded the troop which, although initially well attended, lost support in the seventies as the rural population declined and colour television became widespread. It was now reduced to only twelve, irregular boys and girls. In order to maintain a minimum viable number, some of his members had been recruited through colleagues at work, which meant they relied on their, not always available, parents to bring them in by car.

The brothers approached the brightly lit hall with caution. From inside came the echoing sounds of rough and tumble games and the enthusiastic encouragement of young voices. Aaron hesitated and began to back away.

'You promised!' Joe reminded him.

The wooden hall floor was permanently marked out for badminton – it was a little under size but the players, who were mostly elderly, didn't mind. At the opposite end from the stage was a serving hatch leading to a small kitchen where tea could be made. Those who booked the poorly insulated hall were not well off and their reluctance to feed the meter meant that on winter evenings, the building remained unpleasantly chilly.

Plucking up courage, the brothers went in through the main door. Boys of different ages and sizes – some in full uniform with shorts, others in half uniform and the rest in school clothes – were playing a rowdy game of British bulldog while the girls sat together in a group practising their knots.

A man came towards them; his crisply ironed, epauletted, fawn shirt was covered with different, sewn on badges; brown shoes gleamed beneath sharply creased long trousers.

'Hello,' he said pleasantly, 'have you come to join us? You can attend on a trial basis if you like – it's free.' Aaron and Joe, pleased to be treated as adults, were rendered speechless. 'No uniform is needed,' encouraged the scoutmaster. He put a hand loosely on each of their shoulders. 'Now you're here, come along and join in. We're going to practice for our next football match – it's against the town troop.'

Afterwards, on their way home, Aaron was withdrawn. 'It didn't seem much,' he finally ventured.

'Maybe,' agreed Joe, 'but you heard what he said about camping in Wales during the summer - canoeing and all that. Sounds like fun to me.'

'Sam and Dave never go,' said Aaron with finality, 'why should we?'

Unbeknown to them, their two older friends and mentors were becoming more and more frustrated with teenage life. Dave rather liked Aaron, treating him as the younger sibling he never had and needed to protect, but had recently become a bit miffed at Aaron's infatuation with 'that girl'. At first Dave put it down to a passing fancy but, as the relationship developed, he realised that his young protégé was gradually being lost to the close knit, masculine world.

Dave and Sam had always been bosom pals. Their parent's houses were side by side, each part of a different semi-detached pair – far enough apart to provide some privacy on moody days, yet near enough to drop in unannounced on lonely days. From an early age they had played together in one or another of the generous sized post war gardens. Their urge to explore the neighbourhood had led them into the usual rural escapades, which included bird's nesting, scrumping the farmer's apples, letting off Guy Fawke's night fireworks in villager's porches or placing bangers in tin cans to frighten dogs, stampeding the cattle by targeting them with their home made catapults, chasing the sheep, and cutting down trees to make fires.

Dave was approaching the end of his final school year, a slow starter he had never been able to read properly. Feeling humiliated, he had astutely covered up the problem but succeeded only in making matters worse. Without access to funding for remedial teaching the Denton Cheney junior school had been forced to send him onto the county comprehensive where his prospects were poor and the learning difficulties continued. He would soon be leaving full time education without any formal qualifications, and, as trade apprenticeships had been cut back, with poor prospects.

On the other hand, Sam was a bright boy who didn't bother to apply himself. He had never been encouraged to do so by parents who worked on the land and were unable to envisage any other future for their only son. Secondary school teachers had attempted to convince him that general certificates of secondary education in maths, English and physics, were valuable and well within his capabilities, but he remained unreceptive, resisting their advice, content to drift along waiting for something to happen. A year older than Dave, he tried work at a security company and then a warehouse, but had been laid off – sacked was the right word. Much too late he discovered that, for him, such employment was boring and intolerable. Ignorant of any alternatives he became depressed, which had led to his experimenting with soft drugs supplied by Eddy. Fortunately, he realised that this could only be a temporary solution, not one that was going to benefit him in the longer term.

One cold evening Sam, with Dave in tow, had hung about outside the village hall during a parish council meeting. He envied those inside, not because they were warm but because they had a purpose in life. Big and intimidating, he had jeered the participants and showered stones on them when they left the building. Coming from bright light into darkness the councillors could see little; assuming that they were about to be mugged, they shouted for help. Police Sergeant Smith, who had attended the meeting to provide an update on local crime statistics, was ahead and had already reached his car. The inevitable result was the detention of the two youths and, as insisted on by Jack – who saw the episode as an affront to his dignity - the subsequent issue of an Anti Social Behaviour Order against Sam, who was deemed to be the ringleader.

Sam's mounting frustration with the world beyond school had, by an unfortunate chance, earned him a criminal record; it caused him to feel even more alienated from an adult society into which he seemed fated to be refused an entry ticket.

APATITE - SPRING

The large vegetable garden was flat and empty. During the winter Mrs Oldham had found enough tolerable days in which to clear the bean sticks and turn the whole area over; it was tough, back breaking work for an ancient, but the ground was now ready for improvement. Dick always said they had hungry soil. His original solution had been to collect manure from the Hope's nearby stables, but as working horses were gradually replaced by tractors, they turned to using farm compost which Jones kindly delivered when he cleared his yard. It wasn't as effective as fresh horse droppings but free and better than nothing

She looked forward to this time of year. Seeds could be sown and a bountiful harvest produced, as if by magic, from that humus less waste. After the first, but thorough, fertilisation she added nothing further. Dick used to sow and tend the vegetables after he finished work, enjoying the solitary task, while his wife confined herself to the kitchen, never interfering or offering to help. He was adamant that no watering be done - even in the driest weather, arguing that it would encourage the roots to turn up, causing the plants to become weak and produce a poor crop.

Since Dick's passing, recalling his homespun wisdom had helped her to manage alone.

In those days Mrs Oldham's outside responsibilities had been limited to caring for a few old apple and pear trees, a line of raspberry canes - grown under a fishing net to ward off the blackbirds, and a patch of perennials to cut for the house and church. Confined indoors, baking and country cooking became her forte. Her fruit cakes were much in demand, but she had little spare time in which to prepare them. The secret lay in a recipe handed down by Grandma; unlike many of her age group, she was happy to pass it on to anyone who asked. 'The garden is my priority now, it feeds me and keeps me fit,' was her pragmatic response to any expressed admiration of her laudable efforts.

During her regular trips to the Cecil Day Centre at the edge of the village Mrs Oldham had noticed how badly the roads, and in particular, the pavements, were potholed and breaking up. Elderly friends found the uneven footpaths difficult to walk on. After rain the streets were more puddle than tarmac; it meant that pedestrians were always at risk of an unexpected soaking whenever a vehicle passed by.

The old widow wondered when the village highways had last been resurfaced and cast her mind back for something to link it with. Family history flashed before her eyes, all mixed up with a random selection of national events; it was a like a Pathe newsreel. She could imagine the narrator's posh voice, the war ending, her son and daughter being born, Churchill's funeral, Beecham cutting back the railways, her daughter's marriage at St James, that smart, neo-Georgian close being built in the deCourt's old paddock, the wedding of Charles and Diana. Yes, that was it - the new houses. The council had asphalted the village roads soon after that, she remembered the acrid smell. Since then there had been only occasional patches and random pothole filling.

These days, people made a fuss openly, not just down at the pub. The age of deference had gone forever, but what could an old lady do to change things? Then, she remembered the good work and informative approach of the village action group. Yes, she'd go to a council meeting and say something – if she could summon up the courage.

It was early evening, but still light, as Henry cycled away from the village down Glebe Lane. He was meeting a lorry, parked alongside a galvanised steel, five bar gate. Seeing him, the driver waved, dropped down from the cab, and approached with a clipboard and papers.

'You took a long time. Sign these,' he ordered.

Fred was a local trucker, doing a favour by using the estate vehicle for private business.

'Let's get them unloaded,' suggested Henry without any rancour – Fred was always a bit abrupt. 'Just inside the hedge will do for now.'

The two men heaved wooden frames, in-filled with wire mesh, down to the ground and stacked them on the fresh new grass.

'Thanks,' muttered Henry. 'Them will do as walls,' adding by way of explanation, 'You told me you couldn't find anything suitable to cover the pens, so I've ordered a big rope fishing net - it's due next week.'

Fred climbed up into his seat and manoeuvred the truck carefully back onto the lane. He wound down the window.

'You're lucky to live in this village and still be able to make a livelihood in the countryside,' he observed, looking down enviously at Henry.

'Yes,' he agreed, 'but the parish council tell us the county want to build a big school - right here! Can you believe it? That'll finish us – no more rabbiting or shooting. They say to write a letter. Letters don't do no good.'

'Maybe yes, maybe no,' considered Fred, who was a townie. 'But do it. You ain't got no other way of fighting back.' He paused to engage bottom gear before shouting a final gruff, 'Take my advice and do it, mate!'

Henry watched thoughtfully as the lorry moved slowly away. Fred was a sensible man whose wife worked for a solicitor. Yes, perhaps he would.

* * * * *

A plain, buff envelope lay on the mat, Jeff didn't recognise it. Curious,

101

he slit it open; inside was a letter headed 'Shottle District Council' and signed, very neatly, by an officer with a rather long job title. After reading it twice he translated the 'government speak' as a qualified 'yes' to the request he and Chris had sent in two months earlier, seeking approval for the four planter box locations. The council had raised no objection, declaring that the highways agency and the county council – between them responsible for footpaths, verges and roads, were informed but, so far, had offered no comment. He phoned his fellow organiser who rarely left home.

'Hello.'

'It's Jeff. I've received a note back from the district council.' Having discovered that everything slowed down in a rural area, he read it out carefully, word by word.

'Do we really need to hear from those others?' asked Chris, 'No follow up contact is given.'

'It's nice and ambiguous,' suggested Jeff, 'protects them but leaves us nowhere. I reckon we should go ahead. If we have to move them, we can. Silence means assent!'

Chris was more cautious; after many years dealing with fellow civil servants he preferred to cross every 't' and dot every 'i'. 'We're going to look pretty silly if we have to take them away.'

'Chris, we must back ourselves and press on,' said Jeff, becoming impatient but trying not to show it.

'Right,' agreed the voice, somewhat reluctantly, 'what next?'

'Confirm the price, see if there's any discount, get a delivery date, issue an order and make out a cheque to accompany it.'

'Can you do it then?'

'Yes,' confirmed Jeff, 'I'll send you a copy.'

'It's best to have them delivered to Jones' farm,' suggested Chris. 'Then ask Tony to bring them into the village on his rubber - tyre trailer.'

'Good thinking. You obviously know him. Will he store them for us, plus the compost, plants etc?'

'Yes, it will be fine.'

'Great, I'll go ahead. Progress at last!'

It was raining, admittedly not much, but remained unpleasantly wet as the four of them – the farmer had brought along his teenage son Chad – lifted a square, injection moulded box down from the straw strewn floor of the wooden trailer.

'That's the last,' muttered Jones as he climbed back onto the tractor, keen to be doing more useful work. 'I'll be off.' Always dressed in the same flat cap and long, green waterproof jacket over a well-washed, navy boiler suit and black rubber boots, he didn't appear to notice the weather. Earlier in the day a self-employed, younger friend in the building trade had collected sixteen reject, pressed concrete slabs from the nearest garden centre and, using his employer's transit van, had deposited four at each chosen location.

Progress had been slow. As Chris observed, 'It's difficult having to get everything done by volunteers or for free. Just when it's about to happen something else always seems to take priority.'

Using a shovel they levelled up the final base, placed the slabs and, with a long stake, levered the black planter into place, filled it from the remaining bag of compost and added some liquid fertiliser recommended by the garden centre. With Denton Cheney in bold gold lettering on the side facing the corner, it looked very well. Chris scooped out a hole and planted the central, evergreen mahonia – chosen because it was winter flowering and had spiky leaves to deter possible vandalism, surrounding it with several variegated euonymus and four flowering surfinia which, as spring turned into summer, were expected to grow vigorously and overhang all around.

'All we need now is people to look after them,' he announced standing back to admire their handiwork.

'They'll appear,' answered Jeff encouragingly. 'In the meantime you and I must take turns to water them. With that large base reservoir and the wick system they should last at least a week, even at the height of summer.'

* * * * *

Watched over by caring ewes the first new lambs had been allowed out of the big Dutch barn, almost hidden in the furrows they supplemented their mother's milk by nibbling at the low, fresh green, leaves of turnips. In village gardens the white stars of snowdrops had faded, replaced by the larger, bright yellows and purples of crocuses; along grassy verges, crowds of daffodils were already in fat bud.

For Aaron it had been a long winter. Whenever able to escape from his parents and friends he had set off to visit the horse field, often taking circuitous routes in order to make his destination less obvious. That enchanting schoolgirl face had lodged in his memory like none before. He couldn't forget. It had been a brief vision but one that had drawn him back again and again in the hope that she might be there. He didn't know how to deal with this obsession, didn't understand his own feelings, but had to see her again; his brain could not shake off the compulsion. Deep inside, he realised he would be tongue tied and hopeless if they met, no doubt watching in frustration as one of the more confident teenagers caught her attention and began a friendship.

It was Thursday, school was over and this was the evening Mum worked late and Dad went to his club. Aaron got off the Country Crest bus and waved goodbye to Dave, saying he had to go straight home tonight. In order to avoid any awkward questions he moved quickly away from the village green drop off point. Out of sight, he noticed the light was fading fast which prompted him to run along the High Street. Time was short and he needed to call in at the house to discard his book bag and swap the give away blazer for a pullover – it wouldn't do for her to see him dressed in that humbling school uniform.

Fortunately, his Yale key opened their front door at the first attempt – the lock had been giving trouble all winter and only Mum had acquired the knack. Once inside he dumped the bag on the wooden hall seat and rushed upstairs to exchange coat and tie for his favourite crimson, turtle necked, fleece top. After a quick comb of unruly, badly cut hair, he allowed himself a glance in the dressing table mirror; the reflection almost met with approval.

Within minutes Aaron had reached Glebe Lane, unseen and unnoticed. Ahead he could make out a person in the field, but the silhouette was too broad to be that of his heart's desire. After some judicious research, gleaned by hanging around at the village shop, he had discovered that the attractive young lady was known as Emily and that the woman in charge was called Fiona – this was probably her. Fighting back disappointment he pressed on, his mouth dry in anticipation.

'Hello,' he uttered, somewhat hopefully, over the weathered, wooden, farm gate.

Fiona, who was training a foal on a long tether, paused and looked across.

'Hi, haven't I seen you before?' she said in a friendly voice. 'You're Aaron, aren't you?'

'Yes,' he gulped, surprised, but glad there had been a response.

'Do you go to Wellford School like Emily?'

Aaron had learned something and began to feel more secure.

'No, to Ranwick.'

They continued to face each other but Fiona was occupied and conversation slumped. He returned to feeling uncomfortable and pushed himself to act. It was, after all his first opportunity since the summer; although he had been down there many times, nobody had ever turned up.

'Do the others come here to help you?'

'Yes,' smiled Fiona, noting his shyness. 'Now it's spring there's plenty to do and longer evenings to do it in. We should all be here on Thursdays and Fridays from now on.'

'Oh,' commented Aaron. For once he was proud of himself and already beginning an imaginary chat with Emily, 'Thanks, bye.'

* * * * *

In winter the dog walkers were elusive, appearing outside only for the minimum necessary time; come spring, having a pet needing exercise provided an acceptable excuse for a stroll after work or while dinner was cooking. If good weather tempted earlier in the day housewives abandoned their inside chores and took out their pet in the certain expectation of meeting someone else of the same mindset. As a result their animals walked rather less, mostly sitting still, mournfully watching the adults talk, becoming overweight and more than ever resembling their owners.

Lady was a noticeable absentee and Jeff wondered what had happened to Arthur who, in the autumn, had been struggling to keep up with his bouncy little companion. The non-dog people were excluded from that esoteric club and its discussions about the vet, the house training, the flea problem and the many horror stories about Rotweilers – or similar beasts – savaging babies or youngsters. For the rest of the village the solution to this problem was simple – the owner was always responsible and there was nothing more to be said. Such unpredictable animals should never be kept in homes as family pets; it was irresponsible, apart from being, well, plain stupid.

Jeff found it strange that he had never – to his knowledge – passed Mr Turner walking his setter around the village, but assumed that Turner and Rex either favoured more remote paths beyond the built up area, or that their timing had always remained different from his own. Few appeared to know the man, saying he was a bit of a recluse, most had only heard of him through the Advertiser's article. Unlike many who made the headlines, Turner had made no attempt to capitalise on his overnight fame; Jeff still had no idea where he lived.

Government had recently begun a process of consultation in regard to proposed wider legislation on dog control; Jeff welcomed this, surely it was long overdue. The village was already a 'scoop a poop' enclave where notices attached to lampposts acted as reminders. Generally, the pavements and verges were well maintained and most owners carried their own plastic bags, cleaned up and took the residue home. To reduce the risk, dedicated, regularly emptied bins had been suggested by villagers but, so far, the parish council had not reacted.

Occasionally, a rogue person appeared and it became necessary to instigate a campaign until the very evident recurring mess was no longer there. It only needed one antisocial owner to spoil a pristine rural setting. Fixed fee fouling penalties could now be imposed by parish council nominees but the members had declined to appoint anybody, believing in a small village, this would be an overreaction, and that an appeal by their dog warden in the church newsletter, or a private chat with the offender should suffice.

Parish councils are expected to appoint wardens for footpaths, trees and dogs; the latter was a volunteer who patrolled the streets in the early morning with his trusty lieutenant Gus, regularly reporting back what they had discovered in an always amusing little newsletter entry. It served to keep the problem at the forefront of villagers' minds and led to a decline in the number of unpleasant incidents. The village footpath warden was Ray, a man who loved to walk the local rights of way; he noted stiles that needed repair and signs that were damaged, advising which paths had not been properly opened up by the landowners. Among these rural tracks was the one between Denton Cheney and Dunton which, although it crossed the proposed minerals site, was well trodden by locals and visitors alike, emphasising that such an ancient route should not be interfered with.

Since the appointment of a qualified, full time 'arboriculture officer' by Shottle district council the tree warden post had become a sinecure. The position really needed to be cancelled since the warden had no powers to cutback, plant or trim parish trees without first seeking approval from the new district officer, but reporting to an already overloaded, remote official had proven unproductive.

Whether the dogs brought out their masters or vice-versa was a moot point, it probably depended on the relative health of each. Dogs are supposed to be man's best friend and it was often both alarming and sad to notice owners struggling around the pavements and paths while exhibiting progressive states of decrepitude. One such person could be seen bent over from the waist as he shuffled along behind a large, limping bull mastiff, if spoken to his replies were barely coherent. Yet another villager was drawn along – like a sleigh – by a pair of scrawny greyhounds, the man so frail that mounting the kerb was an effort. This all too visible irreversible decline, caused by the varied physical problems of aging, reminded Jeff that new drugs were being developed based on genetic engineering; from time to time, the press highlighted encouraging news about progress and he rather hoped that a breakthrough would occur before his own body approached the critical stage.

News finally reached Jeff that Arthur was deceased and Lady was being looked after by his brother in town; both would miss those uplifting country strolls.

* * * * *

To Alan, a lot seemed to have happened since becoming involved in village affairs; he didn't regret the decision. Christmas had passed and, soon after, there had been a light fall of snow which survived only until noon. The thatched, mellow stone cottages looked enchanting beneath their sprinkling of icing sugar. With the sun shining from a pale, washed out, blue sky, he had hurried out to collect as many photographs as possible. His wife already had a record of key village views taken at the height of summer, a winter collection would provide an attractive contrast.

Carol singers from the church had toured the streets, decked out in long anoraks with Santa hats and bright scarves, the men wearing green Wellingtons, the ladies, calf length, brown leather boots. Adults carried paraffin lamps, while children from the small village primary school scurried from door to door collecting donations. The scene really did reassemble the idealised Victorian festival depicted so frequently on Christmas cards. Alan hadn't experienced this before and much enjoyed the cheerful family atmosphere; it reminded him of the lantern festival he had been lucky enough to see when on a business trip to China, except that here there was no full moon to accompany the revellers, only an ominously heavy, purple-black cloud.

After the New Year had arrived and the world was moving again, David called to advise that a common date had been set for the district and parish council elections. If they were interested then nomination papers needed to be completed, signed by two seconders - who must either live in the parish or within two miles of it – and submitted at least four weeks in advance. He suggested they get together and draw up a list of seven other sensible villagers whom they could approach and encourage to participate.

'Why a total of nine?' asked Alan.

'That's the full council complement - I've checked. If more than nine are proposed then an election must be called, if only nine then all are deemed to be elected.'

'I see,' said Alan, 'but, surely, some, if not all, of the incumbents will apply again.'

'Perhaps not, they know they're unpopular, the majority may give up.'

'It looks like an election then!' concluded Alan. 'That would be bad – they're all long time residents and will have a lot of friends.' Then, he cheered up a bit. 'However, at the worst, we should manage two places – they're that many short right now.'

'I'm more concerned about obtaining support,' worried David, 'The action group and VASE are one off events, whereas this is a four year commitment and involves not only conflict, but sorting out a big mess.'

'We're away on holiday tomorrow, so let me be the first. If you collect the forms I'll definitely stand,' said Alan decisively. 'Sorry, but I must leave you to find the remaining seven. Ideally, we need a core whose names are already known. I fear that I'm not going to attract many voters.'

When Alan arrived back there was a pile of unopened envelopes by the front door, among them was one which had been readdressed with a red felt tip pen - it was from David; the application form was inside. He phoned his co-organiser, who was inclined to be over enthusiastic.

'Welcome back. Good to hear from you – my soul mate. How are you?'

'Fine,' said Alan. 'Did you get seven more?'

'No,' came the reply, 'six, but all have the forms. I'll check with Shottle to see how many are submitted.'

'Can't do more,' Alan acknowledged. 'Some of that lot you call the Taliban will stand, of that I'm sure.'

* * * * *

Polling day arrived, as usual it was wet and windy. On the second voting paper was a list; Alan found it strange to see his own name printed at the bottom. There were ten candidates. A close read indicated that, as only three of the present councillors had stood for re-election, the newcomers

109

must get at least six places. This would be a solid majority, enough to steer the council in a new direction. He couldn't suppress a smile when the attendants at the village hall polling station recognised him, even permitting themselves a small cheer of encouragement while he stood in one of two private booths to place careful crosses against eight names – including his own. It seemed slightly undemocratic to vote for oneself; initially, he hesitated, then, realising that every cross might be critical, went ahead.

* * * * *

Peregrine sat at one of two matching desks in the modern, single story extension to his parent's ancient home; appropriately, it was called 'Tumbledown'. The name wasn't chosen because the house was in danger of collapse, but because it had been added to in so many clashing architectural styles. His father often remarked jokingly to clients: 'You can choose what type of look you want simply by walking round my property.' Father and son usually sat side by side in identical stainless steel swivel chairs, talking rapidly, discussing designs, solutions and new ideas while moving themselves smoothly around the laminated flooring on large rubber wheels. When working together they rarely stood up; the computers and printers were readily accessed from their mobile platforms, and time was money.

The first concept his father had sketched out showed a round tower of random stone construction with one narrow, full height, slit window - like those found in castles - and a glazed dome roof. It resembled one of the many local grain silos. Inside, was a meeting room and two toilets – one conventional and one for the handicapped – which were linked to St James' unused, north door by a short corridor with plate glass walls. Peregrine immediately liked the idea and couldn't improve on it. It was a simple but dramatic solution, with modern and traditional architectural themes juxtaposed to their mutual benefit. Using measurements taken in situ, he drew up scaled plans and elevations for the parochial church council to comment on.

Their reaction was prompt, without exception they liked it; even Joan,

110

who was known as a notorious 'stick in the mud', gave her unqualified approval. Later, doubts arose - of which there are always plenty in regard to innovative architectural buildings.

Peregrine wasn't dismayed, he knew that patience was essential. Clients invariably had to be educated en route to a final solution - they were, after all, footing the bill. Why couldn't the wash rooms be located within the existing church? Peregrine thought this could be advantageous since it left the extension as a clean, circular space, exactly like the chapter houses at many English cathedrals. But there were other, more difficult points: 'Why have all that glass on a fifteenth century, Grade 2 listed building - it looked out of place'; 'Why a transparent dome - wasn't it preferable to hide the roof behind a parapet and keep a clean outside profile?; 'All this work for just one extra room, wasn't that a bit extravagant - even if it did look great ?'

The revised version, or 'ArchiD2' as his dad, who was a Star Wars fan, grumbled, put all the required facilities - which now included a storeroom - in a connecting, stone walled link, but kept the meeting room circular and replaced the dome with a triangular skylight running exactly east/west to connect with the vertical window. Peregrine regretted the loss of a dome but felt he could introduce coloured glass panels at a later stage to add some drama. He was delighted when the council unanimously gave the changes their support, requesting that he prepare a full presentation submission for the parochial authorities and the district council's planning and leisure department – who would both need to approve it. From past experience, he knew that it would first need sending to the Ancient Monuments Board and English Heritage. The approvals process could be arduous, acceptance was by no means certain - all these bodies had to be satisfied, none of them moved fast and all were averse to new ideas.

Familiar with all the bureaucracy, Peregrine only became seriously concerned when he was advised that the present parish council was likely to be replaced by a set of people who were opinionated and involved - quite unlike their predecessors, who, from past experience, were unlikely to raise any objection. The parish council would automatically obtain a full copy of the planning application from the district, the council had no power to reject the proposal, but, if they didn't offer support, consent from the other authorities was less likely.

All too aware that selling the concept and creating the demand were paramount, Peregrine hadn't dared to broach the sensitive issue of final cost. He began to realise that it would be a formidable and expensive task to obtain the quality of materials and workmanship necessary to ensure the extension still looked good in a hundred years. Perhaps things had been going too well! However, unknown to the two anxious partners, prayers had been offered up by the congregation, some openly and some privately, and God was working out an answer. This was, after all, His church and He liked the idea - it was innovative, set a good example and deserved to succeed. When called upon by believers He moves in mysterious ways. Little did they know it but a saviour was already amongst them.

*   *   *   *   *

The village was isolated but hardly remote. On a summer's day a motorway and a railway were within hearing distance - although access to them was tortuous. Despite widespread car ownership and these nearby connections to the outside world, there existed a wide range of flourishing, well supported clubs, societies, and associations. Surprisingly, for a population of barely a thousand there appeared to be little overlap of membership between the disparate groups. It wasn't that the villagers weren't friendly, they were, but all their social activity existed in parallel worlds. That residents accepted this situation helped explain the remoteness of the parish council and total lack of communication from the village hall trust. Although the hall's facilities were well used, their large, glass fronted notice board, which faced the green and stood close to the village's principle bus stop, remained empty; no information was available in regard to hire charges or what bookings had been made.

The hall fronted onto an extensive shingle area - the beach as Ernest called it, one side of which was bounded by the high stone wall of the chairman's garden. Unfortunately, this wall and the adjacent wooden bus shelter provided an almost light free, nightly refuge for rebellious teenagers, causing Vincent to become focussed on this noisy personal inconvenience at the expense of his duties to the trust. This car park had been invaded by weeds whose seeds found a footing when the prevailing wind dropped them alongside the wall. Last year's messy, brown stalks were slowly being supplemented by fresh, spring shoots and a tall, impenetrable nettle bed had filled a service area to the rear. The hall surroundings had become an eyesore. Did anyone raise an adverse comment, write to the local paper or protest at a parish council meeting? Certainly not, such is tolerant, middle England - more a sleeping than a silent majority.

As the weather warmed and dried out, the hut-like bus shelter relinquished its nightly venue as Denton Cheney's unofficial youth and drugs club, and reverted to employment as a soccer goal – it was just the right size. The day long shouts and bangs, which annoyed the chairman and his wife, were broken only by time outs when the half hour single-decker bus approached, hooting a warning as it rounded the corner. Villagers, who paused to think, found it strange that the hall appeared unaccountable. What did the working group do? The parish council had been bad but it was, at least, an open, publicly controlled body, except that the tyrannical chairman refused to put its monthly minutes on their dedicated notice board - even when asked ever so politely.

A one sheet, double-sided, monthly newsletter was produced and distributed by the church. Typically, on the front, it carried a message from the vicar and on the reverse gave details of: those who were due to pick up and distribute prescriptions to elderly or infirm residents; births, deaths and marriages; women's institute events; ladies responsible for the church flowers, and important notices from the parish councils or clubs of both villages, but little else. Newcomers felt there was a need for more information but soon accepted that most local news was passed on by word of mouth – but, as had always been the case in rural villages, its accuracy was often questionable.

Well meaning villagers believed that steps needed taking to preserve this close knit community, one that was breaking down owing to cheaper cars and the escalating housing prices young locals could no longer afford. There was a widespread but unvoiced concern that, without consensus and organised resistance, the village would soon be absorbed into ugly urban sprawl, as had so many similar, ancient settlements that originally ringed the town.

Government's 'structure plans' were prepared on a ten year basis, in them one's future became set in stone. The only safeguard was to participate intelligently in the mandatory consultancy programme which played a key part in drafting them. It was essential that bodies representing wider village interests such as the parish and parochial councils and the village hall trust became involved to help steer these long term frameworks in the right direction. If such a process was not taken up soon then this beautiful village and its way of life were surely doomed.

*   *   *   *   *

McAlister's normal, rural policing responsibilities did not cease, but with the body case demanding so much of his and his officers' time, he became stressed. Car crime was on the increase - not helped by the casual way in which country communities behaved. Valuable items would be left visible on car seats, even keys in the ignition. At local parks, visitors locked handbags and coats into their boots before taking a stroll, but, these days, the villains were more sophisticated and hung around watching. At pubs or roadside cafes, businessmen in a hurry forgot laptops which soon disappeared when professional thieves made their regular checks.

The Scotsman was realistic. He knew he hadn't the resources to police all these places – nor was it practical. The solution wasn't more officers, it was enhanced public awareness. To achieve this he organised a long term campaign, putting warning notices up at all remote council parking places and obtaining the cooperation of pub and restaurant owners to do the same on their premises. After a year's effort, he was able to advise the chief constable that this particular crime statistic had improved markedly - and all without the use of extra manpower.

*   *   *   *   *

'We can turn the heating down during the day now,' proposed Anesh, steering the heavy saloon into a narrow drive, before passing beneath the newer extension and parking at the rear. It was a sharp, sunny, spring morning and he had enjoyed seeing daffodils lining motorway embankments where some of the skeletal trees were showing just a hint of fresh green. He locked the doors absentmindedly with the electronic 'dinger' as he and Amita walked the short distance to the front entrance of their investment, still engaged in earnest conversation. Once inside he branched away into the small study while his wife continued purposefully towards the kitchen.

'All's well.' Amita had returned to hand him a steaming mug of tea without milk, but with lots of sugar. 'You should give up sweet things,' she chided him playfully. 'You're developing a paunch.' The tea was from a special Indian leaf airmailed to them regularly by his father, and was much appreciated.

'It looks like we've got some carers,' he announced, handing her an opened envelope, 'from somewhere I can't pronounce in Eastern Europe.'

She read the letter carefully, going back over the first page.

'Seems above board, but our next problem is accommodation. Nothing came in from the estate agents I contacted, and that's weeks ago now.'

'Give them a bell,' suggested Anesh. 'If we take up that offer we need to find places for four. Property prices are rising now - especially around here. The action group says we're slated for forty thousand new homes by 2025 - apparently it's in the 'Central Region Study'. I know we don't want such a development, but if we buy now it will almost guarantee capital appreciation.'

'That's a good point,' agreed his wife, admiringly. 'Deductions from their wages will no doubt cover the mortgage. I'll ask about places nearby - if something comes up in the village we want an early alert. There's another, more practical issue,' she added. 'Dorothy has been reliable. We need to keep her informed and make sure she knows we want her to remain the senior staff member. She may not like the idea of a lot of foreigners who could gang up on her.'

'Yes,' agreed Anesh, 'I'll work out a better package and job description. We - maybe you - can put it to her with details of our problems and ongoing plans.'

'Agreed,' flashed Amita as she moved away to begin preparing the residents' lunch.

Anesh couldn't help noticing how slim she was, so lithe, like a panther in her movements, still the sharp-witted, attractive woman he had married half a world away.

The day seemed to pass quickly. Anesh's desk was already tidied and the car keys were in his hand when he looked through the window - he hadn't been outside all day - and noticed that it was still light. British summertime had begun the previous Sunday but he had forgotten. Glancing at his watch he realised he was an hour early and promptly sat down again.

A bright eyed, urgent Amita arrived at the open door. 'Finished already,' she mocked, but before he could explain, began to brief him on her progress. 'There's little to rent, but a house is coming available soon. It's semi-detached, in the council estate on a corner site near the church - only a short walk from here. If we want to view it they'll send someone round with the keys.'

'We 'want',' said Anesh. 'It can do no harm.'

Later that day, back in London, they mulled it over.

'I don't think we can risk losing this one,' proposed Anesh. 'At the asking price, less say four percent for bargaining, it's a sound buy for any family.'

'But only two bedrooms,' cut in his wife. 'These days people expect a room of their own - it's not like when you first came here. We're not employing unskilled, itinerant fruit pickers.'

'Well, there's plenty of space and no garage. I'm sure it could be extended. Loans have become easy to obtain.'

'Brilliant!' Amita was on board. 'Let's get the four staff lined up and place them somewhere convenient until they can move in. If something goes wrong we can always let it to students. There's a big demand now the college has become a university and the bus into town is reliable – every half hour, and cheap.'

After kicking the idea about they decided to make an offer - depending on a satisfactory cash flow projection which Amita would do in the morning. The phone rang – it was Dorothy.

'Mrs Shah, sorry to bother you so late but we've got a problem. I thought it best to let you know.' It was the first time they'd been phoned at home and there was a pause. Clearly, encouragement was needed.

'Yes Dorothy, you did the right thing. Go ahead. What is it?'

The voice resumed more positively.

'It's Gladys, she's not in her bed - I've checked. Nobody's seen her since supper and its dark now. We've searched the home fairly carefully, and the garden, but nothing. What should we do?'

'How many hours is that?' queried Amita, but worked it out. 'Three at most, I guess. Dorothy, did you call that neighbourhood watch police number – the one the community police lady gave us? We know they will react promptly to that.'

'Not yet. I will now.'

'While you wait for them, check again around the garden and nearby streets.' Detecting a wavering of resolution, she added, 'Don't panic - it's nobody's fault. It's a warm night and I'm sure she'll soon be found. Call me back in half an hour, OK?'

'I will,' was the response.

Amita put down the landline handset and looked at Anesh.

'Should we go back?'

He shook his head. 'Wait until the next report and decide then. All we can do is add two more pairs of eyes to the search. When she calls ask her if the police have e-mailed all those villagers who were willing to be contacted for such an emergency.'

'I will,' said his wife in appreciation.

An hour later the matter was resolved when Dorothy called again.

'Gladys has been found not far away in somebody's greenhouse - near the playing field. She was apparently sitting calmly in an old chair, lost in thought, quite warm, and physically sound. The owners – Mr and Mrs Woodcock – responded to the police e-mail and took a look around. I thanked them a lot.'

'Well done,' said Anesh. 'What about the hospital or doctor?'

117

'A doctor will visit soon – it's the night service – and give her a check up.'

'Where is she now?' asked Anesh, relaying Amita's mouthed question.

'She's here in her room - fast asleep.'

'Dorothy, you did well. There's nothing more any of us can do. Ask the doctor to call us direct, after which I suggest you brief one of the junior carers and get along home. We can talk it over in the morning.'

'I will,' was the final reply.

'It's like that with dementia,' said Amita. 'They wander away unpredictably for no good reason, are unable to find their way back but can't tell anybody. It will happen again. We need to establish some means of making it less likely.'

'Yes,' agreed Anesh, 'but we can't lock our residents in their rooms.'

'Maybe a more difficult system for opening the front door, or an automatic alarm if it is opened between certain hours?' suggested Amita. 'I'll do some consulting tomorrow and write up a report for the relatives. A son I recall. He's in Birmingham.'

'Bedtime!' declared her husband. 'Enough for one day is the evil thereunto.'

Amita looked at him quizzically. Was he going all religious now? Perhaps it was another new fad.

* * * * *

The nine - none were absent – recently elected members of Denton Cheney parish council and their paid, professional clerk, assembled for their first meeting. No longer were they in the draughty, uncomfortable hall but at Cecil House – a well managed day centre for the elderly residents of district council owned retirement bungalows adjacent to the old council estate. Also assembled were members of the public who were determined to give them a hard time…but once again I am moving ahead too quickly.

It had taken a busy month for our erstwhile heroes to advance this far, yet caution was still needed because winter nights always conjure up the

118

dark forces - no matter how well meaning one's intentions. Back, back we must go to our conspirators and their temporary elation at being voted into power, albeit along with several residual members of the enemy - and the most dogmatic at that.

When the notice of his electoral success reached Alan, he was surprised and delighted; so far so good, but who else would make up the numbers? He called David, who was already emerging as their natural, energetic organiser-in-chief.

'You're on, I assume?'

'Yes,' came the reply in a strong voice with an upper class accent, 'and you'll be pleased to hear that only three Taliban got in – I called the district's returning officer to obtain the full list.'

'Good,' said Alan encouragingly, 'what next?'

'We need a competent clerk. That feeble Deidre never complained about Jack's dictatorial ways, just did what he asked. You will remember that our county councillor called him 'a Hitler'. By the way, did you realise they had three clerks in less than two years, it was so bad - the others resigned.'

'I don't blame them,' said Alan. 'You're right, but who?'

'Do you recall that big protest at Shottle about replacing a level crossing with a road bridge? No – I don't think you were here then,' said David answering his own question. 'Anyway, their leader was Jane White, and they won! If you agree I'll consult with the others – our lot that is, if they're happy I'll sound her out. She already does two villages so she might be too busy.'

'Sure, go ahead,' Alan concurred. 'We don't even know the rules. We need someone who does, someone who is a strong character.'

'Right, I'll keep in touch,' said the dynamo from down the street – although 'close' might be a more apposite word in this small cul-de-sac.

This conversation resulted in an interview – of whom, by whom depends upon one's viewpoint – at David's house where selected new members, over a glass of the Mosel's best, liberating white wine, sought to demonstrate their good sense and recognition of a need to be guided by a keen professional. In truth, they crawled, and it worked. Unknown to them, it was really because Jane's husband had developed a chronic illness - she required the cash more than any love she had for the anticipated confrontation that was sure to materialise. Step one had been completed.

Step two was administrative, namely - to deal with organising the signing of their necessary 'personal declarations' and 'council code of practice' - without which nobody could take their seats; discover how the chair was given authority – which was through nomination and secondment by any councillor and a majority vote at the forthcoming first meeting; obtain the annual accounts and have them audited externally – this, Jane advised, had not been done during the previous four year term; collect from the outgoing clerk all the ongoing minutes and correspondence – the young clerk revealed that Jack held most of the records at his house and made her alter the minutes to reflect his own views, no matter what had actually been said. Frightened of Jack's physical strength and alcoholic rages Deidre had obliged him. As a single mother with two children to support her behaviour became understandable.

When Jane called at bachelor Jack's, as had been previously agreed, to accept the files, he threw a tantrum, causing her to leave and return with David. She covered up the need for a bodyguard by explaining that she couldn't possibly carry away a whole eight years of records all by herself. None of this original paperwork had been passed onto the district council's legal department as was customary. A quick check discovered that several months of minutes and correspondence were missing. Jack's response was that they were of no use and had been burnt.

By the day of their first meeting in April – always the second Tuesday of the month – the new members had learnt there was much to do in putting the workings of the parish council back onto an even keel; it would be many months before new initiatives could be contemplated. Although already explained by Jane, they hadn't grasped that there was a legal requirement to hold a separate 'parish meeting' on that first day as well as a parish council meeting. Their clerk had prepared two agendas, but, as the session began her pupils failed to understand the difference. Full of good intentions they rushed headlong into the minefield that awaited. Displaced previous councillors knew exactly what the procedure should be, worse still, they were there with public support, well briefed and angry.

I must explain to the suburban reader that, at a parish meeting, only parishioners are allowed to talk. Such an event is the one occasion in a year when residents may gather formally to discuss their problems with a view to resolving them amicably; although usually chaired by the council chairman the councillors have no special status. Afterwards, a parish council meeting is convened and is obliged to consider any issues that have been raised at the parish meeting. In the council meeting there is always a designated 'public session' during which - and only during which - parishioners may speak.

Pending a decision on the new chair, Jack was in charge. Needless to say, criticism and invective from those gathered was forthcoming, even encouraged. After nearly two hours the list of items needing attention was long and the clerk could barely keep up. Finally, she judged that the, so called, Taliban had had their fun, asking politely - but in an authorative, no-nonsense voice - if the parish council meeting could now commence. Cat calls and boos erupted, making the newcomers feel extremely uncomfortable. Many were beginning to wonder whether it had all been worth it. Realising that they could be sent to Coventry in a village which supplied most of their social lives, they began to regret their decisions.

Becoming impatient, the clerk prompted Jack to seek nominations for chairman, but he ignored her – that was, after all, the way it had been for the previous eight years. Jane, fortunately, was made of sterner stuff and, not to be intimidated, announced the contest, much to the surprise of most of the public. The vote went ahead and Jack, although nominated by his two friends, predictably lost by six to two. Advised that Jack had a casting vote if there was a draw, the insurgents had prudently agreed that only David would stand.

The designated public session followed, but the troublemakers called out and disrupted proceedings so much that David was forced to employ his most officious voice and read out the standing orders, making it clear that anybody interrupting would be asked to leave. In an atmosphere of relative calm some good points were made while the, by now excited, onlookers awaited the council's comments. Carefully, but positively, the new chair read out a prepared speech, stating that all the issues raised deserved proper consideration by the whole council and would, in due course, form a part of its agenda. He reminded everybody that all decisions needed to be from the whole council, and that no individual member, including the chairman, could act alone. This was a setback for those bent on mischief who had become accustomed to on the spot rulings. Nevertheless, hecklers continued to make the inexperienced council's first meeting difficult by raising obscure village problems about which the new members were ill informed and open to ridicule.

Alan found the whole session quite tense; he wondered if it would do his heart condition any harm. All that effort to protect the village by giving it a proper voice, only to be treated unpleasantly by the very people one was intending to help. Delving deep, he found encouragement by reminding himself that these were now his constituents, perhaps ignorant and prejudiced, but only trying to preserve their traditional way of life. As he strolled home in the dusk he told himself: 'No pain, no gain,' remembering how badly politicians were often treated on television. It was a new experience for the councillors but they had to see it through.

Right now, patience and tolerance were the keys to damping down the dissent and obtaining approval from the silent, ever compromising, majority, who, he felt certain, would be up in arms if uncontrolled mass housing were to envelope their village. In England, it was necessary to exert one's democratic rights by commenting on government plans well before they were finalised, became sacrosanct and were insensitively implemented. The elected council had a duty of care to look ahead and do this job; by the time Mr Average had woken up, it would be too late for any protest to affect the outcome.

Little did Alan know it, but, for the council tax payer, worse was to come. New Labour decided to streamline what was, admittedly, a ponderous planning approval process by gradually introducing an entirely new collection of documents on the premise that all previous 'structure plans' – the big picture, and 'local plans' – the details, were to be cancelled. The replacement procedure permitted county councils to bring policies forward 'selectively' from earlier plans, even where such policies had been subject to impartial, lengthy and expensive – for the taxpayer – public inquiry and criticism. This change allowed time for developers, and others with a vested interest, to influence officials and steer them towards acceptance of their previously rejected proposals by means of intensive lobbying and, dare it be said, an element of corrupt persuasion.

The new rules were explained – 'spun', as we now call it – to parliament as the overdue reform of a system which had grown, like Topsy, bit by bit over the years into something that worked for none of the interested parties. As always, the devil lay in the detail, which, for example: defined mandatory consultants - who turned out to be almost entirely government's own departments; omitted democratically elected bodies like parish councils; changed the terms of reference for inspectors appointed to head public inquiries, preventing them from being able to hear and consider, on their merits, views put forward by any person or organisation. Objectors could now only comment from the viewpoint of assessing the 'soundness' of a particular plan, with the criteria for soundness defined in a short, entirely bland list. Such redrafting allowed an inspector to reject nearly all objections as 'out of order'…I could go on … thus rendering any so called 'inquiry in public' unable to address genuine public concern.

Denton Cheney was soon to face the reality of a planning system in suspension. Proposals from entrepreneurs and developers continued either to be tabled unofficially or submitted wholesale in order to ensure a 'foot in the door' when the new documentation was finally in place.

After a long absence Alan had recommenced life in the cradle of modern democracy, believing strongly in the fairness of the English way. As he grasped the reality of what actually transpired in the administration of his country, and observed government's cynical manipulation of the consultation process, he became somewhat disillusioned with his land of birth.

* * * * *

Talk in Denton Cheney gradually migrated to less serious topics than the body in the stream. Although the weather was improving and the clocks were about to be put forward, there remained a discernable background noise - perhaps like that left in the universe after the 'big bang', a sort of permanent shock wave, a shared intuition that the mystery hadn't gone away, a conviction that somehow, something had been missed.

* * * * *

The uniformed postman pushed open the shop door and headed directly towards the general counter. During his approach he glanced furtively to the right where Shiva was concentrating on counting out cash for an aged pensioner. 'Post,' he announced quietly to Sunny and passed across a pile of envelopes secured by a red elastic band.

Ibrahim sorted through them, removing two fat airmail letters which bore Indian postage stamps, he tucked them into his inside jacket pocket. The remainder he swept up and deposited on a shelf behind. Their eyes met in a conspiratorial greeting as Sunny acknowledged his friend's confidence with a slight up and down movement of the head.

The replies from Bombay had begun to arrive and Shiva must not see them - yet.

So far, he had to admit, the applicants were unimpressive, but that would surely change when his brother received the latest colour photograph of Ayesha in her elegant, full length ball gown. 'More British than the Brits,' he mused. 'How could she fail to attract a well educated man with prospects and the ambition to become a migrant?'

'Did you realise,' stated Shiva loudly, interrupting Sunny's daydream, 'that the government won't give you cash any more.'

'What?' was the pensioner's startled reply.

'No,' she continued, almost shouting in an effort to be understood, 'you must open a bank account. They will pay your pension into it each month, or quarter – it's for you to decide.'

'I've never had no bank,' came old Harry's outraged response, 'and ah don't need one. Them people will take your money and then charge you for getting it back. It's not right.'

'Not now,' she explained patiently – time was no problem with only a few transactions each day, 'it's free.'

'But where do I go. I can't walk much. I use that machine to get around, though the footpaths are in a terrible state – not been fixed in thirty years as I know of. It were easier when we only had horses.'

'You can have an account here,' Shiva explained, 'it's easy. Only one form - and I'll fill it in for you. All you have to do is sign at the bottom.' Harry muttered and clung more tightly to his walking frame. 'Wait, I'll do it for you now.'

Shiva knew that the cantankerous villager couldn't move quickly and was unlikely to reach his electric scooter without Ibrahim's assistance. Eventually, Harry scrawled his name. When her husband refused to help - complaining he couldn't risk his back now the 'post office was retiring him', the old man was lifted back onto the wide seat of his orange coloured vehicle by the next customer to come in.

Sunny's ill-judged comment was enough to inform the whole village, who took it literally, forcing him and Shiva to spend the following week advising all who enquired that it had been just a figure of speech, nothing more. Whilst it was true that a letter had been received from head office stating that Denton Cheney was being considered for closure under a plan to shut down seven percent of all branches within two years, nothing had been finalised. More importantly, they had been forced to sign a confidentiality agreement; if they broke it and told their customers before it was officially made public, they could forfeit any right to compensation.

Rumours get about: a member of the parish council had already asked Sunny if he was shortlisted, if so, did he want them to write arguing against closure and asking villagers to do the same? Forced to be discrete Sunny replied evasively, and, despite his conscience, not quite truthfully, saying he knew nothing but would welcome support. The well meaning councillor had asked if the shop and newspapers would continue; they were important lifelines for the villagers - especially the elderly, who formed more than twenty percent of the population. Sunny said yes, but privately doubted if it would be financially worth the effort. After the nearest supermarket extended its hours to virtually 'all day, every day' and provided free transport once a week, he had cut back to stocking only staples, and of them, nothing that was time sensitive: a few everyday, household items that villagers had specifically requested; respectable magazines; the post office's own, well designed greetings cards, and treats that mothers could buy for their junior school children to enjoy on their way home in the car.

In his heart Ibrahim felt guilty, ashamed at deceiving and letting down the very people who provided the principal reason why he and Shiva enjoyed living in Denton Cheney, but, if they wanted to remain there into old age, some temporary subterfuge was necessary. The thought of getting compensation for doing what he anyway wanted had become an overriding consideration. Now he must find a good man to take over his other main responsibility - which was for their daughter Ayesha.

*   *   *   *   *

Robert stopped at the parish council notice board, somebody had pinned up an antisocial behaviour order – better known as an ASBO. This one defined the adjacent car park which fronted the village hall as being out of bounds to a certain Mr Simon (known as Sam) Woodley for six months. He knew the youth concerned and wondered what had led to its issue. He failed to see how this 'name and shame' approach could work, rather it glorified troublemakers, giving them paper credentials and making them instantly into potential gang leaders. He had found that a clip around the ears and a little chat with their parents nearly always did the trick. Just then a panda police car pulled in at the kerbside - it was Sheena.

'What's all this then?' he queried through the open window while pointing at the board.

'Oh,' she said, resignedly shaking her head, 'it was unavoidable. I'm not in favour – as you may guess. Sergeant Smith was leaving a parish council meeting when Woodley and a friend shouted rudely at some of the councillors and obstructed them. It was dark and they didn't realise that our sarg was there, he wanted to take names and talk but the chairman insisted on bringing a charge.'

Robert sympathised, 'I see,' he said, stepping back and allowing her to continue the daily drive through ten rural villages. 'Yes,' he thought, 'a quick motor tour in that very visible car is all they do now - and that's called policing! She won't have spoken to a single villager and, if I

126

hadn't been an old friend, she wouldn't have listened to me.' He accepted that it wasn't Sheena's fault, and knew that she was lobbying hard for more visible foot patrols.

Walking on towards the memorial green he found yellow, spray graffiti on the bus stop and again, in the same style, across the face of the village sign at the main road. Scribbling a note in his old police notebook he pushed it through the letter box of the council's chairman. He knew full well that Jack would clean it off himself and the police would not be informed. Jack loved this village and really cared for it in his own simple way, but he hated paperwork and bureaucracy and had, sadly, become ineffective in a modern world. Following the district and parish council elections, Robert rather hoped for a new broom - leaders he could deal with. He still had much to offer.

Robert had followed the saga of the proposed new secondary school, gleaning all he could from the action group's regularly delivered update sheets – good fellows those – and extensive reporting in the Advertiser. Locating a school at Denton Cheney served no logical purpose. He was mighty suspicious that this proposal had resulted either from laziness by the officials responsible for allocating catchment areas, or some sort of collusion with large building companies. These organisations would support the school and then build around it, using the empty fields on which they had already purchased options from hard up, only too willing, farmers. He resolved to check with contacts and discover whether his old colleagues were investigating what smelt to him like corruption - there could be no other reasonable explanation.

At the shop he noticed that the national dailies were all carrying similar headlines which stated that: 'Crime was down overall'. Recalling recent experiences Robert became doubtful. The word 'overall' was significant. New Labour had criminalised so many minor and relatively harmless offences that the statement might be statistically correct. On checking, he was told by friends at the town's police headquarters that violent crime, robbery and burglary were well up. He was disappointed - these were the crimes that affected people most, the ones they worried about. The prime minister had declared he would be 'Tough on crime and the causes of crime', but Robert could see no evidence of the second, more important, long term solution.

He made his way around the village admiring the ubiquitous banks of daffodils. It was the one good thing old Jack had done while chairman, but his initiative had became sullied when it was revealed that he used money from a company that had applied to erect a polluting, ready mix concrete plant on the outskirts of the village. Luckily, planning approval was refused by the district council - even though the parish council had raised no objection.

Robert wondered whether one could really trust anybody who obtained some sort of political power. What motivated them to seek control over the lives of their fellow citizens? Was it really their intention to do some good, put obvious wrongs right, make a fairer community and help those who can't help themselves? As a committed Christian and supporter of the church's proposed extension, Robert had, over the years, almost convinced himself that only the faithful were capable of this sort of altruistic behaviour; regrettably, the rest of them were only in it for themselves – either on an ego trip or lining their pockets.

Down by the school he met Henry. Earlier in the day he had noticed that Henry's hens, which often spilled, clucking and scratching, out of the back garden, up a grassy embankment and sometimes onto the road, were noticeably absent. 'Are you alright?' was his greeting.

'They've put an ASBO on my flock.'

'What?' asked Robert in surprise, 'I thought they were for teenagers?'

'Yesterday, someone reported them and the police came round – that Sergeant Smith. He said I had to keep them penned - danger to highway users. Not like your days, eh?'

'Of course, but that road was quiet in my time,' admitted Robert, 'not even surfaced. Cows and sheep used to wander about. Long ago, there was a village pound to put them in if they caused trouble – the owner had to pay for any damage before he got them back. Nowadays, everybody's got a car and is in a hurry. No bugger would have told on you then.'

'Yes, and what about the teenagers?' said Henry. 'They have nothing to do - all bored stiff. We had a youth group, army cadets, scouts, football, even a drama group – it was great fun. Now the government's too mean

128

to organise anything - result delinquency.'

Robert shook his head wisely, 'I'm on your side, but there's now't I can do to change it. Keep up the good work on the pheasants! It's a pleasure to see the survivors around the streets and gardens - real decorative they are. Who needs peacocks?'

YEAR TWO

ORTHOCLASE - SUMMER

McAlister was weary, his most exciting case so far hadn't progressed; it wasn't going to accelerate the promotion his wife felt he so richly deserved. No connection with local villages had been proven, nobody knew who the body was; it was frustrating. The officers sat on hastily laid out stacking chairs; they knew that something had to change.

'Good morning, I need your full attention.' The voice was accentless, the face unmade up. Despite the crisp white shirt, long black skirt, severe hair cut and butch appearance, for the older officers, having a woman as chief constable still made them slightly uncomfortable. It was nothing to do with not being clever - a university degree in sociology disproved that, or competent - she had worked her way up through the ranks from constable, or a good administrator - the force ran more smoothly than before her appointment; it was just that, for those over fifty, a woman took a bit of getting used to.

'The body found near Denton Cheney remains unidentified. The various tests confirm that violence was used and contributed to death by drowning. Despite thorough enquiries - 'At least we are seen as thorough,' thought

133

McAlister - nobody saw anything suspicious and nothing useful has been found in searches at the site or around the village. We need an independent review of this case which I am upgrading to one of suspected murder.'

There was a rustle of surprise among the assembled policemen and women; it sounded like an autumn wind swirling through a carpet of dry leaves. Nobody spoke.

After discussion with the police authority I have asked our neighbours, the Metropolitan Police to second two senior policemen to us for a fortnight. They will go through all the work done so far and give us their views on the best way forward. This is not a criticism of anybody here, or their commitment and methods, but the case has dragged on and we need an injection of new blood to help solve it before the trail grows cold.'

'No praise there,' concluded McAlister,' but she's right.'

'I will introduce Detective Superintendent Chan and Inspector Patel to you when they arrive. McAlister will continue to lead our investigation and provide a link with the newcomers. Don't forget they will be working away from home and may miss their families and friends. Please give them your full cooperation - I mean full - and make them welcome. Thank you.' She picked up her notes, turned and walked away.

'No, any questions?' noted a tired Sergeant Smith, who anyway didn't have one.

As it crossed the room, the trim figure was idly watched by the mostly male audience.

'How about that,' said trainee Constable Brown. 'This is getting interesting. Proper police work - murder's a serious crime. It's a welcome change from prosecuting dog owners, putting up with lip from rebellious kids and manning the mobile speed camera.'

*   *   *   *   *

'Hello, my friend, my soul mate, my guru!' The caller required no introduction.

'David,' responded the Irishman, 'what can I do for you?'

'I'll come to the point. The parish council want to start a magazine, news-sheet, whatever. We think you're the best man for the task.' There was a distinct pause. 'Hello, Patrick. Are you still there?'

'Yes,' was the reply, 'just wondering if I can fit it in - my new job is demanding. Of course, I'm honoured to be asked. Have you no other candidates?'

'Not of your calibre,' said David, and meant it. 'You're interested in politics and understand people.'

Patrick sought clarity. 'Will this be about council business only, or the whole village?'

'After approval the minutes go on our notice board.' David rarely listened closely enough to answer a question, always sticking to his original point. 'Our idea is to provide general information about what happens in Denton Cheney,' he explained.

'I see,' said Patrick, warming to the idea. 'I suggest that quarterly is enough. If you can agree to that, I'll have a go - produce a draft first issue for your members to review.'

'That sounds great to me. I'll talk to the others and get back. Thanks very much.' With that David ended his call, well satisfied with the result.

It being summer, a few parish councillors were on holiday, but, as most now had an e-mail address, he sent them a message, then walked round the village to contact the rest in person. Eventually, the replies came in; Patrick's proposal found unanimous approval.

'You're not taking that on now!' was Sara's reaction. 'I see little enough of you as it is. Have you forgotten - you have three children to care for?'

Patrick refused to defend himself. His wife had always been 'swift to chide and slow to bless' – the exact opposite of the hymn – and although her initial comments were inclined to be extreme they rarely represented her real thoughts. With this in mind he pressed on but allowed her some consolation.

'It's not decided yet. I've to do a trial for their next meeting. Let's see what happens – I'm sure someone else could manage it.'

'Not as well as you,' retorted Sara, suddenly defending him. 'You have a way with words and could publish it on your desk top computer.'

Encouraged, Patrick outlined his plan. 'If it goes ahead I'll get it printed at Sian's school. The income would help them, and it's good experience for the sixth formers.' His wife appeared pleased.

'I see. On that basis I accept it does become manageable. But don't let it become too grand – there are only a few hundred readers.' She smiled, 'To be fair, this village deserves a voice, with the threats from housing and mineral extraction now is a good time to begin. If you mobilise a majority both could be fought off.' Sara paused, 'Changing the subject, did you know Sian has been approached by Brenda to help the district council transfer its records into a computer data base? It's paid work and will give her confidence, something constructive to do in the long holiday while she awaits the 'A' Level results.

Her husband was delighted, 'If this continues our whole family could soon be working for one council or another!'

*   *   *   *   *

In a busy working life one's mind tends to be focussed either on future tasks or in attempting to sort out past problems; it rarely dwells on the present. For Aaron, it was a novel experience to discover that he was always in the moment, always thinking about Emily. He wondered if she was thinking of him, but concluded, sadly, that she probably wasn't. Was this that strange experience they called love?

Aaron's courtship had moved into top gear in a reflection of the improving weather. When he next visited, Emily was with Fiona. A white van had been driven into the field and a boiler suited man was standing in front of what looked like a black box on legs. As he drew closer he could see the red glow of flames and, close by, the gas bottle which fed them – it was a portable forge. In modern times the blacksmith came out to his clients, bringing his equipment with him.

'Hello,' he called to Fiona, 'can I come in and watch?' Adding, slightly disingenuously, 'I've always liked horses. My granddad was a milkman - had a pony and trap and them shiny, steel churns.'

'Come in,' she answered. 'If you haven't met before, this is Emily.'

Having pushed himself this far Aaron had reached the limit of his resolve and was promptly frozen into immobility. His voice barely issued. 'Hello, I'm Aaron,' he croaked. Emily managed a gentle movement of her mouth – almost a smile - from which he rapidly averted his eyes. So close to the object of his desire he had an inner urge to kiss her on the cheek, to touch her lips seemed far too personal for someone so delicate, someone he only wanted to care for.

The travelling smith began turning a horseshoe in the ruby red heat of the charcoal, extracting the metal from time to time he hammered it skilfully into shape on a heavy, black anvil which was bolted firmly onto a steel table. He caught Aaron's curious gaze and anticipated the question, 'It's the way we've done it for centuries.' Moving away from the fire to answer the ring tone of his cell phone, he added with a shrug, 'Nothing new - just that we're mobile now.'

Looking back, a few weeks later, Aaron recalled how quickly their relationship had developed after that terrifying first introduction; with hindsight, it had all been too fast. The young couple graduated from stolen conversations at the horse field to private trysts at weekends. They strolled, hand in hand, along ancient rights of way, paths which were re-established each spring across acres of rapidly growing crops by the feet of locals who still walked the network of mostly unmarked routes that linked rural villages. These were essential connections, well used long before the advent of bicycle, bus and car.

Aaron's male friends had written him off as a lost cause. He no longer participated in kick around football at the playing field, or under the street lights. Nor did he join them on outings to support their favourite rugby team in town. As a consequence he was forced to suffer endless ribbing, but he didn't care - didn't care at all. At last, the long summer holidays arrived, allowing the young couple the full space and freedom of an abundant countryside which was now approaching its best as solitary oaks and ash added their fresh green foliage to hedgerows already burgeoning with white blackthorn blossom.

It was the wedding that did it. Cousin Alf's invitation made it clear that an accompanying partner was expected; his mother told him that he needed to comply. Aaron negotiated a compromise - he would take Emily to the reception but attend the church service alone. He reasoned that being seen together at such a formal event would be uncomfortable for both of them. When he explained his thinking, Mum agreed. The party afterwards was to be a family affair, held at his uncle's rambling farmhouse on the edge of a nearby settlement. This private function was a good opportunity to show his relatives that he had a lovely girlfriend. The atmosphere would be relaxed and he was confident that, as a country girl, she would enjoy it. Anyway, it was a big do, and free. His dad was buying the present and putting Aaron's name on the card. There would be tasty food, dancing and drinks – nice things he couldn't afford to treat her with.

After the service Aaron walked across the fields and met Emily in her village. He recalled with tenderness her comments about how smart he looked, never before had she seen him in a suit – it was borrowed from yet another cousin, and a trifle large. A half hour stroll along the winding tow path, past recently painted canal boats with names like: 'Steel Away' – registered in Sheffield; 'Dun Wurkin'; 'Floating Assets'; and 'Wild Thyme' – in an appropriate shade of green, brought them to the venue. A large, grey – originally white - marquee had been erected on a flat part of the cow field next to a straggle of barns and outbuildings that flanked the original, brick built farmhouse.

One of the town's student jazz bands was competing with clucking chickens in the freshly hosed down, cobblestone yard where they joined high spirited guests at two long, trestle tables set out on newly purchased coconut matting. The food was basic, but plentiful and filling: cottage pie or steak and chips, followed by treacle sponge pudding. It had been prepared in the farm's cavernous, brick floored kitchen by the groom's mother and sisters, assisted by farm hands and their wives. Aaron knew most of those present, having met them at birthdays, christenings or funerals. His Emily was welcomed enthusiastically.

Draught cider or beer was served to the men folk in pint glass tankards, with tumblers of either Babycham or gin and tonic for the women. Neither he nor Emily had drunk much alcohol but the hospitality and convivial atmosphere meant they could hardly refuse to join in the many toasts. Soon, they were dancing cheek to cheek, navigating the worn wooden floorboards of the farm's biggest room to the sound of currently popular traditional jazz tunes, played erratically by the inebriated musicians who had now moved inside; they didn't care how badly they played - having turned up only for the eats and free drink. Round and round they went, dreamily holding each other tight, surrounded by similarly intoxicated young couples, each pair lost in their own private world.

Something triggered his memory and Aaron tried to focus on his watch. Time had passed by much too quickly and the last bus was almost due. After hastily explaining the problem to his aunt, he caught Emily's hand and guided her to the temporary cloakroom, collected their duffle coats and hastened her down the gloomy lane towards the tarmac road. Before they could reach the distant street lights, a brightly lit double-decker passed across their view; they shouted, but it didn't stop.

'Must go back,' mumbled Aaron. 'Find somewhere in the farm to sleep. Sorry - it's all my fault.'

Emily gripped his arm and nodded, there was no need to say anything. They turned about, retracing their steps back towards the discordant sound of 'When the saints go marching in' and the glowing, curtainless farm windows. Tipsily, they blundered noisily up dimly lit, uncarpeted, wooden stairs. Nobody was around - all the activity was below. They would not be heard. By now Aaron could barely stand and his legs gave way. Emily was relying on him for support and they slumped onto the landing in an untidy heap. He didn't know why but he kissed her, feeling her chilly face against his lips.

'Cold,' he muttered vaguely, 'must find a bed and some blankets.'

On Aaron's left a door stood ajar. He got up shakily and felt around for the light switch. Pulling Emily gently back to her feet, he put his arm around her waist and guided her inside.

A carved four-poster and large free standing wardrobe filled most of the musty smelling space. The bed was unmade, on it tartan rugs lay across a heavy, knitted bedspread; it looked as if it hadn't been used for years. Emily sat down abruptly on the edge, causing a loud creak, took off her coat, swung her legs up and began to drag the covers across them. He watched, unsure what to do next, but his girl friend had evidently decided to make herself comfortable. She rested her spinning head on an uncovered, feather pillow and relaxed; looking up steadily at Aaron were those light blue eyes, eyes which had always bewitched him.

139

'Don't just stand there Aaron. Take your coat off and get in. I'm going no further tonight. It's comfy enough in here, but I need your warmth.' He hesitated. She noticed he was in two minds. 'Don't be silly. Turn off that light and get in. Nobody will bother us tonight.'

Aaron looked down at her for only a moment before accepting that she was in charge. He began to clamber up.

'No! It's too hot. Take off your clothes.'

The command, in an alcohol slurred voice, could not be ignored. Feeling awkward Aaron slowly complied. He placed his duffle, shoes, shirt, tie and suit in an untidy heap on the floor and lifted up the rugs.

'I said put out that light!'

He turned away to obey, reaching clumsily for the switch. Although the small window was uncovered, it was a rural area and total blackness had descended. Shivering a little, more from sexual tension and fear of the unknown than the cold, he felt his way back and slipped in beside her. Feeling a need to reassure Emily with a kiss, Aaron reached a tentative hand out towards where he thought she was, only to be instantly enveloped by sensual, naked flesh as she gripped his shoulders and pressed her body close. He hadn't expected that, but soon began to luxuriate in the all pervading warmth. An erection quickly formed beneath his Y fronts. 'What next?' he thought.

'Aaron, you're still dressed. What's wrong with you?' she scolded.

Having never experienced anything like this before he became nervous, knowing full well that they were at the point of no turning back he became scared of the consequences. Emily was clearly expecting more, the whole thing. How could he refuse? She was ready, and he loved her. He simply couldn't risk losing her by pulling away - which was anyway the very last thing he wanted to do.

'Wait, hold on' he murmured, thinking how inappropriate the words were.

Reluctantly, he released her hold – would this destroy the magic – to get out and search in the pocket of his trousers for the condom he had remembered to bring, just in case.

Some time back Aaron had plucked up the courage to visit town and enter the chemist's shop. He was annoyed that it was still a family business, one not yet bought out by a big, impersonal, high street chain. Once inside his eyes searched desperately for the name Durex – it was the only brand he had heard of, all the while terrified that one of the middle-aged, female assistants would ask him if they could help. Luckily, both were already occupied dealing with customers, which allowed him time to identify what he wanted and pick up a packet. To make his shopping appear less single minded, he rapidly added a tube of toothpaste and some deodorant, before reaching the counter and enduring the usual conversation about the weather and farm prices.

As his purchases were recorded by the till, each item seemed to ring up louder than the last. When the sales person put his final item into a paper bag he felt her eyes lift to scan his face - registering his features for future identification perhaps? Determinedly, he kept looking past her at the shelves. 'Perhaps she knows my mother or teacher,' he thought, 'she's going to tell them, I know.' Some small change was placed in Aaron's shaking outstretched palm and he hurried away without a backward glance. En route to the seemingly distant street door he had fully expected to feel a heavy hand on his shoulder and hear words like: 'Will you come this way sir? We aren't allowed to sell those things to minors.'

Returning, naked and anxious from the unheated room, Aaron's masculinity collapsed. He rather wished the whole episode was over. Hoping that Emily might have relapsed into a deep alcoholic sleep, he climbed back gingerly into the narrow space, careful not to touch her, but aching to all the same.

'Why so long?' she asked dreamily, snuggling up against him once more, but immediately pulling back. 'You're freezing!' she exclaimed in horror.

By now Aaron had collected himself and, as blood once more engorged his penis, he rolled away to pull on the contraceptive sheath he had wisely kept in his hand. Unpractised, it seemed to take an age. He lay back quickly, fearful that she might have abandoned him at that critical juncture. But she hadn't. Surprised at her apparent confidence, he was rather disappointed to think that she might have done it before, but, after consideration, realised that this would make it easier for him. If it was true, he thought, with a surge of jealousy, there must have been someone else, quickly realising that nothing awful could happen if she had already lost her virginity – whatever that really meant.

Now, there really was no turning back. It was too late to ask personal questions, besides which he didn't want to admit that this would be his first time, even if it wasn't for her. If he began talking she might go off the boil and decide not to progress any further, which would be a worse disaster than bloodying his cousin's old bedcover – at least there were no pristine, white sheets to worry about.

He took her in his arms, bringing them face to face, caressing her small, firm breasts until the nipples were hard beneath his fingers. Emily rolled gently onto her back, pulling him on top, and opened her legs, raising her knees high at his side. Now he was inches away and felt for her crotch to ensure finding the expected, softly lined void; it was there, waiting and vulnerable. With a moan of pent up pleasure he eased himself in. Wondering what to do next Aaron was encouraged by the firm grip of heels in the small of his back. He pressed hard as she began a rhythmic movement of her pelvis. More quickly than expected, he experienced a wonderful sense of relaxation and rapture as his sperm ejaculated violently into the condom, and her body reacted by melting into a satisfied limpness. Before he had time to worry if she was alright he heard deep breathing – Emily had fallen fast asleep. Aaron lay all over her, not wishing to forget the moment, struggling to re-imagine that wonderful climax before yielding to fatigue and joining his lover in another, more peaceful world.

The following morning, Aaron woke with the sun, finding that they were still entwined. Now, his penis was small and the contraceptive loose, the foreskin sticky around it. He began to worry.

* * * * *

'MET TO REVIEW MURDER INQUIRY'

The Advertiser soon heard about the developing situation, using it as an eye catching leader; but it was premature - the newcomers hadn't yet arrived which left them with little new to say.

* * * * *

Sensibly, the chief constable deemed that a press conference was essential; it was held at the village hall.

Detective Superintendent Chan explained that he and Inspector Patel were there to do an independent check of the way the 'body in the stream' case had been handled, review the evidence obtained so far - and, in conjunction with the local team, recommend and agree the best way forward. He emphasised that no link to the village had been found but, in order to eliminate this possibility, he supported Inspector McAlister's already voiced recommendation that they begin DNA testing of all male residents within a ten mile radius of the murder site. It was expensive but, given the complete lack of progress, could now be justified.

The hall would act as a collection point and throat swabs would be taken from those who called in. After a fortnight, house by house visits would be made to check on people who had not yet been seen. The process was both quick and painless. He urged locals to come forward promptly which would make the police task easier and, at the same time, prove that they were not involved in this unfortunate death - one which was now being treated as suspected murder. As the nearest police station was eight miles away - and with the full cooperation of the trustees - he was bringing in a mobile reporting centre and stationing it in the hall car park. Constable Brown would be on duty in the mornings as an officer with whom villagers could speak if they came across any useful or suspicious information.

After the briefing - where no questions were taken - background on the village and story so far dominated page one of the Advertiser for two more issues, until usurped by the surprise resignation of the town's latest football manager.

* * * * *

For Bill it had been a good day. In the morning he had enjoyed the sight of his young neighbour sunbathing topless on the lawn – not that he was

143

watching - and now the afternoon post had brought a pleasant surprise –
he had won the village hall draw's, special, half yearly prize. 'Let's go to
the Maltings for dinner,' he immediately proposed to his wife. 'It's going
to be a lovely fine evening. Even I, with two new hips, can walk that far!'

When they arrived the tables around the pond were already filling up.

'Why don't we sit outside?' suggested Peggy.

Bill nodded and promptly ordered two Guinness. 'Help pass the time,'
he stated.

While they were waiting for the food a nearby conversation caught
their attention.

'Is this the village where that murder took place?' asked a woman's
voice.

'Very close,' replied another, 'just a short walk along the canal. Gives
me the creeps - it's not safe to go out in the country anymore. They never
explained who did it, or why.'

Bill looked towards Peggy, opening his eyes wide in mock
astonishment, as if to say, 'What about that!' Their neighbours got up
to leave, and any comment was cut short by the arrival of their meals.
Peggy had ordered a modest spaghetti Bolognaise, but Bill was soon
tucking into his favourite, well done sirloin. Just as they finished, big
soft spots of warm rain began plopping into the water. 'Good timing,'
declared Bill, turning up his coat collar, 'Lets nip inside to pay.'

As they stood waiting for the credit card machine to make its silent
connection, Peggy commented to the cashier, 'All that adverse publicity
must have been bad for business. Has it kept people away?'

'Takings are down this year. But the weather has been so unpredictable
- and we're still suffering from the banking crisis. It's hard to say,' the
man answered very frankly.

'I see,' said Bill, 'It's certainly put Denton Cheney on the map - but
for all the wrong reasons. Our villagers daren't go out after dark.'

*   *   *   *   *

It was early summer as Henry cycled home. His wife had ordered a 500 egg
incubator via the internet; it was due for delivery today. Disappointment

awaited him.

'Has it come?' he asked enthusiastically.

'No,' she announced, shaking her head and continuing to click the mouse while he bent down, looking over her shoulder at the ever changing, coloured images.

'Why not then?'

'I've phoned. They reckon next week, wouldn't give me a reason.'

Henry recovered quickly, 'Never mind, it'll be alright.' All this new technology was beyond his patience. He had tried, but it didn't work for him. Somehow, he always expected the order to go wrong, without a bit of paper how could anything happen? 'It's a lovely evening and still light. If it's alright by you, I'll go down and begin building those pens. Tim's available and Mick can help tomorrow. With the longer days we should get them finished by the weekend.'

She kissed his cheek, 'I'll get some dinner about eight, the girls will be back and it's dark by then.'

Henry grinned, 'Right, I'm off.'

He collected his tools from the garage and pedalled down Glebe Lane in, still warm, April sunshine. When Henry checked the heavy panels he found that some were damaged. He dragged a few onto the ground and used his hammer and nails to effect some rough repairs before walking across to Tim's isolated house; it was one that Henry had built himself and he was proud of it. A knock soon brought his friend to the door.

'Did we get that incubator?' was the greeting.

Henry explained, adding, 'Since I can't install it I'd like to get on with them pens - if you're available?'

Tim nodded, 'Be right over. Just need to get my boots.'

By the time the sun set behind a copse of pollarded sycamores and the temperature had rapidly fallen, one rectangular pen was complete. The panels were braced together, propped by long, four by twos and surrounded with a five wire, anti-fox electrical protective system connected to one of Tim's outdoor sockets.

'The missus says them big nets are also coming next week,' Henry advised. 'Can we put you down as the contact?'

'Sure,' said Tim, 'I'm always here.'

'See you tomorrow then, about five – earlier if I can make it.' Henry waved and rode away into the gloom. His sturdy Hercules bicycle had no lights.

* * * * *

Now a member of the parish council Alan felt even more pressure to bring the management of the village hall – which remained entirely opaque – back into the mainstream. The problem was - how to achieve it without blundering in and exacerbating what appeared to be a personal stand off between David and Vincent - the chairman of the trust. He was unsure exactly how this antipathy had come about, except that it was linked to David's lack of support for either relocating the wooden bus shelter - which was adjacent to Vincent's house - or replacing it with a modern, glass-sided, seatless one in which potential miscreants could be more readily identified. David, with council backing, considered the proposed changes inappropriate and out of character in what was Denton Cheney's designated conservation area, and was much encouraged in his stance to discover that Vincent's ideas did not have police approval.

There was no answer until, on one of his walks, Alan noticed that a 'For sale' sign had appeared outside the chairman's house. Discreet enquiries established that, at the instigation of his wife, they were moving overseas. As a result, Ernest the secretary felt less constrained, declaring that he had been unhappy with the situation all along and was actively seeking a new leader who would be more open. Hamish from the second manor became that person; he had nothing to prove, but mentioned a long term interest in restoring local harmony and getting the village hall back onto a sound financial footing.

Slowly, the facts seeped out. Under Vincent an anonymous working group had successfully raised funds through a series of speciality events including: a 'horse racing night', a blind auction, a 'bring and buy' sale and a new year's dance. Ian, a quantity surveyor, had taken up their cause with the county council who had offered a useful grant against a proposed, and much needed, renovation of the premises. The plan was to remove the wooden stage, which was no longer used for local productions, and replace it with two small conference rooms – the idea being to provide facilities that would generate more income; install double glazing; replace the antique and inadequate heating system; upgrade the electrics and fuse-board; provide separate storage for the various clubs that booked the hall, and bring the interior back to life with a long overdue redecoration scheme.

Ernest advised that June would continue as caretaker but new commitments meant she wished to stand down from the working group, would Alan like to be the replacement? As he had relevant experience in construction, and Ernest had helped Jeff and Chris to organise the planter boxes, Alan felt he couldn't refuse, but compromised by agreeing to begin as an observer until confident that he could contribute something useful. Using the internet – which Alan had eventually acquired when his old 1996 computer finally failed – a meeting was called at the Tudor manor. The prospect of such a visit, not to mention the promised 'glass of ale', was enough to ensure his presence.

Hamish welcomed him at the weather-beaten, grey oak door. Beyond a modern inner screen was a high ceilinged space from which a grand wooden staircase climbed to a hidden second level. In this medieval hall the group were already sitting at a long refectory table. When wine was offered in pewter tankards the prospect of making useful progress suddenly seemed to improve.

Their chairman allowed nobody else to talk, interrupting everybody and filling any gaps by expounding his own, often disconnected views; his main theme being that the village hall should have a grand, post restoration re-opening in September which would, conveniently, be the thirtieth anniversary of its completion. He pointed out that, even if they didn't have to pay VAT on the building work - Ian was asked to check whether the trust qualified for charitable status - and the promised grant was included, they still had insufficient funds to complete the project.

The secretary stated he was no longer sure that the proposed alterations were what the trustees – the clubs and societies who used the hall – now wanted. The plans were four or five years old and comfortable rival venues were available at the new school hall, at Cecil House, at the

Maltings, and, eventually, in St James's proposed new 'chapter house'. All agreed that the situation was unsatisfactory and needed resolving by firstly, calling a meeting of trustees and seeking their updated views; secondly, clarifying the VAT doubts; and thirdly, by confirming that a grant would be provided.

Alan was pleased; the evening had been a revelation. After five years of mystery the renovation project was, at last, moving forward in a sensible way. Even Ernest admitted that it had been a harum-scarum get together but said he would send out the minutes quickly - by e-mail - and set out the decisions made before Hamish changed his mind.

During the meeting Alan had advised that, despite his background in construction, it was impossible for him to manage the potential contractor. Ian, who wanted to step down after many years involvement, had dealt with the builder verbally over a long period but their agreements had never been confirmed in writing. If Alan took over, the contractor would always be referring back to something he understood Ian to have promised.

To Alan, it was clear that the project was not receiving the necessary detailed attention, and it was unlikely that the chairman's target date would be met. Nevertheless, he felt that Hamish, as a self made businessman who operated a profitable cafe bar franchise, made a good leader and would get things moving. The main difficulty lay in persuading, a too busy, but irreplaceable, Ian to spend more of his time on it.

Consultation with the trustees was now crucial in producing a final plan that could be accepted by all. How the balance of funding would be obtained was an open question. Given the rate money had been accumulated under Vincent, unless a major loan was confirmed or a generous donor came forward, they were looking into the far distant future.

*   *   *   *   *

Spherical drops were forming in the corners of Emily's anguished, blue eyes. As Aaron looked down into the upturned face they began to trickle down her cheeks, each one creating its individual, sparkling rainbow in

148

the bright rays of a setting sun.

'I had to see you,' she whispered, her voice struggling to break free from emotion. 'The test... the test... I did at home, was positive.' Having said the unthinkable Emily's head fell forward onto Aaron's chest as she convulsed with sobs. 'I'm sorry,' she muttered, angry now – with herself, rather than him.

Aaron placed his arms gently around her shoulders. She was almost too precious to touch, so fragile he felt she might shatter. He said nothing - his mind seemed to have gone on holiday. This was something way beyond the uncomplicated world of school, fun and television. His constitution went into shock, unable to grasp the reality, unable to contemplate the consequences of something so irreversible. Aaron knew this would not go away, realised that life would never be the same again. His stomach became taught and his body chilled as he began to tremble. Overwhelmed and at a loss, he felt helpless, a failure. Seconds passed. She didn't appear to expect any reply. The effort of meeting and telling him had left her limp and lifeless, nothing further had been considered.

All Aaron could manage was an inappropriate, 'Are you sure?'

He felt her warm body nodding against him. It was what he had expected, but had needed to ask. Emily relaxed slightly and eased herself away - well ahead of her man in the flow of events. Calm now, she wiped her eyes with a tissue taken from the sleeve of her blouse and looked him squarely in the face.

'What now?' she asked.

For Aaron there was no doubt about where his loyalty lay

'We'll work it out.' He expressed the words more firmly than he'd expected the doubt and fear in his brain would allow.

She smiled ruefully, almost happily, 'Silly isn't it?'

Catching her mood, he tried to smile back, noticing that her eyes were wet as further uncontrolled tears welled up. He did admire her. Somehow, he knew it really would work out well. The two of them could manage it, together anything was possible.

* * * * *

The two London based policemen quickly settled in to their allocated office. Detective Superintendent Chan was a workaholic who quickly grasped the detail; he was, of course, soon nicknamed 'Charlie' by the locals - but not to his face. McAlister warmed to the newcomer who was smart, with a lack of humour that matched his own rather dour approach. The thin, bespectacled, ethnic Chinese seemed more machine than man, perhaps more brain than machine.

Patel was tall but chubby and Chan's permanent sidekick; they complimented each other - Chan thought and Patel acted, Chan worried and Patel laughed. Unlike Chan, the inspector had absorbed the British sense of humour, always friendly, he was easy to approach, which helped when it came to discussing the case with the local team. Patel was careful to avoid any suggestion of blame, creating an atmosphere where everybody was keen to contribute, allowing open discussion and joint agreement of the best way to progress the enquiry.

* * * * *

Frank and Angela arrived almost unnoticed; an isolated house near the edge of Denton Cheney had quietly changed hands. No 'For Sale' notices had been erected, even the publican of the 'Fox and Hounds' admitted to having been taken by surprise.

Once established the newcomers quickly made themselves known; they appeared to take socialising as a duty to be enjoyed and encouraged. It soon emerged that Frank was a former member of the diplomatic corps who, because of ill health, had retired early, and that he and Angela had ventured further south to be nearer their children who lived in London. When the locals noticed that both had strong Yorkshire accents and were without any 'side', they were seen as decent people who might - given a few years - integrate and qualify to be treated as proper villagers.

Frank, because he lived up to his name and was ever accessible and cheerful - though invariably accompanied by his less enthusiastic wife, who never let him out of her sight - soon became widely known and liked. The couple spent the early months of good summer weather sorting out and redesigning their neglected, overgrown garden, which was much to

150

the liking of neighbours who, as country folk, endorsed such application.

Some more sceptical locals wondered about this newcomer who had infiltrated himself so rapidly into village institutions. In the country, clever talkers were always treated with suspicion and Frank seemed too good to be true. This supposedly ill man appeared to be quite fit, almost vigorous, which lead to discrete enquiries being made through relatives and friends. The resulting half-truths began to circulate. The most credible being that he had been forced to hand in his notice after a scandal involving a female colleague who complained about harassment. Perhaps this explained why Angela stuck so closely to him and wore the permanent downtrodden look so typical of a loyal but betrayed wife. Nevertheless, most of the better off, who nearly all had something to hide, gave him the benefit of the doubt and accepted the couple at face value, regarding them as 'people like us' and remaining pleased to reciprocate their dinner party invitations.

Just as the new parish council was finding its feet, Jack died. Days earlier Alan had bumped into him leaving the shop - where Ibrahim ensured that a half bottle of Red Label whisky was always available. Jack had looked a little furtive, carrying a brown paper bag which he tried to hide by thrusting it beneath his woolly, naval jacket. Alan deliberately didn't notice.

'I go down to the playing field a lot,' said Jack, 'but there's nowhere to sit. The mums with young children have the same problem. Don't you think the council should get a seat put in?'

A peacekeeper by inclination Alan hesitated to remind him that a previous wooden bench had been vandalised and then stolen – only its concrete base remained. 'I suggest we raise it at our next meeting,' he said as helpfully as he could. It was the last time the ex-chairman was seen by any but his close family.

Alan's phone jangled. It was ten am; David expected him to be available. 'How are you today? It's a beautiful morning. I don't want you to think we aren't keeping you in the picture.' They had last spoken only two days previously, but David always inserted long preambles into his conversation.

'No, no,' insisted Alan.

'Did you hear about Jack?'

'No,' said Alan, 'what?'

'Well our secretary has received some tributes which the senders want appended to the minutes of our next meeting on July 9. I'll bring copies over to you. I would appreciate your considered wisdom.'

'It's a bit odd,' ventured Alan, but David had gone.

Ten minutes later the crash of his brass letter box announced the arrival of a brown, resealed envelope – originally from a stockbroker - on which was written in blue fountain pen ink: 'To Alan from David,' and dated. It contained three fulsome appreciations of the ex-chairman, each nearly two pages long. One implied that there had been an unjustified vendetta against him; none were from people Alan had ever seen at a council meeting.

The man had problems, but, thought Alan, as he was no more, it was perhaps only correct to see his better side. Jack had genuinely tried to improve the village, doing necessary handyman tasks himself and organising the teenagers to raise money for a half pipe skateboard ramp, towards which he had contributed, entirely of his own volition and quite wrongly, a cheque for four thousand pounds from the parish council's limited and painstakingly accumulated funds. This major purchase had never been discussed, let alone agreed. Unfortunately, it was a cheap wooden version and reached a state of terminal decay after less than a year. Worse, the boxy end platforms had been broken into and used as a den. Those whose houses backed onto the playing field gave reports of night time drug usage and wild drinking. Jack's unwise decision resulted in yet more issues for the inexperienced and impoverished council.

In view of the background, and some injudicious wording, Alan concluded it would be out of order to put these epitaphs onto the public record, even though one was from such a pillar of the community as Keith Rector himself. In addition, the texts appeared to be collusive, so he advised his chairman that he would be unable to support the request.

'I've spoken to...' said David, listing all the members but three (I suspect you know which ones) '... and they all concur. It will have to be placed on our agenda but needed sorting out in advance. Don't you agree?'

'Yes,' said Alan weakly as the line was abruptly cut.

A few days later the Church of England news sheet advised that the funeral would be held at the county crematorium on the following Friday. David was on the phone almost as it was delivered. 'Good morning. I hope I haven't disturbed you.' This time, his prologue included full details of the funeral arrangement. Alan, far from trying to listen, switched off – but too obviously. 'Hello, are you still there?'

'Yes,' admitted Alan, wearily.

'Should we go?' came the query.

'Jack was chairman and, despite all the problems he created, someone needs to represent the council.'

'Most of the others agree with you,' replied David. Alan noted that he was always the last to be consulted. It was as if the chair needed his neighbour's assent before taking any action - or was it just that he got up later than the rest. 'I'm going myself,' he continued, matter-of-factly.

'I'll join you,' volunteered Alan. 'It needs at least two.'

The chairman was always the first to offer a lift. Alan took the front seat; he looked down with interest at his dark, pin striped trousers - they were part of his last executive suit, the only one he'd kept - and adjusted the black tie he bought years ago for his father's funeral. The white shirt had posed a problem. The only decent one left was short sleeved, but it would be hidden and, given the present weather, probably an advantage in the non-air-conditioned crematorium.

A surprisingly large number of cars had turned up at this public facility, which, although in daily use, was not served by any bus route. Alan and David walked slowly towards the entrance through lawns and flowering rose gardens. The chapel was dreary, the inner, roughly plastered walls a faded, blotchy green. A small dome, which added character to the exterior, was seen to be nondescript and cheaply built. They moved past rows of crowded, black, bench pews; the three letter writers were sitting together on one of them, seemingly prepared to offer a rival opinion at this last judgement.

The service was in the standard format and colourless. There were no readings or details of the man's life - other than his name and where he had lived – and no hymns. Alan left feeling depressed, not at the death of Jack, but at this perfunctory farewell in a dark, charmless building, one which had lack of funding written all over it.

'I dread my family having to bring me in here,' he thought. 'The one we visited recently in Spain was delightful, what a difference! Maybe I'll donate some cash for a paint job.' His mind wandered. 'The cortege ride here can't be more than two miles. Perhaps I should add a codicil to my will insisting they go twice around the village to get their – my - money's worth!'

Outside, beyond the porch, the sun was bright and Alan's gloomy thoughts translated into physical action. 'Nobody's lingering,' he told David, 'we'd best just go.'

As they strolled away, a closer study of the grass and plants revealed they were ill kept. Individual names on partly knocked over, metal commemorative plaques were defaced by corrosion, giving the memorial garden the look of a run down allotment. 'Oh dear,' he thought, 'not much honour for the dead here.'

By contrast, at St James in the village, massive headstones had given way to either neat, well kept graves or - for the ashes of those cremated - simple, flat sandstone markers set in grassy banks flanking the approach to the main entrance. In his opinion, it was much the preferred option.

On the agenda for the next parish council meeting was an item headed: 'Jack's memorial.' David explained the three requiems, handing everybody a copy before seeking a show of hands for a proposal that they shouldn't be officially recognised; predictably, it passed with the customary dissenters – their chair having checked beforehand that he had enough votes.

A discussion ensued about how, or in what way, Jack's tenure should be commemorated. Suggestions included a brass plate in the village hall – but there was no precedent for this, and permission from the prickly trust would be needed; planting a tree on the green – but this area was already crowded. The issue was finally resolved when the clerk related a phone call from Jack's sister - the wife of a Denton Cheney farmer who specialised in sheep trading and animal trucking. Caroline advised that she was intending to purchase a wooden bench and locate it at a convenient spot in the village. Given this information a contribution of fifty pounds towards an inscriptive plaque was approved by a show of hands, and a cheque duly signed by the necessary two nominated councillors.

Except for sorting out the damaged and unsafe skate board ramp, old conflicts had, at last, been resolved. Apart from its teenage users, this issue was also certain to offend a sector of the old village. With this in mind, it was decided to organise a get together with the police in order to seek their advice and support. Little did the council know it, but the apparently simpler problem of the seat was to drag on much longer than that of removing the skateboard ramp and mollifying those most affected.

* * * * *

In the town, at police headquarters, the fortnight long assignment was almost over.

The visitors had worked long hours to finish on time. A draft report was drawn up which Chan went through with the chief constable.

To her surprise - and well concealed delight - there was only minor criticism of McAlister, his officers and their methods. Chan explained that, even in his wide experience, the case was an unusual one. Despite the silence - unusual in a rural community - he agreed with McAlister that there must be a local connection; finding it was the key. Something was needed to flush out the culprit or those who were protecting him. The stir caused locally by the DNA testing - which he acknowledged would never be comprehensive - might well panic someone into coming forward; as he saw it that was its main purpose. The investigation had stalled; aware of this the murderer must have begun to think that he would never be caught, would have become more relaxed and more likely to make a mistake. It was essential that pressure was raised and maintained; the testing, which was slow but thorough, would serve this purpose. The Advertiser and national papers should be used to keep the continuing police hunt in the news.

'You appear to have decided that it was a murder,' stated the chief constable after listening to Chan's summing up, 'how did you reach that conclusion?'

'The autopsy was clear. I have seen many such reports, this one I have categorised as convincing. The wounds inflicted are the result of a strong blow to the head, only another human being could have done that. Such an action must have been deliberate, though perhaps in the heat of the moment rather than premeditated. There is still the possibility of manslaughter, or a 'while the balance of the mind was disturbed', ruling by a jury. Your force need to assemble the evidence and pass it to the crown prosecution service who will, as always, decide whether any charge you recommend can be brought, - but you know all this. It helps to keep the word murder, with all its emotional connotations, foremost in the public's mind when trying to unearth a suspect. Now, something else. About your team...'

'Yes?' interrupted the senior officer who had no wish to hear any personal criticism.

'You should be pleased. They are motivated and well lead by inspector McAlister who needs to remain in charge. Don't have any doubts about him - he has coped well with this difficult case. Only one change. I suggest you bring in Robert - the retired village policeman, he knows everybody from way back, is well respected and has more to give. Patel met him at the 'Fox' one night and recommends this course of action. McAlister likes Robert, he only needs your nod to brief him and agree a fee for his services until this case is solved - which it surely will be.'

'I will act on what you suggest,' said the chief constable. 'It only remains for me to thank you both. Your findings have been both reassuring and helpful. I regret that you haven't been able to propose any startling new approach, but perhaps expected too much. It's clearly a matter of carrying on as we were with lots of patience and in the knowledge that there is no easy solution.' The chief constable rose to shake hands, 'Mr Chan, I am happy with your report exactly as it stands and presume that you will print it out in London and let me have the usual copies.'

'I will do as you say,' Chan confirmed. 'I regret that we could not come up with some earth shattering solution, but, as it is so often with police

156

work, steady, deliberate, even boring investigation from a competent, motivated team usually gets there in the end.'

* * * * *

Mrs Cecil was woken by the sounds of modern gardening. A strimmer screamed as it attacked the lawn's edges, while a petrol mower roared up and down to produce the traditional, parallel, cricket field cut. 'How ironic,' she thought, 'before the First World War Granddad employed thirty gardeners but you never heard them. Today, the same work is done by two but with the disadvantage of incessant noise.' Hand-held shears had given way to electric hedge cutters, spades to rotavators. She much preferred the old days; after all a garden should be quiet, a place for contemplation, somewhere in which one could admire the seasonal plants and shrubs, not a demonstration ground for new gadgets... and that leaf blower, well... she had made them take it back to the shop.

Now the parish council was staffed with decent citizens it was time for her to step down and let younger villagers become involved. For her, it was important to plan the estate's future, besides which there was an ailing sister to care for and time needed to further her son Auberon's plan to convert the unused and almost derelict 'Home Farm' into housing. Following his transfer to London - serving as a senior civil servant in the Foreign Office – dealing with the estates day to day problems had become her responsibility. She accepted that his idea was sound. Most of the farm's sandstone out-buildings formed an elegant, golden curve along which the village confines line had been fixed; they would make attractive dwellings. Although she considered it appropriate that the buildings should be Grade 2 listed, maintenance had become an expensive problem after they were rented out to Stephanie's husband who used them to garage his many lorries.

Her son had told her about government's decision to appoint a local development authority - Mrs Cecil hastened to remind him that she did not condone such undemocratic 'quangos' - with the responsibility and powers to push through major housing proposals. The new authority was required to meet a large target spread over the next twenty five years.

It had come about because the prime minister was unhappy with the nation's present rate of home creation - a specially commissioned report had stated that it was well below demand. The shortage sparked a bubble in house prices which put homes beyond the reach of most first time buyers, the lower paid and many essential civil servants - like teachers, nurses and the police. The decision resulted in national house building companies offering attractive purchase options on Mrs Cecil's land. She had refused them all, considering it important to keep the village small and intact, justifying her stubbornness by knowing full well that her ancestors would have done exactly the same.

As Auberon had argued, the time was commercially right for converting all those crumbling cowsheds and pigsties, and marketing them to newcomers; many of whom would prefer to live in a village of character - one which also boasted the best rated junior school in the county - rather than move into an untried, socially incohesive estate of brand new dwellings. If they didn't act soon the planning authority might order the family to repair the deteriorating, listed structures, even though they generated but little income.

As a result Mrs Cecil sought out and appointed an architect experienced in designing dwellings appropriate for a village setting and placed the whole project legally under a family trust into which the manor house and their remaining land holdings had already been vested. To make the scheme viable several new properties would be incorporated in addition to those resulting from conversions. On the empty road frontage she asked for a thatched, five bedroom stone cottage, it would face the manor's south front - there was no point in spoiling her view. The farm manager, who was approaching retirement, occupied the actual farmhouse; Mrs Cecil thought he deserved to remain and was arranging for him to purchase it on a long term mortgage. Any replacement would need to find accommodation locally, which, in view of the proposed building boom – especially in affordable housing – should not prove too difficult.

*　*　*　*　*

Laura took the fifty pence coin and handed out three cheeses, stepping smartly aside to avoid the rebound as an inept teenager missed entirely with his first throw and hit the table edge. 'Take your time,' she advised. 'Underhand is better.'

The youngster, egged on by his school mates, paused before trying again. This time, a crash, and tumble of wooden skittles left only two standing. Having partially succeeded he looked towards her for further instruction.

'Carry on. If you knock them all down there's a prize.'

He nodded, reassured, and reverted to round arm, only to hit the canvas back cloth.

'Next please,' she called out to the noisy line of waiting, mostly male villagers.

Frank had enjoyed his first 'fun day'; it provided a welcome distraction from the ongoing talk of murder and mayhem and had helped to cheer up the villagers. Angela had wandered off to tour the small stalls which supported the school; she wanted to see if there was anything suitable for their latest grandchild. This left him to join a long line and buy a freshly prepared hamburger from the sturdy figure of Joan. With sleeves rolled up and wearing a plastic, grease spattered apron, she was busy at a propane gas stove, frying meat patties in an enormous, cast iron pan which had evidently been borrowed from the cavernous farm kitchen. Her helper took the hot meat, placing it in soft, white buttered rolls and adding a pile of brown edged onion slices from a smaller, Teflon coated skillet. The smell was fantastic, and Frank found himself salivating over this culinary treat, it was only two pounds and fifty pence which, he was assured, all went towards the new church room.

Next door, beneath the roof of the same big, black barn, he could hear the continuous, jovial banter that always accompanied a cheeses game and, snack in hand he moved across to get a closer view. In truth, it was Laura he watched. Most women look better when the weather is warm and she was no exception. Her green eyes sparkled from a healthy brown face; considering her age it showed very few lines, and was capped by a mass of naturally curly, light blond hair. It wasn't her face that triggered that inexplicable male attraction, but a pair of well proportioned, long legs and the still firm figure moving beneath a short, red summer dress which exposed just enough cleavage to make him want a closer look. He wondered if the low neckline was intentional.

He swallowed the last bite of the hamburger, wiped his hands on the thoughtfully provided paper napkin, dropped it into a forty five gallon drum marked 'litter' in crudely painted capitals and joined the cheeses line up. Reaching the front he dug a creased five pound note from his pocket and asked for ten goes, explaining, 'I might knock a few down if I keep practising,' wondering aloud, 'Has anybody cleared them all yet?'

'Not while I've been on duty,' said Laura with a welcoming grin. 'Put them up again,' she instructed her son, before continuing, 'you'll need to set them up yourself from now on because Luke has to go home.'

Frank was rather pleased that Laura would be there alone, it might provide an opportunity to establish some sort of private contact. After a third humiliating failure, Angela appeared by his side. Catching his attention she announced, 'I'm going – there's a match at Wimbledon I'd like to catch. You can stay, if you want.'

Frank nodded his understanding as, with a quick wave to Laura, she left. He turned his attention back to the little leather bound table, which had been brought down from the 'Fox', and applied himself to demolishing nine skittles with three cheeses. He concentrated, aware that Laura was watching him closely. She seemed to be willing him onto success. After his final attempt only one was left standing.

'Not bad,' she declared. 'If you want to play some more then pay Janet - I must get back.'

He shook his head and grimaced, 'It's enough. I've had a long turn. Let others have a go. May I walk along with you - Angela has already gone.'

Laura picked up a wicker basket of wild flowers, placed a white, straw sun hat carefully on her curls and handed over the takings to a matronly looking, middle aged woman who, despite the hot sunshine, remained dressed in a thick tweed suit. 'Ready,' she said gaily and smiled up at him.

A frog caught in his throat; it was the first time he had accompanied a pretty lady - other than his wife - for at least twenty years. 'Let's take the longer route,' suggested Frank wickedly.

She looked slightly bemused but didn't hesitate to follow, commenting 'The exercise will do me good. It must be all of three hundred yards further!'

Away from the fun day field and its happy crowd he felt a strong urge to put his arm around her waist, to feel the crisply ironed cotton, to hold her hand in his, but knew that either action would break the conventions of society, and desisted. Laura seemed unnecessarily frivolous. He wondered if she'd drunk a few gin and tonics as a reward for her spell supervising the cheeses game.

The fifteen minute walk was fun. Surreptitiously, he managed a quick look at her breasts, noting the soft line where the golden tan merged into plain white skin, resisting a strong impulse to reach out and touch the nipples with his finger tips. Too soon they reached her gate. Checking that nobody appeared to be looking, he dared himself to give her at least a peck on the cheek. As he lowered his head, she turned her mouth upwards and sideways to meet him. A full, but brief, kiss on the lips resulted.

'Oh!' he exclaimed involuntarily.

But Laura had hurried away, turning only momentarily to glance back at him before disappearing up the overgrown gravel driveway.

'Was that an accident?' he asked himself in disbelief.

*   *   *   *   *

Jeff watched a pair of swans shepherd four young cygnets beneath a hump backed, red, brick arch; the bridge had a separate, horseshoe worn path which had allowed the draft animals to cross the canal. Nearby, a branch arm led off, via a flight of locks, towards the town. At this once busy junction a dry dock had been filled in, immediately behind it was a half timbered inn, resplendent with hanging baskets in full bloom, where drinkers relaxed around rustic picnic tables set out along the towpath. Sunday ramblers leant against rusting, iron railings, watching as holidaymakers wound open sluices, allowing a traditionally decorated long boat to leave the lock and resume its journey across placid water where a family of curious, black ducklings darted hither and thither, supervised by their ever alert parents.

'It's strange,' he thought, 'how, given a summer's day, a bit of water never fails to attract a crowd – especially this far from the sea.'

It was the first time that Jeff had ventured out along the canal since the body had been discovered. As he moved away from the more frequented stretch, the surfaced tow path narrowed into a muddy track along which silent, well equipped fishermen were stationed at intervals amongst the reeds – it looked like an angling club competition. Beyond them, the waterway was less well trafficked. Tree cover and green undergrowth closed in, and he soon reached a hillock which offered a view over the adjacent stream – the one where the corpse had been found,

There was nothing to mark the spot except a small shrine - just a cross fashioned from bark covered branches tied together expertly with tarred garden twine and, lying nearby, decaying bunches of flowers battered by the wind but still in their cellophane wrappings. Villagers avoided this place; they considered it unlucky to disturb a location where a ghost might be waiting for justice to be done so that it could take its final rest.

*   *   *   *   *

'Leave the door open,' called Ibrahim, sweltering, yet wearing only a white cotton 'T' shirt.

The shop had no ventilation and, although global warming had caused small wall air conditioners to appear in hairdressers, doctor's surgeries and locally owned convenience stores, he felt unable to justify one - nobody remained longer than it took to complete the mandatory weather or health conversation and queues were unknown. A breath of cool breeze reached him and he glanced at his watch - it was almost lunch time. Remembering that it was Saturday, and they opened only in the morning, he began to perk up. His wife, who was crammed into the protected and airless post office corner, didn't complain about the heat. Shiva never moaned about anything; he appreciated that she had not fallen into that, all too prevalent, British habit. While bolting the front door and attending to the new triple, mortise locks, he was reminded of the rainy night when he nearly quit.

162

Without a dog to alert them they had been woken by a frightful crash; it shook the whole house. A gust of damp air rushed up into their first floor bedroom.

'Something's wrong,' declared Ibrahim, somewhat obviously, 'I'll go and check.'

Slipping on his shoes and grabbing his son's cricket bat from the spare room, he switched on the landing lights and ventured cautiously down. Considering it prudent to announce his presence and exert some fear of authority into an intruder, he called out,

'Don't do anything rash, we've already called the police.'

Ibrahim opened the connecting door to the shop only to find the front of an old, high revving Discovery Land Rover jammed half way through the outer porch; bricks, plaster and broken woodwork lay across its grey, steel bonnet. On seeing him with bat raised threateningly, two rain-coated, balaclava clad men, who had been ransacking the cash register, quickly turned their faces away and left nimbly through the broken, rain dripping debris. Car doors slammed in unison as the vehicle backed violently out, tearing away more of the wall and accelerating down the High Street.

Shiva appeared alongside him, phone in hand. 'They've turned left - towards Shottle,' she promptly advised.

Frightened and tense, Ibrahim suddenly felt dizzy, reaching for the counter to steady himself, he dropped the bat.

'Sit down over there,' ordered Shiva. 'They've gone, but what a mess! I'll make a cup of tea.'

The police reacted quickly to Shiva's call; with a patrol car already in the area they found the slow moving, damaged vehicle and arrested its occupants. Resulting from this unwanted night time visit were extra locks, and four concrete bollards immediately outside the shop front in an effort to discourage any further 'ram raiding'.

'Life is getting too hard,' stated a dejected Ibrahim as they sat in their small garden enjoying the sunshine. 'All this trouble and they still haven't arrested anybody over that death by the canal. The perpetrators must be living nearby. One of them might come in here and attack me. I'll be glad to give up, really glad now.'

The early evening was still warm and humid as mayflies whirled and twirled around above the lawn, or was it the annual flight of winged ants seeking to establish a new nest? He couldn't be sure. They treated themselves to shop made scones with strawberry jam and double cream, followed by a crisp avocado salad – it wasn't a day for home cooking. Ibrahim couldn't help but notice his increasing waistline.

'Ayesha called,' said his wife, 'she's back tomorrow - about noon.'

'Good,' replied Ibrahim, 'I need to tell you both about the results of my brother's research.'

Although it required willpower Shiva's expression did not alter, but she watched her husband closely before continuing. 'She's got a lift from a friend who lives in Newcastle, asked if he can stay overnight – it's a long drive here, and then up to the north, all in one day.'

'He?' queried Ibrahim, not believing. 'Don't you mean 'she'?'

'No. It's John apparently. I think they may be a couple – she was very shy about mentioning him.'

Ibrahim was gobsmacked. Finally, he pulled himself together. 'He can use one of the boy's rooms then.'

'Yes,' agreed Shiva, who was always matter of fact, 'I'll go change the sheets.'

Saturday morning passed pleasantly as clients from both villages came in to pay for their weekly paper delivery or just enjoy a chat. Ayesha had christened the shop - the 'unofficial social centre of Denton Cheney'. Shortly after they had pulled down the blinds and pushed a mobile set of shelving across the shop entrance – all as insisted on by the police and insurers - an early model MG sports car in British racing green drew up outside. The young occupants folded up the hood and headed for the front door.

Ibrahim heard the engine and glanced towards the blank windows. He was unsure how to react, but Shiva rushed out and threw her arms around Ayesha, before kissing her embarrassed companion on the cheek.

'Come in please, both of you,' she urged. 'Your dad's just closing off the post office. We're so happy to see you.' She had decided to adopt an 'over the top' approach in order to compensate for her husband's reticence.

164

Ayesha smiled, puzzled at her mother's slightly out of character welcome, but pleased never-the-less. 'Mum, this is John – from college.' Unable to delay any longer, Ibrahim came out to be formally introduced. 'Dad, there you are! Dad, meet John.'

Ibrahim noticed immediately that John was plainly but neatly dressed, wore shiny, black laced up shoes, had short hair, and, better still, behaved in a polite and respectful way.

When John left after breakfast and coffee on the Sunday morning, Ayesha accepted a lift to visit a friend in Dunton which was on his way out towards the motorway. Ibrahim pinched himself in disbelief. Was it a dream he'd been in? Contrary to expectation the whole experience had been quite pleasant.

'What do you think?' asked Shiva after waving goodbye from the pavement. She wanted the opportunity to talk.

'Well,' said her husband in wonderment, 'he was English!' He saw that Shiva was at a loss and tried to explain, 'I mean white English with a regional accent.'

'Sunny!' she exclaimed.

'Moreover,' he continued, 'he treated me like a proper compatriot, not some new immigrant. He didn't seem to notice we were… from, from Pakistan.'

'Sunny!' she repeated.

'It was a shock, I'll admit it. I didn't expect Ayesha to be so open with us and have such a pleasant, decent young man as a friend. I'm very proud.'

Shiva laughed. 'You're out of touch. She's a sensible girl. It's high time you began to trust her. You've got a fine daughter. Perhaps you've only just realised?'

'I have,' admitted Ibrahim sheepishly. 'I need to apologise to my hard working brother for wasting so much of his time and energy. He didn't find anyone I approved of anyway.'

'Just admit you were wrong,' concluded Shiva, 'and stop attempting to justify a foolish idea.'

Ibrahim lowered his head and accepted the scolding, but quickly brightened, 'This means we'll be able to enjoy our retirement after all.'

*   *   *   *   *

It wasn't long before the complaints poured in – the British hate change and are often paranoid about it, but usually say nothing. Jeff received an officious call from their clerk.

'Those planter boxes – I like them myself – but I've received several messages saying that they block the traffic sight lines at corners. Can you move them?'

Jeff was a bit irritated; when locating each one he'd considered that aspect and Chris hadn't demurred, but then he was an ex-government man and used to consulting rather than deciding. Although Jane was experienced and had been an excellent choice to guide the new councillors through the formalities of 'the lowest tier of democratic government'- as she had put it to her pupils, when it came to seeking approval from other authorities one wasn't quite sure whose side she was really on.

'Can we get out tomorrow and fix them?' Jeff later suggested to Chris. 'Maybe we can drag them along on a sheet of plastic. We can't wait for old Jones, willing though he is.'

Chris was doubtful but Jeff insisted. After an inspection they were forced to admit that, in some places, the 'rude comments of villagers' had probably been justified. Using a length of scrap scaffold tube they levered the two worst offenders onto an old ground sheet, which, against his wife's wishes, Jeff had stashed in the garage - 'in case it would be useful', moved the supporting slabs and dragged the planters to better locations. The work was back breaking, but knowing that, at the next council meeting they would be able to report it as done, gave him a sense of achievement.

This incident made Jeff realise just how much criticism full time politicians had to bear on a day to day basis - even when they knew they were doing useful work and had made the right judgements. No, it wasn't worth considering any further political advancement - his skin would never be thick enough for that.

A day later the phone rang, it was Chris, 'I've got something that may interest you. Shall I bring it round?'

'Yes,' said Jeff, bemused, but the line went dead.

Chris spread a large folded sheet out onto the kitchen table; it was an undated map of their parish. The most obvious difference was the lack of a railway.

'Wow,' exclaimed Jeff, 'look at all those long rectangular fields, all individually named. There's 'parley pole' I see – isn't that a village house? Now I remember, rood, pole and perch are old English land measurements. Parley – meaning to discuss? The field where villagers met?' Interested, he pressed on, 'The parish boundaries are the same, except on the north side - where they've been adjusted so the motorway lies just inside, and near the county crematorium which is now part of the town. That explains why we get so many lost drivers asking for it in the village. But hey, Chris, why are some of those field corners shaded in?'

His friend grinned, having waited patiently for his say. 'Some time back I wanted to plant trees in the village. I invited Jones - the farmer, and Agnes – the wife of that small nursery man down Glebe Lane – to come round. They knocked back a lot of my whisky and in return identified those places as acceptable for tree planting.'

It set Jeff thinking. 'You might have something. Although the European common agricultural policy is presently orientated towards yield - which doesn't encourage owners to improve their land holdings, a change is imminent; soon it may be in their interest to cooperate. Apart from the fields, what about locating trees in the village verges? I've seen so many leafy avenues in London - all lined with plane trees, and attractive continental towns with jacaranda or orange planted along even narrow streets. What do you think?'

'Trees would complement the predominantly soft brown, stone houses, give our residents more pride in their surroundings and, hopefully, more enthusiasm in protecting them for the benefit of future generations,' added Chris with a smile, aware that he had made at least one convert. 'It could only be good for Denton Cheney.'

After kicking their plan around for a few days, and recognising the need for publicity, support and funding, Jeff asked Jane to put it on the agenda for the next council meeting; he needed to see whether the others were in favour.

* * * * *

Damien was trying to stand up. This time he had grasped the edge of a stool, pulling himself upright on fat, shaky legs. Unfortunately, his feet were twisted inwards and he plopped back onto his bottom; cushioned by the disposable nappy he did himself no harm. The cries that brought Susan running from her ironing board were of frustration rather than pain. She picked him up and a mother's presence provided immediate solace.

'Damien,' she said, laughing, 'you're too strong for your own good.' She looked around, 'We have to get somewhere bigger – this upstairs flat is no longer practical.'

A clatter distracted her as the letter box shut and a copy of the parish council magazine fell onto the bare floor. Still holding her son Susan quickly opened the front door. A tall, lightly dressed figure carrying a plastic bag was heading down the external concrete steps.

'You're on our council now, I hear?' she called towards the receding back.

Alan stopped. 'Yes,' he said pleasantly, glad someone had shown an interest.

'What's happened about the affordable housing?' she queried. Damien squirmed, wanting to be put down. 'Come inside a moment – I need to shut the door.' Explaining, 'When the day's warmed up I fix the stair gate across it so we can both get some fresh air and see the sky.'

Alan's impression was of a drab, sparsely furnished room that had been made into a home by a feminine touch. The curtains were a bright sunflower print with matching settee covers, the plain walls decorated with silver stars and tinsel from a child's party. Susan noticed his approving look.

'I made them myself. I'm good with the sewing machine, but it's difficult to find the time with Damien so active – crawling about everywhere.'

Alan began to feel rather guilty, the last time he had spoken with

Susan her son was tiny, only in the pram. The family were still there. Everything moved so slowly. In local government there was no sense of urgency, nobody to take personal responsibility for bringing issues to a conclusion. He tried to be positive.

'I know you've qualified, which is a start. The district council advised us they are negotiating a land purchase in the parish. A 'housing needs survey' has proven demand; the plan is to build five places – two flats for total private sale, one for rental, and two small houses where the ownership will be shared with a housing society. Don't they keep you informed?'

'So it's going ahead,' she stated. 'Here in the village?'

'Yes, here,' Alan confirmed.

'Really, we get no news - typical council!'

'I'll ask our clerk to raise that with the housing officer. It's not good enough,' said Alan despondently.

Susan cheered up and moved to let him out, 'We appreciate what you're trying to do.'

Just then, a female voice called from below, 'Susan, are you up there?'

'It's Mum,' explained the young mother, before continuing more loudly, 'Yes, just coming down.'

Alan saw a seriously overweight woman of about forty standing at the foot of the steps and immediately realised why she had called ahead. He found it depressing that middle aged British people had become so heavy. Such a look had become an acceptable norm, it was no longer considered unusual. How contradictory it was when teenagers emulated skinny models and tended towards anorexia, but twenty to thirty year olds found no problem putting on excess fat, making them susceptible to diabetes. Perhaps the second problem was caused by a release from the mental discipline of the first! Either approach was equally unwise; it demonstrated the immense influence of constant visual advertising, and television 'soaps' in which both shapes of people appeared regularly as role models.

The morning was set fair, with a cloudless azure sky – an 'Andalucian day' for Alan – and he began to enjoy delivering the magazine. He hadn't acted as postman since being a student, but that had always been at Christmas in cold, often snowy weather. After pushing one through a letter box, he had barely reached the pavement when an elderly householder burst out of the front door behind him.

'You lot,' he accused, 'just playing politics. You don't represent the old villagers. My daughter was treated so badly.'

Nonplussed, Alan stopped, attempting to grasp the point of this verbal attack. Then it came to him. Only a few houses away lived a single teacher who had been on the parish council for ages – latterly as vice-chair. David had labelled her, perhaps too hastily, as 'one of the Taliban', which he felt had been confirmed when she wrote critical letters to the clerk picking up the new members on trivial points of procedure.

Their chairman did have an unconcilliatory approach, made worse by an unfortunate upper class manner and a well modulated voice; residents were often, unintentionally, upset by him. Alan could sympathise with them. He wished David would yield graciously on occasion and build up some goodwill, instead of always defending his position. Like most things, when looked into closely, there were historic reasons for their chairman's intransigence and reluctance to compromise. David had been singled out for abuse: flower pots in his rear garden had been tipped over on several occasions and one was thrown over a wall onto the road; overnight, disparaging notices had been pinned on telegraph poles or glued onto walls and eggs had been smashed against his garage door.

Although the police had been informed, and crime numbers allocated, no culprit had ever been identified. This ongoing war of nerves had affected David's natural generosity of spirit; only time and a lack of further incidents could set matters to rights. As Alan well understood, their chairman was being victimised for criticising members of the previous council, and he, in turn, was being abused for being David's friend; but he avoided taking offence, ignored the man's shouting and replied calmly, offering a reasonable, but suitably contrite explanation. He didn't, after all, want to see the villagers he represented vexed and upset for no real reason.

*　*　*　*　*

The single living room was crammed with photographs; they jostled together on the furniture, marched along windowsills, hung from curtain rails and climbed up the stair treads. All were framed, many in silver, most in wood. The prints covered the whole development of photography; from Daguerreotype plates they passed through sepia to black and white before finally arriving at colour. Many were faded or the worse for wear, all were of people; more specifically they represented Dot's family and her friends through the ages, and very proud she was of them. Each image was identified on the back; when they were lifted during her annual summer dust, she read them out aloud before placing them carefully back into their allotted places – allotted, yes, but with no attempt at a chronological order. Without its gallery of pictures the room would have felt bigger, but, to Dot, very lonely.

Strangely, the portraits seemed to smooth off distinctive facial features, flattening her memories of the actual people, most of whom she'd known as spiky characters in three dimensions. Looking at them didn't conjure up their living being - something she could imagine more easily in the dark of her bedroom. The frozen moments transformed each personality into no more than a visual record, a passport photograph - individuals, but diminished by being fixed into a standard format. It was what one once looked like, but not what one once was.

Dot was glad the warm weather had returned, it made life easier for those villagers in poor health - and there were quite a few of them. Perhaps she was the only one who noticed, but her contemporaries were, never-the-less, succumbing to the problems of old age. On the plus side was the National Health Service, thanks to Mr Bevan and his determination in 1948 - when he needed to overcome massive resistance from the consultants. At the time her parents had doubted it would ever get off the ground. The concept of 'free health care for everybody at the point of delivery' had been radical, Bevan's target of full implementation within six months, wildly ambitious, but it happened. She struggled to recall how old she was at the time – it must have been her early twenties, in a village seemingly full of sick or incapacitated people.

Tuberculosis, diphtheria and polio were not uncommon and nearly every child suffered from whooping cough, measles and scarlet fever;

many didn't survive. Few could afford to call in the doctor. Without a free dental or optical service all the older people were toothless, and many younger ones unable to work in factories because their eyesight was poor and uncorrected. Adding to this local tale of woe were returnees from two world wars, many with missing limbs or untreated shell shock - young men who simply whiled away the hours sitting in a big chair by the coal fire or, on days like today, out in the porch. Yet, change had come quickly. A national vaccination programme eliminated most of the childhood diseases, while regular dental checks and eye tests at schools sorted out youngsters early in life, keeping them healthy. 'They take all that for granted now,' she thought while cleaning the frames of two older sisters, both of whom had died in infancy - unnecessarily she now realised. Dot recalled the figures: by 1958 child mortality had been halved and infectious diseases reduced by eighty percent - quite an achievement.

Of course, more could always be done and it was sad to witness the onset of Parkinson's or Alzheimer's in old friends. To be obliged to watch as they became housebound and less communicative, struggling to walk their dogs around the village twice a day and gradually morphing into personalities she no longer recognised. Some had been fitted with artificial hip joints, while others had lost their clear speech after suffering strokes. Many depended on volunteers to collect their pensions or pick up repeat prescriptions from the pharmacy. Yes, tragedies there always were - always would be - but, thanks to Mr Bevan, their effects were much less devastating than before he introduced the NHS.

Dot, who had begun to polish the silver surrounds – it was always her last job, shrugged her shoulders. It was no use bemoaning age, better to put effort into helping the young. She had spotted Aaron and his brother around the lanes, aware that they were probably up to mischief – it was to be expected from teenagers - and had become intrigued when he suddenly became a solitary loner. Guessing, correctly, that a girl friend was the reason for this changing pattern of behaviour, she made a mental note to try and assist the young couple - provided they stuck together and made a go of it.

QUARTZ - AUTUMN

Laura stood in the newer part of the cottage looking out of the large French window, disinterestedly watching as a male blackbird attacked some breakfast crumbs she had scattered across the lawn. Martin was away walking with friends from the climbing club, which meant she was alone for the first time since that 'fun day' experience. She tried to take stock of her position. There had been no contact with Frank since then. The kiss had been intended, and yes, she did find him attractive. The whole event had rekindled the romantic teenager in her – an aging grandmother to five! For a long while she had felt a need to break the comfortable routine, end her socially predictable behaviour and start on a path where the end result was unknown. 'Funny', she thought, smiling at her reflection in the double glazing, 'I was once so glad to escape from the uncertain, emotion driven adolescent years and settle down. Whatever has come over me?'

'The question is', she asked herself, while making a cafeteria of strong, Kenyan coffee, 'do I want to take this any further – always assuming that he does?' Yes, that stolen kiss had rekindled those pleasurable feelings, perhaps they could be fanned into a flame - even a small one - or would it all end up as a terrible anti-climax? Anyway, what to do? He had done nothing to follow it up – as far as she knew. Perhaps she was only one of his attempted conquests – there were persistent rumours about exactly why he had retired and moved house; it was intriguing. If they began some sort of friendship would villagers suspect it had the elements of a relationship? Villages are notorious for harbouring busybodies with their gossip – true or false – and its impact could be hurtful. What of Martin? Yes, it was selfish of her not to have considered him first, such a situation would disturb the enjoyable yet rather mundane life they had led together for more than forty years.

Overall, there was no logical answer. She had to decide on feeling, or instinct. The very fact she was thinking it over indicated that, deep inside, it meant something to her. It was an issue that couldn't be left unresolved. Having arrived at a judgement the next problem was deciding what to do. Then she remembered the raffle tickets she had committed to sell in support of the extension to St James. Curiosity triumphed over common sense. She would call at Frank's home; it was anyway located in the area she had been allocated to cover. As a prominent local fund raiser that would be expected, nobody would find it unusual.

Frank's house was set on a corner, right at the village edge, and so enclosed by a group of mature trees that the building was barely visible from the footpath; 'Parley Pole' was its appropriately rural name. A high, electrically controlled steel gate displayed a notice saying: 'Leave post in box outside' – without so much as a 'please'. When she looked closely there was a rusted metal tube for newspapers and, near it, a further plate advising that the entrance was only in use between twelve and five on weekdays. The hidden home with its dilapidating security had previously belonged to a toxicologist who worked for a company that carried out drug testing on animals; its name was made into a household word by aggressive animal rights protesters.

Laura had never previously attempted to go in, having always been discouraged by the unfriendly, fortress-like look. Today, there was a reason. Finding no obvious intercom she tried the gate. To her surprise it opened, apparently without setting off an alarm. She paused, ready to retreat, but no fierce dog rushed out to attack her - so far so good. A gloomy, overgrown, curved path led to a porch, but the house itself remained unseen and there were no convenient windows through which to check if anybody was at home. Goldilocks and Hansel and Gretel both sprang to mind. Laura pressed a large bell button and, although she heard nothing, the front door began to move. It was almost an anticlimax to find Frank standing there looking expectant, waiting for her to say something. Her heart took a silly teenage jump – he was handsome, no doubt about that.

'Hello again,' she said, as flatly as her shaking chest would allow. Waving the small, yellow paper books and adding gaily, 'It's raffle time again!' Observing her outstretched hand holding the tickets she noticed it bore some strange, red blotches - without realising it Laura had put on lipstick - something she had given up - using her index finger to smear it into place.

'I'll take two books of ten,' said Frank generously, 'so I owe you ten pounds. Do I need to put my name and address on the stubs?'

'Yes,' agreed Laura, much more relaxed now she had something to do, 'just one for each book will do.'

'Come inside for a minute,' suggested Frank, 'I've got a pen in the lounge.'

She obeyed without a thought, following him into a cosy room with a glowing gas fire on one wall, and, despite her better judgement, chose to sit on the only two-seater settee. Unhesitatingly, Frank dropped down beside her, holding a biro in one hand and a paperback to press on in the other.

'How's Martin?' he asked politely as he wrote out the details slowly in capitals on the back of each little book, peering at each letter through long sighted eyes to check it was correct.

'Fine,' she advised brightly, 'he's gone off walking until Monday.' Quite why she had volunteered such information she couldn't say – perhaps it was fate?

'Oh,' he remarked without looking up,' he's not bothered about your being left alone when this dead body case is still current?'

'It never occurred to us,' she replied, surprised, 'should it have?'

Frank ignored her question and continued, 'Angela's gone to York to visit her sister – back late tomorrow.'

Taking the money out of his hip pocket he ripped off the tickets and passed across the stubs and covers. The transaction completed they stood up simultaneously and she felt his warm hand gently touch her back. Suddenly, they were face to face but Frank dropped his arm and stepped away. 'Now that you're here, would you like to look around?' he asked, adding proudly, 'We've done a lot of renovation. The house was pretty run down when we bought it.'

Again on automatic pilot she nodded, and he led her past a pretty Victorian stained glass window and up elegant, polished wooden treads for a tour of the upstairs. Laura gazed vaguely through an open landing door at a neatly made up double bed, then snapped out of her daydream. 'This is slightly ridiculous,' she thought. 'It's like being in a television soap opera – everything is so predictable. Where is our director hiding?' To Frank she commented weakly, 'It's all very tasteful and private – you're not overlooked, which is unusual in a village.' As they stood at the top of the stairs, looking awkwardly at each other, Laura put a finger to her lips and shook her head, coyly smiling, 'I really must go. We'll meet again. There'll be another time.' Like Cinderella at midnight, she ran nimbly back down the stairs, turned the Yale lock and let herself out, leaving the door wide open behind her.

Frank was disappointed. He assumed that, at the last moment, Laura had simply lost the courage to see it through. He resolved to capitalise on her evident interest in him. It was obvious there was mutual attraction - even if Laura was reluctant to acknowledge it - and looked forward to their next encounter.

* * * * *

Carol was away for two nights visiting her mother. His wife had moved her mum into a care home soon after she had been found wandering the streets, unable to make herself understood. Physically, the old widow was sound but, as her mind had begun to deteriorate, remaining at home alone was no longer practical; that incident had been the final straw.

Alan was in a sombre mood as he returned from the supermarket, but forced himself to check on 1571 for any phone messages – Carol had promised to advise whether she would set off in the early afternoon, or much later to avoid the always frustrating motorway traffic during the peak evening period. It was a voice Alan didn't recognise, one he soon learnt belonged to his cousin Jake; it advised him, unemotionally, that his aunt had died, gave his uncle's number and suggested that a call would be appreciated. As Alan hadn't seen or spoken to either Jake or his father in twenty years, he phoned immediately.

A calm factual conversation began. 'As far as I'm concerned,' began his uncle, after Alan had explained why he was calling, 'she left me three months ago, never spoke - had Parkinson's. I've got cancer – twice. There's a problem in my mouth and in the prostate. I take female hormones for the latter – injected in the tongue, gives me the most awful hot flush. Jake's wife is sympathetic! They are fixing to operate on my mouth – only a small one. Must get to bed now - I had to be up at five thirty to get the ambulance to hospital for my treatment.'

Alan was rather taken aback., he chatted a little about enjoyable visits to his uncle's home for Christmas when he was a child, but, sensing a disinterest as weariness descended, gave his clumsy regrets and rang off. Afterwards, he sat down to think over such an unsatisfactory interaction. It struck him, rather forcefully, how rapidly a useful, decent, eighty year long life had been dismissed. After people we love cease to communicate they begin to be seen as living zombies, from whom we instinctively wish to sever our links - even after a long and happy marriage.

Of course, it wasn't quite like that. His uncle was attempting to move on, to look ahead rather than back. The human spirit has a survival drive which rapidly distances itself from tragedy – especially if nothing can be done about it. We pass through the psychologists' designated stages, beginning with denial but ending with acceptance and a need to make the best of it. It is, of course, easy to put labels on grief but much less easy to cope with something which keeps on re-entering one's thoughts. His uncle was trying to prevent others from worrying about how much losing his wife had affected him, while, at the same time, accepting that his own demise could not be long delayed.

Alan was downcast. He reflected that when a particular human life was over its impact disappeared almost immediately. All that character, all that energy, all that humour, all that day to day enthusiasm - their uplifting effect on others was lost when one could no longer have a conversation. He hated the idea that he might go in the same way; one day alive and considered - because he was talking; the next alive, but mute and effectively dead - as unable to respond. Alan got out the car and went back to the supermarket to buy a card. He knew it wasn't adequate, and it didn't make him feel any better, but it was expected by civilised society.

*   *   *   *   *

It was the distinctive odours he noticed first. Yes, in the plural! Unlike the highly imaginative sales department's 'soft, berry and flower bouquet' waiting to be discovered in wine, these smells were pungent and individual. Initially, antiseptics had dominated but once beyond the reception area, floor cleaner, wax polish and coffee could be readily identified.

Along wide corridors, the endless, mysterious entrances fascinated him. Why did those satin-steel handles point in opposite directions? Some doors wore serious, blank faces; others looked back from small, tinted windows which he wanted to peep through. Double Yale locks appeared in places; he wondered who held the keys. Elsewhere, there were slots for plastic, bar coded identification cards and a few with even more inaccessible, full numerical key pads on which to tap in a secret code. Despite security appearing to be the hospital trust's highest priority, Aaron suspected that such a door would open at the slightest push – not that he had the nerve to try.

Emily hung back, intimidated – everybody else seemed to know what to do. Aaron approached an elderly lady at a desk labelled 'Enquiries'; she was wearing a lapel badge which said 'Friends of the hospital.' Behind her a cardboard notice was stuck untidily on the wall, it advised that the service was staffed by volunteers. Perhaps, he thought, this was some sort of excuse for incompetence, well knowing the government's bureaucratic penchant for avoiding any responsibility.

'We need the ultra sound department,' he stated.

The woman looked at this healthy young man closely, narrowing her eyes. Sensing further explanation was called for, Aaron passed across the hospital's appointment letter. After a quick scan she stared past him, observing, 'It says Miss...' as her eyes alighted on Emily's not quite so slender figure.

'Yes we're...' he began, but there was no need to continue.

'Along there.' She pointed towards a corridor. 'Left at the end, then left again. Look for Radiography reception.'

The letter was passed back; grasping it, Aaron caught Emily's hand as they set off along a rabbit warren of underground tunnels. No wonder they needed directions - it was all a bit Alice in Wonderlandish. At their destination the pass key letter was re-presented and they joined a mixed group of people sitting on wooden benches set in a sort of lay-by just off a secondary corridor.

The staff were busy. Every now and then white jacketed women – nearly always well overweight – walked in calling out names. As the seats gradually emptied he noticed that the neutrally painted walls – what sort of colour was that - had broken out in a rash of notices. Variously sized pieces of white or grey paper with different font printing, but always in black, offered advice and instruction; they reminded him of the wall displays in junior schools. Some said lunch was from twelve to two – presumably there was no service then, others encouraged visitors to wash their hands – but where? No radios were to be played and seats must be given up for older people. Then a more relevant one: 'Scans cost £5.' Aaron was puzzled – Mum had said the service was free.

'I don't have any money,' he said despairingly.

Emily was well informed. 'I think that's only if you want to know the baby's sex – more than just a routine check up.'

'Oh,' said Aaron. Somehow, he never thought the baby would be a girl. Everybody he knew, except Emily's mother, had a son, sometimes two. Finally, it was Emily's turn. After about fifteen minutes she returned.

'Is it alright?' he asked anxiously.

'Yes,' she stated, in that matter of fact way he had begun to admire so much.

'Look.' She handed him a black and white print on which he could make out nothing.

'What's that?'

'See, here,' she pointed with her middle finger. 'Can you make out a head?'

Now he could.

'That's amazing. Can we keep it?'

'Yes, it's the first picture of our baby.'

Aaron found the word 'our' rather disconcerting, but, as Emily was obviously happy, he smiled and put an arm around her waist.

'It will be fine, I'm sure.'

Emily knew there was a long time to go, knew they needed money and a home of their own, knew it was going to be difficult, but didn't want to worry him or spoil the good news. 'Of course,' she said, and gave him a gentle kiss on the lips.

* * * * *

In order to promote their perceived need for more trees, Chris suggested holding an exhibition in the village hall. Jeff liked the idea, and it persuaded him to convince fellow councillors that this project was one they should support over the long term. The council was receptive, not only agreeing to an exhibition but also minuting a formal policy: 'Denton Cheney Parish Council wishes to see the planting of more trees. These are to be small, decorative ones (e.g. prunus, malus) within the village confines and hardwoods (e.g. oak, ash) in the surrounding fields.' A 'tree group' was formed in order to implement the decision; it consisted of Chris, Jeff and a bachelor villager Jim – his being the sole reply to a request in the magazine for anybody interested. Unfortunately, Jim worked shifts, which were mainly at night, and found it difficult to be available during the afternoon.

A Saturday in November was booked at the hall – one that didn't conflict with a home game for the town's rugby team – and, on Jeff's insistence, various organisations were requested to take over a table and make a 'green' presentation. Those coming forward included the scouts, junior school, women's institute, district and county councils and the parish council itself. Display boards were found to be available and duly collected from the 'Association of Rural Councils,' and set up for the exhibitors on the hall's folding aluminium tables. No formal support was forthcoming from the trustees or their chairman.

The three tree group members arrived early in the morning to unlock the doors and assist the arriving exhibitors. Best of all they persuaded a computer literate villager to set up a lap top with a power point presentation about the concerns, and resulting aims, of the tree planting project. There was a good turnout, despite the pouring rain - perhaps because of the advertised free cup of tea and accompanying chocolate biscuit. Jim sat in one corner and collected not only a large sum of money, but many pledges for actual tree donations.

The first to arrive, even before they were officially open, had been Mrs Cecil who bustled in, leant on her stick and expected immediate attention. 'My gardener has potted out these nice laurels for me. Can someone carry them in?' Jeff placed them just inside the entrance to form a patch of welcoming evergreen. The aging aristocrat watched closely, seeming to approve. 'I must go into town, but will return,' she confided. Chris had wanted to button hole her and seek approval for setting trees in her family's land holdings, but she disappeared before he could open his mouth.

Many attendees brought in the requested empty, black plastic plant pots, a few still contained weedy sprigs of ash or chestnut which their owners were perhaps taking this opportunity to abandon. Dot Faulkner entered cheerfully, carrying a specimen, copper beech in a grey ceramic flower vase, 'Been looking after this for a bit, you can have it now,' she advised. 'All this is a good idea. Keep it up.'

To Jeff's surprise Laura arrived alone, greeted nobody and began to watch the presentation; she seemed slightly furtive, not her usual self assured self. He nodded to her as she took out a decorative, blue leather purse and engaged Jim's attention. Shortly afterwards Frank turned up, immaculately dressed as ever, with a diamond pinned silk cravat and open necked check shirt showing above the collar of his Burberry coat, spotting Laura he headed for the tree group's table. Was it a coincidence, thought Jeff that these two people, who rarely left home, should be out without their partners on such a foul day, and arriving within a few minutes of each other? Perhaps there was some substance to the latest gossip.

Small children ran about inside the hall playing noisy games of hide and seek among the stands, while older siblings tried to answer the simple question sheet Chris had prepared in an attempt to prevent them from becoming bored. Meanwhile, their parents and grandparents stood around in clusters talking to friends about the previous night's television programmes, regretting the rain and enjoying their afternoon tea – especially the biscuits. Finally, the weather cleared and they all drifted out onto the adjacent green, where, after a speech by the parish council chairman, a fine young maple - an acer platanoides drummondii - was ceremoniously staked and planted; its hole dug out by the scout troop, assisted by several youngsters who each contributed a shovel of soil to the backfilling.

As they stacked the folded tables and swept up the floor Chris summed up the mood.

'It's nice to see so many villagers participating in something constructive - a relief from all the prevailing gloom and doom about killers and police.'

'Yes,' agreed Jeff, 'a pleasant afternoon, and the support we were so concerned about is certainly there. I found it encouraging.'

'It leaves us with a lot of work to do,' added Jim, yawning. Then, noticing the warning looks of his friends, hastily clarified his intention by adding. 'Enjoyable work, I mean.'

* * * * *

The door opened and Mick came in clutching several magnificent birds. 'There, a great morning's shoot!' he declared triumphantly.

Susan put Damien back on the floor, having scooped him up when she heard the crunch of hobnailed boots on the concrete steps – he did have a habit of rushing across to greet his daddy and risking a bang as the door opened.

182

'So, it was worth all the effort!' she said with a smile. Her husband worked long hours in summer; at this time of year, when the farm was relatively quiet, it was good to see him less tired and enjoying his new hobby.

'I didn't bring many – I know you don't fancy pheasant – but I had to show them to the lad. I'll take a brace across to the butcher at Shottle and get them cleaned up. We need, at least, to try them – they are home grown.'

Susan laughed, 'What happened to all the rest? Surely you lads got more than four?'

'Henry counted a total of ninety - seven cocks, we try to avoid shooting too many hens. Not bad for four guns and five beaters. The beaters got some, and a Chinese fellow bought the remainder for fifty pence each. I expect he sells them to London hotels.'

'Is your shotgun back with Henry?' For safety reasons Susan refused to have any guns or cartridges in the flat.

'Yes, it's been put away.'

'Damien was becoming grisly. I was about to put him down for his afternoon sleep but hoping he could see you first. Your timing was good.' She turned to their son, 'Come on young man. Your dad will still be here when you wake up.'

Putting his boots outside the front door, Mick went into the bedroom to change out of his heavy jacket and cord trousers. When he reappeared Susan was already pouring out cups of dark tea, adding milk and stirring in spoonfuls of white sugar.

'You were quick,' he said in surprise.

'Yes, he rarely makes a fuss now, knows when he's had enough. If it's a weekday I do the ironing while he's asleep.'

'You're so well organised,' commented Mick approvingly, 'like Farmer Jones.'

They sat down in the armchairs they'd bought before Damien was expected, since then little had been added to their meagre comfort.

'How long will he sleep for?' queried Mick.

'You should know by now – only an hour or so at this age.'

That Saturday's Advertiser had carried another article about the mysterious body in the stream and a leader urging those who had not yet been swabbed to hurry up and come forward. It mentioned that a further thorough check was to be organised in the area to see if any evidence had been missed during the first search. Tramping across muddy, bare fields the shooters had gone close to the site.

'Poor bugger,' Tim had said, 'I wonder who she was. You'd think there'd be a nice husband waiting for her at home. Makes me realise how lucky I am to be out here with my mates, and a warm house to go back to.'

His friend's words and the news of the search tugged at Mick's conscience. 'What if the money he had taken was an important clue? Nobody had been arrested and the police were certainly struggling. Although he hadn't been aware of the corpse when he picked up the oilskin wallet, it now came home to him that he may have taken away a vital piece of evidence. Apart from not handing in the money, he had unwittingly obstructed a murder enquiry. As they waited for the beaters to come nearer, the events of a certain day in summer came back to him, vividly.

After a long wet spell the weather had dried out and he'd been combining the wheat since dawn – from the centre out as the conservationists wanted; it was a lonely job and any distraction was welcome. As he reached the margin of the field, seated high up in the cabin he could see over the bulrushes and down onto the stream, now clearly lit by a low sun. From this vantage point he noticed that something yellow near the bank was catching the light. Curious, and glad of an excuse, he climbed down from the harvester, pushing through the nettles to investigate. The object was lying in wispy grass at the water's edge. It was an unmarked oilskin pouch. He bent down and picked it up, inside was a thick wad of ten pound notes, but nothing else. No one was in sight, so he stuffed the find into his pocket, hurried back to the huge, green machine, pulled himself up into the cabin and recommenced work, intending to report his discovery to Farmer Jones at the end of the day.

The sun was a fiery red ball, touching the horizon, when Mick drove the rig back into the farmyard, but there was nobody about, nobody to talk to. He went into the kitchen where a handwritten note said that Joan had gone into town. As the outer door was always left open, he couldn't risk leaving the wallet on the big table. Tired and dispirited, he collected his bike from the barn and cycled wearily home. Late as usual, and with the smell of dinner already wafting out through the door, he changed hurriedly beneath the stairs – his habit in summer, hung up the working clothes and ran upstairs to wash his hands before sitting down to eat. Afterwards, there was only time to watch the televised regional news before retiring for a good night's sleep.

Early the following morning he found that Susan had put out a clean shirt and blue denim overall which he pulled on before heading over to the farm and another long day. When he returned home he remembered the pouch. It was still in his pocket under the stairs – Friday was the day Susan went to see her mum and she hadn't yet collected up the weekly washing. It was also his wife's birthday. They no longer bought each other presents – the money he earned, and the child support they claimed, barely sufficed to support the three of them. Worse, he hadn't had time to get a card from the village post office. Feeling bad he came up with an idea; why not use the windfall, give it to Sue - she deserved it. Nobody would know it had ever been there.

Having set his conscience to rest, he presented what turned out to be nearly two hundred pounds to his wife, saying it was a bonus for the extra hours he had put in to get in the harvest before it rained - which would have given Jones the additional cost of drying all that damp grain. Susan was delighted - she had a list of things that they and Damien needed. Mick cautioned her not to talk about it – even to friends. Not everybody had received any extra, and he didn't want to embarrass old Jones who was notoriously tight fisted.

Out in the chill air Mick's mind had cleared, now he knew what to do. It was wrong. He shouldn't have kept his find a secret, shouldn't have taken the money. He must go to the police, he couldn't live with his guilt; his find might help them discover what had happened and who the murderer was. First, he needed to tell Susan - that would be the worst bit.

'I've got something to confess,' he began awkwardly.

Susan looked up from her knitting. Thoughts of infidelity flashed across her mind but were as quickly discarded – her Mick wasn't like that.

'Yes,' she said encouragingly.

'You know that birthday money I gave you.' He glanced across at her, 'It wasn't mine.'

'Whose was it then? Should it have been split with the others?'

'No. It's a long story. I'd best hurry before Damien wakes.'

Mick related the day's events as well as he could remember them. Susan didn't interrupt.

'So, that's it,' he concluded just as a cry came from the bedroom.

His wife stood up to fetch their son. 'You'd better call the police straight away,' she advised without a moment's hesitation.

'What about the money,' asked Mick, 'we've spent it all?'

'Never mind,' answered his wife as she emerged with a sleepy Damien draped over her shoulder, 'we'll just have to save up and repay it. Did you make a note of exactly how much?'

'I did,' he paused. 'They may accuse me of theft.'

'You should have thought of that before. Call them now,' instructed Susan. 'Let's get it over with.'

*   *   *   *   *

The plastic banner had been fixed along the school railings for several weeks; it advertised their biannual fete. This fundraising event had been well heralded in both the council's magazine and the church circular. Robert didn't need any reminder, having attended these events since he was a boy. During his time as a rural policeman he had found such informal gatherings very useful, during them he could chat with relaxed villagers and find out what was really going on; after being co-opted by McAlister to assist with the enquiry he had even more reason to be there.

In line with Agatha Christie's detective novels there was always a lot of harmless gossip but, sometimes, among it, matters that were better dealt with by the law. He had never worn his uniform to a fete, not that he wanted to disguise his profession, only that dressing for work didn't reflect the spirit of the occasion. It wasn't a disguise; in those days Robert had walked the beat every day and nearly everybody was familiar with the tall, reassuring figure.

The autumn afternoon was glorious and he wandered around alone, looking here and there, missing nothing, noting everybody's movements and their contacts, recalling the faces of newcomers and regretting the villagers who were no longer able to attend. This time, the parochial junior school had made a bigger effort; 'friends of the school,' led by Emma, had mobilised a wide variety of stalls. Some sold donated car boot items, like paperback books, videotapes and soft toys; others offered demonstrations of traditional country crafts, including basketry, embroidery, crochet work, tapestry, weaving and lace making - the latter having been the predominant occupation of village spinsters in the early nineteenth century. All the hand made products sold well, helping to accumulate funds for a proposed computer room. Little else was new but the event was, nonetheless, well supported by parents and villagers alike.

Robert recalled that, in years gone by, like the harvest festival and village fun day, it would have been one of very few occasions when agricultural workers laid down tools, in this case, to support their children rather than enjoy themselves. He chatted for a while with Joan and Mrs Oldham in order to catch up on the latest happenings but they had nothing new to reveal.

Suddenly, he spotted two scruffy young men with their arms full of beer cans, recognising them as Sam and Dave. Robert knew, from past experience, that they were potential trouble makers and withdrew into the heavy shadow of the school porch to keep them under observation, hoping that his acquired policeman's sixth sense of trouble had let him down this time.

The two youths were moving fast, weaving erratically through the loitering villagers, who ignored them. It was attention they craved – some meaningful contact with an adult world from which they felt excluded. Dave stumbled on the rough ground, lost his balance and fell against the tea stall, causing a clatter of crockery and a clamour of anxious shouts as the purveyors held tightly onto the hot urn. Sam quickly hoisted his friend onto his knees, standing over him defensively and adopting an aggressive posture. The English, in their mannered way, blocked out the disturbance and, apart from helping to right the cups and saucers, behaved as if nothing untoward had happened. Robert could imagine the older people's thoughts: 'We've lived through the war, what's the problem?'

Frustrated to be surrounded by so much apathy, Sam yelled out and pushed over a table. Events were getting out of control. As the visitors backed away into a cautious circle, Robert, deliberately moving slowly, strolled across and entered the ring of tension. Aware that these days youths often carried knives - 'for their own protection,' as they told the courts - he carefully kept beyond striking distance, even from there the stench of beer was overwhelming.

'Fuck off, you queer,' jeered Sam. 'You're not a proper copper now.'

The silence that followed was broken by Robert's calm voice. 'You're correct on both points,' he agreed. 'It was an accident. Now, move away from there, please, and let the ladies tidy up.'

As the situation was diffused and onlookers began to melt away, Robert edged closer. When the crowd had dispersed he put protective, but authoritative, arms around both of them. 'Come on down to the entrance. I can help you.' The two lost souls meekly complied, falling into step behind him. 'Look,' he said, 'you've been drinking - all morning, I'd guess. That's illegal, as you well know, but I'll not report it.'

'Thanks,' mumbled Sam, realising that they were being let off – Dave was still incoherent.

'There is one condition though,' the old policeman continued evenly. 'Listen well! The parish council needs help around the village – picking up litter, cutting back nettles, painting fences and so on, we call it community work. If you report to my house every Saturday at 9am for four weeks I'll come along and direct you. Three hours each time - that's all. Agreed?'

Sam mumbled, 'Yes,' in evident relief.

A moody Dave just nodded.

Just then, a distinctively marked yellow and blue Cortina caught their eye as it pulled up outside. Sheena got out, locked the doors and greeted

Robert over the school gate. The PCSO was thick set, strongly built and, if her accent and cheery demeanour were anything to go by, of West Indian extraction.

'You still on duty?' queried Robert.

'Not really,' she replied, implying that her work never stopped, 'but I always try to attend these summer events.' She turned her attention to the boys, who she knew. 'Hello guys. You been misbehaving today?'

Neither spoke, but Robert took up their cause. 'No,' he said reassuringly, 'all's well here Sheena.'

'Good, I'll just take a quick walk around and be gone,' she decided, accepting the obvious cover up at face value. 'Cheerio.'

Sam was clearly relieved, gaining new respect for their saviour, beginning to trust him.

'You won't tell her?' he asked.

'Not if you help me the way I already said,' Robert emphasised. 'Now, off you go and don't come back.'

Later that evening he phoned Sheena at her home number.

'It's me. I owe you a call. As you will have guessed things weren't as straight forward as I made out.'

'Yes, the sheepish looks told me something had been going on.' Robert related the whole story.

'You and I are in agreement,' said the PCSO. 'What those kids need is motivation, not punishment. Your idea of compulsory 'voluntary' community work is better than putting them before a juvenile court or a judge, also cheaper for the tax payer and less trouble for us.'

'Can you suggest anything I can get them into by way of training or apprentice- ships?' queried Robert, who wanted a long term solution to the causes of crime and vandalism.

'I'll try,' promised Sheena. 'They've just opened a free construction industry training centre in town – bricklaying, steel fixing, joinery, the lot. If you persuade them to take it seriously I can recommend them for the new intake in the autumn. What do you think? Is it a goer?' The old bachelor reckoned it was.

'Thanks Bob, I'll get onto it. It will be done.'

No sooner had Robert put down the phone than he began to realise what he had taken on. The first step was to talk with Sam and Dave; they owed him a favour and would at least listen. If that worked he still needed their parent's approval – acquiescence would suffice.

'Small steps,' he told himself, 'begin long journeys.'

* * * * *

Cecil House was warm, perhaps too much so since colds and sore throats seemed to take a hold on Jeff soon after council meetings. The reason became clear when his wife pointed out that they were using a day lounge for the oldest and least healthy people in the village. Moving the venue away from the village hall had not only saved a few pounds, it was much more comfortable, especially in winter; although in summer, after a hot day, an early arrival was essential in order to pour out glasses of water and throw open the large windows. After their first few sessions the warden, who lived in a flat upstairs, advised she had received complaints about the chairs which had not been put back into their correct places – elderly people wanted their favourite seats to remain exactly where they had left them. This recurring problem was finally resolved by taking a digital camera image at arrival and referring back to it after they had finished.

After the councillors had attended a training course - which emphasised that their job was to come fully briefed and make decisions, the meetings began to shorten. Issues useful for the whole village started to be raised and resolved; that is those not requiring any money. The previous incumbents had failed to make any provision against depreciation of council owned property – such as the playing field swings, slide and roundabout. Given this lack of capital it was agreed to increase the parish's annual per capita precept – which formed part of the annual, county council tax - as it had fallen well below the level charged by rural villages of a similar size.

On the plus side, the council enthusiastically took up the critical ongoing work of both VASE and the action group, allowing both to be disbanded and their remaining small funds transferred into the parish account. Jane was asked to harass the county council over the badly deteriorated state of Denton Cheney's roads and pavements. Having neither love nor respect for that organisation she took up the cause with relish. The area around the war memorial had become unkempt and its soft stonework was defoliating, so competitive quotes were obtained from gardeners for regular weeding and from masons to sand blast the monument and repaint the names of the fallen. Work was to commence as soon as the precept was received and be completed before the upcoming eleventh hour of the eleventh day of the eleventh month. The clerk also spent many tedious hours having all earlier accounts she could lay hands on independently double audited. This enabled a line to be drawn and allowed the new members to move forward constructively without risk of criticism from central government.

The most important innovation was to form small working groups that could deal with different aspects of the council's delegated responsibility and bring their solutions to the full council for ratification. This decision recognised that, at monthly meetings there simply wasn't sufficient time to discuss everything in detail, but, as Jane pointed out, it was still necessary for the council – which always acted as a whole – to make any binding decisions. 'Groups' were preferred to 'sub-committees' because the latter's meetings were required to be prearranged and held in public, something which was neither practical nor really necessary for the minor matters being considered. The initial divisions were - planning – which needed to respond within 21 days to any parish planning applications; community relations – covering the playing field, grass mowing, street lights and the burial ground; the magazine - for which Patrick was confirmed as editor; crime and disorder – which dealt with the police and aimed to reinstate the defunct 'neighbourhood watch', and finally finance – whose function was self evident.

Planning was the most demanding because, firstly, the village was within a few kilometres of the town, which under a government policy initiative, had been designated to expand by some forty thousand homes over a twenty five year period, and secondly, owing to the rapid rise in house prices many applications were being submitted for infill housing and extensions of all shapes and sizes. Alan took charge of this group, ably assisted by the chairman, and brought to bear their previous experience in resisting the school – something which remained an ongoing concern.

Freed from the previous council's cloying shackles of prejudice,

Brenda, their district councillor, suggested that the village develop a 'parish plan' and sought approval, which was given wholeheartedly. Apparently, the Countryside Agency was not only offering grants and guidance but encouraging residents to plan for the future by producing a detailed document that would capture the villagers' views. A lot of input was required. To ensure credibility, as many households as possible - certainly a majority - needed to be visited and interviewed – rather like the national census had done - and the same list of questions put to all. Brenda offered to lead this venture, gather together her own team of assistants and report back to the parish council with a draft plan for review and endorsement. With the threat of major development hanging over them and a very real risk of being absorbed by the town's urban sprawl, members expected such a plan would provide tangible proof that Denton Cheney's inhabitants wanted their home to remain a small village surrounded by its green field parish.

Unexpectedly, the Open University offered David a series of free, basic computer training sessions on their well equipped 'learning bus'- always provided he could guarantee fifteen attendees for each visit of an eight week course. Rushing into this with his customary energy and tenacity he soon had enough signatures, and several reserves – David's approach was best summed up by a volume in his bookcase which bore the inscription: 'To the most enthusiastic man I know.'

*　*　*　*　*

The knock at the door was respectful. Checking through the windows, Susan saw two station wagons parked at the kerb, a man standing, half hidden, in the back garden and a further pair outside on the landing. It was Sunday and Mick was catching up on his sleep in their bedroom. The authorities hadn't taken much time in responding to his call.

Taking a firm grip on Damien's hand, she alerted her husband before opening the front door.

'Is Mr Cox in?' asked the caller whom she immediately recognised as Brown – the constable who was stationed in the village. 'We received a call from him.'

'Here,' said Mick, opening the bedroom door.

Brown stood blocking the stairs as his boss came forward, 'Mr Cox - I'm Inspector McAlister. I think you know me - I've been leading this case for quite a while. I believe you want to make a statement.'

'To tell you what I saw, yes,' answered Mick.

'It's more convenient if you can come along to the town headquarters and write it all out for us. I've a car waiting outside.'

Mick nodded, 'Let me get my coat and I'll be right with you. How long will it take?' he asked looking towards his wife.

'A couple of hours,' advised McAlister, 'I'll arrange for you to be brought back.'

'Right, I'll follow you.' He kissed Damien on the cheek. 'See you later Sue.'

*   *   *   *   *

Ibrahim closed the shop. As there was no cricket coverage on the television, he sat down to compose a letter to his much put upon and, by now, thoroughly confused brother. Having blown hot and cold for three months and had endless rows with his loyal and ever patient wife, Sunny had finally been forced into an acceptance of events over which he no longer had any control.

'Dear big brother,' he began - Ismail was two years his junior but while they were together in Islamabad his sibling had always been the taller and a more natural leader. Ibrahim went on to admit that his recent experience had reminded him that Ismail was, in social situations, the more outward going and practical, even though he had lived in two relatively traditional countries. After moving from Pakistan to India, Ismail, as a minority Muslim in a country of Hindus, was forced to adapt, whereas, in laissez faire England, Ibrahim had been able to cut himself off from society and retain all his old ideas.

He could have used the telephone but that was expensive. His brother advised him that, if he bought a computer, there was something called 'Skype' which he could access for free via the internet. But Ibrahim was wary of new gadgets and intimidated by all types of technology, besides which he had heard that the world-wide-web was all about pornography and he didn't want Ayesha to see that sort of thing. Writing was easier, it allowed him time to collect his thoughts and, if the shop was busy, to build up a letter over several days.

'I'm sorry,' he wrote, 'for wasting so much of your time. I was dead set on Ayesha marrying a good Indian boy from a respectable family – one shortlisted by you and selected by me. Shiva was sent here by our father, and the marriage - though late in life for me - has been a success; she's a wonderful lady. So, seeking to do the best for our daughter, and wishing to avoid all these divorces that western people resort to at the drop of a hat, I decided that the old fashioned way would give her a better future. Shiva has opposed me all along but I ignored her, and Ayesha was disinterested. For a long time their resistance only served to make me more determined. Now, things have changed. Ayesha brought home an Englishman – white - whom she likes and, after meeting him a few times, I have to admit, so do I. Shiva tells me they want to get engaged but that Ayesha won't go ahead without my permission. What more could I ask? I'm delighted that I was consulted – she's so mature, and a loving child. I should have known. Ayesha will become a real British person - not just an immigrant like me. She belongs here. I'm so proud that our family has completed the leap from the subcontinent to England in only one generation. So, that's the story. If all goes to plan, I shall expect you and Moona to come over for the wedding. I will pay for the air fares and you are welcome to stay at the shop with us – it's the least I can do to recompense you both for all your effort. Shiva would like to arrange the wedding here in the village church, even though we are nominally Muslims I believe that may be possible.' Ibrahim signed himself off as, 'Your affectionate small brother.'

Feeling well pleased with his script, he added a stamp and airmail sticker to the envelope and placed it in a half full, canvas letter bag behind the post office counter.

* * * * *

As the mornings became frosty, a small group of volunteers, well wrapped up in long coats, woolly hats and scarves, waited patiently

194

in the Malting's car park for the arrival of the yellow single-decker. They discovered that the learning bus was thoughtfully designed; it had rows of monitor screens - set on shelves along both sides - which were connected to a central processor. The pupils moved inside and sat on chairs almost touching each other. Gradually, as body heat built up – the driver was not allowed to run his engine when parked - they shed their bulky outer garments while two tutors passed out work sheets. Most of the attendees were retirees who had never experienced the age of the universal desk top computer with its user friendly software, and were delighted to accept the offer of a third party introduction that would be free from any risk of humiliation.

Sitting side by side were Frank and Laura, both had dashed in first and taken the innermost places. Frank was already solicitously engaged in clarifying the instructions and helping her find the right keys. In the initially, chilly air Laura's ample breasts pressed round nipples against a tight, blue cashmere sweater; it was a sight which met with instant, but unspoken, approval from the male members as they filed in, but became lost to view as soon as they sat down.

'Are you all ready?' It was a woman's voice. There was a mumbled 'yes' as localised chats ceased. 'Right, has everybody got a work sheet that's suitable for their experience?' Silence followed. 'Please begin and we'll come round and help.'

Outside, the sun broke through early mist, inside, there was by now a cosy atmosphere with the gentle sound of key tapping interrupted only by an occasional call for assistance.

From his work days Jeff was familiar with computers and their capabilities, but felt an update would prove useful since he was thinking of trading in his old model for something that could handle the recently available broadband internet. He was seated next to Fiona from the horse field - whom he'd never met, finding her close proximity and strong scent distracting. During the lesson there was no time for socialising but when it ended somebody suggested that cafetieres of coffee at the pub would warm them all up - it was, after all, time for the retirees' customary mid-morning break.

Inside the Maltings a recently set log fire crackled in the ancient brick hearth as they pushed tables together and drew up chairs. Frank and Laura, who were the last to arrive, deigned to join them. Fiona commented on Aaron, whom she evidently liked.

'I've asked my husband to find him something at our estate agent business in town - it's easy to get there by bus. I'm sure he can assist somewhere, or be taken on as a trainee. There are always odd jobs to do, especially in this present boom.' A thought crossed her mind and she paused, 'Does anybody know if he can drive?'

'Sorry - I'm fairly new around here,' said Jeff, pouring out the cups. 'Can Aaron drive?' he asked, repeating the question more loudly for a wider audience, but nobody knew.

Fiona was a strongly built country woman, yet, close up, Jeff realised she had lovely hazel eyes with long lashes and a playful, humorous way of expressing herself. He began to look forward to the following week's session. Since retiring he missed the daily presence of the kooky female secretaries with their bright, fashionable clothes and constant giggles, but had to admit that, when trying to concentrate, he found them quite irritating. He and Jean had only one child - a son – who was, so far, unmarried; as his wife was also an only child they rarely met new people. Fiona's presence had reminded him that women could be fun, making him aware that a void had developed in his daily life, one which needed to be filled; but how?

*　*　*　*　*

Looking back, the wedding had gone well, but the preceding weeks had been stressful. Yes, all that attention to detail had been worth it. Everybody appeared to have enjoyed themselves - and that included families and friends, few of whom had been acquainted before the big day; but wasn't that always the case? At thirty two their second daughter was no longer a concern, and the younger one already had a husband and twin sons. A feeling of relief swept over him.

Mike was well aware that people found him rather conservative. It was, nevertheless, a fact that Janice had needed steady moral and financial support ever since leaving the family home. For her parents it had been a burden. From their perspective she usually pushed things that bit too far. Just when he was admiring his daughter for being so sensible and well adjusted, she would fail to pay back a 'loan', give up a good job, change her degree course or move in with doubtful characters. Yes, Janice had always been on the margin, endlessly self centred, willing to take a bit more rather than exercise self restraint. If anyone, even her mother, ventured to suggest she might be wrong, she descended into a flurry of recrimination. Being aware that Janice was, by mental make up, often on the edge of depression had made dealing with her a long process of biting one's tongue while suspecting that any help might be taken for granted.

Janice and husband Nigel, who was in the oil and gas prospecting business, were currently based in Aberdeen. Mike admitted to Sandra that he, for one, wasn't unhappy that Scotland was a long way away. He was glad at no longer having to put up with Janice's repeated, but now less frequent, complaints about being victimised. For many years their daughter had been convinced the whole world was against her, making amends by a life of over indulgence in her many leisure time pleasures and interests. On the downside, he would miss her company which was always intelligent, well informed, and warm. As their eldest child Janice was a delightful and likeable daughter, but very domineering; when small she had constantly reminded her sister, who was only two years the junior, that: 'She was talking'. Now they were adults they got on well, but to his disappointment, kept well apart and led their own lives.

Sitting alone at a wooden table Mike looked down onto reflections in the limpid water of the Malting's attractive lily pond and smiled. He, and especially Sandra, had brought the children up to be independent and self motivated. After their parents had gone they would be able to cope with the inevitable accidents of life, of that much he was certain. Surely, he pondered, that is the best one can do for offspring. Appreciation and thanks don't come until old age arrives. Yes, he thought, when it's too late to pass on any gratitude they will probably look back and realise how much Mum and Dad had done for them – just as he had with his own parents. At least he hoped so.

Mike had woken early; he couldn't get the annoying scenario out of his mind - new housing developments had been proposed and, seemingly accepted, on fields lying between the village and town. The parish council's strident and persistent protests had apparently been ignored. Somehow, the system refused to acknowledge villagers' letters and comments; this was wrong. He understood it was a legal requirement to consult, but – one had to be cynical - perhaps not a legal requirement to take any notice of the results. A drive out to take a look confirmed his worst fears, a large area of land had already been fenced off and concrete was being poured into foundation trenches. Surely, this couldn't have happened so quickly?

Still half asleep, he had begun to feel annoyed, punching the air to release his anger, only to wake up fully when Sandra scolded him for prodding her arm. 'Sorry,' he mumbled incoherently, 'it all seemed so real. Must have been a dream.'

'A nightmare more like!' she replied and promptly departed for the spare room.

It was only then that he realised just how much this struggle with the authorities was taking out of him, the frustration was always in his subconscious mind. He had come close to giving it all up, but it was the wrong time – the council had just heard that, by a small majority, a specially convened scrutiny committee of the county council had finally refused planning permission for the school. Despite the many options taken out on land surrounding the proposed site at Denton Cheney, the committee had decided to build the school on the plot Shottle district council had long ago set aside for it. The chosen site was right in the centre of the one thousand house estate whose children would form the majority of its intake.

The deciding factor had been the cost - at half a million pounds per annum - of transporting children into the village. He and Alan had been in the public gallery throughout the debate and were astonished that the councillors responsible for the education portfolio and their officials had defended the nonsensical proposal to the bitter end. At no time had they heard any valid reason why sites in Denton Cheney had been both first and second choice, they could only explain it away as some sort of corrupt arrangement, it certainly wasn't incompetence.

For the present they had won, or, at least bought time. The threat of the town's expansion remained, but there was now one less excuse for it. It was necessary to remain vigilant and respond in detail to each and every planning consultation and to raise supporting letters from parishioners whenever there was a serious issue. Otherwise, in a few years time, the authorities could argue that the village had made no adverse comment and 'that would be that'. Mike had no delusions - they were fighting well-financed commercial interests. The only way, in still democratic England, was to motivate local residents to resist by convincing them that under the present system they could still triumph. Even though central government was gradually changing the rules to make planning approval easier, he knew that mobilising people power and the press could, in a politically aware country, still provide a path to success.

* * * * *

The 'baron' leant against the marble mantelpiece above an empty fireplace, he was fingering a small, leather-bound volume. 'If Richardson had used modern methods of printing and distribution he would have become a millionaire! It's a great bit of literature, probably the first real English novel and very popular in its time, but his agent struggled to produce enough copies to meet demand.'

Hamish had interests in publishing and was a collector of original, early volumes.

'Who are we waiting for?' he asked of those present, but, without waiting for an answer, carried on his discourse. 'In 1740 this man had it right on war crimes and marriage – to address two dissimilar issues.' Unaffected by the puzzled looks, he rambled on. 'Listen to this bit: '*People, I don't know how they shall act when their wills are in the power of their superiors. I always thought it became me to distinguish between acts of malice and of implicit obedience…though no commands of others should make us do an evidently wrong thing'.* Doesn't that sum up the quandary of junior officers in any disciplined service? Here's another gem: '*I told you before, her fine person made me a lover; but it was her mind that made me a husband.'* First the sexual attraction that draws people close, then the companionship that binds them together. It's no different today.'

'What book is it?' ventured somebody.

'Pamela,' revealed the baron as he strode across the flagstones to answer the bell. 'Ah, Alan, you're late. Come in, come in. You know the others.'

'The others' were members of a reformed village hall working group. After a frustrating year putting up with the bus shelter vandals Vincent and Sanja had decided to make their main home in Croatia, retaining only a small flat in town. Their cottage had been put up for sale and Vincent had succeeded in persuading Hamish to take on the chairman's duties. Several fundraising events had been organised by Sanja and her friends, but the amount collected had barely dented the renovation budget - even allowing for the tentative grant offers which had now been passed onto the baron. Chris had volunteered as secretary and had roped in Alan. June no longer attended meetings; Ian had resigned, and a woman called Harriet appeared to be their accountant.

Alan had gone to the manor house somewhat reluctantly, chiefly to discover just what Hamish intended to do and where the money was coming from. Once inside, he continued to drown them in rhetoric, listening little and delivering his own ideas on everything but the one thing that mattered - the future of the hall. The baron seemed to assume that the group already knew everything. As a result Alan found it hard to contribute, but managed, gradually, to piece together the story of what had happened previously.

Harriet tabled a set of figures which indicated a price for the proposed work – whatever that meant – and announced, 'Assuming it's still valid, the county council grant will cover about 30% of the cost. At the present rate of fund raising, it could take twenty years to find the rest.' Despite this bad news their chair appeared totally relaxed, insisting that a meeting of the trustees be called to review and approve the plan and its budget before they went any further. Funds were lacking, and, with competition from the proposed extension to St James – a popular, rival cash seeker – it was difficult to see how they would ever be found. After this gloomy prediction Hamish declared the meeting closed. Alan went home, more puzzled than ever; he would ask Chris to let him know what was really happening.

* * * * *

The smooth predictability of Mrs Oldham's life had been disturbed, it was making her grumpy and she hated that. Questions and doubts had arisen. Little progress seemed to have been made in collecting funds for the church meeting room - a project that was close to her heart. Added to which there was the ongoing unease caused by that drowning and the subsequent press interest, but no indication of when, or whether, light might be shed.

The police reporting station was still in the hall car park, but nobody went there. Until she disappeared, Constable Brown used to spend all day chatting with the caretaker – neither of them had enough to do. It was rumoured that June was tired and had checked herself into Phoenix House for a spell. That June was a strange woman, always on her own - until Brown came along; she appeared to have neither family nor friends, yet usually knew more about what was going on than anybody - and willing to tell you too. The fibreglass cabin, in bright yellow and blue, was an eyesore; it reminded Mrs Oldham that her peaceful village had begun to resemble an Orwellian state - with swabs, door to door visits and that shifty Smith always snooping about. To cap it all the car had been giving trouble, refusing to start now that winter was nigh. Thank goodness for that nice Mick, he understood mechanical things.

She knew there were good things happening, but, in the current climate, they went unreported. However bad the world seemed, decent people were always trying to put things right. That was how freedom and democracy worked at a grass roots level – provided one was well away from this zealous, do-gooding, rule producing, government. The parish council were useful - one could talk to them now, its members all seemed well intended and honest. She'd lobbied them to control speeding which, given an economic boom, was becoming a problem again. One youngster, 'whose car went out of control' - weren't accidents always so described, the driver never taking any responsibility - had taken the hump back bridge at the stream so rapidly that he'd ended up on top of the adjacent stone wall; another had cornered wildly and her car had become lodged half way up a hedge. Both these drivers had escaped unscathed, but a third one, who collided with the railway bridge buttress, had been less fortunate.

These incidents were worse than irresponsible; they were avoidable and a danger to others. To address this issue the parish council had organised volunteers to use a police speed gun during the morning and evening rush hours when vehicles made 'rat runs' through the narrow lanes. The resulting records indicated a high percentage of law breakers, fortunately, not many were locals. As a result, the police had clamped down by issuing tickets, and she felt, more sensibly, had installed a flashing thirty mile an hour reminder sign at the village entrance. Mrs Oldham had stood on the verge for an hour to evaluate the sign's effect on drivers, discovering that a large majority slowed down - it was a step in the right direction.

* * * * *

Nearly a year had passed since the project to build St Michael's room – for that was the, somewhat unimaginative, chosen name – had been launched with such enthusiasm, now, support was wavering, and he knew it. A quiet realisation had dawned on Keith Rector that funds and pledges received so far amounted to but a fraction of Peregrine's budget, after taking into account declared legacies, the total was barely ten percent. Perhaps he had been overambitious, forgotten that his previous benefactors were successful graduates, many of whom had made their fortunes in industry or banking. Mobilising enthusiasm was the easy bit – he was good at it – but in Denton Cheney the ability to pay was limited and the potential catchment much smaller.

Keith began to feel uncomfortable. He had arrived as an outsider, a prophet bringing the vision of an impressive, in character extension to their lovely church, but now his project had become a burden for the whole village. What to do? It was important to discover what the locals really thought. Keith kicked himself. He hadn't undertaken any sort of systematic consultation on the viability of his plan but had rushed ahead, applying his motivational skills and force of personality to obtain a consensus. It would be sensible if he mentioned his growing doubts to someone outside the parochial church council, someone who was a long term resident and regular churchgoer; Dot Faulkner fitted that description very well.

After a hollow sounding rat-a-tat on the shiny brass, horseshoe door-knocker Keith was welcomed in by 'Auntie' Dot and promptly marooned beside the log fire in a capacious, chintz covered armchair. The springs were badly worn and he felt he'd never be able to stand again. Well educated visitors were infrequent and, as it was late afternoon, tea was served. After he'd taken a few sips Dot enquired politely as to the purpose of his visit. Slightly intoxicated by wood smoke - which seemed to fill the low ceiling room, Keith struggled to muster his thoughts. 'I don't know how to put this,' he began clumsily, 'but it's about St Michael's room...'

'Do you want a bequest?' cut in Dot, unabashed. 'I'm getting a bit decrepit. I suppose I could give something - though I'd rather it went to the grandchildren.'

'No,' he continued, 'I don't want to talk of that – though it's very generous of you. It's a bigger problem.' Dot frowned and reached for the teapot. Keith shook his head, ashamed of his reluctance to make the point. 'It's like this. I feel bad. I'm beginning to doubt whether we can ever raise enough money for our project – well, not in my lifetime anyway - and I'm embarrassed at having got you all involved.' His confidence building, Keith grasped the nettle. 'Frankly, I think we should call it a day and, with the donors' approval, give the amount collected to the church maintenance fund.' Relieved to have confided in someone he ended with a question. 'What's your view, Dot?'

The widow was straightforward, 'It's not going to happen. Everybody's too polite to tell you.' Keith felt a sense of relief, maybe his ego had been punctured but it appeared that nobody had been deceived. 'Don't look so downcast,' she smiled. 'It was a grand idea, got us all going, but there aren't enough churchgoers these days to provide the funds – it's all we can do to fix the roof.'

Dot lifted the latch and let him out. Much reassured, he felt he could now approach a fellow councillor.

In the hot farm kitchen Joan was baking on an industrial scale. She talked to him over her shoulder.

'What is it then?' Keith explained his concern but didn't mention Dot.

'Give it up,' was her immediate retort, 'unless you can find someone to pay for it. We can't afford it.' She repeated her summary, emphasising the 'you' and 'we' before continuing, 'I'm not saying it's impossible – there's plenty of rich around here, believe me, but they keep it for themselves. The church isn't in their lives any more.' Keith said nothing, just stood there. 'Can you let yourself out?' she called, 'I can't stop right now.' Joan had been her clumsy but honest self.

Chastened, Keith mumbled a quick, 'Thank you,' and stole away as inconspicuously as he could. Now, he knew what to say at the next meeting, and what response to expect. He realised that they had respected him enough to let him try; it was a sort of consolation for what had been a misjudgement. Keith was left with the problem of ensuring that Peregrine was at least paid for the work he and his father had done, that would be difficult and he wasn't looking forward to it.

Prior to his speech at the parochial church council, the whole village became aware that the plan had been abandoned. Nobody was more relieved than the village hall trustees and the parish council, both of whom were seeking support for initiatives of their own; each well knew that a pool of invaluable good will and cash had once again become available.

For Keith it was another setback. Soon after arrival in Denton Cheney he had lobbied for the formation of an historical society. His reasoning was that a small book, printed only recently, which updated the story of Denton Cheney as written in the twenties by a previous vicar, had been well received. After meeting his costs the author wished to donate the balance of the proceeds to a relevant ongoing cause. Keith thought such a gift would serve to kick off the society which could then draw members from a village with a heightened awareness of itself and its past role. The organisation had thrived, so much so that Keith had suggested opening a museum in which relevant artefacts – such as those from past trades and industries – could be put on permanent display. As a precedent he quoted a similar successful venture at a village in the same county.

Pressing on with his customary energy he had discovered a small, run-down building behind the 'Fox' which, once refurbished, would provide a suitable venue right at the heart of the village; better still the owner was prepared to contribute it for a peppercorn rent. In public, the society baulked – or at best was apathetic. Outside its meetings, reasonable doubts were expressed: what would they exhibit? Only a Victorian nail factory was known to have existed. Who was willing to put the building in good order – it needed a lot of skilled work; who would man it on a daily basis – the society only had forty members, and, most pertinently, who would visit – the village was not on any tourist route and those interested would only be ramblers or those from passing canal boats. Finally, he raised the issue at the annual general meeting. Nobody would openly criticise the project, but Keith managed to filibuster it away in front of a vacuous gathering who, nevertheless, agreed with him – albeit in silence.

With two failures so close together Keith Rector began to feel downhearted. He resembled an expatriate who, fresh in a moribund foreign society, had arrived full of good ideas which, although initially accepted by the locals with enthusiasm, had finally succumbed to the cold breath of ever prevalent reality - much to everyone's disappointment.

* * * * *

The news of Mick's collection from home by McAlister and visit to the town's police headquarters, became morphed into his arrest and release on bail by villagers anxious for any scrap of information. Speculation was rife and his wife wasn't denying anything - Susan was concerned that he might be charged with robbery and unable to tell residents what had really happened.

* * * * *

Although situated on a prime site at the centre of Denton Cheney, hidden behind its tall wall Phoenix House remained as isolated as any Greek hill top monastery. There was some similarity - human and vehicular traffic circumnavigated the retirement home but very few travelled the final thirty yards to the car park or front entrance. Those that did were usually assisting a relative or booking a room. Like the monks, Amita and Anesh received them kindly, basic food and, if needed, a night's lodging were always available. This well intentioned, competently managed establishment functioned almost independently of the village which surrounded it. Now that the carers, apart from Dorothy, consisted entirely of new arrivals from Poland, the home had become a real retreat. Usually, little disturbed the daily routine, which was the way the residents wanted it.

Cloistered for much of the day in the office or car, Anesh kept abreast of the world outside by having two daily papers and an assortment of medical journals. When the administration was up to speed, and Amita had no call on his time, he read avidly; his was a genuine interest in matters of health - for Anesh their business was more than just a way of making a living.

He deplored the standard of medical journalism in the popular press. How many times did articles highlight 'research' which proved, for example that taking Vitamin C supplement was a cure or preventative for the common cold; cholesterol was directly linked to heart disease; margarine was preferable to butter; more obesity had led to an increase in death due to cancer; that the critical, childhood MMR vaccine could lead to autism, making it safer to have the constituents injected separately. When one examined these claims – often used as front page headlines – either no proper large scale trial, with a placebo control group for comparison, had taken place; or the conclusion had been reached after a phone call survey of less than a thousand people; or the article had reinterpreted the cautious, qualified report of a properly published scientific paper by the cherry picking of dramatic phrases. Even worse, the oft heralded miracle cure or wonder drug was, almost always, based only on animal testing in the laboratory with no human trial having yet commenced.

It especially annoyed him to observe the effect of pills or medicines prescribed for his residents by the local practice at Dunton. Many did suffer from degenerative conditions which sometimes resulted in strange antisocial behaviour, clearly a problem when strangers had to live together in a closed community. Yet, despite manufacturers' claims that their products slowed or mitigated the deterioration, to his eye all they did was act as sedatives, sometimes changing quite bright and communicative people into living zombies. Perhaps such drugs made life easier for less scrupulous carers, but to Anesh that was immoral and unacceptable. Knowing his father would never have tolerated it, he spent time recording his observations in letters to the General Medical Council and several other professional medical publications. So far he hadn't even received an acknowledgement, but he wasn't deterred.

Anesh was an intelligent man and his thoughts had inevitably turned to the strange case of the unidentified man, or was it a woman? He cut out and kept all the Advertiser's reports, together with brief references from the national press, and had made notes on the content of commentary in the television news and on the radio. To him, it seemed strange that the police didn't know whose body it was – they must have lists of missing persons. Everybody knew somebody. What about dental records, surely that would work? Judging from evidence in the public record he was convinced there must be a local connection, but, for some reason, nobody had found it. Yes, they had asked questions from door to door, and Inspector McAlister with PCSO Sheena had called in to talk with residents who had been brought up locally but none had been able to assist.

Anesh reckoned that McAlister wasn't so smart. If he were in charge it would be his priority to interview the residents again, this time more thoroughly - especially the older ones; some could provide useful background, some would have their suspicions. It was a matter of gaining their confidence, posing the right questions, and persistence. Inspector Patel, who had only been in town briefly, had been born in the same city as Anesh - a sort of distant cousin it turned out. He had put his thoughts to Patel, but his fellow countryman had remained non committal. Was something going on behind the scenes?

Anesh surmised that the county police and their London visitors must have fallen out - something which would explain the total lack of progress. He discussed it all with Amita, but she brushed him aside.

'It's nothing to do with us – we don't even live here!'

Yet, he couldn't allow the mystery to rest, after all a dead person had been found within a mile of Phoenix House. Such awareness made him feel uncomfortable - the murderer might live close by and could strike again.

*　*　*　*　*

During his work as editor Patrick discovered that he was more natural wordsmith than natural scientist. Never a sporting type, the children, Sara's political ambitions and his input to the parish council, filled up his leisure time.

Sergeant Smith from the enquiry team had asked him to publish police reports in the quarterly magazine and he had appealed at police behest for cooperation and participation in the DNA exercise. Later, with Patrick acting as webmaster, the council opened a web site which was used to inform villagers and request information. The replies were to have been sent directly to Smith - how many there were, and whether any had been of use, the police had never revealed. By mistake, a few respondents had written directly to the editor. One submission was interesting - it was a piece of basic verse:

> 'A crime there has been,
> It's there to be seen!
> Look close at hand,
> It's all about land.
> Remember the main,
> It's mid - summer again.'

Patrick identified a local postmark on the envelope, but no name was attached; the writing was in hand crafted capitals, the stationary a brand in common use. Patrick passed it promptly to McAlister, but was intrigued. Was this a clue or just a prank, and, if serious, what did it mean? The inspector was decisive, ' I need to think about it. Meanwhile, print it in the magazine – we might trigger some local response.'

When Patrick's mind was disengaged he couldn't help but notice that the present government were poor managers, skilled at getting elected and holding onto the popular vote but never finding time to formulate and pursue long term policies with which to improve the country. This realisation made him more and more exasperated and his characteristic, cheerful willingness began to deteriorate into bouts of petulance. Sara noticed the trend and asked him if there was a problem. Her unexpected awareness was refreshing and he immediately felt less stressed.

'Why don't you take up a political career?' she suggested. 'I think that would satisfy you. You've always had strong principles, added to which it's now clear that you're also a good communicator. Frankly, I'm jaded - a bit fed up with it all. If you want to replace me, I'll suggest it to the party. It would enable me to lecture part time at the town college and put more effort into guiding the children, who would benefit. I've left too much to you.' Patrick looked concerned. 'It's just a switch of roles,' she explained, 'and quite common these days. It could help us stay young and remain sharp.'

A week later, Patrick decided that his wife's proposal made sense. His job was flexible, with good forward planning he would be able to fit in most of the party's requirements, and his work and parish council colleagues would not detect any change. He decided to give his increased involvement a six month trial; if all went well he would ask Sara to let the local political agent know of his recently discovered enthusiasm to replace her and, hopefully, be shortlisted as a potential parliamentary candidate. They both wondered whether the Liberal Democrat hierarchy would agree. Sara had anyway lost her interest in politics, even if they didn't, nothing was lost and exciting new opportunities might arise.

Patrick enquired whether anybody had progressed directly from a small parish council to becoming a Member of Parliament. It was an unlikely scenario, but the flame had been lit. While supporting Sara, he had mixed with political insiders for years but, having never met someone he really admired, became convinced that he could make a better fist of it. On a local level Denton Cheney was under threat, its thousand years plus way of life at serious risk of extinction. The village needed a high level representative to speak for it, becoming a candidate would certainly help its cause.

Beyond the sliding French windows a riot of autumn colour glowed in the sun. It was Sunday and, as Sara had just left to take the children to a party, he felt duty bound to get out and clear up the accumulating piles of dead leaves. As he raked up the soggy, multihued harvest his mind wandered back in time. In their friendship it was Sara who had always been the leader. Patrick wondered why he'd been content to follow her, putting it down to a continuation of the natural obedience and ingrained respect every boy has for his mother. Yes, he'd been ambivalent about getting married – apart from the tax benefits that then existed – and content to drift along at his own pace, his head full of organic chemical formulae and improbable theories about the origins of matter and time.

At university, where they'd met - both aged nineteen, he'd been a virgin. His desire ran high and he knew he had much to learn - if he could only make a start. Gradually, their relationship moved towards sex. She neither encouraged nor discouraged him; but by simply being available, turned making love into a pleasurable routine. At first this wonderful new experience was everything to him. He couldn't wait for the next occasion – usually in the afternoon after lectures. As time passed he began to notice that, following the stunning climax, the world remained the same and there was still the rest of the day to fill in – which could seem a long time if stuck in the wrong person's company. This aspect of their lives became more important, and it dawned on him that, if they decided to live together, then the time away from sex would be the crucial part of their relationship. Both found the other's presence easy and pleasant and, when their affair became almost unremarkable, Patrick knew it had to be permanent - there simply wasn't enough time left in life to start looking for someone else, someone he may never find. Added to this he was aware that after graduation his friends would scatter and he might be left very much on his own - not an experience he would wish on anybody, least of all himself.

TOPAZ - WINTER

The village was small; local news travelled by word of mouth – at the pub, in the woman's institute, after a church service, in the post office, or simply on the lanes. As a result, wise folk had suggested that Aaron should meet with Mick who was in a not dissimilar family situation.

Of necessity, Aaron's life had moved away from his earlier gang of teenage village boys without responsibilities, he had almost forgotten their existence. Nevertheless, he shared with them the difficulty of getting into steady employment; for him it had become essential, for them only a nuisance and a means of obtaining some pocket money. To Emily and Aaron, the Job Centre Plus now meant something – hopefully a lifeline to coping. For Sam, and Dave, it was just an annoying, form mad part of a bossy bureaucracy which seemed intent on walling them into the world of conformity.

A pressing problem was finding suitable accommodation for themselves and the baby. Aaron had noticed Mick around the village. A chance meeting usually warranted a passing, 'Are you alright?' to which the expected reply was only one word, 'Alright!' This ancient, greeting routine seemed to reflect the all important issue of health in a poor farming community. It was essential to be fit in order to handle the only available work - which had long hours and was physically demanding. Aaron was the younger by about ten years, and at an age when such a difference forms no effective upwards barrier but presents more of one in the opposite direction.

Mick and Susan, having qualified for affordable housing in their local area, had now received a more detailed and personal questionnaire from the district council; it was designed to identify their preference – whether rental or part purchase, and financial capability. Hearing a little of Aaron and Emily's background, Mick called in at Aaron's home one evening to explain the couple's own housing needs and their approach to solving it. Aaron was touched, he grasped the importance of his senior's advice, which was to obtain the necessary forms and return them quickly in order to secure a place on the ever growing waiting list.

'You're a needy case,' he had assured Aaron, 'and should qualify. The parish council have become quite active and are pushing for a few houses and flats to be built right here in the village. It will take time – maybe years – but will happen. You can always refuse if something better comes along.' Mick left, as quietly as he had arrived, adding, 'It's a no-brainer Aaron. Good luck. See you around.'

Only now did Aaron and Emily begin to realise how fortunate it was that the scan had not shown twins. Slowly, they became aware of a baby's basic needs, like a Moses basket; a pram; bath; bouncer; cot; bottles and bottle warmer; nappies; suits; formula milk; it was a shock to contemplate such a long and expensive list. Yet, unknown to the perhaps undeserving youngsters, help was on the way. String tied, brown paper parcels began to arrive with each rat-a-tat-tat of the door knocker. From them emerged play suits, vests, socks, hats, and hand knitted cardigans, along with scrawled biro notes wishing them well. Aaron discovered he had a lot of previously unknown, but kindly, relatives – Mum had done her work on the phone. Nobody queried their circumstances, which pleased him. Owing to a predominance of girls in his family, most of the clothes were pink. Emily, now forgiven by her relatives, had a parallel experience, except that nearly all her acquisitions were blue. Until then

Aaron had never thought to associate any particular colour with boys or girls, he didn't care, but it was apparent that all the womenfolk did.

'You two are well provided for either way!' concluded Mum wisely.

'Auntie' Dot - who wasn't really related – knew and liked the two engaging teenagers, and used her membership of the women's institute to roister up some of the heavier items. A dusty, chipped wooden cot, with one lifting side and a stained but sound mattress, was discovered in someone's attic; others contributed a black carry-cot, an Ikea plastic high chair with tubular aluminium legs. and, best of all, a well used but serviceable, old fashioned pram with springs, chromium plated trim, rubber tyres and a folding hood – Mick had offered theirs but Susan had cautioned that she might be pregnant again.

Mum made out a comprehensive list and Aaron learnt a lot. Within weeks most of the items were ticked off and, under strict supervision, Aaron and Emily spent a long time producing hand written letters of thanks, for which Sunny was persuaded to contribute free postage.

'You're fortunate to live in a small village like Denton Cheney,' observed Emily's mother. 'What would we have done without all this support, and you two not even married.'

Once more Auntie Dot turned up trumps. 'I've got the very place for them to stay,' she said after calling round to see Aaron's mum. 'You know - that old coach house we converted into a garage years ago?'

'Yes,' said Mum politely, wondering what was coming next.

'Well,' Dot continued, 'above it there's a room – used by the family groom when I was a child. It's got a sink with an Ascot heater - which works, mains water, a cooker and the electric light. It's a bit grimy but can be cleaned up. The outside wooden staircase is safe - but slippery when it rains. There's a bit of furniture – bed, couch, table and chairs. If you're interested have a look. You can use it - no cost, of course - until they find somewhere better.' Realising she'd made the room sound unattractive Dot continued, 'It's private and quiet. The baby wouldn't disturb anybody up there, and if help is needed I'm only yards away.'

Aaron looked at his mother, it sounded like the answer to a prayer and his face immediately lit up. 'What do you think?' he asked her.

'Very generous offer, I must say.' Mum had already decided. 'You did mention we could take a look – just to be sure?'

'Come round on Monday – anytime,' invited Dot, who was delighted to see their reaction. Excusing herself quickly before the evident gratitude became embarrassing she headed home feeling good about life.

*　*　*　*　*

Laura sat at the computer looking to her left through the tiny cottage window. It was nearly dark. As little could be seen past the distorting, cast glass panes she got up with a sigh and put on the light, how she disliked these gloomy afternoons.

Martin was at a meeting in London, before leaving, he had switched on the server and brought Microsoft's 'Word' up onto the screen - 'booting up' he called it. She took out an orange 'post it' sticker and wrote herself a pencil reminder to ask him how to do it. The screen contained so much information – 'icons' she recalled – that her mind went blank. It was difficult to know where to start. Diligently, she picked up the last exercise paper from the learning bus and applied herself to the keyboard, realising that, apart from the alphabet, it contained many other buttons whose functions remained a mystery.

Using one finger she began to type, but a letter appeared on the screen in error, it was an 'F'; as this had guilty associations she hastily pressed the 'back' key and deleted it. After continuing for a few minutes to tap out the test paragraph, she stopped and forced both hands onto the keyboard; the task became easier as other fingers began to find a use. The problem was she lacked any instinctive feeling as to where the different letters lay, needing to search for each one individually; patience would be required.

Laura's concentration began to wander off onto more personal matters. Martin had always appeared rather stiff and distant, but she knew this didn't represent his real attitude, aware that his diffident manner had been brought about by the unfortunate combination of natural shyness and a strict upbringing. In truth he was warm and kind; she just wished he'd show it more. Perhaps that was Frank's appeal, he was ever cheerful, looked you in the eye and was instantly engaging, with him one soon felt comfortable, embraced by a world of physical pleasure, easy conversation and intellectual stimulation. She told herself there was nothing wrong with their friendship, but acknowledged deep down that she was deceiving herself. She liked Frank, wanted him to hold her - perhaps even more.

The screen faded away as her heart raced like that of a teenager, causing her to press the wrong keys. 'Oh dear,' she thought, 'how do I get the lesson back?'

After reading through all the accumulated help sheets and then her notes, she was none the wiser, deciding to abandon her efforts rather than trigger something that might damage Martin's costly set up. Laura began to worry that, in her meanderings, she might have inadvertently typed Frank's name onto the screen and was aware that experts could always find these things on your hard disk – or so the crime programmes indicated. Perhaps Martin would see it! The only answer, but a humiliating one, was to phone one of the tutors from the learning bus. It was an issue that couldn't be left unresolved.

* * * * *

'Did you hear the news?' asked Dot when Aaron and his mother called to make their expected visit.

'What news?' said Aaron.

'Mick has been arrested.'

'You mean Mick Cox?' queried Mum, and received a nod in response. 'I don't believe it. What on earth for?'

'Something to do with the murder - that's all I know,' said Dot, 'Quite a shock!' adding firmly. 'He didn't do it.'

* * * * *

An oppressive darkness had stolen the last few days, creeping in at keyholes and sneaking past curtains. Heavy rain drummed on the roof as the downpour continued into a third day. Puddles formed on saturated ground and every further drop ran off quickly into the already high brook. Along Glebe Lane the abandoned, manorial fish ponds were replenished, soon, even this temporary reservoir overflowed.

Alan and his wife took an early morning walk – anything to escape from the house. 'Noah must have felt like this,' he thought, 'but he had forty days and nights to put up with.' They headed towards Lower Lane, only to stop in surprise - it was a river, no longer a road. Muddy brown water was rushing into the back doors of two bungalows and leaving via the front with unstoppable haste. 'Poor people,' said Carol, but there was no sign of the occupants who had already left.

The tiny village stream had become a torrent. Where it went underground the pipes were too small and the water had nowhere to go except along the street and through the houses. In an adjacent field, where a herd of disconsolate sheep had been cut in two, matronly ewes were calling out to their marooned lambs.

It took a week before the water subsided to normal levels. Rainfall records were unexceptional and there had been little building in the catchment area, yet in town the river had burst its banks and large parts had been inundated - the worst flooding since the thaw of 1947. Alan found it all inexplicable, until the Advertiser came up with a story about two boys getting lost in the river's floodplain and the sluices being closed to assist the eventually successful rescue operation. 'That's it,' he thought: 'There had to be a reason. It almost proves the 'chaos theory' – children go missing, flow is restricted, the river backs up, its tributaries have nowhere to go and, many miles away, innocent householders have their homes made uninhabitable.'

Despite questions being asked, reports being commissioned, and promises made about ensuring it would never happen again, no official explanation was ever forthcoming. Nobody in authority accepted any blame. 'Such is government today,' he thought, 'it's never anybody's fault.' Concerned to avoid a repetition of the damage, the parish council took up the issue of the stream with the Environmental Agency and county council. Their answer explained that such a small brook was the responsibility of no government department - it was the duty of adjoining landowners to keep it clear. This wasn't the point - clearly some authority had to assess the capacity of the drainage system as a whole. Alan considered the response to be a nonsense - stretches of the stream's natural course had been put into man made channels and pipes which needed checking regularly to see if they were able to cope with additional building development and today's warmer climate. Bureaucracy and regulation had, once again, colluded to avoid a pragmatic, commonsense approach. To this day, Denton Cheney lives with the unassessed threat of further flooding.

Each winter the parish council organised a 'litter pick'; it was always well attended.

The heavy rain had made matters worse and it was an opportune time to clear up unsightly rubbish before fresh spring growth disguised it. A local cleaning company had prompted this popular event by donating a dozen 'picking sticks' and several boxes of plastic gloves and black bin bags. In view of the ongoing police enquiry Jane advised McAlister, who requested that any personal items they found - such as clothing, letters, credit cards or jewellery, should please be kept separate and handed in to the police for checking.

On Saturday afternoon Alan met the assembled volunteers inside the village hall. He allocated areas to different teams and gave their leaders a plan, passed on the police message, warned of the traffic danger and asked them to bring back their bags by four o'clock latest in return for a well deserved cup of tea. Their efforts resulted in lots of healthy winter activity and eighteen full bags – which the district council agreed to collect – and, for the police, a plastic covered bus pass, a pair of ladies gloves, a cheap, silver-gilt bracelet and three sodden, empty envelopes on which the handwriting had smudged and become illegible.

* * * * *

Only rarely had Jim's sleep been disturbed by Damien; there had been just the occasional piercing baby cry and a few outbursts as he succumbed to the inevitable, two year old tantrums. He was aware that Susan was on edge in the mornings - knowing he was downstairs trying to get his rest - and realised the problem affected her more than him.

On the afternoon when the police had taken Mick to town, Jim had just woken up. He heard heavy shoes going up the steps, wondered if Susan needed help and had gone outside to check what was happening. No marked vehicles were in sight, so who were the visitors? Back in his flat, watching from behind the net curtains he had seen Mick walking away, apparently relaxed, in the company of two men. They wore no uniform but, from their upright bearing and confident demeanour, he identified them as police officers.

A lifelong bachelor, Jim had cared for his aging mother in this same small council flat, following her death it had passed into his name. He felt fortunate to have his own home, although the warehouse shifts didn't pay well he managed to make ends meet. Mick and Susan had been good neighbours, so he wondered what to do. Should he go up and enquire politely if anything was wrong, or would it be better to wait a bit? Often, folk don't like to discuss their problems – at least not immediately.

The weekend arrived. Apart from occasional toddler noises, upstairs had remained quiet. Allowing his good neighbour intentions to overcome his perception of the English wish for privacy, he walked up the steps and knocked, calling out reassuringly, 'It's only Jim.'

The door was opened promptly. Susan stood there holding her son's hand. 'Come in,' she urged. 'It's cold.' Hearing Jim's voice Mick emerged from the bathroom.

Jim was embarrassed, he had listened to too much village gossip. Remembering that Mick was good with engines he found an excuse.

'My old car is giving trouble again! I need it for work - no transport at night. Could you take a look at it? '

'Certainly,' responded Mick, 'I'll come down tomorrow. Is around ten OK?'

'That's fine,' said a relieved Jim. He stepped carefully over Damien - who was making engine noises as he played with a bright red, toy car - and let himself out.

* * * * *

Representatives of the clubs and societies, who jointly formed the trustees, were duly convened. During a rambling speech, in which the details could barely be discerned, and in which he didn't stop or seek comment, merely meandering on and allowing nobody a word in edgeways, justifying and rejustifying what he'd already proposed, Hamish fed them his plan. Frustrated, Chris, as secretary, seized a gap in the interminable dialogue and suggested moving onto item two of the agenda. Their chairman barely reacted, continuing to repeat that it was a sound plan and they needed to move ahead. No mention was made about where the cash was to come from, and nobody asked.

Afterwards, the working group remained behind to be advised that: 'Everybody agrees, so we can appoint the contractor.' It was an example of filibustering at its best.

Harriet shook her head in wonder, 'But Hamish, we don't have the money. It's not reasonable to commit the villagers to such a massive debt. I, for one, can't support this.'

Following her uncharacteristic outburst an awkward silence descended on the proceedings – in England, nobody spoke up in this way, and rarely did the baron cease talking long enough to provide an opportunity.

Alan took up the issue, 'One of the trustees, I won't say who, has already expressed the same concern to me.'

'Typical,' ranted Hamish, and shrugged his shoulders, 'when they sit here they say nothing, - only mention it privately.' Then he calmed down. 'Very well, you may as well know. I'm going to fund it – provided it's not more than…' and he nominated a figure which when added to the expected grant covered the likely full cost…'but I'm not happy with the central heating proposal, I'll work that out myself.'

Quite what was intended remained unclear. Alan wondered if their chairman knew - Hamish had, after all, repeatedly stated that his background was in marketing and publicity - but, as a generous offer had been made without which nothing could be done, he decided to hold his peace.

'I'll pay the contractor direct,' Hamish rambled on. He turned to Chris, 'Come round tomorrow at 6pm and bring the grant stuff so I can finish it off.' He looked around the expectant faces, 'I don't want this around the village. Just put 'anonymous' in the minutes.' His flow ceased for a moment, but began anew as he selected a bottle of good wine from three on the table, uncorked it expertly and poured the rich, ruby liquid into pewter tankards which he had brought along in an old, cardboard shoe box. 'Drink up,' he admonished, 'its cold out there!'

*   *   *   *   *

Wearing gloves, Inspector McAlister examined the items that the parish council had collected during their litter pick, but he wasn't optimistic about discovering anything that might be relevant. Their bombastic chairman, David, had come up with the idea that Jane had relayed to him, and he wasn't a man one could easily refuse. The empty envelopes appeared to have blown away when the household refuse bins were collected; as far as he could decipher the writing they were all village addresses but none related to anybody likely to have been involved. The bracelet and gloves he put aside - did these belong to the corpse? Many women carried gloves and most wore some sort of jewellery. Perhaps an owner could be identified. He noticed that the bus pass was valid for the year of the incident, but otherwise it was water damaged and illegible; placing it in a plastic bag he decided to ask the forensic experts if there was an address, number or name on it.

*   *   *   *   *

Some days later Alan received an e-mail from Chris asking that he check a proposed draft of the minutes, which he admitted: 'Had been difficult to write.' The note concluded with a date for completing the renovation and a brief description of the work to be done. This was a relief to Alan. The scope had always remained undefined but, as the baron was footing most of the bill, he couldn't see much point in trying to assess whether or not it represented value for money.

After about three weeks Chris phoned; he had organised for a shipping container to be placed in the car park, into which items belonging to the scouts like tents and camp beds; the bowls club – the short mat and woods; the badminton club's net and stands, and so on, could be placed while the work was done. He needed help to carry the items out and sweep up afterwards. Alan obliged and learnt that the existing stage would go and be replaced at the opposite end by a large, wooden cupboard in which each user organisation would have a lockable section for their exclusive use; the badminton court was to be relocated and remarked, and the floor varnished; a new boiler with additional radiators would be installed; double glazing fitted into all windows, and the internal walls repainted - though the colour was still the subject of a disagreement between the badminton players and the other users - one advocating a light shade against which it was easier to see the shuttlecock, the rest favouring a darker covering that wouldn't show the dirt.

On his customary daily walk Alan bumped into some of the long serving trustees who were out with their dogs, conversation turned immediately to the hall. 'I feel sorry for Chris,' said one. 'He produces a good agenda and tries to keep our meetings under control, but Hamish just ignores him. It must be most annoying. Still,' she continued, 'we did agree with his proposal that the hall should only aim to break even, and that, rather than increase our subscriptions to build up funds, each group should recruit more members and organise an annual event whose proceeds can go towards a capital reserve.'

'Maintenance is needed,' added her companion, 'and things do go wrong, but the income from outside bookings and the monthly draw – to which the majority of villagers contribute – only just covers the costs. Hence, we all have to do more.'

'Yes,' said Alan, wondering if he'd been at the same meeting. Whilst what he'd just heard was eminently sensible, nothing similar had come up during the two hours they'd been sitting together around the big table. 'Things in villages get done by a sort of osmosis,' he concluded. Maybe Hamish's methods were smarter than he had realised.

* * * * *

White frost covered the pavement and long icicles hung from guttering. While Robert waited for the two youths he pushed mitten protected fingers further into greatcoat pockets, stamping his feet to keep the circulation

221

moving. It was 9am on Saturday morning and unpleasantly cold.

They arrived exactly on time, both having realised that the ex-bobby's offer was their last chance. They had grasped the fact that Robert no longer solely represented authority, understanding that he was involved in a wider, more personal way. He appeared to provide the stern, but caring father figure they both had lacked.

'Good lads!' he acknowledged, handing them each a black bin bag, a pair of plastic gloves and a litter picking stick. 'The council want us to do some more rubbish collecting.' Thinking, 'It's not long been done, but does get bad quickly along the through route.' He looked over his two charges; they were inadequately dressed and palely shivering. 'At least it will keep us warm!'

Robert took a set for himself and led them out towards the main road, 'We'll do this first – it's the worst area. Dave, you and me will take this side. Sam, get across there and we'll work our way all along. Take care near the edge – them cars come by at well over the speed limit.'

The two friends had said nothing, just following like sheep. Suddenly, Dave came to life, 'I heard they covered this bit only recent like,' he announced. 'Why do we have to do it again?'

Robert wore his patience on his sleeve, he didn't command, only explained. 'You're right, but people throw drink tins and fast food boxes out of their cars all the time. Disgraceful, I think. Anyways, winter – when the grass has died back - is the best time to see it all.'

Dave, slightly surprised to be treated as a rational person, acknowledged the facts. 'I see,' he said, adding, 'That's a disgusting habit.'

Sam just wanted to get on with the job, 'Let's crack on,' he suggested. 'I'm shivering.'

As the frost began to thaw the verges changed from firm to unpleasantly wet, and the trainers the youths were wearing became soaked. It added to their misery, but they daren't complain.

Robert was proven correct. Beer cans lay everywhere, some crushed underfoot others intact and shiny, many with their contents still inside.

'What a mess!' exclaimed Robert to himself as he smelt the stale ale lager from the tin he was emptying.

'What's that?' queried Sam, half hearing and assuming he was being criticised. 'I'm doing my bit. There's not so much over here.'

Between passing cars Robert explained what he'd mumbled, setting Sam immediately at ease. After another unprovoked incident, he realised that the big youth was unusually touchy and wondered whether he had something on his mind.

Back at the hall's car park the semi-retired policeman placed the three full sacks alongside a row of plastic bins, from where the district council had assured him they would be collected by their rubbish truck as part of its usual Monday round.

'It's only been two hours today,' said Robert, 'just the road and playing field. More next Saturday when we'll also do some hedge trimming. Meet me again, same time same place.'

'Can we go now?' asked Dave in an unusually contrite manner.

'Thank you both, yes,' agreed Robert, who wanted to ensure that the youths were treated as volunteers rather than penitents.

Dave rushed off quickly, but Sam lingered, he seemed about to say something. Robert leant towards him in anticipation, his breath forming a white cloud in the still air.

'There's something I need to get off my chest. You won't shout at me, will you? I haven't dared tell nobody else.'

The old policeman smiled, 'Of course not.'

'It's like this. I fell out with Eddy. He got mad, said I'd end up in the stream if I wasn't careful. At the time it meant nothing, but later, when we heard about the body, I wondered if he'd done it – otherwise, why say such a thing. I've avoided him ever since.'

'Can you remember when that was?' asked Robert.

'It were the summer before last, but I don't know exactly when. Late on I think.'

'Did you know that I've joined the enquiry team?'

'I did,' acknowledged Sam. 'Sorry it took so long, but until you came along I had nobody I could talk to – my dad would just have hit me, said it was all my fault, and that I shouldn't have had no argument with Eddy.'

* * * * *

Constable Brown was lounging in the reporting box toasting his bare feet by the fan heater; it was almost as cold inside as outside, where sleet was lashing against the single small window. A series of knocks disturbed his reverie. He stood up, slipped on his boots - it might be McAlister - and opened the door slowly. Outside was a stooping, anorak clad figure, its hood pulled well down over the face.

'Let me come in,' a female voice requested. Brown stepped aside and allowed the unidentified caller to enter. 'Please shut the door,' she continued, 'I don't want anybody to know that I've been here.'

'How can I help?' asked Brown, adding, 'won't you take a seat.'

The woman sat down reluctantly on a wooden bench against the wall and opened her coat a little, 'It's a bit better in here,' she remarked. 'You know about the poem?'

Brown, searched his memory, 'You mean the one in the magazine?'

'Yes, that's it. My mother, who has been at Phoenix House a long time, wrote it. One of the residents has been talking in their sleep, mentioning the same things everyday- they generally have an afternoon nap in the lounge. Old people often ramble and nobody takes any notice but this one becomes almost hysterical and talks about 'being sorry they fell out, not meaning to strike so hard, not meaning to kill' – it's quite explicit. Other residents cautioned my mum not to get involved or tell the owners. In order not to annoy them - she has to live there full time - Mum decided to answer the appeal in the magazine by sending in the poem which - she tells me - contains clues that lead to the person I mentioned. Mum has always been good at crosswords and puzzles of all sorts. She reckoned that the police would have acted by now – it's almost three weeks since it was posted. Worried that it may not have reached you, or not been understood, she asked me to tell you direct.'

The speaker stopped and Brown gathered there would be no more.

'Inspector McAlister realised it was a genuine lead and has been working on it. How far he has progressed I am unable to say. Your evidence is very valuable and we thank you for coming in on such a miserable day. Tell your mum that it will be followed up. Before you leave, I must make a note of your name and address, and a way of contacting you discretely if it becomes necessary. We won't approach your mother; assure her that she will be allowed to remain incognito. She

224

will not be needed as a witness.'

After the brief interview Brown began to wonder if he had promised too much, but knew a lot was at stake; he only hoped that McAlister would see it that way.

* * * * *

Since deciding to leave the parish council Mrs Cecil had not spent much time at the manor. When she was there the days were spent liasing with her son in their joint effort to convert the disused Home Farm buildings into a residential development. Their original ideas had not progressed well. Shottle district council's planning and heritage officers, although extensively consulted, and with a competent architect representing the family, always seemed to find fault with their applications.

The latest difficulty had arisen over the pigsty. It was an ugly, long disused, two- storey, concrete building with a rusting, corrugated steel roof, which they wanted to replace with a large, stone faced, thatched house. This attractive improvement had been refused because the sty was an existing farm building right on the village 'confines line' and as such it could not be demolished, only converted. Mrs Cecil was well adapted to a changed world in which the lady of the manor, despite acting as the nominal guardian and benefactor to villagers whose predecessors had provided her family's wealth, could no longer do much as she pleased. Yet, for her, the convoluted planning system was petty and unhelpful. As she put it to Dot, 'I really can't stand this silly palaver and all those bothersome, rule bound people.'

The problem dragged on, partly because her son no longer had his heart in it, but also because Mrs Cecil refused to compromise and wouldn't accept what she considered to be utter nonsense. At length, the architect arranged a joint meeting between Mrs Cecil, herself and the council's head of planning. After a long discussion it was agreed to leave the pig sty in place and resubmit the rest of the scheme. On the positive side was a strong letter of support from the parish council and no real opposition from nearby residents.

The weather had been poor and, while she was away, a length of the perimeter wall collapsed onto the road. This had resulted in a phone call from Jane to the Lake District, and a request that the old lady quickly arrange for a further unstable length to be pulled down before it fell onto a child or passer-by. Mrs Cecil knew that these walls, though apparently of solid, natural stone, were just skins in-filled with soil and liable to burst if heavy rain penetrated the capping. How she wished the major was still there to deal with it all! With assistance from a local builder she managed to get it fixed from afar, receiving a nice thank you letter from the clerk in return. It confirmed her earlier judgement that the new councillors were, once again, 'people like us', and that she had been correct to let them get on with it without any need for constant supervision.

To her way of thinking, a shadow had fallen across Denton Cheney soon after that awful morning when the dead person had been discovered. One couldn't pin point the change, or name it, it was a matter of attitude. Certainty and predictability – once taken for granted in this rural hamlet - had turned into caution and an irrational fear of the unknown. Perhaps the villagers were nurturing a criminal in their midst? Despite early police attempts to portray the incident as a routine lost person enquiry, it was apparent to all that some sort of violence had taken place, but what? With no known motive, uninformed opinion turned to the idea of a possible serial killer or psychopath who might strike again in an unpredictable way. It was an angle that the red tops returned to at regular intervals when real news was in short supply, one which only served to fan the flames of more lurid imaginations.

When Mrs Cecil did visit the manor she observed small changes in the residents' behaviour, things that people who never left the village probably wouldn't notice. Fewer people walked their dogs, and those that did rarely ventured beyond the buildings; the village hall was almost unused; the guides and scouts suspended until further notice; residents drove to friends' dinner parties when previously they would have walked; little groups collected on street corners and were often seen in the post office; parents both took and collected their children from the primary school; situated in a dark part of the village, the 'Fox' lost evening custom and those who persevered rarely left alone. Overall, a siege mentality had gradually taken hold. Yes, it was winter now – a season when there was always less activity - but even allowing for that, the villagers had noticeably modified their habits. It was, she recalled, a bit like living in Germany after the Nazis took over - an insidious change for the worse as private terror steadily infected the population.

Because information about progress remained scant, and no end appeared in sight, Mrs Cecil became impatient. Going to the top she called Inspector McAlister, expecting to be put straight through. When the telephonist heard such a confident, well modulated voice, her wish was granted and the inspector had no prior warning.

'What is happening in this body case? I want to know,' she demanded, aggressively coming to the point.

The inspector had met this bluff, thick set, upper class lady before, he knew she was formidable, not one to tangle with. He also recalled that a friendship with the chief constable was talked about - something he could well believe.

'There's not much I can add to what's been in the papers, Ma'am,' he stated, buying time, but well aware that his answer would prove inadequate.

'Not much? Let me hear it anyway.'

'Well Ma'am, be assured that I do relate to the uncomfortable situation that has arisen in the villages. You know, I'm sure, that we have been pursuing the DNA testing scheme. I'll be frank. Detective Superintendent Chan and Inspector Patel reviewed our work and endorsed what we had already been doing. It was they who helped push through the costly DNA scheme, on the basis that there is no alternative way forward. I believe such an intrusive programme will eventually flush out the murderer who, we all agree, must have a local connection.'

'I see. It's all about sticking to one's professional judgement, staying positive and not being sidetracked - a solid British approach. Good luck,' said the lady of the manor, 'you will need it.'

McAlister relaxed, his promotion prospects were on the mend. He knew it was crucial to stay on the right side of those who wielded power and influence through class or appointment.

* * * * *

'Newspapers, magazines, leaflets, glass bottles and jars!' The word sequence had a natural rhythm, thought Brenda, like the street cries of old one felt an urge to shout them out. It echoed the calls of the itinerant rag and bone men she recalled from her childhood, and the unforgettable, but chilling, one from the plague years: 'Bring out your dead.' Yet, it was only the district council's list for that Monday's recycling box.

Household collection had recently been organised into a fortnightly scheme - garden waste one week, household waste the next, a green and black bin respectively. As a district councillor she was pleased to find feedback indicated that the system had, except in summer, worked quite well. In very hot weather the two week wait could lead to unpleasant smells, while for those with large gardens, and no storage, their grass cuttings mounted up too rapidly. Apart from these problems, which the council had decided to discount, the villagers, in what was predominantly a rural area, had welcomed the system.

Brenda realised that the UK lagged well behind Europe in the introduction of recycling; on holiday recently in France and Spain this had been all too apparent. She felt ashamed that a country which used to take a lead in social reform had fallen so far behind its neighbours. The issue had been well debated by her own council, during which she pointed out that further public education and more publicity were essential. Among her constituents she had observed a natural, in-built resistance to change, especially in the smaller, more isolated communities. Yet, it was this very refusal to acknowledge progress, and a certain pride in the past, that contributed towards making villages attractive places in which to live.

Brenda saw her main duty as giving the district's small settlements protection against overdevelopment and their residents a deciding voice in what they wanted to be built or not built within their own parish. Some sort of 'localisation act' was essential.

* * * * *

'It's busy countryside around here,' noted Robert as he and McAlister walked slowly along Glebe Lane and back into Denton Cheney. They had taken a quick visit to the crime scene, hoping to be rewarded with a flash of inspiration in what had become a frustrating investigation.

'Yes,' agreed McAlister, 'and town folk – like me - have no real understanding of how it all works, how it holds together socially, how it adapts and continues through the generations.'

Robert beamed, 'That poem well summed up our intuition so far. The reference to land – it's all around us.' He gestured with both hands. 'Acres, hectares, whatever - the bedrock of any farming district. Own the soil and you own the people – hence the French and Russian revolutions.'

'You are well read!' said the Scotsman. 'Yes, the reason for most long term problems can be obtained by a close study of history. You've convinced me that it probably is all about land – greed mixed with heredity, rights and responsibilities. 'Who does it all belong to?' pondered the inspector.

'The short answer is that, for most of it, only the present owners and their families will know. Why? Well, the Land Registry Act is quite recent – it dates from the fifties, only land changing hands after that time needs to be officially recorded. The Registry is aimed primarily at house building – so the buyer can make sure that the seller really has legal title to the plot. If you identify an exact street address you can look it up on the Registry's website – for a fee, of course. One can also ask the Registry about ownership of specific areas of farming land which, if it has changed hands recently, they can advise. Unfortunately most rural land is privately held and stays in the same family for generations – often in a nominee trust, there's no change of owner and hence no public record.'

'Nevertheless,' said McAlister, pursing his lips, 'ownership could provide a motive. Land and its usage is what this country is all about.' He paused, 'Come to think of it, isn't this whole area slated for development? Such an expected huge increase in value could lead to a difference of opinion on when, or whether, to sell, perhaps resulting in jealousy, blackmail or corruption?'

'Indeed,' Robert agreed, 'I've checked out all the options taken out on farmland around the village, but must confess that none have rung any bells.'

'Our walk and chat has pushed me back to that elusive local connection.' McAlister continued, 'I've some new information. A woman from Denton Cheney called in to see Brown. She claims that her mother - who is resident in the village care home - heard another incumbent become deranged and talk wildly about 'not meaning to kill' someone. Reluctant to become a whistleblower her mum composed the poem you mentioned and sent it to the magazine, confident that we would find the person concerned by solving the clues it contains.'

'Wow,' was all Robert could manage. 'Apart from the land bit we haven't unravelled it at all!'

'The mother has asked to remain unnamed, which we must respect. She was born in Denton Cheney and her whole life is here; she doesn't want to suffer any recrimination for giving the culprit away. How to proceed? I suggest we organise an urgent meeting with the Phoenix House residents. We must attempt to trigger particular memories, and hope the person accused panics and breaks down. Have you a better idea?'

'I'm of the same mind,' said Robert. 'Let me organise it, I know some of the residents quite well.'

* * * * *

Amita took the call. 'Surely you don't suspect anyone here of being involved?' she protested. 'Most of them never leave.'

'No, no,' laughed Robert, in his good natured way. 'I know that Inspector McAlister and PCSO Sheena have already interviewed the residents, but that was a long time ago. Mr McAlister and I would like to see them again. It's about their recollection of long past events.'

'Some have become rather vague,' responded Amita, pointing out the problems of senility very discretely. 'Can I suggest something? It could be more productive to address them as a group, that way one may prompt another.'

'Advice accepted,' was the reply. It was exactly what Robert wanted. 'Can you assemble them in the lounge – no television please – at say, 2pm today?'

'I can,' confirmed Amita. 'We will expect you then.'

The residents, the majority of whom were women, sat in their favourite armchairs. In defiance of the grumbles, Amita had rearranged them to point away from the television – the usual focal point – towards the empty fireplace where the policemen placed two upright carvers which they had carried in from the adjacent dining room. Low winter sun illuminated the full height side windows, giving the rather threadbare lounge a warm glow, but emphasising the grey pallor and deeply lined faces of its occupants.

Anesh explained why the police had returned. 'Mr McAlister, who is being helped by Robert from the village, is short of local background, typical things about the village and its people - old disputes, past acrimonies, apocryphal happenings - that sort of thing. Our guests believe that you, as long time locals - many of you born here - might recall something which could help them.' He turned to the inspector. 'It's better if you move closer and all join together. I'll ask Ellen to repeat and 'translate' your points sentence by sentence - if you don't mind.'

McAlister didn't; he realised that having the most forthcoming incumbent as intermediary could help draw out people who had formed a community of their own, one which greeted those from the outside world with suspicion, regarding them as intruders.   In order to break the ice, Robert began by apologising for the setting resembling a scene from a denouement by Monsieur Poirot, which brought a ripple of laughter. It told him that most of those present could hear and had, at least, listened. Then, he handed over to the inspector who formulated his queries with a dry, but precise voice before allowing Ellen to rephrase them.

Aided by cups of tea all round, conversation began to flow. Family disgraces and disputes were recalled, and intriguing stories - half fact, half fiction - once again saw the light of day. After an hour, Anesh indicated that, like the sunlight, the residents' concentration was fading. McAlister, polite as always, deferred to the owner, gave his thanks and called it a day.

McAlister had taken notes, more as a reminder than a record of fact. Robert had just let the words flow over him, seemingly remote from the

231

task in hand. Although the inspector found it difficult to follow the harsh local accent, especially when used by the women, only occasionally had he sought any clarification.

As they left the village Robert suddenly braked hard, allowing a large black and white bird with a startling red crest to clear the car's bonnet.

'Pheasant,' he announced.

'You are knowledgeable about the countryside,' said McAlister admiringly, 'but I always understood such a game bird to be brown.'

'Usually, they are, but a villager, Henry, has introduced overseas breeds and that's one.'

McAlister became quiet, thinking, 'We failed to cause an incident, failed to get a confession. Perhaps we have no choice but to ask the informer for a name?'

'Somebody mentioned the Don family,' pondered Robert. 'The village hall caretaker who left was a Don - June Don. 'The last line of that poem - 'It's mid-summer again'. Mid-summer is June! '

'Well done, Robert! It fits. It's a matter of getting on the right wavelength with word puzzles. I can see another piece now. Don is a Spanish word. 'The main' could refer to the Spanish Main. It should have had a capital letter - but all the letters were capitals.' McAlister became upbeat, 'This June Don can only be the one at the home. We have our prime suspect but still need the proof.'

*　*　*　*　*

It was a brittle morning. Overnight snow had banked up on the window ledge, putting a felt around his thoughts. On such occasions the world became suddenly small, his mind inhibited; it could look only inwards towards the past, to events he regretted and couldn't change, but which always made him sad. Away from the compulsive tonic of daily work he had time to realise his good fortune in having had good parenting. Now he could admire his mother. Suspecting her son had ability she transferred him to a better primary school. Later, she encouraged him to sit for an open scholarship at the region's public day school, for him it had felt like fun rather than a stressful experience. Now he had children of his own he realised how well his parents must have managed that particular ordeal.

Mothers are special, especially to boys. While at university his mum had avoided telling him she was having a hysterectomy, insisting to his father that her son shouldn't break off his term to visit her in hospital. The worst event of Alan's life had been while he was living overseas when his father had informed him by airmail – there were no trunk lines then – that his wife had been diagnosed with inoperable lung cancer. For weeks he couldn't take it in. His brain refused to acknowledge the awful inevitability and he immersed himself in work, trying hard not to imagine how such a condemned person must feel. Yet, his mother wrote a cheerful aerogram note to say that Dad had taken her to visit the hospice into which she would eventually be accepted, adding that the staff were pleasant and the buildings very nice. For him the whole long range experience was awful. He had offered to come home, at least to talk face to face before it became too late, but his mother had issued an agonising, 'no' – she didn't want him to see her now, only to remember her as she once was. His father advised that the patient was always right and they must respect her wishes, but it was hard and against his instincts.

After such melancholy early morning thoughts Alan had been glad to get some physical exercise in the wintry, yet featureless countryside. Suddenly, a dark brown shape moved against the frozen, all white background; it appeared to have a hump – no, two. Alan knew the area was sandy because Denton Cheney straddled a glacial river bed. This geological fact was evidenced by the large number of wells, now disused after a mains water supply had reached the village. But, this was impossible - it had never been a desert!

As he approached, the unmistakeable odour of camel proved that, even after a liquid lunch at the 'Fox', he wasn't fantasising. Behind a leafless hedge two dromedaries were munching contentedly away at a pile of fresh hay. They paused momentarily to glance at him, in their typically haughty manner, before continuing to chew. Decorated, wooden caravans stood near by - the owner's name just about visible in faded paint.

During the afternoon's wandering he noticed that the five horses and their later companions – two bad tempered, braying donkeys – were no longer in the paddock, and that Fiona's caravan, complete with its jarring red curtains, had vanished. On the way back he caught up with a heavily coated figure draped in a multicoloured head scarf. It was a woman; she turned towards him sadly for empathy, observing, 'Them horses have gone.'

'Probably only temporary,' he suggested. 'Taken inside?'

'No,' was the certain response, 'gone – had a row with the landowner.'

'Shame,' commented Alan, 'I'll miss them.'

'Yes, but it'll save me money. I used to buy carrots for them,' she explained ruefully.

'Even the cut off world of Denton Cheney changes,' he thought. 'But so does everything. It's just that during our short lives we don't expect it and are surprised, when we really shouldn't be. 'Cheers,' he mumbled.

Damp breath hung in dry air as he walked on over a thin, patchy covering of brilliant snow, but the sun was setting and the temperature dropped rapidly; home beckoned. It was time for a return to gas central heating and television.

At first, Carol pooh-poohed his story, but enquiries established that Viner's circus had over wintered in this farm at the edge of the village for many seasons. Apparently, they used to own more animals - including an elephant – but new regulations had reduced their menagerie to this pair of old camels which were now more household pets than sawdust ring performers.

*   *   *   *   *

For the regular, year round walker Denton Cheney provided several, different non-repeating loops; Bill knew them all. When Alan had first met him, the ex-sergeant major revealed that he needed two artificial hips; one of them was to replace an earlier substitute which was showing too much movement. Alan wondered if the problem had been caused by all that drill, but guessed the damage was more likely to have arisen from excessive football or rugby in his youth. In need of regular exercise Bill had worked out the exact length of every route and could bring them to mind in an instant. He'd done it so that, after each operation, he could slowly increase his walking distance and provide an exact record for the surgical team.

Always cheerful, and always alone, the old soldier unfailingly did his circuits, never complaining about the year and a half waiting times he had been forced to endure under the National Health Scheme. Despite his problems, and slender means, Bill remained a gentleman. The latest replacement had upset his balance, forcing him to retire as lead player and chairman of the indoor, short mat bowls club. This he did regret, having discovered, late in life, that he was rather good, and had a mantelpiece of trophies to prove it.

But what am I saying? The problems of advancing years affect all of those who are lucky - or perhaps unlucky - enough to live through them. Identifying further individual villagers might be hurtful, so I will continue this discourse without naming the actual people involved - otherwise, they could be reminded that others see them in a humiliating state of unavoidable decline.

*   *   *   *   *

Soon after their arrival in Denton Cheney, Alan and Carol had attended several Conservative association events. One of these, now long defunct occasions, was an annual summer fete held in the delightful gardens of yet another of the village's grand stone houses; it had allowed them to meet and recognise a number of locals. Since these 'does' were open to all and sundry - who treated them as a good afternoon out - those present represented a cross section of rural life, from the very old to the very young. Given happy memories of vital residents in 'T' shirts and cotton dresses it was chastening, years later, to see the self same people in a much less healthy state.

One, who had retired from the intelligence branch of the foreign office, remained fixed in Alan's memory as a bright man with an engaging mind. This ex-civil servant who had joked, seemingly out of character, about the attractive legs of their host's French wife - he lady had been flattered - could now to be seen struggling around the narrow lanes with a huge, old dog of indeterminate pedigree. His handsome, white haired head was permanently bent towards one shoulder and his back fixed into a stoop which served to induce a pronounced limp and shuffling steps. On being greeted he could manage but a flicker of interest and a few faintly forced words which Alan usually failed to catch, resorting to smiling and nodding, feeling uncomfortable and hoping he'd got it right. This prematurely old man still managed to circumnavigate the village in the morning and evening, come rain or shine – his dog ensured that commitment. Alan wondered what he did during the rest of the long day, and how his wife was coping.

The tall, well turned out senior had every appearance of being from the Edwardian age of affluent, middle class professionals; perhaps it was the expensive hat that gave him away. Alan had first noticed him soon after moving in - while he was unpacking tea chests by the big window upstairs. Keeping out of sight – we British don't approve of prying neighbours – he saw stiff, laboured steps and a robotic bearing as the man mechanically turned to cross the quiet cul-de-sac. The routine was repeated at the same time on alternate days and Alan came to expect it. When Carol discovered it was their neighbour - who was totally blind, it explained his observation, filling him with both respect and sorrow. Over a few years the short outings declined in frequency, finally ceasing when the arrival of an early morning ambulance added another resourceful widow to those that already surrounded them – in the village widowers were in a minority.

Alan had little to do with next door, but he couldn't avoid observing how well women took these unfortunate accidents of life. They appeared better reconciled to accepting the insignificant, short life span of humans; somehow, deep inside, they believed themselves an essential part of something bigger, something permanent. Perhaps it was the joy of being able to produce children, an inner satisfaction derived from knowing that your genes were being passed on and would continue eternally via the offspring you had conceived and nurtured. This philosophical calm was something men could never relate to, they wanted to leave a legacy, make some sort of permanent imprint on the world.

'I've given up running the rugby club now,' announced the man with an emphasis on the 'now', and the hint of a hidden reason that Alan was expected to grasp without the need for further explanation. It was inherent in the statement that no further details would be forthcoming. But he didn't understand and imagined the cause must centre on some sort of unpleasant power struggle within the club, the minutiae of which, as a newcomer, he was unaware. With the exception of short spells working in Australia and Africa his unnamed acquaintance had spent his whole life in Denton Cheney. This was the same man, Alan later discovered who, prompted by the death of a favourite aunt had sought donations towards researching and writing the modern history of the village; in it he had traced families and buildings back to the advent of photography. The success of the resulting little book had led directly to the founding of the Denton Cheney historical society.

Days later a villager, stopped Alan and made a point of telling him that the local author had recently been diagnosed as having Parkinson's disease, it was obvious that his ignorance had been noticed and an intermediary despatched to bring him up to date. Alan reflected that this quiet, third party way of passing on bad news provided a good illustration of the refined social ways of close knit village society.

You should have no doubt that Alan's sensitivity to the health problems of his friends and acquaintances mirrors the hard wired decency of English people. I have the utmost respect for the stoicism and courage with which the villagers - and humanity in general - face up to their mental and physical problems.

* * * * *

McAlister was in his office quietly rereading Mick's statement; he was fairly sure that the wallet had belonged to the deceased - it was on the stream bank close to where the body was found the stuck in the reeds. Mick's recollections fixed the latest date of death; he was due within the hour for an informal interview with himself and Robert. The old rural policeman had proven a useful calming agent when dealing with villagers - they respected him, and he spoke their language. He was pleased that Chan had persuaded him to bring Robert into the enquiry.

The oilskin had been sent off to the laboratory for testing but McAlister doubted that anything useful would be revealed on such a surface after so long. He had already found the assailant - who was safely at the care home - but for a conviction to be obtained proof was required, proof he didn't yet have.

On the pretext of thanking her for organising their visit at short notice he called Amita. 'Hello, this is McAlister. We appreciated your help the other day.'

'It seemed to go well,' commented Amita, 'at least there was no disturbance. They were very quiet - trying to help, I think. Was it of any use to you?'

'In police work we can never be sure,' answered the inspector, 'it's all about collecting information and painting a picture. Sometimes little things assume importance days, even weeks later.'

'I understand, I expect you need a lot of patience.'

'We do!' agreed McAlister. 'While I've caught you, one query. I understand that the village hall caretaker checked into your home for a rest; would that be a Mrs June Don?'

'That's right, June Don - she's not married. We've had elderly villagers do this before, picks them up to be looked after for a while. Then they go home and are able to take care of themselves once more. I shouldn't say this, but June is unlikely to do that. She's deteriorated rapidly since joining us - something's gone terribly wrong.'

'You mean physically?' asked McAlister.

'We have a close relationship with the surgery at Denton; Doctor Otto has attended her several times already. It's not physical - June's as strong as an ox. She regularly rambles on, mumbling to herself, becoming agitated, shouting out, repeating phrases, clearly in some sort of mental anguish. A few residents say they can follow what she says but I've never managed it - the rural accent doesn't help. I was pleased she didn't make a fuss when you and Robert came round. I'm surmising, but it might have been because she would have known Robert when he was the village bobby.'

'You may need her to be seen by a mental health specialist. A transfer to hospital seems the likely end result,' postulated McAlister

'I am afraid so. Doctor Otto is arranging for such a check up. It's a

238

big concern for Anesh and me. We don't want her problems to affect our other residents.'

'You're doing what's best for her. These things happen,' said the inspector reassuringly. 'Nobody should blame Phoenix House. Thanks again. I'll let you get on.

*   *   *   *   *

'I'm sorry we needed to ask you in again,' McAlister began, sitting opposite Mick at a small table. 'On my right is Robert, someone, I'm certain, you already know. Please understand, I don't for one moment think you were involved in that death.'

'Good,' said Mick, 'but aren't you going to charge me with stealing the money?'

'Before we come to that I need to ask if you are still in possession of any of the bank notes? '

'I did check before I left home. The short answer is, no. As a farm worker I'm not well off. Susan can't work - she has to look after Damien, who like all small children, is expensive. The money came in very useful to set him up with all the essentials. I was stupid. I shouldn't have kept the cash, should have handed it in. I feel so bad about it all. Sue is disappointed in me, which is the worst of it. Maybe, it's 'out of character', as they say, but I did it, now I deserve the consequences. Can we pay it back - slowly that is?'

Brown entered carrying three steaming mugs of tea, one without milk for Robert - who had a dairy products allergy.

'You've shown remorse. You did own up - better late than never.' McAlister continued, 'Never mind. I just thought that there might be traces of DNA or fingerprints on them. I'm short of evidence to build a credible case. Returning to your earlier point - no, we are not going to charge you with anything.'

Mick showed immediate signs of relief. 'That's marvellous news. Can I phone Sue - she has been so worried?'

'You can - as soon as we're finished,' agreed McAlister with a smile. 'You may be wondering why. I will explain. The money almost certainly

239

belonged to the unidentified dead body who appears to have neither family nor friends; despite massive publicity nobody has come forward to claim it. The cash will not be missed. There seems little point in using expensive public resources to pursue a case which would result, at worst, in a suspended sentence. I will check with the Crown Prosecution Service but cannot see them raising any objection.'

Robert liked Mick and was pleased with the interview. He considered it was a fair result.

*   *   *   *   *

The demise of the parish council's former chairman prompted Auberon to suggest his mother might now reconsider her decision to resign. She disagreed. 'Things have settled down in the village,' she announced, adding, 'Anyway, I'm getting too old to contribute much. I need to spend more time on this development of ours and looking after my sister in the Lake District.'

Her loss was accepted with regret, but she could not be dissuaded. This left the council two short but with its necessary quorum of six. David checked the rules. The vacant positions had to be advertised on the parish council notice board and, if there were more than two applicants, an election - which would be managed by the district council - must be held. As their chairman, David volunteered to approach a short list of suitable villagers. A salesman by trade he soon persuaded Patrick and, to balance him with a woman, the president of the women's institute, Emma, was prevailed upon to join. The councillors found both acceptable and no further candidates came forward.

District councillor, Brenda, was keen to deal with the reformed council, she suggested they support the development of a 'parish plan' - this was something government had been promoting through the Countryside Agency. She proposed forming a separate working committee which would include one council member to act as a link. This group would collect the guidance notes, do a house to house survey asking villagers how they wanted Denton Cheney to look in twenty years time and draw up a detailed, but pragmatic 'wish list' of proposed actions for their council to implement. In order to make the result credible, and hence useful, it was important that input from a majority of residents was achieved.

Emma volunteered her services, which was a relief to the rest, and Patrick suggested that his seventeen year old daughter Sian, who had already worked with Brenda, would make a useful assistant before leaving for university in the autumn. A grant was obtained and, over a three month period, the raw data collected for collation. Finally, a concise document was produced - based on an above eighty percent household response rate. The plan set out a list of twenty or so necessary actions together with residents' replies to a series of crucial questions, such as: 'Do you want your village to remain a village separate from the town and other villages?' On this vital point there was an overwhelming 'yes', thus handing the parish council a democratic mandate to resist unwanted or inappropriate development and mass housing. A similar majority wanted Denton Cheney to keep its rural character by retaining the surrounding parish as an area of farming land

* * * * *

After Jane advised that only four plots remained unsold in the parish council's burial ground, an urgent meeting was convened with members of the parochial church council in order to agree a way forward.

It was a chilly day in the old churchyard when, dressed in warm headgear, thick anoraks and overcoats, David and Jeff discussed the problem with the vicar, Laura and Mrs Oldham. Jeff suggested that a monument free area, close to the church, be reused under the 'fifty year rule' – which was acceptable provided no living relatives objected. He pointed out that, as the council owned no land, acquiring a new area somewhere in the parish would take time, need money and was by no means certain.

The vicar wasn't too sure, but Mrs Oldham had checked the regulations and agreed that this was the most promising, and perhaps only way forward. She considered that, with demand for sites at only two a year, it was inappropriate to set aside a new field remote from St James. Jeff advised that two ancient graves would need moving when the proposed extension went ahead, so the problem of disturbance had anyway to be addressed. The elderly clergyman confirmed that his was only a fill-in posting before retirement, but promised to check with his diocese. Although a further appointment was unlikely in the near future - there were simply insufficient people in training to cover all the positions – he felt it important that the Church quickly find a workable solution.

At the following council meeting, prompted by the graveyard issue, Jane related a macabre story. While at the supermarket check-out she was approached by a stranger.

'You're the clerk at Denton Cheney, aren't you?' was the statement.

'Yes,' she had agreed, placing her shopping on the belt and wondering what was coming next in such a public place. The woman advised her that at a recent funeral the sexton had opened up a grave at St James in order to inter a wife beside her husband, but found, to their astonishment two women's bodies. The vicar and close family were in total shock and disarray. The mourners had to wait in the churchyard while a vacant plot was identified and a new grave dug so that a proper burial could be completed. When asked, the previous clerk advised that the records were muddled which meant that the extra body in the opened grave remained unidentified, as did the whereabouts of the husband. The lady asked if Jane, whom she knew to be competent, could assist in resolving the mystery, but, after careful checking, the new clerk could only confirm that there were indeed no proper records.

The new councillors were reminded by their clerk that, apart from the burial ground and paying her wages, they were also responsible for such things as the street lights; village green; grass mowing; seats; litter bins; the old village pound; the war memorial; any surviving trusts for the poor (of which there were two); the main bus shelter; trees and playing field, and empowered to recover any costs relating to them through the annual levy - or precept.

Patrick's experience in starting up the magazine led him to advise that he was getting more than sufficient material. He recommended increasing the sheets from an initial four to twelve, and to continue issuing it quarterly. The councillors were delighted to see his enthusiasm, and pleased they had someone with the skills to produce it so attractively and economically. An informal survey had discovered that the response from villagers was positive – a majority relied on it to keep them informed about past and future village events. Despite the increase in printing costs councillors decided to stick with a policy of no advertising as they felt it would detract from the content. At a stiff, A5 size, the magazine went through letter boxes easily, making it popular with the volunteers who delivered it.

As the months passed the number of vociferous critics – still known as the Taliban - who had made a point of attending every public session, dwindled steadily and finally dispersed – perhaps because they always received a polite hearing and any points raised were properly recorded and considered by the council. When it became indisputable that the 'new lot' - even though they didn't qualify as 'old villagers'- were working in an open, even handed way and in the interest of a majority of residents, there was no longer any point in going along simply to antagonise them.

Encouragingly, as time passed, previously unseen residents called in to listen and discover how things worked, while 'old villagers' either made sensible observations or asked about issues which the informative magazine might have overlooked. Growing public support from the usual 'silent majority' allowed the council to cease being defensive, giving it time and space to look ahead and plan ways in which a neglected Denton Cheney could be improved.

* * * * *

The inspector called in his team, with Robert, for a confidential briefing.

'What we are about to discus must remain within this group,' he began. There were nods and serious looks from the assembled officers who were aware that the 'body case' had, at last, moved forward. 'To sum up: We can now pin a name and address on the murderer but not the victim, but lack a convincing case to put before a jury.

So, what is still needed and how do we go about getting it?' A few of those present indicated that they wanted to contribute. 'I'm pleased to see you're still keen - even after all those months of work. Nevertheless, I am so sure that I'm going to tell you.' He paused. 'Our prime suspect is a woman - Ms June Don - who until recently worked as caretaker at the village hall. I need to find out more about her- any family; past life; education; friends and enemies; age; income; property; everything. As Robert is of similar age and has lived and worked in Denton Cheney as a rural policeman he is best placed to follow this up. Alright Robert?'

'Certainly, I can handle that. How long do I have?'

'Three weeks at most,' replied the leader. 'I'm aiming to wrap this up in about a month and take a spring holiday. I've promised my wife a trip to Spain and there's no going back on that.'

'What else?' asked Sergeant Smith.

'A confession is essential, without it I doubt we can collect enough evidence. Leave that bit to me and Robert. Otherwise, anything at all about the victim - who she was, where she lived; how she came to be at the stream; why she was killed. All this should have been straightforward but has proven difficult. Of course, I may get information from the culprit but she has become unbalanced and I can't count on it. The victim is your responsibility Smith. A lead might be unearthed when forensic report on the bus pass found during the village litter pick, but it could have belonged to anybody.

'What about a motive?' asked Brown. 'We need a motive, surely.'

'That we have,' stated McAlister, 'remember the poem, 'It's all about land'.

'So those are the specifics. The rest is knocking on doors, talking to residents, observing and thinking - steady police work which always brings results. That's it, you can go home early tonight!'

CORUNDUM - SPRING

As the days became longer so Emily became heavier. Naturally athletic and slim of build, she didn't show it and, as a consequence, received very little sympathy from neighbours and friends - even Mum went on about how lucky her daughter was. Emily admitted to feeling physically fine but, whenever her thoughts turned to what was about to happen, an unwelcome realisation dawned that this was a voyage into the unknown, instantly making her tense and tearful. Yet, there was no bad news. The checks had all been positive, and 'baby' – not wishing to tempt fate she had declined to know the sex – was the right way up. Provided there was no activity five days before the due date, the birth was scheduled to take place 'at home', which meant in Dot's old, coach house flat.

A team of mid-wives, and mid-men, had been allocated, one of whom would attend the birth. The Polish lady whom she'd met – a mother herself - had been pleasant and reassuring, but the older generation argued that, for a first child, she would be better off in hospital. 'What if something went wrong,' they worried. Emily was all too aware of seemingly endless press reports about nasty bugs with funny names which the NHS had failed to eradicate from its wards, and didn't agree. Despite Aaron's nervousness she knew she would be more relaxed in familiar surroundings.

As the big day approached Aaron's mother became detached and remote, causing him to become more and more concerned, with only younger brother Joe to confide in, his imagination lacked any restraining influence. Worse, the midwife with the foreign accent had asked him to be present at the birth, insisting that his assistance was required. For him the whole event had acquired an air of unreality and he couldn't force himself to think beyond the ever looming date. Having seen a baby calf born in a field, he was aware how much the cow had suffered, but remembered more vividly the tenderness and bonding when the mother nudged her offspring to its feet and began to lick it clean. That cow was big and strong, whereas his Emily was so slight. Nevertheless - he had to admit it - she was ready, and had become totally composed. For this steadfastness he admired her even more. Having taken up the only offer of remunerative employment – which was at Fiona's estate agents, mornings only - he worried constantly about how he would support them all.

Then it happened. 'Aaron, Aaron! Call that number! I'm going into labour. My contractions have begun.' Ashen faced he tapped out the figures on his mother's mobile, getting them wrong in his haste and having to start again. Emily smiled calmly at him,

'It's alright; this may take hours yet.'

'She's coming right away,' Aaron relayed the information with a sense of relief. He'd read accounts of apparently nerveless fathers delivering their babies unaided in cars at the roadside because the ambulance was stuck in traffic, but knew that, if the midwife was delayed, he would be unable to cope. Conveniently, the baby was only two days overdue and they could remain 'at home'. He wouldn't be given the added difficulty of a long cold night in hospital.

'Tell my mum,' said Emily, 'luckily it's a Saturday and she's not at work.'

With the supporting cast and equipment all assembled the tense wait began. Baby finally emerged at about six pm. It was big, at eight pounds six ounces, and healthy with a thick thatch of black hair. Aaron noted

246

that babies were still announced in the more traditional pounds, rather than the kilograms he had been wrestling with at school. Emily was exhausted but, when the newborn was handed to her, she glowed. Aaron had remained in the background doing jobs as instructed. Although birth might be taking place every second all around the world, for him it was both a shocking and amazing experience. Afterwards, somewhat ashamed, he dashed off into the toilet to be violently sick. When he returned the women laughed, but in a kindly way, and he realised that he had just become an adult, one of them - a teenager no longer.

While the midwife reported back to base, his mother-in-law showed Aaron how to make up bottles in case her daughter found breast feeding a problem. The phone call became prolonged and Emily learnt that the tools for clearing baby's nasal passages, if necessary, had been mislaid - another member of the team was supposed to have brought them but failed to arrive. The midwife was upset and very relieved that there had been no problem, she apologised profusely. Emily simply couldn't find the energy to feel dismayed - she had a beautiful daughter and was recovering rapidly. Her mum, however, was more detached and became angry about an incompetence which might have been life threatening, deciding to follow it up with the hospital as soon as she got home.

*　*　*　*　*

Business was slow now that the post office was closed. Ibrahim didn't mind, he was nearly sixty five and his state pension was soon due. There were some benefits. He had moved their second television into the area where the GPO counter had once been and, sitting on his favourite high stool behind the till, was enjoying the final test match at Lords – England against Pakistan. Sunny had always liked cricket but, in the past, had usually been too busy to see much, now, with the door propped open and cooled by a delightful breeze, he had time to concentrate on it, time to appreciate the finer points.

Ibrahim was concerned about how his regulars would cope. The parish council had responded positively, using their much improved magazine to seek support for a major letter writing protest while, at the same time, floating ideas about how the service could best be maintained. Councillors had also investigated the availability of government's official options, which were either to provide a part time postmaster for one or two days a week based at the pub or village hall, or supply a fully equipped visiting bus - a service already available in more remote parts of the county. However, as with so many of New Labour's schemes, Denton Cheney didn't meet the necessary criteria which were set out in the usual 'tick the box' list; he wondered if anywhere did. The villagers - annoyed that they were being abandoned, either accepted that there was a post office at nearby Denton or were too apathetic to have an opinion. Such polarisation meant that no organised campaign became viable.

There was an unexpected hitch in arranging Ayesha's ceremony and the whole process had kept Shiva so occupied that Ibrahim had been obliged to run the shop almost single handed. He said he could manage – he could, but he did find it lonely. Apparently, a 'special wedding licence' was needed. His immediate, ill considered reaction had been that it was because they were from the subcontinent and the authorities now labelled all such people as terrorists. The prejudice he had endured during his early days in the UK came flooding back to slant his thoughts.

Shiva sought to reassure him that the issue was only about where one lived. She had spoken to the vicar who had consulted the ecclesiastical authorities. A lot of tedious forms needed to be completed but she was assured that, subject to the betrothed being satisfactorily interviewed by him, the young people would be accepted. It was explained to her that, being from another parish, John didn't qualify. However, even though Ayesha wasn't a practising Christian and, being in full time education, was deemed to be living elsewhere, permission could still be granted because her parents had lived in the village for more than twenty years – hence the special licence thing. When her husband learnt that such a dispensation dated back to Henry the Eighth, and heard that the young couple would receive a finely written, paper scroll - which set the date for early June - he became fascinated by the historical connection and proud to have been officially accepted as an Englishman.

Brother Ismail arrived and was immediately impressed with the higgledy-piggledy, ancient, stone built village, basking, sleepily under a hot summer sun; never before had he seen such luxuriant green growth. The wild life caught his wife Moona's attention: 'So many small birds, and all with their own individual songs. Back in India we see only squawking crows and silent vultures circling high above the Parsee 'place of the dead' on Malabar Hill.'

After the standard marriage ceremony, at which Mum and Moona wore their brightest silk saris, the newlyweds lead their families and guests in a colourful procession that wended its way slowly towards a huge marquee set up in one of the village's two central fields. Fortunately, the grass was dry underfoot and Farmer Jones had diligently removed any remaining animal droppings. The villagers came out in force to witness the happy scene. Against a background of church bells, cheers of approval rang out as the bride, in a traditional long, white dress, passed their vantage points. Many had watched Ayesha grow up and knew her as a polite, attractive young lady who had assisted in the shop at weekends. A cash bar was provided and, to serve its inevitable result, mobile 'luxury' toilets had been stationed on the grass close by. Caterers were carefully selected and the wedding feast had an oriental flavour - except for the sweet which was a very English 'summer pudding'. After the customary photographs, socialising and dancing continued until it grew dark, at which time the happy couple departed in a shower of confetti, bound for a hotel in the Cotswolds.

Ibrahim felt a great sense of relief – his only daughter was married. He was well aware that the English - compared with some nationalities he could think off - usually made good, faithful husbands. It gave him confidence that this union would last.

His brother admitted to liking the social stability and prevalent attitude in the UK, having felt accepted from the moment he arrived. 'You know, if we'd visited years ago I would have been hard pressed not to join you. Now the bank has transferred us to Mumbai – still Bombay to you Brits - we've become part of a prosperous middle class and the future looks bright. To move at our time of life would no longer be worthwhile. We're very glad we came, and wish you both a successful retirement with new interests. It's rewarding to see you so well settled – part of the fabric. We found it difficult to understand why you insisted, for so long, on finding an Indian husband when back home those out of date traditions are already in decline – and rightly so. But you asked, and it was our duty to try.'

'I was so wrong,' admitted Ibrahim, who grimaced and hung his head. 'Off you go. Keep in touch. I'll try hard to get into that new interest thing once we've retired.' Moona was sceptical, 'Promise?' she insisted.

* * * * *

Emma discovered that Mike had just received application forms for a possible grant towards new playground equipment. He phoned to ask if, in her role as leader of the 'friends of the school', she could take responsibility for organising the required 'launch and celebrate' item. Since many of the members were also in the Women's Institute, she saw little difficulty in obtaining support for something the village mums all considered a worthwhile goal. Most of the parents had spent hours pushing their children on the swings or roundabout, where 'faster and higher' were always the commands. Later, as the youngsters grew in stature and physical strength, they had helped them up the steps of the pedestal slide, only to watch when they faltered at the top, turning back into the safety of their mother's arms, but willing to be lifted onto the steep part and slide a few feet to the end.

The concept behind modern play equipment was one of providing an element of risk which youngsters slowly learnt to manage. When sufficient confidence had been built up the child could obtain a rewarding thrill by carrying out an activity on their own while still being watched over by a parent or sibling. In case of misjudgement they would be protected from injury by a properly engineered impact surround of poured rubber or tree bark. The village's existing play items, although unimaginative, remained serviceable and could be retained. Councillors had seen more adventurous designs at playgrounds elsewhere which they knew their own offspring, or grandchildren, had both liked and benefited from.

The WI members had long been in favour of installing seats. How many times had they been there when the grass was either too damp or too cold to sit on, but were desperate for a rest while the kids continued to run around and burn up their energy? They also supported landscaping and the planting of trees and shrubs to enhance the area and make it into an attractive venue for the whole community. Emma resolved to pass on these wishes to Mike and encourage him to make them part of a long term, overall plan that the parish council could approve.

Presidency of the joint Dunton and Denton Cheney Women's Institute continued to absorb most of Emma's spare time. Fortunately, their meetings were always close to those of the parish council. It meant one hectic week each month but at least left the remaining days free to fit in grandchildren, essential visits to older family members, and her one indulgence. Strangely, for a couple living about as far from the sea as was possible, Ray and Emma owned a thirty foot, Bermuda rigged keelboat which lay moored at a non tidal marina in one of the east coast's many river estuaries. Her husband had been introduced to the sport as a lad when crewing for his father in a wooden, clinker built National 12 dinghy. While they were working, sailing provided a stimulating weekend escape; in retirement, it had become a serious, full time summer pastime.

Given a need to consider safety afloat - which had led to the purchase of a life raft, floatation suits, flares, a radio and a safety beacon - the dangers of water had become uppermost in Ray's mind. The likelihood of an adult drowning in a brook no more than two feet deep puzzled him, surely it could only be explained by some sort of foul play. The police appeared not to have reached such an obvious conclusion, he wondered why. There must be something going on that the village wasn't being made aware of. Perhaps a serial killer was on the loose and they were expecting him to strike again. After talking it over with his wife they suspended the long country walks they enjoyed so much in the warmer weather, deciding not to venture beyond the village confines until this crime had been solved and an arrest made.

Of a kindly nature Emma found it easy to agree with the opinions of others, readily settling into a cautious way of life. At the parish council, although refreshingly diligent in reading and responding to the e-mails that members circulated in order to secure an electronic consensus on which Jane would then be authorised to act, she lacked the resolve to veto anything that was self evidently bad for the village as a whole, preferring to sit on the fence. Such a hesitant approach to problem solving had, in Alan's opinion, slowly become a national way of life. It was engendered by political leadership whose style of administration was a charade – lots of consultation and discussion was disguising a dearth of principle and a reluctance to do things that were in the long term interests of the majority. This day to day, indecisive management at the top had become accepted as the way to handle policy at all levels, especially in local government where a concentration on reports containing thousands of words, but which never led to any useful action, was the standard pattern. It left those who liked to get results, or prevent stupid things from happening, tearing out their hair in frustration.

Alan didn't hold government's attitudes against Emma and other councillors but considered the United Kingdom was badly in need of a whole new political direction. Unfortunately, he couldn't identify anybody – like, say, the emerging Senator Obama in the USA – who might provide leadership based on common decency, principle and real achievement.

*　*　*　*　*

It was mid morning and Robert, Smith and McAlister were drinking coffee and eating Danish pastries at a table in the rather bare police canteen.

'Have you anything for me?' asked the inspector.

'On the suspect,' Robert began, 'records show that June has an elder sister called May - we can guess in which months they were born - and no brothers. Her parents farmed in Barnswell - where Aaron's partner, young Emily hails from. June was born in the town's original Barrett maternity home in 1934. Educated at the village school, she went to the secondary at Wellford but left early in order to help her father on the land. June appears to have remained with her parents until they died, and never married. Her sister was more academic - passing the eleven plus, attending the girls' high school in town and going on to have an independent life as a nurse in London. Like June, May also remained single. Ownership of the farm and other land holdings appears to have been incorporated into a trust with the parents and children as the only trustees.'

'Useful background,' commented McAlister, one can see big differences in their personalities and room for disagreement over the land income. Can you find out what shares each of them had?'

'I'll try,' offered Robert.

'Now Smith, what have you got?'

'Robert has already covered May, so I will pick up on other lines of our enquiry. The bus pass has been examined; we were nearly lucky - it is in the name of Don but without a legible first name. I'm trying to trace it through the bus company's central records but nothing thus far. The bracelet is a common, silver plated type which could be bought at the Saturday market; it carries no name or inscription. The envelopes have rain damaged village addresses but none are relevant - they probably blew away when the bins were collected. The laboratory advises that none of the finds carried DNA or finger prints.'

'Let me know soonest if you get anything on the pass,' urged McAlister.

Smith continued, 'Aaron, who Robert mentioned, has started a job in town and came into see me - he didn't think that Brown was much use, but told me that Eddy - that twenty something lay-about and suspected drugs dealer - had threatened Sam - he's the lanky youth with an ASBO, and had ended up saying something like, 'Or you'll end up in the stream.' Aaron's story has been corroborated by information passed on to me by Robert - he's trying to help Sam and has gained his confidence. Eddy's warning was given back in summer, a year ago. Aaron was there and mentioned it to his new wife who urged him to report it to the police. He couldn't fix an exact date, but knew it was just before the longest day – which was, of course, June 21. That fixes the latest possible date of May's death.'

'Why so long coming forward?' asked McAlister.

'Aaron's frightened of Eddy - thinks he may have been involved, wanted us to keep the information a secret in case of reprisals against his family. I persuaded him that we had to check it out and offered protection if needed.'

'Oh dear,' commented the senior man.

'This Eddy had already given his DNA – he volunteered - but none was found on the body. We had him in and, to get his confidence, told him he wasn't a suspect. During questioning he remembered using such words, but admitted he was only putting on an act to impress the younger boys.'

'So how did he know?'

'Ah, Eddy was reticent about that. He says he was out for a stroll by the canal and noticed the clothing. Realising it was a dead person he decided, in view of his known association with criminals, that it was wiser to say nothing.

'Do you believe him?' queried Robert.

'All things considered, I do.'

*　*　*　*　*

Between meetings council chairman David worked hard to develop a constructive working relationship with the police. His efforts had been bolstered by Sheena's appointment as PCSO and later, by the request for cooperation from the investigation team. Sheena had provided some welcome local continuity while the county force was being endlessly reorganised at central government's behest.

Modern cars have become fast, relatively cheap, and with generous credit, easy to obtain. This caused a big increase in traffic 'rat running' through Denton Cheney - especially during the morning and evening rush hours - creating a potentially dangerous situation. Following a series of complaints, David, employing every bit of his bulldog tenacity, persuaded the police mobile camera team to attend during the critical times over a three week period. Results showed that a majority of motorists exceeded the 30mph speed limit, with many timed at above 40mph. As this was a trial period warning letters, rather than fines, were issued. The problem was proven, and the chair followed up by organising teams of volunteers to use a speed gun at different times of the day in order to obtain a more comprehensive picture. Many, including Mrs Oldham - who thought it was akin to spying on one's neighbours - were not supportive. David prevailed and the results indicated a pressing need for action.

Some councillors favoured doing nothing since any restraint would lead to 'urbanisation' – they thought in particular of 'speed bumps' which had been employed extensively in the town's Victorian streets, but were unpopular with both residents and the emergency services. As parish council decisions needed to be passed by a majority – but were preferably unanimous - discussion about the best way forward had continued for many months. 'Repeater' signs to flash a warning if one was over the limit were suggested by the police, except that the working part would be detachable and shared with six other parishes throughout the year. Jeff and others felt that, while this was a start, some sort of physical restriction – or 'calming' - was essential at the two worst locations. This could be a mini roundabout; a road narrowing with one way priority, or a chicane – any one of which would force motorists to slow down. Finally, after seeing rough budgets for each option, the council opted for a simple narrowing of kerbs with a signed directional priority as the least intrusive and most cost effective solution.

The request was carried forward onto the county council's list of future road works, but with no commitment or target date. Jane suggested that lobbying was needed if the project was ever to become a reality. As a result, letters seeking support were sent to their county councillor and Member of Parliament. After about six months a promise to include the works in the following year's budget was obtained in writing; – it fitted with Jeff's observation that everything in local government took at least two years from request to implementation.

VASE, as part of its campaign to keep sand and gravel trucks out of the village had begun to keep a photographic record of all the overweight trucks – some with trailers – that regularly ended up lost or jammed in the narrow, winding lanes. A long list was soon compiled. The predominant reason given by drivers was an error in the route provided by their satellite navigation systems, which were either of poor quality or had failed to choose an alternative route because the village did not have an official 7.5ton weight restriction. Having identified the key problem the clerk applied for signs to be installed at the junctions of all the minor roads that led into Denton Cheney. More promises were received, but no action taken and no answer received to any follow up queries. The responsible officer was persuaded to attend a meeting at David's house, and following an unpleasant, tetchy confrontation, the best that could be obtained was a verbal commitment. Eighteen months later the direction signs were all in place, but the most important one - at the motorway turn off – remained unlit.

Jeff had found most local government officials to be pleasant and open, but lacking any motivation towards achieving an end result within a reasonable time frame. Having always worked in private enterprise he wondered how they ever obtained any satisfaction from their employment, but came to realise that the officers were part of a bureaucratic system, one which was, nearly always, beyond their personal control or influence. Local council positions evidently attracted the sort of indecisive personality that could tolerate such a mind numbing hierarchy.

*   *   *   *   *

The unruly, high pitched shouts of youngsters echoed around the hall. When Mike pushed open the door he was almost knocked over in the ensuing stampede. As part of the 'consultation with children and young people' required in order to satisfy criteria set by government in regard to the parish council's 'playmaker' grant application, he had managed to organise a twenty minute session with the scouts. It was the first time he'd been inside the building since completion of the upgrade and his immediate impression was one of brightness – the badminton group had triumphed – and uncluttered space; it was also noticeably warmer.

At scoutmaster Ray's urging the restive boys and girls settled down on the shiny floor and prepared to listen. Schooled by his wife, Mike had prepared a series of yes/no questions aimed at unearthing their preferences for alternative equipment from different manufacturers – designs needed to cover the basic functions of climbing, rotating and swinging. Finally, he asked what play items they had used elsewhere, and which ones they would like the council to buy. Surprisingly, this open question brought little original response, but the earlier points demonstrated clear preferences that could be compared with the results of consultations made with the school council and youth forum. Mike advised the scouts that, if the application was successful, he would talk to them again and try hard to incorporate their favoured choices.

The whole grant thing came about by chance. The reformed parish council had agreed to set aside an annual amount from its precept towards depreciation of the existing, rather old equipment at the playing field. The annual, independent safety report had recently condemned the roundabout and advised that the seesaw was nearing the end of its useful life. This left only the pedestal slide and a set of four swings in good working order. When members urged the immediate purchase of replacements, the council's 'community and environment' group hastened to produce an overall, long term plan aimed at making the area more attractive for the whole village. Their plan was adopted; it envisaged making progress by phases as savings became available from the precept, and had final completion targeted in seven years time.

Following an initial consultation with the suppliers of the present equipment - which had lasted for well over thirty years - the whole approach was accelerated when they were advised that government had recently launched a scheme of major grants. A set of criteria were hastily obtained and a quick read confirmed that Denton Cheney would be eligible. Although the closing date was barely eight weeks away, extensive consultation and community engagement were a mandatory condition. Mike dropped everything in order to concentrate on this application - it was too good an opportunity to forego. It would be competitive but deserved their best shot before the money ran out.

His visit to the scout troop was one result; another was a questionnaire, delivered to all village homes. The latter had sheets of separate 'tick the box' questions for children and their parents. It commenced by asking whether the existing play facilities were adequate, this received an almost unanimous 'no', thus confirming an 80% similar response when the parish plan was produced. A 'need' could be proven! Now, he could address the other key requirements, which included better access and an innovative choice of equipment for girls in the 8-13 age group.

Three quotations were obtained, and then, in the light of the various usage surveys, modified to meet majority views. The final layouts were placed on the council's website and set out in the spring edition of its magazine, with a single question: 'Which one would you like?' Response was encouraging and a clear favourite emerged to be included in the application form as their 'preferred contractor'. A project management team was nominated, a site survey completed, and letters of support from various village organisations attached to the text as 'supporting documents'. Mike was exhausted, but had the satisfaction of knowing that he'd done as thorough a proposal as possible in the limited time available. The 'playmaker' form was signed by Jane and submitted by e-mail to the county council.

An answer had been promised within three months. It was eagerly awaited by the villagers who had, by now, become enthusiastic about the project - in particular the plan to landscape the area, plant trees and provide picnic tables. Optimism had to be tempered by the knowledge that their application was one of many - not everybody would succeed. If Denton Cheney won, would the council receive the amount required to complete the whole project or only a part? Now began a tense period of waiting.

* * * * *

Frank hadn't set eyes on Laura for some time but was encouraged by their last encounter. A mutual attraction had been confirmed; he recognised it, even if she didn't. Laura had been friendly – very warm and friendly – until something had distracted her and a retreat was beaten. The absence of any contact only served to make him more certain that a 'relationship' - as they called it these days - had been cemented. It was like being at school again and finding it quite impossible to act normally with a girl one fancied; the result being that no progress was made. Sadly, the object of one's affection remained totally unaware that they were seen as attractive because their admirer was far to shy to let them know. Was this retiree love – puppy love under another guise? Frank was starting to feel desperate.

For Laura, the long interval had enabled her to rationalise the situation, which had been assisted by Martin's ever more distant persona and independent lifestyle. After retirement she had anticipated that he might take up golf, which would have allowed them to play together and socialise at the county club where she had been a lady member since the children left home. Laura wasn't a low handicap player and disliked the competitions which she thought brought out the worst traits in people's nature – all that falsifying of handicaps to gain an advantage in the Stableford point's events. It was an unwritten rule that nobody raised any objection, but she considered it hypocritical not to acknowledge what was, let's face it, cheating. As a result she played only with a small group of like minded friends, enjoying the exercise and challenge but without any pressure to score well and the fraught atmosphere of artificial politeness that obtained during serious rounds.

Left mostly on her own she lacked pleasant, like-minded male company, concluding that if maintaining a friendship with Frank required a need to indulge in the sexual side, then so be it. In a small, introverted village, opportunities for already married couples to engage in clandestine courting are few, but with both parties well disposed to finding a solution – albeit it unknown to each other - something was bound to happen.

*   *   *   *   *

It was now late February and the first lambs were already gambolling around the small field in which stood the black barn. Their frail bodies and white coats contrasting with its dark bulk as anxious ewes eyed an overpowering, grey sky, knowing there was still the chance of a significant snowfall. They were right. Soon after midnight Farmer Jones was out in a blizzard. He and son Chad manoeuvred the big trailer into where gangs of tiny lambs lay huddled together against the wall, seeking shelter from a cruel wind and frequent snow flurries. Offering little resistance they were scooped up in the glare of the tractor's headlights, two at a time, and placed, bleating, onto the trailer's straw lined floor. Their mothers watched in silence before accepting the status quo and following them reluctantly up the ramp.

'Shut it up,' shouted Jones. 'Let's get out of here while we still can.'

Come dawn, the new arrivals woke in a warm outhouse amidst a crowd of pregnant ewes; the villagers a little later, to find that nearly a foot of snow had obliterated the usual view and a dawning realisation that they might be cut off for a few days.

*   *   *   *   *

Martin phoned Laura; he was safe at a hostel in the hills where he had been on a group walking trip, but wouldn't be home for a couple of nights. Angela called her husband to advise that, although the weather wasn't too bad at her mother's house, she would stay on until the pavements were cleared and it was safe for Mum to walk unaided to the supermarket.

Marooned in the house Laura enjoyed the wintry landscape. She felt strangely exhilarated. Her small world was black or white, positive and well defined rather than grey and indecisive. Beyond the windows the village was pristine, beautiful and still, all the usual noises had been muffled. Feeling little inclination to go outside, and aware that the children would have a day off school, she decided to delay this adventure until later when the promised sun had broken through and the lanes would be full of high pitched voices, toboggans and snowmen. For the present, it was enough to sit in comfort, switch on the television and enjoy dramatic news coverage of this freak fall.

Then, a thought occurred; at the last Women's Institute meeting she remembered Angela mentioning that she was about to visit her mother. Realising that she would not now be returning, Laura wondered how Frank was coping, whether he had sufficient food in the house – men didn't deal with this sort of practical problem. A frisson of anticipation and excitement revitalised her. Perhaps she could go around and check. Yes, she would – first thing tomorrow morning.

Frank's house looked as if it was somewhere in the Alps. The surrounding firs were overloaded with snow, their branches bent low beneath its weight. Snow stretched from the big gate, unbroken and unmarked - apart from the track of some wild bird - right up to the porch, nobody had gone either in or out since the blizzard. On the top rail the name - Parley Pole - was almost obscured by a sparkling, white capping.

Laura hesitated; somehow it seemed intrusive to break the surface,

260

to mar the perfection of it all. Finally, she pushed the gate open. It was harder than expected owing to a deep drift which had accumulated behind it. Luckily, the soft white blanket failed to reach the top of her Wellingtons, by picking her knees up high and trying not to let the boots slip off, she managed to reach the front door. Her mission clear she took off a glove and pressed the button. In the hollows of the hallway the bell sounded strangely muted. Nothing was quite real today.

Frank appeared quickly. His welcome was matter of fact and without any awkwardness.

'Laura, glad to see you. Take those boots off. I'll get some slippers for you - they should fit. Angela is at her mum's.'

She banged off the wet slush and stepped into a pair of lamb's wool lined bootees. 'These are great!' she laughed, adding, 'Martin's away too.'

They'd exchanged crucial information without feeling in the least bit embarrassed. Often, when there's a common, unforeseen problem confronting them, people become less individual, less isolated, more of a group; Frank and Laura were no exception.

'Have you got provisions in?' she asked as they wandered into the kitchen. This time, the layout of the house was familiar, no longer restraining.

'Not a lot,' grinned Frank. 'Only what's already been organised for me, but that was on the basis of two nights away and it's going to be at least four!'

'I guessed as much,' smiled Laura as she unloaded her shopping bag. 'Look, here are a few meals for two, a pile of vegetables to go with them, some soup, butter and bread rolls. We should be fine.' Without intending it she'd said 'we,' had indicated she was staying, it all seemed so natural. 'What about a light lunch?' she continued. 'I haven't eaten since breakfast, and I'm not struggling back right now.'

'Great,' agreed Frank. 'Can I assist?'

Between them, they formed a natural team and had soon enjoyed a hot meal, scraped together from the contents of Frank's fridge and her basket. Afterwards, they sat facing each other at the kitchen table, the room unusually bright in reflected light from the snow covered garden.

With the radio tuned to desert island discs they felt like pioneers, alone in an inhospitable world, but one that was outside and unable to influence their relaxed joviality. Time passed quickly and, as the light finally faded it prompted another makeshift meal, this one concocted using the soup and a bowl of pasta with added fried bacon pieces and lots of Brussels sprouts. Frank opened a bottle of red Rioja wine.

Glasses in hand, they settled down to get a free, vicarious thrill by watching the nation's suffering on the television news; it wasn't good. Roads were blocked, power lines down, schools closed and trains disrupted, but the sight of well clad, happy youngsters in bright waterproofs and knitted, Balaklava helmets enjoying rides on hastily improvised sledges, warmed their hearts. It was a bit like going to the cinema - an uplifting escape from the reality of daily life. For Laura the only jarring note was the coffee mugs that Frank favoured. She had been on the W I's day trip to Windsor Castle when Angela had bought them, and still didn't like the shape.

Frank who, unlike Laura, hadn't thought through the further development of their friendship, began to feel uneasy; by now it was pitch black outside and eerily still. When was she going to go leave? He ventured to express his thoughts, even though it was the last thing he wanted to broach after such a pleasant day. 'Won't Martin be calling – he'll worry if you're not there?'

Laura fielded the question without demur. 'The answering machine is switched on, but he probably won't bother. We've never been a couple who phone each other every day, it seems pointless. I'll stay – if that's alright? I don't fancy going out again at night, and all that snow may be gone by morning – if the weather man is to be believed.'

Frank was cautious, but pleased. 'No problem,' he said. 'Let's take a look and see where's best.' Being with Laura had been easy - she didn't find problems, only solved them, enthusiastically.

They traipsed upstairs where Frank dramatically flung open every door on the landing and Laura made a show of inspecting their contents. Both found it fun - like exploring a strange, rented holiday home for the first time after arrival.

'This will do,' she pronounced decisively. The walls were painted

262

grey-blue, the bedspread, cushions and curtains all in matching pale blue, the fitted carpet and furnishings in mat white. The ambience was crisp and cool, not usually appropriate for winter, but today enhanced by a pale background of moonlight which seemed to have permeated the whole room. 'It's lovely,' Laura exclaimed, 'I'll leave the curtains open.'

'That's the one I usually use when Angela is away,' said Frank hesitantly.

'Never mind,' she continued unabashed, 'I need company. If not I'd may as well trudge back home.' Slightly intoxicated Laura threw herself onto the double bed. 'It's comfy. Tonight I'm staying right here.' Getting up again she went down the stairs and delved into her shopping bag, only to return with a pink toilet case and something that looked to Frank like a pair of pyjamas. 'Time for bed,' she announced, indicating that he should absent himself for a while.

Funnily enough Laura, the positive one, had found her mind full of questions and self doubt. She had no close family to confide in. After identifying a need to talk with somebody sensible, she chose Jane whom she knew was held in respect by the parish council; previously, they had discussed local events, never anything personal. Until recently she had considered Jane much too decent and practical to engage in gossip or give advice on affairs of the heart, but who else was there? At the very least, she could expect an honest answer.

Jane was a little surprised at Laura's visit – even though she had phoned to make an appointment – and had assumed it must be about a problem affecting Denton Cheney. When Laura explained her boredom and attraction to another, unnamed person, Jane was aghast, her reaction prompt.

'You'll ruin your marriage and maybe upset your children. It will all come out,' adding, in case of doubt, 'not from me, you must understand.'

Laura had anticipated something like this, but already knew it wouldn't cause her to deviate from the course she had embarked upon - though she really didn't understand why.

Frank knocked discretely on the bedroom door. He hadn't expected Laura to be so compliant, so casual about coming to this – Angela's – house, and getting into bed. It must have been preplanned – she'd even brought a book and her winter night wear.

'Don't be silly,' she scolded, 'it's your place not mine.' Frank entered wearing a hooded, woollen, Japanese dressing gown which was tied at the waist and reached to the floor, he'd found it very practical for cold mornings. Laura was sitting up on the left side of the bed absorbed in her book, away from home but completely at home. 'It's a bit chilly in here,' she remarked. 'Don't you have an electric blanket?'

'No,' he admitted, standing beside the bed, but feeling very uncomfortable. He and his wife had long ago ceased sleeping together and the presence of a live, attractive woman was unnerving. 'I'll get a hot water bottle - if you like.'

'I do like,' she commanded impishly.

Soon, Frank reappeared with two rubber hot water bottles. 'These are old but still serviceable,' he said. 'They've been in use since the war. Look, the blue one has got the utility kite printed on it.'

Laura accepted the pink one and pushed it down towards her feet. 'That's better – my toes are always cold.'

Once again, Frank stood awkwardly at the bedside, this time clutching his bottle.

'Get in,' ordered Laura, pulling back the sheet. 'I'm tired. One more chapter and that's it.'

He discarded the yukkata and climbed in. Although the loose fitting pyjama top disguised Laura's ample figure, he could see the curve of pink cleavage where a button was either missing or undone. His desire returned. Laura put her foot against his leg, 'See what I mean. It's a lack of circulation. Lights out!' she called out like the enthusiastic 'brown owl' she had once been.

Frank reached out towards the table lamp. When he turned back it was straight into contact with a topless Laura who pulled him down firmly against her warm body. Aroused, he knew what came next but remembered to check. 'Did you have that operation after Luke was born?'

'I did,' she confirmed, finding time to elaborate, 'he was a surprise,' as she tugged at the pyjama cord. 'There's nothing for you to worry about.'

Frank relaxed both physically and mentally, savouring this long missed, still wonderful sensation; attempting to make it last as long as possible he worked slowly back and forth. Suddenly, she jerked violently away, leaving him frustrated and disappointed.

'My feet are wet!' she shouted in shock. 'What's happened?'

'The bottle must have leaked,' he mumbled in a voice of utter despondency.

Laura laughed out aloud, then again, higher and higher. Soon, Frank joined in, and a hysterical gale of sound filled the silent world.

'I don't believe it!' he called out, 'I really don't.'

*　*　*　*　*

A silent line of men in dark, green garb stood along the top of a ridge which still bore the rotting remnants of the rape seed crop. Spaced out at about thirty yard intervals they waited patiently, fading into the grey-black, wintry background. It was the last day of January and the final shoot of the season. Nothing much seemed to be happening - perhaps the birds had all gone. Then, mixed groups of women and youths appeared at the edge of this huge field, heading steadily towards the summit beneath a weak evening sun which highlighted their pink hands and faces.

It still didn't look promising. The shotguns remained broken and lowered, the dogs at heel. Suddenly, that familiar whir of wings was followed by a series of soft putt, putts as two finely plumaged cock pheasants fell to ground. The beaters remained quiet but moved relentlessly forward. The remaining birds ran away from them over muddy ground but were finally panicked into flight. One led and the rest quickly followed, only to be met with a volley of shots as soft, feathered bodies collapsed to earth. The dogs had been restrained by helpers, but now, on a signal, they were released, scouring deep, earthen furrows to collect up the dead game. Within minutes the disciplined shoot was over.

The participants re-joined their families. With dogs leashed, and each carrying several plump carcasses, they assembled at the crest before heading down the slope as a long, silent crocodile. There were no exultant cries, only the quiet demeanour of folk who live on the land, bend to its seasons and enjoy a rare social event at a time when farm work is at its least demanding.

In Glebe Lane a row of pick-up trucks, Toyota Land Cruisers and other, well used, utilitarian vehicles awaited them. Behind one was a small, hand built, wooden trailer with four cross members from which hung, head down, the afternoon's harvest - lines of cock and hen pheasants, most with rings on their legs, and a few unlucky wood pigeons.

'How many is it?' asked one of the flat capped farmers.

'Total, sixty nine,' said Henry.

'Not bad. That makes five hundred and seventeen for this year - out of a thousand hatched.' Chad was keen on figures and had taken over the farm's accounts from his father. Jones himself never came to these events - he'd seen so many animals born he couldn't kill anything.

'It's been a good year, good shooting, good fun,' said Mick.

Soon, a convoy of dirty vehicles was moving slowly towards the farmhouse. Once there, the ruddy cheeked land owners and agricultural workers stood sipping mulled wine or light ale around a log fire that flamed and banged in the huge kitchen grate, discussing the chances of better commodity prices in the coming summer. They didn't linger, and, after collecting their dogs from the barn outside, were soon on the way home. Dusk was approaching; many had cows to milk, or beasts in the fields awaiting their evening feed. All too soon it would be lambing time again, and with it that familiar, twenty four hour a day slog.

As the light faded Jones came in, shedding his boiler suit in the porch. Only the organisers were left. Joan handed him a large mug of real coffee. 'That's better,' he announced, sitting in his favourite chair by the fire. Jones never drank, having copied his father who became a teetotaller when machinery replaced horses. He could still hear the old man's voice. 'This mechanical stuff's right tricky. You need to be fully in control of yerself.' Comfortable, he looked up and ventured a question, 'Good year?'

'Yes,' said Henry, 'we reached the national average on birds shot. About eighty percent were those we had reared and tagged. We don't trim their wings, but a lot still stayed in the area.'

'It's all that feeding what kept em ere!' Jones declared. 'What's it all cost then?' As a farmer he was always interested in the money.

'Break even, I reckon,' Henry continued, looking to see if Chad

266

disagreed - he didn't. 'But I need to sort out what our guests put in the jam jar. We used up four ton of wheat this time – that's the main outlay, and it's doubled in price since we began.'

'Aye,' nodded Jones, 'now we're out of the old European Union rules, that's what I'll be concentrating on growing next year.'

'Now Henry,' chipped in Joan, who knew how generous the chief organiser was, 'Make sure you're not out of pocket.'

Henry's response was simply to widen his eyes and smile – he wasn't about to change.

'And what about you Mick?' asked Jones. 'You've been having a right time of it - that we all know. None of us here ever felt you had owt to do with that body.'

'Well,' replied Mick. 'It wasn't good, but Sue had the worst of it.'

'The police came in droves to take you in, made you sign a statement, then called you back again,' said Chad, who didn't like authority. 'That was heavy handed. You should get a claims lawyer.'

'Now, now,' continued his father, 'young people watch too much telly - you live in a compensation culture. Don't forget that Mick here did take the cash, which was wrong. OK, it was understandable, and,' he added with a chuckle, 'I liked the bonus bit.' Mick blushed. 'Don't take on Mick – you're a good lad and I'm pleased to have you. Anyways, they didn't charge you with anything.'

'More changes tonight,' advised his wife. 'The vicar has taken Keith's advice to drop the fundraising for St Michael's room. He's nearly retired, so I don't expect he's sorry. I thought it was a great idea, but they're right – we're not going to get there. Overall, it's no bad thing. The village has other needs – like putting all the cables underground in the conservation area or a better playground for the kids, with trees and picnic tables - though the parish council seem to be getting on with that.'

'What about the money collected so far?' queried Mick.

'That will be kept and go towards a repair fund,' Joan explained. 'With so few churchgoers we need every penny to look after the building. Oh, and part may be given to that new village trust fund the parish council have set up – it has tax advantages and can only be spent on things that are for the benefit of all residents.'

'Nothing ventured, nothing gained,' agreed her husband, who looked meaningfully at his watch – it was only seven. 'Before we turn in, I need a couple of hours on the internet to bring my paperwork up to date. Goodnight all!'

A strong wind greeted Henry, Tim and Mick as they went out into the covered yard to collect their boots and waterproofs.

'Come on, Mick!' urged Tim as the former turned back, pulled the outer door open and called inside. 'Thanks for letting us use your land, Mr Jones. See you tomorrow.'

There was no response from within the thick stone walls where the farmer and his wife had already moved onto other tasks. Greeted only by silence, Mick hurried off down the gloomy track where two dark silhouettes could just be seen leaning into the weather.

*   *   *   *   *

Having had some construction experience Alan was leading the parish council's 'planning group'; this made recommendations to the district council on all proposed extensions or new developments within the parish; comments on government proposals for changing the planning system and on relevant long term strategic plans - an amazing number of thick volumes fell under the last two headings. No sooner had the school been fought off than Westminster decided to speed up the national rate of house building by designating two major growth regions, one of which was centred on the adjacent town. This 'white paper' was bad news, serving only to make official and encourage what was already happening.

The documents that formed separate parts of the new planning policy appeared to have been issued without interconnection, and by people or committees dissociated from reality; they were surely the work of thirty year olds at unnamed consultants, factual but without depth or perception. 'Consultation' was the mantra prescribed by government, but, after a considered look, it soon became evident that this was only a word, a box to be ticked off by the planners. 'Did you consult?' 'Yes'. The time and application required to provide sensible, locally relevant answers to the points raised was far beyond the majority of those who attempted to wade through these tomes.

Although it was confirmed Denton Cheney was one of very few parishes that always responded to the plans, there was rarely any evidence in the next issue that notice had been taken of even the planners' own policy recommendations. Delays to deadlines were typically explained away at briefings by: 'We will be unable to meet the final report date because the government office has asked for some changes.' The process was appallingly long, wasteful, repetitive and expensive, opening it up to manipulation by major developers with the time, money, expert advice and public relations consultants to deploy for intensive lobbying. Nevertheless, Alan concluded that the English system was still democratically based. Hence, it was crucial to get arguments against imposition of mass housing onto the official record - this being the only way to achieve any sort of commonsense protection for the village.

Yes, it was tedious and unrewarding, a repetitive, never ending task as the dates for document review and the finalising of planning policy slipped back year by year. Despite this Alan had decided to see it through – in particular to divert the town's 'preferred direction of growth' away from Denton Cheney by not allowing it to cross the nearby motorway. The requirement to be constantly vigilant was tiring, nothing related to planning ever seemed to be finalised - it was constantly in flux. In order to overcome the prevalent, unthinking NIMBY (not in my backyard) reaction, the system built in a presupposition in favour of the proposers of planning applications. Developers, but not objectors, could appeal to the Secretary of State, whose office was always likely to say 'yes' since government wanted the rate of house building to meet identified demand - or they could request a judicial review which, being legally based, invariably found in favour of the proposer who could always afford the better advocates.

As the dice became more and more loaded against any reasonable compromise, Alan knew he had little choice but to carry on, even though the parish council tended towards being disinterested and apathetic, content to just accept whatever happened – it was the detached English way. Alan was desperate to see a bit more 'get up and go'; of the members only David was supplying this, but in such abundance that it kept him motivated.

'Come in,' she called, but noticed immediately that her invitation had become redundant - the front door was already being eased gently open. It was common knowledge that Auntie Dot always left her house unlocked, though it was deemed polite to bang the brass knocker before looking in to see if she was around. A slightly bent but broad shouldered figure stooped to cross the threshold where it was immediately identified as someone she had known since she was a schoolgirl.

'Hello June,' she said, in a matter of fact voice. Hating abbreviations Dot always used a full name - felt you were entitled to it. Her visitor pushed both leaves of the stable door back into place and hesitated, seemingly seeking approval to proceed. 'Take the big chair,' she instructed, though the direction was unnecessary, the woman well knew which one was Dot's favourite.

'Alright, then Auntie?' she greeted the aging widow, who nodded slightly, as if to say, 'What a silly question – I always am.'

It was too early for afternoon tea so Dot seated herself opposite. They were hemmed in by the dominating, ever watchful photographs, some of which featured the villager as a young teenager.

'I've got something to tell you,' she began very slowly, wanting to check that Dot was listening, but hearing and attentiveness had never deserted 'Auntie'. It took only moments to assure her before gabbling out the seven words she had steeled herself to say.

'I done it Dot. It was me.'

That seemed to be it. To Dot's surprise the woman slumped forward, becoming smaller, shrinking into the high backed armchair, as if loose in her own skin.

'I know,' she confirmed gently, looking June straight in the eyes. Eyes which immediately became uncomfortable as they moved to focus on the snapshot of a village outing where Dot stood side by side with two girls; the children were in different school uniforms. The visitor got up and took it down from the shelf.

Dot watched her carefully. 'I haven't seen May for ages, but then she always was very independent - so that's no surprise. I don't suppose I'll

270

lay eyes on her again. Am I right?'

The hunched up figure remained silent for a few minutes, clutching the silver frame in trembling hands. Dot sat still, patient – during winter in the countryside, time wasn't allowed to press. At length, using the familiar form of address only her family and friends were allowed, she replied, 'Auntie, how did you find out?'

'I didn't,' she admitted, 'but the body had to be someone local. As time passed and the police got nowhere, I fell to thinking. One day it just came to me, no reason really. Of course I couldn't be sure, wouldn't anyway tell on one of my villagers. It wasn't till you came by today that I was certain.'

Dot had no fear, no concern that a murderer might be sitting only a few feet away in her best, chintz covered chair. To Dot, June was just an overgrown teenager still playing truant, this time from the care home. May, the elder by only a year, was a girl who kept to herself, intelligent and determinably independent, a spinster who left the village after qualifying as a nurse, never to return.

'You'd better turn yourself in,' advised Dot. June was calm, apparently far away, perhaps back along the tow path on that summer's day. 'Did you quarrel?' she ventured to ask.

'Yes, Auntie - May was always difficult. But, it's all over now. I can't live with it no more. That Constable Brown was good company, and I like Bob - he was a good old fashioned bobby, only doing a job, but always decent with it.'

'I've been here all the time,' announced the man in question, stepping out of the kitchen. I'm so sorry it ended the way it did.'

His words were stilled by a gentle click of the latch. The weary woman and her elderly confessor looked towards the door where, as if on cue, McAlister ghosted silently into view. Behind him, Brown took up position by the cottage's only entrance, whether to protect his boss or block the means of escape was a question nobody asked.

The dry Scotsman's sharp eyes flickered around the room like a serpent's tongue, missing nothing, before coming to rest on the photograph in June's lap. 'Ah,' he said in a soft voice, 'your sister, but taken in happier times.'

271

After a long moment of tension, June convulsed into sobs, her whole body racked with anguish. Robert looked on sympathetically. Dot turned away. McAlister and Brown moved silently closer. The latter sought direction from McAlister, who inclined his head towards the armchair.

'Come along old friend,' urged the young officer, helping June to her feet, putting an arm around her waist and guiding her towards the open door where a car was waiting to return her to Phoenix House. Robert followed a few steps behind in case he was needed, but could already see that it was unlikely.

The inspector watched dispassionately as they left. 'I believe you knew before I did,' he remarked to Dot with a certain amount of admiration.

'When your technical team came to make copies of my photographic memoirs, asking me to date them and identify all the people, it started me thinking,' she explained. 'It was then I reckoned it had to be someone with a local connection.'

'What did you make of that poem in the parish council magazine,' probed McAlister.

'It gave me goose bumps,' she replied. 'I do crosswords and immediately understood the references. It reinforced my suspicion. When I thought about it, the wording frightened me. I realised that someone else had reached the same conclusion. After that, I decided I must do something, but, as you've seen, I was reluctant to tell you. Stuck in my ways, I guess. The villagers are my life. It wasn't for me to report someone I've liked and known since she was a child. Did I do wrong?'

A slight smile played around McAlister's lips, 'Your loyalty is quite understandable.'

'Did the verse help?' Dot wondered.

'It did.'

Dot was persistent, 'So, who sent it in?'

'Someone who wants to remain incognito,' answered the policeman. 'I do appreciate your cooperation and patience in helping me set this up. When I learnt of her strong attachment to you I expected she would, sooner or later, find her way here - it's just across the road. Asking Amita to prompt June while she was in one of her calm periods worked well; it allowed us to be on hand to witness the critical confession. I have one more routine task and that is to take June to headquarters and make a formal charge. I will ask Amita to organise a day when the suspect is next in a stable state.

* * * * *

A few days later Amita called to advise Robert that Ms Don appeared to have regained composure and was almost her old self - June's confession seemed to have lifted an intolerable burden from her mind. Amita had consulted with Doctor Otto who considered it a temporary reprieve, recommending that McAlister call her in quickly before a further relapse. As a result Robert and Brown had collected June from Phoenix House. At police headquarters she was sitting comfortably in their smartest room.

'Can we get you anything?' queried McAlister.

'No thanks. Bob told me why you wanted me.'

'I am duty bound to remind you of your right to remain silent and to have your legal representative present,' continued the detective. 'Anything you say may be used as evidence.'

'That I understand. I don't need nobody.'

The inspector was disconcerted at how well she looked and spoke - compared with when he had first seen her, but knew it could only make his task easier.

'Then I'll proceed. I would like you to tell me - in your own words - what happened at the stream on that summer's day.'

There was a long silence, June seemed to be wrestling with a mind stuck between wanting to tell her story and the survival instinct to say nothing, the former won.

'It seems a long while back - like in another world. I wrote to my sister asking her to come over and discuss winding up the family trust which she controls. I was fed up with living on a small income in that awful room at the back of the hall, while land values round here have soared. We never got on - Dad always favoured May - and hadn't met or spoken in twenty years. Anyway, she agreed to come. I met her from the bus. The sun was shining so we walked across the fields. Ready to compromise, I suggested she give me a bigger share of the income from

273

the tenants rather than sell the land. She refused. As we continued along the tow path I became desperate, pressed her to sell and split the proceeds. She brushed the idea aside, turning towards me and shouting 'no way' in an aggressive manner. I flew into a rage, picked up a broken branch that was lying by my feet and hit her. May was always frail, she lost balance - that old foot injury may have done it - and fell in the stream. I must have passed out. All I remember is running back across the fields to the village. I hated her - so many times I asked for money but always the same intransigence. I didn't feel any need to go back and check what had happened, just somehow thought she would be alright. Didn't realise she was no more till I saw the newspaper headline...' Her words trailed away, but there was no obvious remorse, no tears.

Finally, McAlister spoke, 'June Don, I formally charge you with the murder of your sister May Don.'

In the silence that ensued the accused appeared distracted but remained calm; nobody moved.

'It's best if Robert and Brown take you straight back home,' said McAlister in a kindly voice.

* * * * *

The following afternoon McAlister assembled all the officers who had worked on the 'body in the stream' enquiry and brought them up to speed.

'My thanks for all your hard work. You will be pleased to hear that this case has been solved.' There were a few cheers amid a general air of relief. 'For the record I will read you my draft summary in an attempt to sum up the trail we followed.'

- *'A dead body was discovered by a dog lying in a stream by the canal towpath. The dog's owner - a villager - said, 'it seemed familiar' or words to that effect - I fail to see why. The Advertiser printed the finder's impression - based on the 'flat hat' - that it was a man. He was wrong - it was once common for country women to wear such headgear.*
- *The ground was hard baked after a dry spell, there were no footprints and nothing was found after a fingertip search. It's a*

remote area and no witnesses have come forward. There were no identification marks or personal items on the garments or body. The corpse had not been hidden or disturbed. Initial signs pointed to an accident. The features were somewhat damaged which precluded a photo identity. As a result thorough local house calls were organised which failed to discover any witness or anybody known to be missing. Signs of violence were noted. The autopsy concluded that they were made by a heavy blow which had led to death by drowning, and that there had been no attempt to drag the person out of the water. Forensic found no useful fingerprints or DNA on the body or clothing and no match in our records with the corpse's own DNA. The enquiry was upgraded from missing person to one of murder.

- The village isn't on any tourist route and there is no accommodation. Strangers from outside are rare; the main ones being holidaymakers on canal boats during the summer months. This angle was followed up, took a lot of time, but produced no results.

- We were stuck, so I recommended DNA testing of male residents within a ten mile radius. The chief constable was under pressure but reluctant to endorse such an expensive measure, instead she called in the Met to do an independent case review; this approved our methods, seconded the testing programme and added Robert to our team.

- Motive. At this stage I couldn't rule out a robber who had panicked and fled - most women carry something valuable - watch, jewellery, cash, credit card. The testing proceeded, but progress stalled until Mick came forward and told us he had taken a wallet - no doubt dropped during the attack - from the stream bank but hadn't noticed the body.

Then we got lucky. The strange poem was published in the parish council magazine. A person who wants to remain anonymous told us that someone at Phoenix House had written it because a resident had gone of their head and ranted on about having killed someone. Robert picked up the idea of a possible land ownership dispute which made us take the poem seriously and we managed to solve it. The name of the distressed resident, June Don, fitted the poem.

Although fairly sure we had the culprit and a motive - but not yet the victim's identity - we lacked the facts necessary to bring a case. A confession was the only way to back up the circumstantial evidence. How best to obtain it?

- The suspected killer's name enabled us to discover details of her background, family, and only sibling - May. Both sisters were unmarried. In order to put June under pressure and spark an admission, Robert and I, at short notice, addressed the residents in Phoenix House but with no immediate result.

- Robert found that June had a very close relationship with Dot Faulkner - known as 'Auntie' in the village - when she was a girl; we decided to capitalise on this. I sent our photographer to Dot's house, which is only yards from the care home, and he brought back a record of her snapshots of village people. Dot agreed to cooperate with Amita of Phoenix House who would suggest to June that she should pay a visit to her old friend 'Auntie' who would love to talk to her. Amita had noticed that June - in her more lucid periods - always preferred someone familiar to comfort her and Dot's house is only a short walk away. June responded. Amita alerted Dot and myself before guiding June over there. The rest, as they say, is history.

- The following scenario then became plausible: June wanted to sell the land holdings bequeathed them by their parents - who owned a large farm. Some of the land had considerably appreciated in value following the formation of the local 'development authority'. May, who had a controlling share, would not agree - it seems they never got on and hadn't communicated for years. June asked her to the village where she was caretaker at the hall, in order to talk it over face to face. May came - reluctantly, I imagine. Given lovely weather, they walked out towards where their holdings are located. They talked by the stream and a quarrel ensued. June became enraged over May's intransigence, lost her temper, picked

276

up a branch lying on the towpath and struck her sister a furious blow. May, who was fragile and has a damaged foot, lost balance, her oilskin wallet was dislodged into the grass and she fell unconscious into the stream - which is not deep but fast flowing. June probably fainted after realising the enormity of what she had done. When she came to there was no sign of her sister whom she had no wish to look for. Deciding to leave the area as fast as she could. June only discovered that she had killed May when she read the Advertiser's headline. Soon afterwards she went into mental decline, left the village hall working group, then, unable to cope or tell anybody, resigned her position as caretaker and checked into the care home for a rest, where her babbling gave her away.' McAlister looked up, 'Any questions?'

Smith had one this time. 'What about the various items found by the litter pick?'

'The bus pass was in the name Don, unfortunately, records showed it to be June Don. If it had been in May's name and found earlier it would have speeded up the enquiry. The other stuff was of no help,' added the inspector.

'What about that Eddy, where does he fit in?' asked Brown.

'Good point,' began McAlister.' He saw the clothes but didn't notice the wallet. Although aware it was a dead person he didn't want to report the finding because of his previous criminal record. The police were the last people he wanted to see. The knowledge stuck in his head and was used to threaten Sam; when Sam asked what it was all about he managed to avoid a direct answer.'

'Why did nobody miss May?' queried Robert.

'One wonders,' said McAlister. 'She was a retired recluse, who lived in a top floor flat in London. Her only neighbour said she often went away unexpectedly for long periods. She didn't communicate with her sister and had no known friends or other relatives. This sort of thing happens more often than the public thinks, it's a result of today's lonely big city world.'

There were no more questions and McAlister brought the meeting to a close.

'Like so many family crimes it's a sad story. Whilst I have some sympathy with the killer, it is our job to uphold the law of the land and flesh out a case to put to the Crown Prosecution Service. The recommended charge has to be one of murder.'

* * * * *

After a week or so of intense national publicity about 'the murder that had finally been solved', and a lot of gossip in the shop and at the 'Fox', the unpleasant incident, which had affected the villagers' whole way of life, passed rapidly into history. It allowed attention to focus once more on the threats to Denton Cheney, threats that had never gone away but been forced to play second fiddle to the understandably, more topical excitement and distraction caused by a faceless body in the stream.

The proposed sand extraction site was a prime example. In an attempt to speed up the snail's pace, planning approvals system, government's set of interlinked new documents had begun to be distributed for comment; predictably, introducing this change had become a painful process. In Jeff's opinion the increased paperwork was little different in content from its predecessor, except that in future public inquiries the inspector's brief limited him to adjudicating on a plan's 'soundness' - which could only be criticised if it had not been developed from an 'evidence based assessment of reasonable alternatives'. By comparison, the previous system had permitted protests of any sort from anybody, resulting in lengthy reviews dogged by ill thought out, even malicious objections and deliberate time wasting. In the meantime old, already approved plans still obtained. This was helpful in regard to the threatened sand extraction site since the first inspector had placed restrictions on its usage – like a long haul route avoiding Denton Cheney, and a need to control the water table. These requirements increased the commercial cost of winning the sand and made the site less viable, endorsing the parish council's strategy of trying to prevent it from being taken up by the aggregates industry.

The replacement documents had duly been issued and commented on by both Denton Cheney and Dunton parish councils in an attempt to force the county council to reconsider it as an 'allocated minerals

278

site'. A press campaign was followed by a public meeting at which their Member of Parliament had spoken strongly against a proposal that would downgrade the amenity of several thousand residents over a ten year period. He maintained that a site of greater capacity was available well away from any population, and argued that the current plan made no sense. His speech drew a sustained round of applause from the packed residents of both villages.

The county council's only public reaction was to point out that the village could put their case at the forthcoming 'second inquiry in public' which would address them. Behind the scenes, a furious political row had developed. All the councillors were soon up for election; those in the majority party suddenly realised that their own county wide, site assessments did not actually favour the Denton Cheney site, putting them in the wrong and making them likely to suffer in the voting.

'Nearly two years has passed, but without any progress,' thought Jeff. He and Mike would soon be back sitting before a new inspector - whose first visit this would be to the county - in order to examine exactly the same issues. Except that, this time, there would be severely limiting guidelines which seemed to have been cynically designed to ensure that government always got its way.

To an outsider, nothing affecting Denton Cheney or its villagers had changed since the previous inquiry. Yet, much was different: an affair had been confirmed; a marriage celebrated; a murder committed, and solved; a church extension cancelled; Phoenix House had better carers; planter boxes had been provided; a baby born; a daughter married; pheasants reared, and shot; people had died; the secondary school would be elsewhere; a new politician had emerged; the parish council was functioning well; the post office had closed; the village hall had been renovated; a grant had been sought for the playing field; children had moved from the village school into secondary education at Shottle and been replaced by nervous beginners.

'Such a waste of taxpayers' money,' commented Mike as the two of them prepared their arguments for the first round table session.

Both parish councils had been invited. Armed with nearly a thousand

279

letters of protest, the determined campaigners felt that right was on their side, and knew they had a compelling case to present. Would they succeed? The two men doubted the impartiality of a system in which the county council was its own planning authority and could readily approve the final proposal. The village's only hope was for the inspector to discover that the proposer lacked the credible evidence necessary to support its decision making, in which case the site selection process could be declared 'unsound' and the whole document withdrawn. Such an outcome was quite possible because requests for back up documents under the Freedom of Information Act had failed to unearth anything that justified the choice of site.

Two weeks later, much to the delight of attendees Jeff and Mike, the second inquiry was declared suspended in order to allow the county council, who had performed poorly in the early sessions, further time to gather together all the requested information. The inspector decided that he would use the delay to make an accompanied site visit and the two friends agreed to meet him in the Malting's car park. They waited for the morning of his visit in a cheerful mood. This new inspector had allowed them to speak freely during the inquiry and their arguments had been considered. It was a surprise when, by using the proposed Denton Cheney site as an example of the promoter's illogical approach to selection, the inspector had accepted their points. Better still, he had sought an immediate explanation - one which had not been forthcoming from the county council's planning team.

It was with a feeling of pronounced deja vue that the founders of VASE stood in the sunshine watching the new inspector's grey Volvo estate turn in from the main road: 'Wasn't life always like this?' thought Jeff. 'The big, world changing issues remain unresolved while people struggle with the day to day problems of making a living and simply surviving.'

Soon, they were following the new inspector through fields of growing green wheat, walking slowly towards Dunton. Jeff broke the silence of a lovely spring day, 'This right of way is ancient. It was used by the Saxons and appears in the Domesday Book.'

Glancing back over his shoulder the new inspector smiled slightly, but continued walking.

DIAMOND

Several years have elapsed since we last intruded into the lives of those diverse villagers and their hamlet, Denton Cheney. In case you are curious to discover what has befallen them, I offer a brief update.

AARON and EMILY now have two children, but remain unmarried; they manage the 'Fox and Hounds' - it was an opportunity too good to miss. They have cleaned up and replanted the long disused rear garden and made it into a 'bring your own' barbeque area. As a direct result of having this popular, local couple as joint landlords, the 'Fox' is more frequented by villagers than ever. After complaints that SUNNY stocks so little, they are considering whether to open a rival store in an outbuilding. On the bar is a large jar for donations to a charity for terminally ill children; it has already been filled many times over.

MICK and SUSAN COX, with son DAMIEN and an infant girl – I don't yet know her name – have just moved into affordable housing in the village. Ironically, the downturn in the property market encouraged a landowner to sell a suitable small site to the district council - previously, he had been holding out for a much bigger market development. The flat they partly own is on the ground floor and, with a private fenced in garden, is ideal for children. Their son has enrolled at the village junior school which continues to be oversubscribed as it guarantees entry to the best secondary in the county.

After an on, off relationship with FRANK, LAURA has separated – for a trial period - from MARTIN who, like the local gossips, is still in shock. Laura feels she has a few good years ahead and that to carry on with what to her had become a stale and boring marriage was pointless when a more vibrant and attractive man really needed her; the sex was enjoyable to. How all this will work out is anybody's guess, and everybody's favourite speculation.

Sadly, 'Auntie' DOT FAULKNER, who had always appeared indestructible, has passed away. She lost her elder sister ALICE and brother in law ROY a year earlier and, from then on, faded both physically and mentally. Both of the village's internal fields were filled with cars on a beautiful June day when the funeral took place. She had given Aaron's young family continued support, and it was her letter of reference to the brewery that tipped the scales when they applied for the vacancy at the 'Fox'.

JUNE DON'S case was finally allocated a time in court, but a panel of medical experts assessed her as unfit to stand trial. Deterioration has continued apace. As she is no longer considered dangerous Amita has agreed to keep her under observation at Phoenix House. McAlister was not sorry that his case had ended that way, he thought that manslaughter would have been the most likely verdict.

JOHN, the founder of the Denton Cheney action group and its first chairman, has continued to suffer from medical problems. Recently, he was diagnosed as having prostate cancer. He and his wife continue to live quietly in their mansion, the Grange.

Under the paternal guidance of Robert, DAVE is a changed person. He knuckled down to the construction industry training board course and qualified as a bricklayer. Following graduation he has been employed by a small Dunton based house builder. Robert is concerned that he may not be retained when the industry turns down as a result of the credit crunch, and has already asked the owner to treat him as a special case.

Sgt Major BILL is pleased with a second double hip replacement and now strides confidently around the village carrying his stick, but no longer needing it. He took the trouble to ring up the surgeon: 'Sir,' he said, always a respecter of rank, 'I thought I should just say how well it's gone. You and your team did a magnificent job.' If only more of us showed an appreciation for the skilled professionals who work in the NHS, rather than treating them as a free service that is our right. Peggy is delighted with his progress.

The local Member of Parliament came out poorly in the Daily Telegraph's revelations about expenses; it seems that, while using a hotel for necessary nights in London, he was also claiming mortgage interest on a non existent second home. The local constituency party has lost confidence and is refusing to let him stand at the next general election.

In the economic downturn fewer people were prepared to pay to join shooting parties which caused layoffs at some of the local estates. As a result HENRY has suffered from a reduced income. The consortium consisting of Henry, Mick, Tim and Chad have continued to rear their pheasants. Having decided to increase egg laying and collection to one thousand, it became necessary to send about half the eggs to a friend's incubator for hatching. By selling more slots on their shooting days this larger enterprise has been made to break even.

RAY has continued to lead the scout troop. It is hard work but, as some of the parents take turns to assist, the numbers have increased to twenty. Following the arrest of June Don, and often accompanied by wife Emma, he recommended his work as village footpath warden. Despite her doubts about the workload EMMA remains president of the women's institute and also leads the 'friends of the school,' which she admits to, 'rather enjoying'. Work for the parish council, and organising an update of the parish plan, she considers, 'more of a duty'.

Farmer TONY JONES continues with his annual cycle. Now the European Union has taken the emphasis off production he has organised to leave unploughed strips at the edge of his fields. Butterflies and skylarks are beginning to return to these permanent grassy borders, which are full of wild flowers and provide a haven for pheasants and partridge. CHAD has begun a course at agricultural college, but returns to work on the farm during his holidays. Their tractors and trailers navigate the village streets as they travel from farm to field; both seem to get bigger and faster, making Glebe Lane an ever less attractive proposition for a quiet, but convenient, walk in the countryside.

Mike's daughter JANICE separated from husband Nigel less than two years after getting married. She blames the fact that he failed in his promise to find a five day a week job on shore, with apparent deceit about his fertility as the final straw. Without the facts her father is unable to apportion blame, but is disappointed. He had reckoned that the relationship would, on balance, survive. He sees the life of a bright, attractive young lady being somewhat wasted and is unhappy that ultimate responsibility has, once again, returned to an aging man. His wife SANDRA remains phlegmatic, saying: 'Give it two or three years and she will have found another partner.'

Much to the delight of villagers, horses have returned to the fields along Glebe Lane, this time only four, and no bad tempered mules. FIONA mended her differences with the land owner and may once again be seen attending to her brood, or hacking around the local bridle paths. As SALLY has gone away to university and Emily is too busy at the Fox, Fiona is now accompanied by some new, teenage helpers whose identities I don't yet know.

For a brief period, encouraged by Keith Rector's enthusiasm, the Reverend JOHNSON believed his final posting would end with the satisfaction of completing a rare, in character, extension to an ancient church. Its failure convinced him that retiring was his best option and he refused the bishop's entreaties to stay on. He and his wife now live quietly in Brighton where they have opened a small summer holiday home for the children of poorer families who are referred to them by the Anglican Church.

MRS WOODCOCK vividly remembers the winter's night she discovered Gladys in her greenhouse. When she opened the door there was the sound of laboured breathing. Scared, she switched on the light to discover an old lady, laid back, fast asleep in the basket chair her husband sometimes took a rest in after working in the garden. 'Thank goodness for that e-mail system,' she thought, 'without it Gladys might not have been found before it was too late.'

The CHIEF CONSTABLE emerged with credit from an internal inquiry initiated by the county police authority. The Advertiser had run a leader criticising the police for their slow and incompetent handling of the case, but was not supported by local residents, large numbers of whom wrote in to disagree.

JEFF sometimes finds his parish council work rather tedious as it centres on dealing with the various bureaucratic and unimaginative arms of government. He preferred the time when he and Mike were running their campaign as a two man team without any need to take account of outside opinion. Nevertheless, he doesn't regret joining, realising all to well that a poor council could quickly undermine any achievement they might have made independently. He is wondering whether to step down on completion of the present four year term. At the suggestion of Fiona, whom he still fancies, he has taken up riding lessons, but lacks any natural affinity with horses.

After her work on the parish plan SIAN spent three years at Nottingham

University where she was awarded a BA in Media Studies. Her father helped her to obtain work experience in the housing department at Shottle district council. Brother PADRAIG is at secondary school and sister KIRSTY has joined the village school.

The impressive blacksmith's anvil which, much too heavy to move, was built into the wall of the disused forge and stolen overnight when the price of metals was driven up by unfulfilled demand from China.

DAVID continues as chair of the parish council; it's a post he's always aspired to and his enthusiasm remains boundless. Members are sometimes reluctant to let him mobilise them for his latest crusade, but it's like water off a duck's back – he simply doesn't notice and does all the work himself regardless. Alan is his 'soul mate' or 'guru' depending on the task at hand. The two make a good team, with the more cerebral Alan seeking to prevent David inadvertently offending people and getting involved in too much micro management.

After the wedding, Aaron's cousin ALF and his wife settled down in one of the Hope's old, unused gate houses on the estate where he has just been appointed assistant farm manager. He intends to learn all he can in order to be in a position to take over the running of the family's land holdings when his father retires in a few years time.

DIEDRE became parish clerk at Dunton when the long serving incumbent eventually retired. She expects it to be a pleasanter experience than when she was working with Jack.

Under the enlightened management of ANESH and AMITA, Phoenix House continues to provide a safe haven for the elderly of the area. GLADYS died at 98 without achieving her ambition to receive a telegram from the Queen. ELLEN is now, not only the most active, but also the oldest resident. DOROTHY finally accepted the position of manager at the owner's smaller and as yet unnamed annex in Dunton. After overcoming her initial fear, taking lessons and passing the driving test, she reaches it on a Vespa scooter which has been provided free of charge by ANESH.

SHEENA, the Police Community Support Officer, continues as an effective influence around the village, dealing with, now rare, episodes of anti-social behaviour in her own quiet but firm way. After the murder case was concluded the team indicated their satisfaction with her work by recommending she apply to become a police officer but, as there is no role for a village policeman and she would be consigned, at least partly, to urban duties, she is resisting.

BRIAN the local supermarket manager - like the vicar, I struggle to recall his name - has continued to fulfil his duties at the parochial church council. Unconfirmed rumour is that he has recently become engaged to Sally.

The village hall accountant HARRIET has taken well to the job. As the hall is now financially viable and has built up a capital reserve, the task has become less onerous; it has allowed her to take on the accounts of the historical society as well.

JIM is still working the night shift. He did look around for a position with more regular hours, but the economic downturn forced him to continue in his present employment. A keen environmentalist, he is a strong supporter of the parish council's tree group, and has become godfather to Damien, whom he dotes on.

EDDY was shocked by events surrounding the body's discovery, and didn't much enjoy the close attention paid him by the police. After being given a suspended sentence for robbery, Robert - whom he has come to like and trust - was allocated as his parole officer. So far, Eddy hasn't reoffended, appears to be trying to mend his ways and meets Mick regularly for a game of cheeses at Aaron's pub.

Local trucker FRED still works for the Hope's estate. With cut backs taking place, he wonders how long it will be before they will have to manage on his wife's salary; fortunately, it is a good and reliable one.

After more than thirty years most of the roads were finally resurfaced but only a few of the footpaths. The parish council has been trying to extract promises of further work from the county council, but government's over borrowing has delayed the chance of anything happening for several years.

PATRICK was selected as a Liberal Democrat candidate but did badly in the general election, losing to the incumbent Conservative who had an increased majority. He enjoyed the experience and intends to try again. On the home front he has continued to edit the magazine which, deservedly, won an award in an open government competition. As she promised, SARA has spent more time at home and the children have benefited.

The MALTINGS has had a change of ownership, becoming part of a large pub group. After a re-branding exercise the new management replaced all the signs, but without applying for planning permission. As they are in the village conservation area and out of character, the council objected but retrospective approval was anyway granted. Villagers say the food has suffered and the service is poor, but it continues to be fully booked at weekends and bank holidays.

VINERS CIRCUS has managed to continue in business by becoming more of a travelling funfair with only acrobats, clowns and trapeze artists performing in the big ring. The remaining animals have either been retired or given to zoos. The camels live in Denton Cheney all year round.

Aaron's mother gave the aging BARRY and ROBIN to her son; the dogs have accompanied the young couple to the 'Fox' where they live permanently in the rear walled garden and are spoilt by all the regulars.

Mr TURNER continues to walk his setter REX along the country footpaths. After all the unwanted media attention he has no wish to discover another dead body.

As its usage was minimal, the parish council accepted British Telecom's suggestion to stop their service at the village green and has agreed to purchase – for the princely sum of £5 - the now empty, traditional red telephone kiosk as a permanent reminder of a time before mobile phones and the internet. I think it looks very well.

Laura's youngest LUKE is, as predicted by Jane, shocked and appalled by his parents' behaviour. Having previously congratulated himself on being brought up in a loving and stable, if conventional, family, he has found it difficult coming to terms with a potential father-in-law he doesn't like, and a father whom he respects but sees becoming increasingly embittered.

VINCENT, although sorry to leave the village – which he did at his wife's urging – has settled well in Europe. He enjoys the better climate and the challenges of coping with a different culture and new language. This pleases SANYA who, although keen to go, was concerned about how well her husband would adapt. They return to a flat in the town for a month or two each year. Both were pleased to see the progress on renovation work at the village hall and, on their last visit, called in to say 'hello' to the baron, who took the opportunity to thank them for their fund raising efforts.

Alan's cousin JAKE was overcome by his wife's death, writing in a Christmas card to say that he talks to her all the time and sees her around the house. Eighteen months later his grief remained but time had healed some of the wounds and he is reconciled to making the best of his remaining years.

Architect PEREGRINE, and his now semi-retired father, put in a very modest bill to cover their work. They have yet to receive any payment from the parochial church council who, having no funds, have referred it to the diocese. What with this lost commission and the banking crisis, the two are struggling to make ends meet. It is the first time since leaving university that Peregrine has experienced a major downturn and has cut back on what he now sees as an extravagant lifestyle. His father is pragmatic, reminding his son to save some money and widen the scope of the practice.

Keith RECTOR remains a chastened man, but having applied himself to improving Denton Cheney and changing its way of life, has slowly regained the respect of villagers.

Owing to a severe lack of ordained priests he has been helping out by presiding at christening, marriage and funeral services in St James. A year ago, with the help of the school, he organised a very popular 'living nativity' procession through the village streets which ended up in a field at a real stable.

The parish council failed in their initial bid to obtain a grant towards play equipment but applied again for the last available tranche. This time they were successful, but received only about half of the required amount. During further consultation a big majority of villagers reconfirmed their wish to see better play facilities. Money to improve the access path was obtained from another awards source and a contribution towards provision of seating – an almost unanimous requirement - made by the village trust fund. The county council offered money for tree planting which was earmarked to enhance the playing field. With the help of a professional landscape architect it is the council's intention to realise its aim of providing an attractive venue for the whole community. Construction work is now in hand, but on a reduced scale.

Mrs OLDHAM's station wagon finally expired and she is the owner of a curvy new Volkswagen. As she said: 'It is characterless but has the advantage of starting on a cold winter's morning when I need to get to St James to do the flowers.' In good fettle, and although very upset by her friend Dot's death, she remains a churchwarden. As far I can ascertain, she is now the oldest person still living independently in the village.

JOAN is about to organise a further 'fun day'. This time it will be at the revamped playing field – now justifiably renamed the 'village park'. Her baking continues to supply the farm, and the whole village at Christmas time - hers and Mrs Oldham's fruit cakes compete to be the best around. In her spare time she remains a churchgoer and stalwart of the Christian community. Two years ago her father was buried in the reused part of the original churchyard.

Despite husband BERNARD's infirmity, JANE has continued as clerk to both Denton Cheney and Dunton parish councils. Following the House of Commons expenses scandal her respect for democratically elected representatives at all levels of government - except parish councils which are non political - has fallen; so much so that she has ditched her membership of the Conservative party and will stand as an independent for Shottle district council at the earliest available opportunity. Such principled, decent people are in short supply.

Detective Inspector McALISTER met his holiday commitment in Spain. He continues to enjoy his work, especially since promoted to Detective Chief Inspector. His wife is delighted.

AYESHA and husband JOHN have bought a Victorian terraced house in Wimbledon, only a short walk from the tube station. John has joined an international bank in the city, while Ayesha teaches at a nearby secondary school. After the banking crisis they became concerned that their property had been purchased at the peak of the market and apprehensive John might loose his job. Well educated and with the confidence of the young, they are planning to start a family in the new year - regardless of the situation – and will emigrate to New Zealand should opportunities in the UK remain bleak.

BRENDA has continued to represent the two villages as district councillor. She intends to stand again and rather hopes that Jane might join her as the area's second member in the now expanded ward. She is pleased with the energy and enterprise of both parish councils and has strongly supported their case to remain as villages separate from the town and other rural settlements. A majority of her fellow elected members have been converted to the cause, which is good news for both Denton Cheney and Dunton.

HAMISH decided that the rambling manor house and its extensive gardens were wasted on only himself and his wife and has arranged to exchange homes with his son and family of four - who are all under ten years old. He has, thus far, continued to chair the village hall trust and its members hope that - since he will be living only seven miles away – it will remain that way. This year the 'baron' became excited after acquiring an original print of 'Alice in Wonderland' to enhance his collection of old books. Now that security has been improved and a new, resident caretaker hired, he is considering placing some of his volumes on permanent display in the village hall.

Simon Woodley, better known as SAM, drifted away from the younger Dave. Encouraged by Robert - who found him a free tutor - he passed seven GCSE papers, and has enlisted in a sixth form college. His natural intelligence is at last being put to good use. As a consequence his frustration with the world has subsided.

Unlikely though it might have seemed MARTIN and ANGELA have become good friends. Martin forced himself to confront the awkward situation and arranged to meet her openly at the Maltings for a lunch. With the ice broken they found more in common than unfaithful partners and the threat of a lonely existence. Both have benefited. They joined walking holidays in France and Nepal, where treating them as a permanent couple seemed to come naturally to the groups they were with; it was something both found refreshing.

Sunny IBRAHIM and his wife SHIVA have continued to run the village's only shop - but on a much reduced scale. Delivering daily and Sunday papers provides the bulk of their income, which, when added to their index linked post office and state pensions, allows them to manage quite well. The poorly maintained house – Sunny is no handyman - has begun to show signs of dilapidation, so much so that John has spent time, during his and Ayesha's visits, filling and repainting the doors and window frames; unfortunately the woodwork has begun to rot. One of their sons obtained a first class arts degree and is working in the BBC's production department, his brother got a 2/1 and has enlisted in Sainsbury's graduate training scheme.

After collecting together the various records of speeding traffic in Denton Cheney the parish council presented a strong case to the county council for the installation of traffic calming measures. The work has been put on the Highway Agency's list and is expected to be completed during the year after next, but depends on money being made available from the Coalition central government who have inherited a very poor financial situation.

Jack's sister CAROLINE is pleased with the help she received from Jane in regard to getting his memorial seat placed on a verge near the Grange. She has organised for it to be varnished on a biannual basis and has affixed an inscription plate which reads: 'In memory of Jack from the village he loved.' Stephanie suffered a further loss recently when her husband died unexpectedly. Their son has added the management of his father's business to that of his own farm in Dunton.

CHRIS, has been invited to join the parish council, and although encouraged by wife SANDRA, has declined, preferring to continue with his efforts to improve Denton Cheney without favouring one group to the detriment of another. His unsung work and commonsense has been invaluable in encouraging others to support village activities in which ever way best suits them. Rather than making decisions himself he has been content to act as a catalyst.

After attending their niece's wedding and finding England surprisingly charming, ISMAIL and MOONA returned to take a two week autumn coach tour of the whole country. This holiday failed to satisfy their curiosity and, two years later, Ismail organised a fortnight's stay in Scotland where his brother and sister in law joined them. Such family reunions seem likely to continue.

AGNES from the Glebe Lane flower nursery has assisted the tree group by looking after their donated young saplings until they are large enough to plant out around the parish.

FIONA has added a year old foal, with its mother, to her collection. She also dry cleaned the caravan curtains. Aaron managed to retain his position at her family's estate agent business, but the collapse of the housing market led to a reduction in his hours of work. She likes Jeff, but finds his attempts to handle a horse rather pathetic – he just won't assert himself and the animal always takes control.

ERNEST wasn't unhappy to have stepped down from the village hall working group and be replaced by Chris, whose original help - on a 'stop gap basis only'- has continued, owing to a lack of volunteers. He admires the new management's bustling activity and achievements, but finds Hamish's overwhelming manner and bogus title quite insufferable.

Sergeant SMITH, although a conscientious policeman, has remained rigid and awkward when dealing with the public. As a consequence, the chief constable transferred him to the county's centralised, operations control room, where his computer programming skills and attention to detail have been better appreciated.

Jeff's wife JEAN, inspired by her husband's work for the village, decided to become more locally involved. Having already joined a regular tennis four playing at Dunton, she has now volunteered to assist the hall's working group.

One summer, the village's fine chestnut trees were attacked by some sort of moth which reduced their leaves to a blotchy, yellow mess. Experts warned that this was a national problem and most would need to be taken down, sadly, some householders took advantage of the advice and cut down mature trees which had been obstructing their view. After an unusually hard winter with lots of snow, the following year saw a partial recovery as the moth's predators began to follow it across the Channel.

Aaron's brother JOE didn't shine at school, left as soon as he was allowed, and has been found a post at their cousin Alf's farm. He remains single, rides a big red motorbike - far too fast for comfort - and spends most of his evenings helping out at the 'Fox'.

LADY, although still tiny for her breed, became more active, such that ARTHUR's BROTHER could no longer cope. One of the village coteries of middle aged dog walkers heard about the problem and offered to give her a home in the company of a red setter and a cairn terrier. Lady is enjoying all the canine chit chat.

Young BROWN completed his training period and became a full constable. Involvement with top brass from the metropolitan police inspired him to commit to the force. It is hard to find a politer, more helpful public servant.

MRS CECIL finally received planning approval for the first phase of her family's development. She and AUBERON have sent out enquiries to four carefully selected builders, who, despite the construction downturn declared themselves still in business and have promised to respond. Quotations are due back. Given a reasonable price, and some cooperation from the bank, they hope to start work soon and complete in time to catch the inevitable recovery. Her son has agreed to take on one of the new properties in order to be nearer his mother.

MIKE has continued as Jeff's main golf partner, though their abilities are in evident decline. Their fight to have the sand extraction site deleted went well when the second inspector ruled that the county council's minerals strategy was unsound as it could not be justified by the evidence presented, and asked for it to be done again. As a result the elected member who held the minerals portfolio has resigned.

Henry's wife, KELLY, lost one of her two jobs. Given more time at home, she has succeeded in teaching both daughters to become computer and internet literate. One is now working at an accountant's office in Shottle and the other is employed at the Maltings; the extra family income has proven useful.

ALAN and CAROL still live in Denton Cheney; he often wonders why, but the effort of moving has, thus far, deterred him. On optimistic days Alan likes to think he has contributed to improvements in the village and its social cohesion. At other times he accepts that they might well have occurred without his influence. He and David have begun identifying the next generation of potentially, decent parish councillors, and intend to make them aware of their responsibility to stand for election when the present aging membership either decides to step down or is voted out of office.

FOOTNOTE

Whatever you may have concluded about the desirability, or otherwise, of living in a village, the concept is hardly a recent one.

As Waugh observed in 1942: 'Most of Mrs Sothill's Garden-Party-Only list were people... who, on retirement from work in the cities or abroad, had bought the smaller manor houses and the larger rectories. To these modest landowners the rural character of the neighbourhood was a matter of particular jealousy... the lawns were close mown, fertilised and weeded, and from their splendid surface rose clumps of pampas grass and yucca... year in year out gloved hands snipped in the herbaceous border... These good people fed the birds daily with crumbs from the dining-room table and saw to it that no old person in the village went short of coal...'

Lightning Source UK Ltd.
Milton Keynes UK
UKOW04f0058090415

249345UK00003B/323/P